I0819558

Also by Caitlin Mullen

Please See Us

HEATHER

A Novel

Caitlin Mullen

CELADON
BOOKS
NEW YORK

This is a work of fiction. All the names, characters, organizations, places, and events portrayed in this work are either products of the author's imagination or used fictitiously.

www.celadonbooks.com

Designed by Donna Sinisgalli Noetzel

The Library of Congress Cataloging-in-Publication Data is available upon request.

ISBN 978-1-250-40057-4 (hardcover)
ISBN 978-1-250-40058-1 (ebook)

First Edition: 2026

10 9 8 7 6 5 4 3 2

For my mother, Kimberly

HEATHER

In the minutes after the baby is born the doctor bends low to your ear.

A first-degree tear, she tells you. *You won't need stitches. Though I noticed an older scar.* She cuts her eyes across the room to Ben, who is on the phone with his sister, then back to you. You don't dare acknowledge her and what she knows, though you had thought about this, during those sleepless nights of the last few months when pain shot through your hips every time you shifted and your stomach rounded so much it seemed like the skin might split down the faint gray line that divided you in half. You had wondered what record your body might keep. The mind is one thing, the little black box of Before locked tight. But the body, as you well know, is a traitor. The body undoes and reveals, has an agenda all its own.

"Such a fast labor for a first-time mother," the labor nurse remarks, now that the chuck pads have been shucked into the garbage, the epidural drip removed, the mess of birth—blood and amniotic fluid, shit and vernix—wiped away from your body's and the baby's. The air smells of rubbing alcohol, sharp and punishing. The labor nurse wears tie-dyed scrubs and rubber clogs printed with black-eyed Susans. You force yourself to smile while counting the petals on one of the flowers. Ben beams at you and you can sense his thoughts. *You're already such a good mother.* Your generous, happy husband, eager to attribute good qualities to you, whether you've earned them or not.

Ben has suggested a name for this child, one that belonged to his grandmother, who used to drive him to swim lessons, who taught him to shape blueberry scones, whose pearl earrings your mother-in-law loaned you for your courthouse wedding two years ago. Blair. You never knew your own grandmother, had only seen one photo of her. A woman already white-haired and raisin-wrinkled at fifty, squinting out from her farm stand beside a heap of zucchini. The right name, you think, could give your daughter an inheritance, one so different from what you have to offer—a history of women who run, who disappear. And your own past, too dangerous to look at squarely. Better to pretend it doesn't exist at all.

You turn your gaze to the baby on your chest. Her fingers, the joints inside so small and intricate they must be like jewelry findings, curl around yours, claiming you, and you have to remind yourself to breathe. Her skin is so soft, the finest velvet under your fingertips. You cup the tender curve of her skull with your palm, putting yourself between her and this room filled with hard surfaces, blunt, sharp corners. You hadn't noticed it before but now you can't help but see it, how everything around you teems with danger. The pen in the doctor's jacket pocket. The floor tiles, with their sickly yellow hue. The ledge of the whiteboard where the nurse made notes during your labor, circled numbers to indicate how dilated you were. You had thought of the chart from the birth book Ben brought home. Five centimeters, the size of a mandarin orange. Six, the top of a soda can. Ten, a donut.

You try your best to cover the back of her head with one hand, her spine with the other, the spine you grew inside of you, taking your folic acid like a kind of communion all those months so it would form true and straight. In the light streaming through the hospital windows you make out the fine coating of down along the baby's small body, even along the ridges of her earlobes.

That downy hair, in the bright light, is a miracle. This is not a word you've had occasion to use before, and one that feels weighty and overwrought in your mind. But today, it feels right. You hold her tight, her skin against yours, and think Oh. Oh, oh, oh.

Downy white hair on the ridges of her earlobes.

It had been so dark, before. How could you have known?

Part I

CALLIE

September 2023

Callie's uniform chafes, even after six weeks of filling in on patrol. She can't stop scratching at the place where her collar hits the back of her neck. She thinks of the suits she amassed while she was working her way up as a narcotics detective in North Jersey. Dark fabrics and crisp lines, garments that helped her feel neat and orderly and in control in the face of whatever came her way on any given week. Seizing tens of thousands of dollars of Mexican heroin from a warehouse outside of Newark. Prepping an undercover unit for a buy-and-bust on a big mafia-run cocaine operation. Now, in her patrol car parked along a sandy stretch of shoulder on Route 206 in the Jersey Pine Barrens, rashes blooming at her wrist and collar, she longs for those suits, the cool, silky linings of the jackets and the way they slipped along her skin.

Frank told her it was a good idea to wear her uniform every day, a gesture to show the guys she considered herself one of them. And she's needed on patrol: The Pine Lakes squad is down an officer now that Sergeant Jimmy Nichols resigned when Callie was named Chief of Police. According to Jimmy the job should have been his. Callie had been out of the area too long, only got the job because she's in with Frank Caputo, her best friend's father-in-law who served as chief until he retired in 2011. On her bad days she's not sure Jimmy is wrong.

But, until she hires a new guy, every Monday she takes the oldest patrol vehicle with the shrieking brakes and spends her hours answering calls, completing her reports from parking lots between traffic stops, doing her best to enforce order among the endless trees, the circuits of dirt roads, in a place that she knows from her girlhood has a secretive, untamable heart.

Her shift has been quiet so far. A broken taillight on someone's boat trailer. A few speeding tickets. She staked out a convenience store for an hour, acting on a tip from a kid they arrested last week for possession. The biggest problem she's inherited: a local drug ring that has been trading in dirty heroin, packages everything in green glassine baggies stamped with pine boughs. Overdoses ticking up and up and up, and with the hospitals so far away, long drives for EMTs, and patchy cell service, many of them are fatal. One of Callie's first initiatives as chief was distributing Narcan to every officer on her squad and setting up a pickup spot outside the station. But still, it hasn't been enough. Not by a long shot.

She's restless, hungry, scratches again at the back of her neck. It's that time of night when the sun is setting but she can't make it out other than in the way the light shifts from behind the trees. She rolls her windows down, dials the radio low. It's so quiet that she can hear the brush of pine boughs against her roof, stirred in the breeze. *Shhh shhh shhhh.*

Ten minutes pass that way, then the silence is cut through by the grumble of a muffler-less engine from around the bend. A white Nissan Altima comes into view and Callie sits up. The car swerves over the centerline, overcorrects and veers onto the shoulder, straightens out again. No headlights, despite the way the daylight is draining swiftly toward the ground. A drunk.

Callie clocks a wide dent in the vehicle's left front bumper as it approaches, consistent with striking something large head-on. A deer. A tree. A person. A thirty-year-old woman with a three-year-old at home.

"You bastard," Callie says. A second later, her siren screams through the quiet and her lights send blasts of red into the dark.

As she approaches the Altima, Callie spots a six-pack of Budweiser in the back seat, two cans short. She raises her eyes to the driver, a woman with a matted nest of a bun at the nape of her neck.

It takes Callie a second to feel it, that chime of recognition. Proof of how long they have been strangers to one another. The red hair less vivid than the last time Callie saw her five years ago. It was once so similar to Callie's own, but now its streaked through with much more gray.

She takes a breath. Straightens the nameplate on her uniform.

As she approaches the car, Nirvana's "You Know You're Right" wails from the speakers. Callie clears her throat. "Would you mind turning that down?"

The driver holds a finger up to Callie. "Hold on, hold on. You know this is the best part!" She leans over and cranks the volume higher.

Callie has to shout to hear her own voice. "Turn the music off."

She gets a peal of laughter in response.

"Jesus Christ, Mom! I said turn it down!"

Jenna shrugs, does as she's told. "My god. You've always been so uptight, Calliope." There's a glassiness to her eyes and a looseness to her speech. More than two beers in, then. And the use of Callie's full name always riles her. Jenna, nineteen years old when Callie was born and still hanging on to her hopes for a music career, had saddled her infant with the name of the muse of music and song.

Callie widens her stance, puts her hand on her holster.

"Whose car is this? What happened to the Trans Am?"

Jenna waves her hand. "Got rid of that thing years ago. Marcus traded me this one for it, lots of miles on it but you know me, don't need to go far. So tell me, my girl. What did you do to get tossed back here in the woods?"

She digs her nails into her palm. Before Jane's accident she had been a few months shy of being named commander in the drug trafficking unit. It was as good as hers, she had been assured, once Greg Holloway retired.

"I called you. Left you a voicemail. Twice. I told you I was coming back. You know why I'm here. I'm chief of police, Mom."

She leaves out the rest: the eight-man team who can't stand her, a drug ring ratcheting up business while her budget is slated to get slashed, and days filled with that tired old litany she thought she left behind in her rookie years. "License and registration, please."

Jenna rifles through a mess of receipts in the center console and produces a driver's license that expired two years ago. "Don't know where the registration is." Callie catches the hot waft of cheap beer on her breath, and something else that is all Jenna. Aussie-brand hairspray, sickly sweet, with notes of grape Jolly Rancher. Underneath that, the scent of her body metabolizing the booze, an ineffable smell but one that Callie would know anywhere. One that triggers alarm bells in her body, and even all these years later, makes the muscles in the back of her neck go tight.

Callie walks back to the patrol car, willing herself to take deep breaths. She runs the license and can't help thinking how Jenna looks a decade older than her forty-nine years. Cheeks sunken, mottled with bright bursts of spider veins. Stained teeth, one of them chipped, bumped too many times on the lip of a beer bottle.

The license number is attached to a laundry list of infractions, everything from disorderly conduct to urinating in public, petty larceny, another DUI last year. Some Callie already knows about, some are new to her, but none of them are particularly surprising. This is the woman who, the year Callie turned fourteen, said she was cooking them a big Thanksgiving dinner, went out to shop, disappeared, and returned three days later, a rotting turkey carcass in her trunk.

When Callie returns to the Altima she takes her time walking around the front bumper, crouches to touch her finger to the dent.

"Do you consent to a breathalyzer?"

Jenna rolls her eyes. "Can we just skip that part?"

"Then you're looking at an automatic DUI, and with your record that would mean—"

"I know what that would mean." Jenna's focused on her fingernails, bites at a strip of loose cuticle.

Callie sighs. Jenna is looking at hefty fines, 180 hours of community service, anywhere from two to ninety days in jail. Even with all of her varied infractions, she's never done jail time before. "Okay, well then I'm—"

"Yeah. You're going to have to take me in." It hits Callie sideways, like an unexpected blast of wind: a sadness so profound it nearly makes her rock on her heels. As an adult, she gave up on hopes that Jenna would stay sober, would rehabilitate herself, would mother her. This sadness is the sadness she used to feel as a girl, before she taught herself to hope for so much less.

"Please step out of the car, Mom. I'm going to cuff you, read you your rights."

The door creaks open and Jenna stands, stumbles a little until Callie catches her under her arm. Jenna's feet are bare, her toes pale against the dark road.

"Where are your shoes? In the back?"

"Nope."

"Where were you going with bare feet?"

"Nowhere. Just one of those nights. The devil's out tonight, and hell if I was going to sit around and let him catch me. Only thing to do when you feel the devil coming is to run."

She isn't going to touch that one. Her whole life Jenna was busy blaming the devil for her afflictions rather than choosing to take accountability for anything she'd done.

Callie flicks her flashlight in the direction of the dents. "What's the deal here?"

"Hit a deer."

"How long ago?"

"Few weeks, maybe."

"You gonna get it fixed?"

"You gonna loan me the money?" Callie snorts. She's made it a policy not to loan Jenna money ever since she moved out at eighteen. She knows well enough where it all goes.

"You sure it was a deer, and not, say, a person? Someone like you who tends to drive around after a few drinks . . . It doesn't seem out of the question, does it?" There's an edge in Callie's voice. She tells herself to calm down, to just cuff her, read the rights, and get on with it, the way she would with anyone else, but she can't help it.

For the first time Jenna seems rattled. "You're talking about Jane.

I had nothing to do with that. My own fucking daughter. Unbelievable. I was sober. Ask anybody. Three months and counting."

She almost has to give Jenna credit for sticking to her lines. *I was sober, I'll stay sober, I was sober but . . .*

"I'll tell you what's unbelievable. It's that you're still pulling the same shit you've been up to my whole childhood. Like hell you were sober. It's been twenty-five years since you tried."

"Oh, you know everything now, don't you? I could fill a goddamn book with all that you don't know."

Callie doesn't say anything, just rolls her eyes, guides her mother's hands behind her back, and cuffs her. She thinks for a second about keeping them loose, before clicking them one notch tighter.

In the cruiser Callie radios HQ, lets them know she's bringing in a DUI.

Jenna sighs from the back seat. "He's watching us now. I can feel it."

"Who?" Callie asks, thinks of the string of men Jenna would bring home, guys with names like Butch and Skeeter, who would stay for a few weeks or months thinking it would be nice to have a place to crash rent-free for a stretch, before Jenna finally drove them crazy. Rusty, who inexplicably took their electric skillet and VCR with them when he left.

"The devil. Out there, stalking through the trees in the night, looking for souls to prey on. But even in the day you can feel him. Lurking. That itchy feeling like something bad is about to happen. That's him."

"Enough with the superstition, please." In the Pines you can't escape the lore of the Jersey Devil. The creature was born in these woods, a mess of a thing: bat's wings, a goat's head, forked tail, hooves, and claws. There's a local brewery that makes a decent IPA with a cartoon of the devil on its label, but for most people, rational people, the devil was more of a mascot than something anyone arranged their lives around, like Jenna did. When Callie was young Jenna liked to tell her stories about a hunting cabin that belonged to her family for generations, where the men in their line used to keep vigil, guns in their laps, should the devil show his face. If the cabin is real—when pressed, Jenna could never tell her where it was—Callie thinks it's more likely it was a hiding place for the men who didn't want to go home and face their wives after a bender.

"I've seen him myself. And let me tell you, you hear that devil scream, you'll never be the same again. You think you're safe? No. No gun or badge is going to help you."

Callie doesn't say anything, just takes a long inhale and tightens her grip on the steering wheel.

The drive to the station is twenty-five minutes from where she pulled Jenna over. Every few miles the moonstone glow of animal eyes catches in her headlights. Deer, mostly. Occasionally, a pair of eyes closer to the ground—something stealthy, a predator on the prowl. Raccoon. Fox. Nothing but blackness in the rearview. It's so dark it looks like someone's thrown a cloth over it.

"You feel it too," Jenna says. "Nothing good coming from a night like this."

Callie itches at her neck, knows that when she finally gets to take this stupid uniform off that the skin will be welted, angry underneath.

"It's a good thing I got you off the road before you killed somebody. That's the real evil out there. Careless people who think nothing of hurting someone else." Callie's voice is harder than she intended and Jenna flinches.

"How is she? Jane?" Jenna asks.

Callie chooses her words carefully. Wants them to hit like a dart. "They're hoping she'll be able to walk on her own again in a few months."

Three months ago Callie's best friend, Jane, had been out at dusk foraging for wildflowers when she was mowed down in the road. Looked up to see the car nearly upon her, no headlights, Jersey plates. Silver or white, Jane couldn't remember when she came to, hazy with the aftereffects of anesthesia and the mind-rearranging drip of pain meds. Her face remade by bruises and swelling, a broken leg, metal plates and pins holding her left arm together. Nerve damage that might be permanent, causing migraines that make her whimper, shut her eyes to the slightest change in the light.

"Frank and Lorraine helping her?"

"As much as they can."

"Always playing the martyr, that Frank."

"What do you mean by that?" She's never heard anyone speak ill of Frank. As the former chief of police his word meant everything when it came to recommending Callie for the job after his predecessor suffered a major heart attack. Cops and civilians alike revered him, and he had only gotten out of the game when he hit sixty-five, mandatory retirement. He still hangs around the station all the time, the guys pumping his hand and slapping him on the back like he's the star quarterback striding into the homecoming dance. There's a local park named after him near the lake, Frank Caputo Greenspace, complete with a shining new playground.

Jenna groans, drops her head to her chest. "Nothing," she mumbles. "Don't listen to me. Can't trust a word out of my mouth."

More darkness, thick and resinous as sap all around them. Jenna is quiet for long enough that Callie wonders if she's fallen asleep. But then Jenna starts to sing. It takes Callie a moment to recognize the Nirvana song that had been playing when she pulled Jenna over—Jenna's made it her own, something low and plaintive and pretty. *Coulda been the next Lucinda Williams,* Jenna used to gripe. If Lucinda Williams had wasted all her time falling off bar stools. Jenna sings until they pull up to the station—a small log cabin in a wash of fluorescent lights.

Callie cuts the engine and they sit in the quiet for a moment. It's Jenna who speaks first.

"Come on, Calliope. Why don't we finally get this over with?"

The word *finally* sounds odd, until it occurs to Callie that maybe

Jenna has been chasing this fate, something she considered a forgone conclusion. Fucking up again, getting sentenced, paying her dues. Callie knows that feeling too. Willing the bad thing to just happen already, so you can get on to facing it.

At the station she asks Latour to book Jenna. He grumbles to Collins on his way to do her processing. "She's back?" he mutters. "Like shit you can't get off your shoe."

"What was that?" Callie asks, swiveling hard on her way to her office.

"Nothing," he says, holding her stare. The younger guys might not know that Jenna is her mother. For some reason Jenna gave Callie her father's last name—before he split for the West Coast. As a kid she hated the division between them, the distance it created, like Jenna never wanted to claim her. But as the chief of police it's useful. Maybe they can book Jenna, charge her, and no one will have to know anything about the whole unpleasant business.

"Clock out after you process her, please. No overtime."

"You got it, Hauser."

"It's Chief!" Jenna calls, from down the hall. In the small station you can hear most conversations unless they're conducted at a whisper, another thing that irks Callie—this feeling that she's always being watched. "My only daughter is gonna end up a cop, at least get her title right, dickhead."

Latour and Collins turn to Callie, Collins with his mouth agape and his eyes lit up with questions. Latour doing his best to hide the smirk tugging at the corners of his lips.

"Like I said. Book her and clock out," Callie says, through clenched teeth.

She retreats to her office, reviews a stack of reports and duty logs, but feels restless. She can hear her mother singing again, low and a little bit more gravelly than when Callie was young. She must be driving Latour crazy. Despite herself the thought makes her smile a little bit.

She sighs, stacks her reports, powers down her computer. She's been on for twelve hours. Time to call it a night.

She grabs her bag from the back of her chair and slips out of the front door, but halfway to her car she realizes she left her keys on her desk. When she leaves her office for the second time she sees Latour and Collins outside the holding room when she returns, their backs to her. They are talking in hushed tones, so she stays still for a moment, listens.

"According to Mac, her problems started when she found a body."

Callie waits a beat. The guys on the squad like to make a lot out of the Pines's reputation as a mafia dumping ground, all the thugs from the big North Jersey gangs trundling corpses out to the woods, like that episode of the *Sopranos*. Paulie and Christopher stumbling through the trees.

"Oh shit. What's the story there?"

"Your girl Jenna? She found a dead baby."

As if on cue, Jenna starts to sing again. This time, Bruce Springsteen.

Callie waits for another punchline, the guys messing with her. Maybe they know she's listening. Jenna sings on. *Like a freight train running through my head. Oh, oh, oh, I'm on fire.*

"You're serious?" Collins asks.

Latour clears his throat. "She was out delivering papers and there was a newborn. Side of the road."

The detail makes Callie's breath catch in her chest. She figured Latour and Collins had their wires crossed, were thinking of some other sorry soul. But Jenna used to tell Callie about her job delivering papers as a teenager, how her fingers were always smeared black with ink. And that it was the best job she ever had, because all she needed to do was to walk and sing, walk and sing, sling a paper here and there. Peaceful.

"What's the deal? Whose was it?"

"Nobody knows. Just one of those things. Case went cold."

The back of Callie's neck gets hot. *One of those things?*

"How old was she? Jenna?"

"Sixteen, I think. Frank always told us to take it easy on her. Guess Hauser didn't get the memo." He lets out a rough little chuckle that makes Callie ball her fists. She leans against the wall, wills her shoulders to relax, but when they do her keys slide out of her pocket, slap against the floor.

Latour and Collins turn toward her. Latour stares at her, insouciant, holding back a smile. "You look like you've seen a ghost, Chief."

She clears her throat. Draws herself up. "I want all the files we have on this Baby Doe case on my desk by the time I come back in the morning, Latour."

Before she leaves she microwaves a cup of water and dumps a packet of Swiss Miss in it, stirring hard to work through the clumps. Latour is nowhere to be found—probably out back, playing some stupid chiming game on his phone while he smokes—so Callie slips into the holding room, delivers the mug.

Jenna wraps her hands around the warm drink. She must have been picking at her cuticles again. Dots of fresh blood on her thumb. Callie stares at her. *Why didn't you ever tell me?*

"What?"

"Why were you out there tonight, Mom?" Jenna must have heard the guys talking in the hallway. Must have heard them address Callie once they realized she was there. Knows that Callie knows now.

Jenna looks up at her from underneath that unruly tangle of hair. "I told you. Sometimes you just feel the devil at your back and you've gotta run."

"Right."

She knows this mood of Jenna's, the shame sinking in, turning her stony and defiant. But something about the thought of leaving Jenna here, with Latour and Collins, and knowing this awful Baby Doe thing, makes her wish she had something to offer her. A sweater. A solid meal.

Jenna's feet are still bare on the cold linoleum. Callie undoes the laces on her boots, peels the navy socks from her feet, lays them on the table.

"Come on, I don't want those," Jenna says, wrinkling her nose.

"Mom, just take them, would you?"

Jenna just juts her chin, petulant.

Callie stares at the clock behind Jenna's head, watching the twitchy tick of the second hand. "Look. You've had a long day. I've had a long day. But maybe once you're out . . . once you're booked and you get through all that, detox again . . . we can talk? About this thing that happened? The baby?"

"Is that why you're being nice to me? Because you feel sorry for me, Calliope?"

"No . . . I . . . but I think—"

"I know what you think of me. You accused me of hitting Jane. Of letting that girl bleed out in the road. So this dear daughter act? It's bullshit. All cause you heard some rumors about something that happened thirty years ago?"

"Tell me what happened."

"I'm not talking about it, Calliope. I made my statement and I'm done doing anything for the cops in this town. It's the shame of my life that you've become one of them."

In an instant the room feels too small and hot, the ticking of the clock so incredibly loud. Callie worked so hard, so much harder than anyone she knows in the force, to get through high school, taking every shift she could at the pizza place to stay up on rent as her mother lost job after job. She got a full ride to Rutgers, graduated summa cum laude. She's pursued extra training as often as possible, made herself valuable to her team. She's done so much to be able to stand on her own two feet and not feel the world spinning beneath her, like it did when she was a kid. She clears her throat. The words emerge like the low growl of a cornered animal.

"I'm sorry you feel that way. Best of luck with your sentencing."

She passes Latour in the hall, who mimes eating popcorn.

"Oh fuck off, would you?"

Outside the station she stares at the tops of the trees for a long time, barely distinguishable from the black of the sky. Her heart is racing. Her bare feet rub against her boots. And for a second, she feels it. Something primeval, a force moving through her body. Seeping into her and out of her. For a second, before she shakes the feeling off, she understands it. How Jenna would believe there's something malicious lurking out there, something you can't escape.

Callie heads home to her little one-room cabin on the lip of a cedar water lake so small it doesn't warrant a name, or like many places in the Pines, goes by a name only the longstanding locals know, something that no one bothered to codify, label on a map. Through her bedroom window the water, with the moonless night, is dark as tar.

In bed she struggles to get comfortable, can't unclench her fists, relax her jaw. Callie was a bad sleeper as a kid—always on alert for the thump of Jenna tripping over something or falling down the stairs—but as an adult, deep, restful sleep had become one of her few pleasures during her grinding ascent in Narcotics. Up north, Callie installed a home security system in her apartment, had a personal weapon locked away in a safe on the off chance of an intruder, and worked out hard four days a week so that her body was strong and her reflexes were good. Adult Callie slept soundly, knowing she only had to look after herself and that she could do it well.

All that has gone to shit in the Pines and she spends the night tossing and turning. She could have just driven Jenna home, let her sleep it off, no one the wiser. Now, all the guys know she's the kid of the biggest mess in town. Now, she's got this case in her head from thirty years ago. *One of those things*, the guys had said.

She turns over, looks at her phone. 2:00 A.M. The woods eerily still outside her window, a quiet that makes her every thought ring out, echo back to her. And she decides then that no, that's not good enough. It won't be *one of those things.* Not on her watch.

CALLIE

Her mood is sour when she gets to the station in the morning and gets worse by the minute. The younger guys suppress smirks when she addresses them. She stops by the breakroom to find Jenna's record printed out on the table and her mug shot stabbed to the corkboard. Someone has written *MOMMY DEAREST* in black Sharpie above Jenna's head. And now, in that spaced-out stare, and in between the lines of Jenna's many infractions, Callie sees it: this Baby Doe story, unspoken and yet bearing down on everything.

According to Collins, they released Jenna at shift change, asked if she wanted to call anyone for a ride. But Jenna had said no thanks and simply walked out the door in her socked feet. Christ.

She pours herself a cup of coffee and studies a flyer behind Della's reception desk, asking for volunteers to work the dunking booth at the Cranberry Festival. Frank used to do it every year, he told her, with a note of expectation in his voice. Wouldn't they all love that? She can practically feel the surge of water up her nose, the wooziness that would overtake her as the guys on the squad lined up to take aim, plunging her into the tank again and again and again. No thanks.

She takes another sip from her mug, waits for the scorch of the heat and the first hit of caffeine to sharpen her bleary, swirling thoughts. Robbins approaches her from behind—she can smell him before she sees him: the Axe body spray that makes her throat itch, and under that, a whiff of cordite and mud. Some of the guys go hunting in the mornings before work, when the ducks feed at dawn. It seems like an awful way to start the day, hunkered down in a blind, watching the dark stars of birds fall from the sky.

Robbins clears his throat. "Got something for you, Hauser."

"What's that?" She says, aiming for nonchalance, but she knows this can't be anything good. The last time Robbins had something for her it was deer jerky that he had killed and dried himself.

He holds out a file. "Heard you were looking for this one."

She sets her coffee down on the nearest desk, flips the folder open, aware that Collins and Latour are watching from across the room.

"Maybe a big shot like you can finally help us simple Pineys sort this one out."

Dread takes the form of an ache in her molars, a tightness in her solar plexus. But she won't let them see that. Just takes a breath and flips through the file as though it's nothing. Meaningless as a traffic stop report.

The crime scene photos are arranged on top, even though it is standard for the report to come first. Her guts twist. Heat surges in her chest. She forces herself to take a sip of her coffee, swallows it against the knot in her throat, a double burn.

She picks up one of the photos. Robbins, Collins, and Latour stand in a half circle behind her, their arms crossed. She can practically see the cartoon thought bubbles over their heads. *We'll just see what this lady detective can handle.*

She rolls her shoulders, exhales. *You dare me to look, I'll look, you stupid motherfuckers. I'll look harder and longer than any of you.*

She lets her eyes skim the images, wills herself not to feel. A skill she learned as a child, honed on patrol. Senses on, emotions off. Assess first. Act next. React later.

She touches the edges of the pictures with her fingertips to make it seem like she is trying to see better, trying to look closer at rather than away from. But her old tricks aren't working today. She's not seeing the photos as a cop. She's seeing them as her mother, sixteen years old, a watch cap pulled down over her ears and a sack of newspapers heavy on her shoulder. A sick mother at home and a father working two jobs to pay the hospital bills.

She has to speak. Has to show them she's not rattled. Even though she is angry. Even though she feels she is going to be sick.

She clears her throat. "I'm assuming the state agencies stepped in at some point?"

"Someone from Major Crimes was involved for a bit. But you know how those guys are."

"Sure," she says. Those guys. Her former colleagues. She holds up a picture from the back of the stack. A scatter of beads, amber spheres bright against the dirt. Half of them still lined up on a broken string, the others yellow against the pale sandy soil.

"What's this?"

"Found near the scene."

"Huh. We know who it belongs to?"

"Nah."

A small note in the report: The broken bracelet was recovered five yards from where Jenna found Baby Doe. The metal clasp is connected but the string is snapped, as though someone had pulled it off.

Robbins breaks the silence. "Good luck, Hauser. Maybe a woman's intuition is just what this one needs."

"Well it sure as hell doesn't help that you all have been scratching your balls for three decades on an unsolved homicide."

There's a slight flutter in her fingers as she closes the file. "And it's Chief," she says. "Or do you need to be written up for insubordination to help you remember?"

"No," Robbins says, his eyes bright with rage. "Chief." The word comes out ugly. Spat out like a piece of gristle from between his teeth.

She tucks the file under her arm and takes it to her office, sits with it in her lap before she works up the nerve to open it again.

From the forensics report: Cause of death was exposure. The baby was born alive but a few hours old at most when she died. She googles the medical examiner who did the report—maybe she could get more info, the report shockingly sparse—but the first hit is an obituary from ten years ago. No crime scene technician support, the scene secured by local cops with backup from the State Police an hour later. 1991, so the case predates the CODIS database that can be used to connect DNA profiles to crime scenes and chances are slim that someone went back to it and entered the DNA into the records. Maybe there's a sample somewhere that the labs can work with, though chances are it's degraded down to nothing. Stuff from the '90s kept in the worst conditions, exposed to unmitigated humidity and roiling heat. DNA technology was more like alchemy to most people back then, and only the most well-funded departments invested in it, for the biggest cases. The pretty, white prom queens. The bankers bludgeoned to death in dark corners of Central Park, signet rings ripped from their pinkies.

Alone, she turns back to the crime scene photos. That broken bracelet tugs at her. She had been prepared to feel fury directed at the mother of Baby Doe, for doing what she did, for the damage it caused Jenna. But maybe the story is different from how it looks. Maybe the mother hadn't meant to abandon the child. Maybe something had happened to her, too. And no one has ever bothered to ask the right questions about it.

She picks up her phone, calls an old friend from her rookie years who is now working cold cases. Benny Healey, a brusque guy from Cherry Hill with a penchant for Italian shoes and a slight dramatic flair as though he learned to be a cop from the movies. But, she concedes, he does good work. Cold cases is lucky to have him.

"Hauser. To what do I owe the pleasure?"

"Hey, Healy. I'm looking into something and was wondering if you might see if anything has made it your way. Maybe something that wasn't shared here with the department."

"Shoot."

She runs over the details of the case and he tells her he'll see what he can dig up. His department has been working through backlogs of cases from the '80s and '90s, hundreds of them. Untested rape kits, unsolved murders, unprocessed evidence. Thousands of loose ends, thousands of questions left unanswered. It makes her mouth go dry just thinking about it.

"Why are you going after this one?" he asks. "Gotta be lots of unidentified bodies in those woods."

She pauses, stares at the slim file on her desk. Flicks at the flimsy bent corner of the manilla folder. She can't tell him it's because of her mother. She thinks of those amber beads in the soil. Whoever they belonged to. That there's a bigger story to tell about what happened here. "I've got a hunch that it could be a double homicide. But we'll need more hard evidence to go on while I work stuff on my end."

"You're not wasting much time down there, huh? I know they're hurting on Narcotics. They miss you."

"Look at you, you big softie. Well, who knows, maybe I'll be back on it soon enough."

"Oh yeah? How's the friend, the one you're helping out? She doing better, then?"

"Yeah," Callie says, reflexively. "Yeah, she is doing better. I'm headed over to her house tonight." What she doesn't say is that the doctors can't yet be sure about the difference between *better* and *as good as its going to get.*

Jane and Damien live in a two-story Cape Cod off a dirt road. Callie manages to hit the same pothole in their driveway every time she visits, swears to herself as her Jeep bounces hard in the rut.

Part of her still can't believe that this is where Jane lives. Private, Jane had said, when they first bought the house. Peaceful. The house itself is charming, and Jane did a lot of work planting flower beds around the front and side yards, filled the inside with thrifted furniture that she reupholstered herself. But every time she cuts the engine and walks the flagstone path to the front porch, Callie still can't shake the sense that this wasn't quite how the story was supposed to go, for either of them.

Jane and Callie have been best friends since they were assigned as roommates their freshman year at Rutgers. Both children of alcoholic parents, they used to dream out loud to one another about what their lives would look like after they graduated. They'd run a coffee shop in a small town, bake the scones themselves every morning. They'd move to New York and stay out until 3:00 A.M. every night, teetering on their high heels to the best late-night pizza place and laughing about the lame guys who had tried to pick them up at the bars of the Lower East Side.

But then, the spring of senior year Jane met Damien while she and Callie were away for a weekend down at the shore. It was March, the beaches still wind-whipped and gray, but a group of them went in on a house together—Callie and Jane and anyone else who didn't have parents chipping in for a spring break week in Cancun or Clearwater. Damien was already in his forties then, the Caputo boys a generation older than Callie, but she recognized him right away as he chatted with a group of men clustered near the beer taps. Everyone from Pine Lakes knew the Caputos, Captain Frank and his family at every ribbon cutting and ceremonial tree planting, the two Caputo boys sharing their father's easy, confident grin. She had never really spoken to him around town, but when he caught sight of her standing next to Jane at a high top near the door, he walked right over and asked, didn't he know her from somewhere?

After a little polite small talk Callie had to excuse herself to use the bathroom, hoping Jane would forgive her for leaving her alone with some random older guy from the Pines. But by the time she waited in line and made her way back to the table, Damien and Jane were standing close enough that the rims of their beer glasses nearly met and they both looked a little startled—and she registered, with no small amount of hurt, disappointed—to see her appear next to them.

After graduation Jane moved to the Pines with Damien, and three years later he got down on one knee on a canoe in the middle of Atsion Lake. Callie was promoted from patrol to Narcotics, got her own apartment near Secaucus that she rented with the cheap beige furniture the realtor used to stage it for viewings. And even though they were still young, Callie had the feeling of a chapter being closed. Their youth already over.

Opal throws herself at Callie's knees the second she's through the front door. She's the spitting image of Jane, with her sun-streaked blond hair, gray-blue eyes, blond eyelashes.

"Hello, love bug," Callie says, running a hand over Opal's head. Her fingers catch on a sticky patch of hair. Callie pulls back, her heartbeat in her ears.

Opal cackles, mouth open wide to reveal tiny pearls of baby teeth. "Daddy let me help make a cake!"

Callie relaxes. Cake batter. Just chocolate. But the Baby Doe case has her mind canted toward the ugly and brutal. Those pictures. The blue-tinged skin. The small curled fist.

Jane is on the sofa, raises a hand in greeting. Callie still isn't used to the dark circles under her eyes. Jane says she can't sleep more than a few hours at a time because of the pain in her legs and hips. She doesn't want to take more meds, though, because of the way they make her feel like she's under water; says she doesn't want to be too drugged out to play with her kid.

"That sounds delicious. What do you say we give you a bath though, get that mess out of your hair?"

Thank you, Jane mouths from across the room, sweeps her hand at the mess of the living room, rolls her eyes at Damien's back as he loads the washing machine.

Opal races to the foot of the stairs. "Let's go, Auntie Cal. I have new bath toys!" Callie follows, has to step over splotches of spilled batter that have somehow strayed from the kitchen and into the hall.

There's a rush of water through the pipes as Damien punches the start button on the laundry, then a grinding noise from somewhere deep within the belly of the machine.

"We've got to get that looked at, Damien," Jane says.

Damien doesn't answer, but Callie catches him grimace before he turns to greet her, forcing a smile. "Chief Hauser, good to see you, as ever."

"Hey. None of that Chief Hauser shit." The irony isn't wasted on Callie. That the only people who use her title are the ones she wants to be familiar with her.

"What's shit mean?" Opal asks.

"Stuff! I meant to say stuff. No Chief Hauser stuff, please." Callie feels her face getting hot. Damien laughs, to her relief.

Opal pulls at the hem of Callie's T-shirt. "You said a bad word!"

"Mom and Dad will be over for dinner tonight too."

"Great."

"Dad mentioned that the guys have been giving you a hard time."

Callie hadn't said anything to Frank about it but clearly she didn't have to. "It's nothing. Cops are always giving each other shit. Stuff!"

"Shit shit shit," Opal says, skipping around the coffee table.

Callie winces. "I'm sorry. I've been here for less than five minutes and I've already corrupted your daughter."

"Eh. She's heard a few choice words over the past few weeks." Damien lays a hand on her shoulder. "Everyone always asks me why I didn't follow in my dad's footsteps. Those guys are assholes is why. They'll back off."

"Not all of them are bad." She hasn't wanted Jane to know about her issues with the guys, knows it would make her feel guilty. But she also means it. There are eight guys on the squad and only three of them are giving her any real hassle.

Opal puts herself between Damien and Callie, pulls on Callie's arm with her sticky hand. "Come on, Auntie Cal. Let's go!"

Upstairs in the bathtub Callie floats yellow plastic boats on the surface of the water, uses foam letters to spell out *AUNT* and *CAT* and *DOG* against the green tile.

"Mommy is going to get better one day."

"She's already much better, isn't she? She's really strong. You should be proud of her. She's working so hard to get better for you."

"She still has to use a chair in the shower."

"That's true. But she won't need it forever."

Don't look, Jane had said about her scars the last time Callie helped wash her hair. Callie had been tempted to tell her that the injuries didn't unnerve her, but Jane's voice had sounded so uncharacteristically small that Callie had only said okay.

Sounds rise from the entryway: the creak of the front door, Frank and Lorraine greeting Damien and Jane. At the sound of her grandparents Opal jumps up so fast her feet nearly slide out from under her, and Callie barely manages to catch her under the arm, keep her from smacking her head against the lip of the tub, her little body soap-slick and slippery. The moment passes in a half second and Opal is fine, unfazed, but Callie's heart races.

As she catches her breath, runs a towel over Opal's narrow shoulders, she wonders if this is what Baby Doe's mother felt when she left her child behind. How dangerous it was to love someone so small, so vulnerable and prone to harm. How she might have looked at the baby and her only thought was *I can't.*

She's putting the bath toys away while Opal stands on a step stool at the sink, squeezing a tube of toothpaste into a dixie cup, when she hears another voice. A man's voice, but not Damien's and not Frank's.

It must be Luke.

"Shit," she says, not realizing she's spoken out loud until Opal peers over at her, a conspiratorial glow in her eyes.

"Oh god, Opal. Sorry! I—Ugh. Don't tell your parents, okay?"

The hint of collusion pleases Opal even more. "I'm really good at secrets," she says, and holds her little finger out to Callie. Pinkie swear.

Opal leads her to her bedroom and Callie is relieved that Opal takes a long time picking out her pajamas—more time for Callie to steel herself.

During Jane and Damien's wedding weekend, Luke, Damien's older brother, had been strange around Callie, alternately solicitous and aloof. As soon as she thought she was making inroads with him—landing a joke, exchanging a knowing glance as Lorraine straightened the already perfect flower arrangements in the reception hall—in the next conversation he'd find an excuse to refresh his drink. When they were meant to walk together as a part of the recessional he wouldn't put his arm through hers, just held out a hand for her to walk ahead of him. Then, he asked her to dance as the band started up. His hands were firm on her back, but as soon as the song ended he turned away from her.

Opal gets herself into her pajamas, then goes skidding down the stairs shouting for her grandparents, leaving Callie to catch up. When she walks into the dining room she's glad to see Jane sitting at the table. She pauses behind her chair, smooths the back of Jane's hair where it's tangled from the hours on the couch.

"Thank you," she says, gripping Callie's hand in hers for a second. "No one else was going to tell me I looked like a hot mess, huh?"

Damien comes in carrying a salad bowl. "Janie, you're recovering. No one cares what you look like."

"I care," Jane snaps. "I need to feel like I'm a person and not just another lump on the shitty sofa."

"That shitty sofa cost four grand because you insisted on a sectional."

"Stop fighting! You guys always fight," Opal protests.

Lorraine smooths a napkin across her lap. Even Frank, used to conflict in his work, looks adrift, uncomfortable, and crooks a finger at Opal, bends to whisper in her ear. Across the table from Jane, Luke takes a sip of his beer and raises his eyebrows at Callie.

Callie tells herself to get it over with. And someone has to break the tension, shift the conversation. "Good to see you, Luke."

"How goes it, Hauser?"

She does her best to hold his gaze.

At the reception she eventually lost count of how many glasses of Pinot Grigio she had. She had passed Luke on her way back from the restroom and clumsily reached for his hand. She had never been with an older guy, but Jane looked so happy all night, and whether it was the booze or the forlorn feeling of being left behind, Callie was strangely, liberatingly, not herself. She was never that brazen with men but she wanted to know, one way or another, how he felt about her. Was she offensive, repulsive? Was she worthy, wanted?

She had pulled him toward her.

He dropped her hand and walked away without a word.

She figured that moving back here, spending so much time at the house, would mean a run-in sooner or later. Luke runs a plant nursery twenty minutes south. He's still unmarried, no kids, older than Damien by four years. He must be in his mid-fifties by now. As he turns his head to watch Opal dance to "Baby Shark" she sees that he's got some threads of gray in his eyebrows, at his temples. It suits him.

After dinner Damien takes Opal up to bed while Callie sits with Luke, Jane, Frank, and Lorraine, poking at the last of the lasagna Lorraine made, draining their cups of Chianti.

"How's the work compare to up North, Chief Hauser?" Frank asks Callie.

"Already plenty to keep me busy."

"Yeah, only difference out here is you need to also watch for coyotes, wolves. Bears too." Frank warns.

"Oh, come on. Haven't been bears around here for a hundred years."

Damien has come down for a stuffed rabbit Opal demanded, chimes in from the hall. "They spot one or two a season. Up near Batsto last fall. Ask Janie. She made me get a gun at headquarters. Actually she's a really good shot."

"Used to be," Jane says, gesturing to her legs. "Before."

"Janie's got a gun? You got a permit for that?" Callie asks.

"Yes we do, though someone should arrest you on the basis of that pun alone. A Winchester semi-automatic, fully compliant with all legal requirements, thank you."

Callie looks at Jane, surprised. She hadn't known anything about Jane learning to shoot. Jane just shrugs.

Callie shifts in her chair, restless for an opportunity to talk to Frank about what she learned about Jenna. He had been chief when Baby Doe was found. "Speaking of legal matters, I had a run-in with my mother yesterday."

"Oh, no work talk." Lorraine flaps her napkin. As though to shoo away a fly. Jenna, a pest, something that could spoil their dinner.

Lorraine, with her smooth French twist and gold jewelry: the diamond studs, the locket with her boys' school pictures inside, an elegant little watch on one wrist and a charm bracelet on the other, heavy with mementos. A woman with so much good fortune to commemorate it nearly weighs her down.

"I heard a story about her, something I hadn't known before. About a baby. Cold case. Is it true?" She tries to keep her voice light, even though she's brimming with questions for Frank. What were his theories? Why didn't he push this one more when he was chief?

Frank tents his fingers. "Unfortunately, yes. It was an awful thing."

"That is a horrible story. Do we have to talk about this?" Lorraine says.

Having crossed Lorraine once already, Callie figures she might as well press on. "No leads ever on this one?" Jane gives her a look from across the table. She knows the expression well. *Tell me later.*

"No work talk! Do I need to remind you that you're retired, Frank?"

Retired, Luke mouths at Callie, making air quotes with his fingers. Callie can't help but smile. As she was first getting settled it was nice that Frank came by the station so often, or called in to tell Callie about a disabled vehicle or illegal hunting activity. But lately she wishes he'd give her a chance to find her footing, do things her own way.

Lorraine rises, clears their plates, and waves her hands when Callie tries to help, her jewelry jangling.

Lorraine retreats to the kitchen and Frank leans forward, conspiratorial, his hands knit together. "We didn't really have the resources or the manpower to go deep on it, the Baby Doe case. We sent it up to Major Crimes, but of course those guys . . . well, you know how it is. Bigger fish."

"Enough, I mean it," Lorraine says, returning from the kitchen, waving a cake knife. Luke widens his eyes as the knife flashes in the candlelight and Callie can't help but laugh.

"Jesus, Mom. Talk about Major Crimes."

Lorraine sighs, but reaches out to ruffle Luke's hair. "Who wants cake? Or tiramisu? Callie?"

"Definitely, Mrs. Caputo."

A vibration in her pocket. Jane. Luke's got the hots for you. He keeps looking at you. When she looks up, Luke's eyes are on her, and he doesn't look away when he's caught.

After dessert Callie stands, bids everyone goodnight, citing an early morning.

"That's right," Frank says. "You've got a lot on your plate. How'd things work out on the tip from last week, by the way?"

"Nothing came of it, but I'm hoping to brief the guys on some new protocols for cultivating informants. I think it will be useful."

"I'll come by. I'd like to hear about that."

"Sure thing." She squeezes Jane's shoulder as she passes her chair and tells her to text her tomorrow, that she'll do their grocery run and come watch Opal after she gets off.

She's just stepped off the porch when the screen door creaks behind her.

Luke.

"You leaving too?" she asks.

"I'm going to wait around until Damien's done with bedtime duties. Just came out to smoke."

"I didn't know you smoked. Your mom can't be a fan of that."

It was a complaint Jane made often. Lorraine Caputo was always on the side of her good, precious boys, who could do no wrong. "Not cigarettes, not anymore at least, and she doesn't know." He pulls a skinny joint from the front pocket of his jacket, a silver zippo from his jeans. "I grow a little too. You think planting flowers and bushes pays this well?" He juts his chin toward his truck. A new Ford with a four-door cab, all the bells and whistles. Must have cost at least seventy-five grand.

"You've got a license to do that?"

"Eh. It sounds like you've got bigger problems than a guy like me growing a little grass without paperwork."

"Your dad know about this enterprise of yours?"

"Nope. Between you and me, please and thank you."

She shoves her hands in her pockets, looks up at the sky. It's one thing she likes about it down here. The stars crisp and clear, like something you could reach up and touch, come away with fingers skimmed with glitter.

"It's nice you're here, taking care of Jane."

"She's family. No-brainer." A cliché, but true.

He sparks his joint. "You miss North Jersey? Heard you were kind of a big deal up that way."

"Eh. Most of the time they had me dressed up, pretending to be a sex worker, so the boys could nail someone in a sting."

"You're a shit liar, Callie Hauser."

She laughs. It was true, sometimes she had to dress up, especially earlier in her career. Stilettos, sequined top, a rush of wind up the back of her miniskirt every time a truck blew by. One time her team was loaned a red Porsche so they could pretend to be big-time cocaine traders, though her partner got to drive it and she was in shotgun, playing the kingpin's girlfriend. But she misses it. She misses it all the time.

She raises her hands in the air. "You got me."

Luke takes another drag, exhales. "You know what they say about lying. You've got to tell a lie that's as close to the truth as you can get."

The screen door creaks behind them. Damien, who casts a quick look between them. Luke holds the joint out to him but he shakes his head.

"No thanks. Gotta lead a moonlight hike in an hour."

"Was that on the schedule, Damien? Your website isn't up to date, my dude."

A look crosses Damien's face, a shadow like a cloud blowing past the moon. "Private party. Don't put those on the site."

Luke stares at Damien over the top of Callie's head and Damien locks in and stares back. They're telling one another something, some shorthand here that Callie can only feel the edges of.

"What are you two doing out here anyway? You keeping good Chief Hauser here with your stoner ramblings?"

"I told you, knock it off with that Chief Hauser shit," Callie says.

Luke cuts in. "We're talking about lying. What's the last lie you told, Damien?"

The dare hangs in the air a second, then two, three.

Damien glowers at Luke before clearing his throat. "I told Jane she pushed a tennis ball two inches with her foot at physical therapy yesterday. But she probably only moved it a quarter inch."

The image makes Callie wince. She knows what Jane looks like when she's throwing all of herself into something, whether that's an 800-meter race or studying for her Organic Chemistry final, the way she bites down on her right cheek and narrows her eyes. She can picture Jane in the physical therapist's office, shaking with the effort it takes her mangled nerves and muscles and bones to coordinate together. Luke looks between his feet, chastened.

Callie can't decide if it's cruelty or kindness, lies like that. Letting someone lie to you. On Jane's third night in the hospital she left Callie a voicemail, her voice a ragged whisper. *I was going to leave him, Callie. I was saving money. I had a plan. Now what do I do?* When Callie asked her about it Jane said she didn't remember calling her at all. Blamed the morphine.

"Opal has started to lie. Or not lie, you know. But invent. They say it's a kid's way of learning to tell stories."

"What kinds of stories?" Callie asks.

"Ah, you know. Kid stuff. That she has a secret house in the woods and a barn full of zebras who talk to her. That she has a friend named Olivia who comes over at night when everyone is asleep."

Callie thinks that they sound like the stories of a kid who is lonely—Opal should be in preschool, but Damien and Jane have kept her home. The nearest preschool is nearly forty minutes away. One more bill.

"Speaking of Opal, thanks for your help tonight, Cal. She adores you."

"Really, it's a pleasure. She's the best part of my day."

"She's a sweet kid," Luke says, and Damien's face goes stormy.

"Like you're around enough to know."

"Been busy."

"I bet."

Callie freezes. Had they always been like this, and she just hadn't noticed? Luke had been Damien's best man at the wedding, had clapped him hard on the back before Damien turned to Jane to say his vows. He gave a toast that night, and it had seemed genuine. *Loyal, will do anything for his family. And now, Jane, you're family too.* So what's happened? Another thing she'll have to ask Jane the next time they're alone together.

The brothers have gone silent, each staring into different pockets of darkness in the trees. Callie clears her throat. "Well, I'd better get going. But I'll bring dinner tomorrow, Damien. You or Janie let me know what you need from the store."

"Yeah, I'm about to shove off too. See you soon, Cal. Thanks again."

Luke pinches the end of his joint. "Until next time, Chief."

Before she pulls out of the driveway she texts Jenna. Tries to strike an easygoing tone. Just making sure you got home okay. Let's talk soon?

Three dots appear on the screen, disappear, then silence.

CALLIE

Another night of restless sleep, moonlight leaking through the blinds. In her tossing and turning, she comes to a decision: She's got to talk to Jenna again. The sooner the better. She'll drive to her house, early, before she's due in at the station. In the bright light of morning it could be a real chance to hash things out, before Jenna's gotten started on the day's drinking.

But when she pulls up to Jenna's rancher she has to resist the temptation to rub her eyes, double-checks the house number, which is formed from gold-toned metal, not the peeling hardware store stickers of her youth. There are two glazed pots of impatiens on the steps leading to the door. The flowers are lush, hardy. The door has been painted a glossy red.

On the steps she stares at the flowers and feels a sense of vertigo. Is she at the right house? Did Jenna move and not tell her?

Callie knocks once, waits a beat, knocks again. She's got a key on her ring and lets herself in, half expecting it to not fit in the lock. But it gives, and for the first time in five years she's inside her childhood home. She calls for her mother but her voice rings out in the empty space.

She does a quick circuit of the rooms—the old habit of making sure Jenna hadn't passed out, hit her head, choked on her own vomit—but no one's there. Instead, she finds the coverlet has been replaced on Jenna's bed, which is made, and not the nest of ash and empties she's accustomed to. A new lamp on the bedside table.

The kitchen is similarly tidy. The trash isn't overflowing. The table is wiped clean. There's a coin on the surface, dark against the wood, but when she stands over it she realizes it's not a coin but a chip from AA.

Three months sober.

Jenna had been telling the truth.

"No goddamned way," she says out loud. Jenna had always said AA was for losers, that a room full of sad sacks telling their tales of woe only made her want to drink more. But she must have changed her mind. *Maybe she's at a meeting now*, Callie thinks, embarrassed by the stupid hope that bubbles up in her chest, the kind of hope she thought she had mastered a long time ago. She scrawls a note onto a Post-it pad she finds in the kitchen drawer. *Call me.* A second later she adds two more words. *I'm sorry.*

As she turns to leave she finds herself staring face-to-face with her own photograph. An article taped to the fridge.

CALLIE HAUSER NAMED FIRST
FEMALE CHIEF OF POLICE IN PINE LAKES

At thirty years old, Hauser is the youngest Chief of Police to serve Pine Lakes as well as the first female chief. Retired Police Chief Frank Caputo hails Hauser's narcotics experience and says he has confidence that Hauser is the right person to help them tamp down the proliferating drug trade in the Pines.

The article is dated three months ago.

She turns back to the table, stares hard at the chip.

"How about that?" she says out loud to the empty rooms.

The call comes in at 1:00 P.M., just as Callie takes a moment to stare out the window of her office.

Suspected overdose.

Another one.

Callie slams out the station door, climbs in her cruiser, peels out of the lot. The afternoon is cloudy with occasional patches of weak, filtered sunlight breaking through. The lethargic weather is at odds with the pounding of her heart, the urgency flooding through her nerves as she speeds away from the station, braces herself for whatever she's going to find at the scene.

The call came in from the owner of the paintball park ten minutes up the road. When she pulls in there's a cluster of men milling around in the parking lot and the owner has the entrance gate pulled shut. His huddled form emerges in front of her, a skinny guy with a hooded sweatshirt draped over his body, and it takes him a minute to get the padlock on the gate undone with his trembling hands.

"She's in bad shape. It . . . I don't know, man."

Callie clenches a fist around one of the vials of Narcan in her pocket. "Paramedics will be here soon. Take me to her. Now."

The owner—guy called Kirby Lewes—is wiry, quick, with a slink that makes her think of a ferret. Callie has him slide in the passenger seat of her cruiser and they bump over paint-splattered fields, more dirt than grass.

"She's on the bus. Nobody's supposed to actually be on the bus, you know? It's just like, a feature. It's locked. But these kids, man, they're always forcing the door open, climbing in there to smoke up or touch each other."

"What bus?"

"It was my uncle's but the transmission went, so he had it towed here. Cool part of the park, adds some detail and something different, you know? Up here. Just past the barracks."

They pass through a row of huts supposedly made to look like an Afghan village. On the side of one of the buildings someone has scrawled *OPERATION ENDURING FREEDOM* in red spray paint. She speeds up at the sight of the bus up ahead, squatting on flat tires. All of the window glass has been removed and there's a little bit of the original yellow paint showing through Kirby's attempt to blot it out with a sickly green she guesses is meant to be camouflage.

"Do I have to go back in there?" Kirby asks, shivering.

"Please don't," Callie says, her body feeling heavier as she closes the distance to the bus. "Just make sure the EMTs know where to find us."

She mounts the steps and the frame creaks a little under her weight. In the second to last row she sees the girl's legs draped into the aisle, gangly in denim cutoffs, a pair of red Chuck Taylor high-tops on her feet. The left shoe is missing its laces, used to tie off her upper arm. Her lips are pale and her face has a gray cast to it. Callie doesn't need the needle for confirmation but she spots it on the floor, just past the red Converse. She's not breathing and her eyes are closed. Maybe already gone.

Callie whips the Narcan from her pocket, administers a dose in each nostril, moves the girl onto her side to keep her from choking when—if—she regains consciousness. Feels for her pulse, catches a light, sporadic beat.

"Come on," Callie says, softly as she can. "Come on, come on, come on." If three minutes pass and she doesn't wake, Callie can administer another dose. She feels every second. It's the closest she ever gets to praying, standing over people like this, waiting to see if they'll rejoin the living. Feeling death in every one of those long intervals between each breath, each heartbeat.

One minute ticks by, then two. She finds herself holding her breath, and just as she starts to count the seconds until she can give the second dose, the girl's narrow shoulders jerk and she lets out a long, low groan.

"There we go," Callie says, letting herself exhale. "There we go. You're okay."

The girl rubs the heels of her hands into her eyes. "Fuck you," she says, her voice thick, her teeth clenched. She backs away from Callie's touch. "Get your filthy cop hands off of me!" Callie raises her hands gently, tries to show she means peace. Sometimes they come back this way. Angry after losing their high, ripped out of a sweet delirium and called back into gritty, dank reality, withdrawal symptoms already setting in.

"You overdosed. I just administered Narcan. The EMTs will be here in a moment and they'll take you to the hospital for monitoring."

"No way."

"You need to be supervised. This dose I just gave you could wear off and you'd be right back to the way I found you. Almost dead, in case that's not clear."

"I said I'm not fucking going."

"You're not in trouble. You have my word."

"You don't know what the hell you're talking about."

Callie sighs, drops her eyes to the girl's red sneakers. Kid probably still lives at home, doesn't want her parents to know. "How about this? I'll give you a ride to the hospital. Help arrange a ride home when you're released. But I need to know you're going to be okay."

The girl shoots her a furious look, dark eyed, mouth tight with contempt.

"I'll let you think about it for a few minutes. I'm going to go talk to my friend out there and then I'm going to check on you, see what you've decided. Me, or the EMTs."

She steps off the bus and finds Kirby, who is pacing in a twitchy way that makes her wonder if he doesn't have a habit himself. "Who was she here with?"

"They all left, the dudes. Three of them." Of course. Shot up with her or hooked her up then peeled off when shit hit the fan.

"How'd you know to check the bus?"

"One of the kids she was with. He turned in all of their gear, left, then came back in and told me I probably wanted to look at a problem on the bus. He didn't say anything else; I didn't think it was urgent or else I woulda ran over there. Instead I took a phone call, checked in a few dudes for a bachelor party. Fuck. She's dead, right? Fuck fucking me."

"Not dead. But close. Minutes away, if I had to guess. If you feel bad about that, why don't you help me out. You hear anything about who is dealing heroin around here?"

"Nah. I don't know," Kirby says, his eyes darting over her shoulder in a way that makes Callie think the opposite.

"You sure? You don't want me to have to come back and take a look around, see if there's anything I missed this morning that might be relevant to my case."

He turns and looks over his shoulder, making sure no one else will hear. "Rumors are Fauver is in on it. But you did not get that from me, right?"

"Who is Fauver?"

"Billy. Billy Fauver. But please. It comes down to it, I didn't give that name to you." Callie looks him over. He's really scared. There's a new neediness in his voice, his jittery movements and that evasive stare have turned focused, intent.

"Why are you afraid of him?"

Kirby looks at Callie with disbelief. "You wanna stay alive? You don't piss that guy off."

Back at the station she shuts the door to her office—something she almost never does—and dials Jenna. She wills herself to concentrate on something blank, simple: the cup of pens on her desk; the patch of wall discolored from where someone had once hung a framed picture.

She gets Jenna's voicemail again.

"Mom. Please let me know you're okay. I just . . . Just call, all right? Or text. Anything."

The girl—whose name was Layla Hart—let Callie drive her to the hospital in the end, silent and seething. Callie had walked her to the check-in desk at the ER, offered her her cell phone number if Layla needed any help down the road. But she still can't shake it, the chill that runs through her every time she has to pull someone back from the edge.

A half hour passes before another call comes in, Keegan asking for backup on an accident scene. Robbins and Latour are engaged on a theft issue at the Stop and Shop. Or so they say. Callie will be sure to look for that incident report. She sighs, gets the details on the accident location, and tells Keegan she'll make her way over there.

She drives west, passing a cranberry farm. A yellow school bus in the parking lot. A field trip—though she can't help but wince at the sight of the bus. There's a row of kids toeing up to the edge of the bog in bright sweatshirts. One of the mothers on the trip bends over her daughter, smears sunscreen on her cheeks, as the girl tries to duck away.

At the accident site she finds Keegan standing next to a conversion van that wrapped itself around a tree on the town's little Main Street, where there is a general store, a gas station, a pizza parlor.

She approaches the vehicle. In the back, stacks of long, narrow cages.

"Muskrat traps. One of them got loose. Driver tried to catch him without pulling over first," Keegan tells her, gesturing at the twisted van, more stacks of traps lined up on the side of the road. She squints and can make out fur between the bars. She toes closer until she can see the muskrats' twitching whiskers and hand-like paws, the long snake of their tails.

"What's the plan for these guys?" Callie asks.

"We can't tow the vehicle with them in there. Let's free them and call it a day," Keegan says. Keegan and the older guys give her shit, but the tenor is different from the younger cops. Something if not quite avuncular, at least not pointed.

She puts her fingers on the bars of one of the cages.

"Careful you don't get bit. They can have rabies."

"Why do they trap them?"

"You can dye the fur, make it look like mink."

"There a lot of money in imitation mink these days?"

"It's resourceful, I'll give them that."

She waves a sedan around the flares and cones, though she can tell the driver wants to linger, rubberneck. "I guess."

She waits a beat to ask the next question. "I've been looking into that Baby Doe case from the '90s. You were on patrol when they found the baby, right?"

"Rookie. Just took my test the year before."

"How about my mom? Did you know her?"

Keegan falters. Takes a minute to put together his thoughts. "Not really. I was a few years older. But I knew it was a kid who found the baby." Keegan shakes his head. "God knows how that would mess with you."

"It just seems like in a small town, people would talk a little more. About something like this. They would have theories about who might have been involved."

"I think people wanted to put it behind them. The idea that someone here, one of us, did it? No one wanted to sit with that." Keegan rubs his chin. "But there was a name, for a little while. A high school girl."

"That would track." Can't tell her parents, no access to medical care.

Keegan springs another trap. The muskrat scampers off.

"Help me with these last few traps and we can call it a day, yeah?"

Keegan lifts a trap from the stack, sets it on the ground, slides a bar from a latch to spring the door open. A brown ball of fur slips out, disappears into the underbrush.

She releases the next one, the mechanism snapping open fast and hard, nearly catching her finger. She gasps louder than she means to, louder than the moment warrants, her nerves sizzling, her exhaustion getting the better of her.

The muskrat doesn't move for a moment, not until she taps the bars, and then it skuttles out, nose twitching.

"Will they be okay? This close to the road?"

"Oh, Christ, we'd be doing everyone a favor if we let them get hit. Mean little bastards. They'll find water soon enough, that's how they're made."

"Keegan, what was the name of the girl?" she asks him. "The one people talked about back then?"

He rubs his knuckles into his eyes. "Shit. I forget. Back at the station we'll ask one of the others during shift change. I don't exactly remember that much about a teenage girl from all those years ago."

Of course not, she thinks. Teenage girls, so similar as to be interchangeable. Paper doll cutouts. Forgotten, disposed of, left behind.

At the station Keegan holds the door for Callie, then cups his hands around his mouth and yells to McIntyre, who is at reception talking to Della. "Hey, Mac, what was the name of that girl who lived out in the big colonial off of 206? By the paper mill? She was your brother's age I think."

"Her? He used to say she'd blow people behind the school for weed."

Callie tries to catch Della's eye, but Della only stares at her computer monitor.

"Shawna something?" McIntyre offers. "She was real cute. Blond, little."

"No that's not it. Susannah?" Keegan says.

"Maybe that. Riley! That was the last name."

"Susannah Riley?" Callie says. "We're sure that's it?"

"Yeah, yeah that sounds right," Keegan says.

"Why do people think it was her?"

"Because she was a slut," McIntyre says. "Odds were pretty good someone knocked her up and she didn't know who the dad was." The word *slut* hits Callie like a slap. He looks at her as he says it, a satisfied gleam to his eye that tells her he relishes the chance to aim this word her way.

"She went AWOL right after the baby was found. She had dropped out of school before so it was hard to tell when she went missing, but no one ever saw her around here again. Innocent people—they don't run."

Something about that timing doesn't sit right with Callie. A teenager, vulnerable, had just given birth, somehow finds the resources and the wherewithal to start a new life somewhere else? But she humors Mac. "I'll look into that."

"Look into it? You actually trying to solve the case?" McIntyre shakes his head, fixes her with a pitying look.

"Asking questions. Sometimes with cold cases time shakes things loose a little bit." She bites her tongue about the bracelet, about the sense she has that there's a bigger story here.

"Sometimes some high-horse detectives think they can show some Pineys a thing or two about good old-fashioned police work. Like one of those HBO shows. Keegan, you going to the Tavern?"

"I was going to have one, yeah."

Keegan gives her a look—sheepish—but his loyalties are his loyalties. The guys all drink together in the one-room bar up the road. She sees their cars parked in the sandy lot every time she leaves a shift. Frank used to go—he's told her as much—but no one has ever asked her along.

Back in her office Callie searches Susannah Riley in the system. No records. Nothing online, no social media—or rather, too many Susannah Rileys that social media is of no immediate use. Girls twisting their torsos to pout at a camera. A Susannah Riley in England who posts pictures of her garden. Gnarled wisteria vines heavy with flowers. Tulips so purple they are nearly black.

Fuck it, she thinks. She'll use the bathroom, then get out of here. Her limbs are suddenly heavy with exhaustion.

In the stall she lets her head drop to her hands, lets her body go limp. She texts Jane, asks her how her day has been.

Jane sends her a link to a TikTok video. I've been going down such a rabbit hole with this one. Oh, and Opes made you a necklace. It's hideous and she's so excited to give it to you.

I'll wear it with pride.

Maybe wait till you see it first.

Callie clicks on the link and watches the first few seconds of the video. A lipsticked young woman with glossy hair explains that a woman was found dead in a field in 1979 in Western Pennsylvania, the cops looked at all the wrong people, but she's got a lead that is about to blow this thing wide open . . .

Callie closes the video. She can't deal with these internet detectives, their affected righteousness and thirst for gore. She texts Jane: Wanna know about the real life of a cop? I just spent my afternoon springing twenty-five muskrats from traps.

She puts her phone away, washes her hands, and when she turns to the door she finds a blue Post-it note on the back, eye level.

Sabrina Riley, it says, in Della's looping script.

Sabrina Riley she finds in the system. An arrest at seventeen for disorderly conduct in front of a bait shop where she was employed at the time. Time of arrest, 7:00 P.M. No mention of drugs or intoxication. A broken window. An altercation with a one William—Billy—Fauver.

"No shit," Callie says, lets out a little whistle.

Billy Fauver is in the system, too. His record is lengthier: one arrest for marijuana possession a decade ago, for which he did community service; poaching; a handful of traffic violations; arrested again, five years ago, in relation to a domestic dispute, battery; charges dropped by his ex-wife, a woman named Angela Harris.

Good guy, she mutters. Violent toward women. Nineteen years old to Sabrina's seventeen, not much of a difference but old enough that he would have the upper hand. Or want to have the upper hand. Wouldn't want to give her time, money, sacrifice his independence, his will to do what he wants when he wants.

What was it that Kirby had said? *Don't piss that guy off.*

In his mug shot Fauver looks offended. Chin thrust forward, mouth drawn in a tight line. Handsome, in a sneering way. Maybe Sabrina Riley would have found him magnetic, before she understood that he was really just mean. Maybe Fauver was a boyfriend, maybe a one-time hookup. Maybe she felt like she couldn't raise the baby on her own. The fight with Fauver might have been about paying for childcare. About getting him to help out. It would have been three months before the baby was found. The clock ticking. Riley getting increasingly desperate.

She cross-checks Sabrina Riley's address in the system with the location where Baby Doe was discovered, on Jenna's old street, three-quarters of a mile away from Sabrina Riley's house. Not inconceivable, if the girl had gone into the woods for privacy. Maybe she carried the child to the road, left it somewhere she hoped it would be seen before it was too late. A Safe Haven law wasn't passed in New Jersey until 2000, which made it legal to surrender an infant at a police station or fire department. She probably thought she would get in trouble for asking for help, or for leaving the child where the authorities could find it. And she was probably right.

She looks forward to dinner, to a glass of wine, to the simple, bare walls of her cabin, but when she gets home there's a dark stain at the base of her mailbox. She follows it upward, a trail of red up the post, the mailbox door hanging open.

She flicks her Maglite over it and makes out fur.

Inside the mailbox are the bodies of three muskrats, all of them slit open along their stomachs, revealing the wet ropes of their insides.

A message. A warning.

It could be any of them: Latour, Collins, Mac. Could even be Jimmy Nichols before he came around the bar to have beers with the old boys, the man they all think should be in her job right now, getting his payback.

She takes a breath. Methodical. Act first, react later. Heaves the bodies into a trash bag. Hauls a bottle of bleach and a roll of paper towels from under the sink. Scours the metal insides of the mailbox until the blood seems to lift. Bleach, bleach, and more bleach, until she is woozy with the stink of it.

Her appetite is gone by the time she peels the rubber gloves from her hands. She showers, needs to wash her hair but can't muster the energy. Instead she leans her head against the tile. She wills her mind to go blank but she can't shake the feeling of Layla's pulse going fainter, slower, underneath her fingertips. The life draining out of her face.

Her hands shake as she towels off, grabs her phone.

She tries Jenna's cell phone again, but this time it goes right to voicemail. She calls the two watering holes Jenna used to frequent but the bartenders she speaks to tell her neither have seen her in months. "Never thought I'd say that," one of them says, laughing as he hangs up.

An hour later her phone buzzes, but when she looks at the screen her relief is replaced by dismay. It's not Jenna, but Deveraux.

"Out with it." She likes him, but her reserves of patience dried up hours ago.

"Hey there, Chief. Uh, we've got something down in the station you should see."

"Can I get some details here?"

Deveraux sighs into the phone. "It's your mom's bag. Her wallet's inside. Her phone. A hiker found it in the woods off the Batona Trail an hour ago, about a mile from the Buttonwood Camp."

She tells Deveraux she'll be right there, even as a part of her is convinced he's gotten something wrong. Why would Jenna have been on the Batona Trail? That's fifteen miles from her house and her car is still impounded. And Jenna of all people was never one to hike.

There's something Deveraux isn't telling her. She can hear it in his voice, or not so much in what he says, but the careful way he's choosing his words. There's nothing she can do but climb into her Jeep and make her way back to the station again.

She finds him in the interview room. The purse is indeed Jenna's, an impractical straw bag with a fraying handle that belonged to Callie's grandmother. Deveraux hands her a box of latex gloves. She slides a pair on and removes the wallet. Inside she finds a twenty-dollar bill, a Stop and Shop card, Jenna's invalid license behind the clear plastic pane. A tube of lip gloss in a frosty pink—Jenna gave up lipstick years ago, too hard to apply when you've got the shakes. A package of Tic Tacs. She places each item on the table and once the bag is nearly empty she understands why Deveraux was so hesitant on the phone.

She shuts her eyes for a second, steadies herself with a deep breath before she pinches the green glassine baggie between her fingers. There's a scrim of white powder inside.

ANNABELLE

July 1990

You are walking back from the convenience store when the car slows at your side.

Your guts bottom out as he rolls down his window. A man. It's always a man.

"What are you doing out this way?" he asks.

You ignore him, or try to. You can't help but sneak a glance out of the corner of your eye. He's an impression. Dark hair. White T-shirt. Blur of a face before you turn your gaze back to the road, your cheeks already burning with shame and interest.

You and Sabrina have been stopped this way before. Twice, two different men. One slowed and in a gentle voice told you he was lost. Did they know if the parkway was this way or that way? Oh, weren't they such sweet girls, such kind girls. You hadn't even noticed his hand working up and down or his unzipped pants until Sabrina gripped your forearm so hard that her nails bit into your skin.

Pervert! Sabrina had screamed, and picked up a rock from the side of the road, threw it hard against the passenger's side door.

You little bitch, the man said, his voice changing then. Deeper, ragged, as though something rough was caught in his throat.

Sabrina didn't blink, just picked up another rock and sent it sailing, then a third, that dinged the man's bumper as he sped away.

You had stood still the whole time, stupid and silent as a cow. Always finding the words for things at least a beat too late. You envy this about Sabrina, her scalding quickness, her castigating temper. Her ability to draw up the right words at the right time while you find yourself haunted for days, weeks, by the retorts you could have made, the slights you should have addressed.

The man is still beside you, the smell of exhaust making you a little woozy. His car is creeping along so slowly that you can hear gravel pop under his tires, the creak of the rubber on the road.

"Hey. Come on now, don't be like that," he says. His voice sounds familiar, but there is no reason for a man who is not your father to be talking to you like this unless he is like the others. You steel yourself to use the words Sabrina did before—*pervert, creep*—and scan the shoulder of the road for suitable rocks but can't make out anything bigger than a pebble.

"You giving me the cold shoulder? Really?" A tinge of annoyance in his voice this time.

You stop walking and look, really look. He's handsome, so handsome that his anger makes sense. He's a man used to getting what he wants. Dark-haired, dark-eyed, with a belt of stubble along his jaw. White T-shirt fitted to show off the muscles taut across his shoulders and chest. Despite yourself, you feel a flutter between your legs. The same one you felt the other times, with the other men who pulled over. You knew enough to be ashamed, to not tell Sabrina, but it didn't stop the feeling from creeping in, a little fizzle in your veins that lingered even after the men sped away.

Your stupid, traitorous body. The same as Sabrina's in every way, and yet, Sabrina crouched and gripped the rock. Sabrina found the right words, sharp as arrows.

And then, just in time, you understand. He thinks you are Sabrina. His voice is familiar because you've heard it on the other end of the phone, when you've picked up upstairs and tried to decipher your sister's new life. The way Sabrina disappears around the curve of the driveway at night, her new habit of spending hours in front of the mirror, turning her face back and forth, her mouth ringed with lipsticks nicked from the drug store or from other girls' backpacks while they're busy finishing their homework or gossiping on the bus.

It has been a long time since someone confused the two of you. You've gone to school with the same sixty kids since kindergarten, kids who know that Sabrina is left-handed, that you bite your nails down to nothing. Sabrina wears her hair down, loose and wild, while you can't stand the feeling of it on the back of your neck. You look at the man again. Lock eyes with him. So much about your life just happens to you, the chime of the bells escorting you through your days at school, the obligations of homework and studying that rule your afternoons. You and Sabrina shopping for the cheapest cereals every week with the paltry stack of cash your father leaves you, while you eye mounds of fruit or read off flavors of popsicles you can never have. It occurs to you that you, for once in your life, have a decision to make.

"Okay now. There we go. Is this about last time? Come on, don't pout."

And you want to know. Want to know everything Sabrina has been keeping from you. Where she goes when she disappears down the driveway and waits out of view of the house. About what happens with this man when she gets into his car. What Sabrina does with him, who she is with him. You don't even know his real name. Sabrina won't tell. She calls him the Coyote and won't even say why.

The decision was always about Sabrina.

"I'm not mad," you say, trying to get the same lilt in your voice as Sabrina has on the phone, tilt your head a little for good measure.

"Good girl," he says. "Now get in."

In the beginning you hadn't believed that he existed. Sabrina said she met someone at the bait shop where she worked on the weekends. But then the phone rang at home a few weeks later and she lunged for it, and while she talked you tiptoed upstairs to your father's room and picked up the other line.

"I'm not that young." Sabrina's voice high and fluty in a way you didn't recognize.

"I bet you still have stuffed animals on your bed."

A giggle.

"And honor roll certificates on the wall."

"Merit roll."

"Well it's no fun being perfect, is it?"

"Definitely not."

"I'd love to see that room."

"Maybe you will someday."

A groan from the man like he had bitten into something delicious. You lowered the phone back into the cradle, your cheeks blazing, your back prickled with sweat. A flush of shame at your own honor roll certificates taped above your desk, at your stupid, naïve pride.

He speeds past the turnoff to your house. You don't ask where you are going. He's got the windows down, the radio on. Do they usually talk, Sabrina and this man whose name you don't know? You scan the car for something that will tell you. A work badge like the one your father clips to his shirt. A keychain that says John or Lou or Harry. Nothing. Just the litter of pumpkin seed shells on the floor of the car. A half-empty roll of wintergreen Life Savers in the cupholder between you, the same ones that you and Sabrina used to crunch in the dark of the bathroom, giggling as the mints sparked in your mouths like a magic trick.

Then, he's guiding the car off the main road, onto a dirt path. Past a sign that says PRIVATE PROPERTY. You, the rule-follower, are brimming with questions. Whose property? His? A stranger's? What will happen if someone finds out you are here? You bite your lip and stare out the window. You pass a cedar swamp, a layer of sphagnum moss dense at the base of the tree trunks—or what looks like the base. Your mother taught you long ago how the moss can grow in layers so thick that it looks like solid ground, but if you were to step on it you could find yourself in water over your head.

You can't hear any passing cars from the road where you turned. He's had to slow the car to a crawl to navigate the tightening path, the trees at the edge of the road brushing against the side view mirrors.

Finally, you stop in a small clearing. Out the windshield, bright-blue water.

You don't know where you are, but you know that color and what it means: aquamarine, jewel-bright. The Pine Barrens is known for its cedar water, the tannic creeks and lakes the color of tea left to brew too long. This water, though, is a Caribbean blue, the beckoning blue of tropical islands. Of warmer places studded with palms and home to easy, soft breezes.

But here? The color of the water is a warning.

Sinkholes. The woods here are riddled with them. Blue Hole is the most well-known: Every other year some high school kid or out-of-towner from Philadelphia takes a swim on a dare, having heard the stories but not believing them. Not believing that water that looks so inviting, so placid, can be home to deadly crosscurrents, that blue holes are really as deep as people say. One hundred feet to the bottom. The water can be cold enough to cause hypothermia, to make your muscles seize and your lungs tighten and your blood go to ice in your veins.

When you turn to him his eyes are on you, that same play of a smile at the corners of his mouth. The windows are still down but he's turned the engine off. Without the music there's just the sound of the woods. The trill of birds from up above and the *crack-crack* of squirrel patter in the trees.

A second later and his mouth is on yours, the moment shifting so quickly you wonder if you missed something, your brain skipping forward like a stone skimming the surface of a lake. It is so different from your first kiss, a chaste, dry, spin-the-bottle peck from Gregory Lepone last year. His fingers are cold up your shirt before he takes it off.

It is jarring, to see the pale of your body exposed in bright sunlight, to see the contrast of his tanned hands against it. He touches you through your jeans and you whimper, but too soon he takes his hand back, starts working at his belt buckle and then his fly. You feel embarrassed when you see him exposed, have to fight back the urge to giggle and wonder how he's not embarrassed too. But he only grabs your wrist and clamps your hand where he wants it, guiding you up and down and up and down. His head drops back. His hand—your hand—moves faster and faster.

This can't be it, you think. This can't be the reason Sabrina takes so much time choosing her outfits, why she roots through the Goodwill looking for new T-shirts she can knot at her hip, slash the necklines with scissors. Why she spends hours in her room, prodding and poking and posing. You wrestle your hand out from under his and for a moment he looks at you with such disdain you are worried he might slap you.

And then, that smile again, the half smile that makes you both excited and nervous. "I know what you want."

He reaches into the back seat for a blanket, opens his door. You don't know if you should wait for him or not, as you watch him spread the blanket on the ground next to the car. In the end he opens your door for you and guides you to the ground. A pebble bites into your shoulder but you forget it as he unbuttons your jeans, the zipper so loud in the silence. With a single hooked finger he gets your underwear off too. You watch it move down your thighs, over your knees, your shins, your ankles, like it is happening to someone else.

It feels good, his mouth on you, his hands wrapping around your thighs. It helps you understand why Sabrina has pulled away from you these past few months. There is so much in life that you both want, so little you can claim as your own. And here is something to want, this pleasure, that you can reach out and take, just like that.

He stops, positions himself so that his pelvis lines up with yours. You know what comes next and yet you can't believe it will actually happen. You are afraid and you wonder if he notices, the way your fingers have started to tremble. If you don't say anything now, today will be the day you lose your virginity. You will be transformed, remade, by him, a deep crack running through your life, Before and

After. The Coyote. Why does Sabrina call him that, you wonder. The thought costs you a few seconds, and before you can resolve whether or not you are ready he is over you, and then inside of you.

The pain is immediate and shocking, and instead of making you cry out it makes your voice crawl somewhere deep inside you, small and hidden. You hardly notice him moving above you, the sounds he's making. All you can think about is Sabrina. Had Sabrina felt pain like this? How did she survive it? How did she get to the other side?

Your eyes prickle with tears. You count backward from 1,000 and reach 364 before he shoves into you one last time. He makes a high, loud sound, not the groans you've seen in the movies, or that you once heard from your parents' bedroom at night. You aren't sure whether you want to laugh or cry. You want, most of all, to tell Sabrina that you understand now. That you are in on the joke. The Coyote. It suits.

As he stands you turn your head to one side, notice a single blond hair caught in the weave of the blanket, and wonder whether it is yours or hers.

He drops you off, your face raw and stinging with stubble burn. Already the afternoon has taken on the feeling of something unreal. Something that you will tuck away in your mind until you have the time and space to make sense of it.

"You might be even crazier than she is," he says, that rough chuckle again, a sound that makes the hair on your arms stand up.

"Who?" The word emerges as a mouse's squeak. Because you already know the answer.

He juts that cruel, handsome chin in the direction of the house.

Your throat constricts. You thought you had him fooled. But if he had been confused, it had only been for a moment. You had been ready to give yourself away when he didn't know exactly what he was taking. But he knew. He knew the whole time. *Crazy.* That word sticks to you, a burr. Are you crazy? Is she?

You turn your face away, fumble for the doorhandle.

"See you around, kid," he says, his mouth around a cigarette before you get out of the car, the silver of his lighter flashing in his palm.

You hoped that Sabrina would be busy, but she's in the kitchen when you come home, leaning over a bowl of cereal. Your stomach rumbles at the smell of sugar and milk and you realize you must have left your bag of food in his car.

"Where were you?" she asks.

You have no time to fortify yourself. Even if you could come up with a convincing lie, you are worried about the way the story will tell itself in your gestures, will play out on your face. The two of you have always been able to read one another this way, sometimes unwillingly. Twinship a forced sharing of thoughts, moods, pain. When you were girls, Sabrina would wake from across the room if you had a bad dream, climb next to you in bed, and stroke your hair until you fell asleep again. You could always feel Sabrina's headaches coming on, a change in the atmosphere of the room.

It takes you too long to answer.

"A walk," you stutter. Whatever decisiveness or boldness that possessed you when you climbed into the man's car is gone. You are back in your own body, your sore, damp, lonely-feeling body, where the words get caught in your throat.

Sabrina stares at you, unspeaking. It's in the air between you, the ionic crackle of a secret. Only now, seeing Sabrina in the flesh, do you think about what you have done as a form of betrayal. So little, nearly nothing, has ever belonged to one of you or the other—until the Coyote. You had merely been trying to right the balance, return to your equilibrium.

Sabrina finishes her cereal, clinks her dish into the sink, which is piled high with other bowls and plates, water cups clouded with fingerprints, coffee mugs whose rims are printed with lip gloss.

You run the water, hot, so hot it is nearly steaming. You start to scrub, dish by dish, taking your time, until the countertops are covered with wet, shining plates and slashes of glistening knives and forks. Until your hands are red and raw and no longer look like your own.

ANNABELLE

She knows. You know she knows. She can sense it off you, the alchemy of what he's opened up, the crosscurrents of shame and desire that now flow through you.

You await your punishment, slinking around the house, penitent and full of dread. A slap that lands hard and fast and aching when you least suspect it. Your bedroom door flung open, a scream like a hawk that has circled patiently before seizing its pray. Or a sly revenge that happens while your back is turned. Sabrina slitting all your clothes with a pocketknife. Tossing your notebooks into the fire.

Instead, she's quiet. Aloof, all the rest of the day Sunday, then Monday and Tuesday too.

On Wednesday night she walks down to the end of the driveway, her hair swishing loose on her back as she disappears around the crook that leads to the road, where you can just make out headlights—his headlights—through the trees. It's a heat wave and the oppressive weather makes everything worse, like you can't take a deep enough breath, a hand pressed against your sternum.

You lie awake that night until you hear the knocker on the front door—the lion with the brass ring clenched in its teeth—jangle. Until you hear her feet on the stairs.

You are relieved that your long days alone together are broken up by your shifts at the ice cream stand. You walk the mile there, the grip of the heat relentless, humidity thick in your throat. You avert your eyes from the heather blooming along the roadside, a plant your mother loved. Not especially pretty, but she always said she liked Pine Barrens heather because it was hardy and unique to where you lived. She used to cut the longer branches and arrange it in mason jars on the kitchen table. *Bright and strong, like my girls.*

Most days by the time you get to work your T-shirt—Sundaez and Cones!—is soaked through with sweat and you have to pull at least one tick from your ankles, then stomp bits of ground glass and gravel from the treads of your shoes. You never feel clean.

Work turns time slow and languorous, like the hot fudge sauce you dribble over custard. You often go an hour at a time between customers, without speaking to another soul, so you find small acts to perform to confirm that you still exist. Crumble a sugar cone in your fist until it looks like sand, push it around in piles. Spell your name in M&Ms. Sometimes you spill maraschino cherries on the counter and watch the bees glut themselves on the syrup until their bodies turn red with whatever dyes and chemicals constitute the sugary sludge.

But come Friday you have a day off, and so does Sabrina, which you've dreaded all week. In the few moments you've been in the same room as your sister you feel something charged between you, like air collecting humidity before a storm. A gathering of energy that will soon demand release.

That morning you eat in silence, you with your bowl of cereal, Sabrina with dry toast she mostly picks at. Out of nerves you pour yourself a second helping, so that you might have an excuse not to speak.

"What should we do?" Sabrina asks suddenly. The old assumption of your girlhood in play again, that you would spend the day together, every minute, a fact you'd taken for granted until she met the Coyote. For a moment, you tell yourself that everything will be okay. You try to keep your smile in check.

"We could play with Hannah and Iris?" Hannah and Iris are the dolls your mother gave you for your seventh birthdays, the few years when money wasn't tight and your parents could buy you Christmas gifts. You mean the suggestion as a peace offering—it has been years since the two of you played with them, but you think it could feel good. A return to your old selves, to the way things were. Entire afternoons lost to the worlds you created, the dramas unfolding nearly wordlessly between you, because you were so often thinking the same thing.

Sabrina scoffs. "Annabelle, we're not kids anymore."

"I was joking," you say, trying your best to keep the hurt out of your voice.

At Sabrina's suggestion, the two of you decide to pick mushrooms in the woods behind your house.

Almost as soon as you bend to pick your first mushroom, Sabrina finds hers. She scans the edge of the woods ahead of you and she crouches down low. An unspoken competition blooms, making the air throb. Every few minutes you'll straighten from picking one and find Sabrina watching you. Measuring something in you.

You find one mushroom, Sabrina finds two. You point out that one of hers looks like a Destroying Angel, which can cause your guts to turn themselves inside out, make your liver shut down, so poisonous that by the time the symptoms set in it's too late. You're dead. You warn her that she should probably dump her whole basket. Just to be safe.

"It is definitely not a Destroying Angel," she says, a hand on her hip.

"Eat it, then." You cross your arms, sure you have her, but then she opens her mouth and shoves the entire mushroom inside. She hasn't even cleaned it, so crumbs of soil collect at the edge of her lips. You are stricken, your mind already racing through the what-ifs. You picture yourself carrying your sister's limp body through the trees, to the road, flagging down a passing car. Sabrina only laughs, open-mouthed, at your shocked expression, the pulp of the mushroom spotting her tongue.

You resume your hunt and aim for blitheness, even though you are watching carefully, for beads of sweat to burst forth at her temples, for her skin to go yellow, for her eyes to glaze over.

"Well. That was stupid. Now you have one less than you did before."

"It's okay. I know places you don't know. Mom showed me."

You stiffen. Your mother has been gone for over two years. You came home from school to find two delicate heather flowers and two wooden animal figurines—a cat and a horse—in the gap in the brick wall of the old factory building, where the three of you would leave notes and trinkets for the others. A two-line message in her angular print on one of the rough scraps of paper she would make herself: *I love you. Forgive me.*

You and Sabrina pocketed the flowers and note, carried the carved animals inside, set them on the kitchen table, and when your father came home from work and asked where she was you gestured to them. He understood right away, walked over to your mother's favorite footstool, covered in blue gingham cloth and trimmed with bric-a-brac, and raised it over his head, slammed it against the wall until it splintered. Afterward he seemed both satisfied and shamed by this display of rage. You placed your flower between two sheets of wax paper and piled your textbooks on top to press it flat so that you might always keep it, this last tender, living thing that held your mother's touch.

Neither of you ever said it out loud, but you knew that in your heads you and Sabrina tussled over the note. That *you* of the *I love you* felt so small. Trying to make it cover both of you was like two people sharing a too-small umbrella in a thunderstorm.

Not long after your mother left your father took the night shift job down at the prison, his presence in your life reduced to little more than the heap of his boots by the door, the occasional stack of cash left under the brass letter opener that had been his great-grandfather's. Sometimes you see his car at the tavern up the road. Sometimes, you make out his slumped form in the front seat.

The mention of your mother stings, a sharp, astringent pain. You understand that Sabrina has been saving this statement, hoarding this knowledge, waiting for the right time to deploy it. The pain of it, and your exclusion, hits like a fist in your guts.

"She did not. When?"

"You were at school and I was home sick."

You inventory your memory for days in which you and Sabrina had been apart, back then. The list is short. But, you think you know. May, before your mother left, Sabrina woke feverish and flushed. It unsettled you all day, that something was happening to Sabrina that was not happening to you, and you could hardly pay attention in class.

You are still watching for signs that there is a poison coursing through her bloodstream when she turns abruptly on her heels and starts to walk back to the house.

"Let's go out to the factory," you call desperately at her retreating back. You ache for the afternoons you passed there as a trio, your mother with her fistfuls of wild plants that she turned into tinctures and salves. She hadn't grown up here but was more at home in the woods than your father, could break the land down into something that could be tamed.

Ahead, Sabrina swings her basket. A glittering thread at her wrist catches the light, and that's when you realize Sabrina is wearing your mother's old bracelet, cool spheres of amber that turn a bronzy gold in the sun. The surge of anger that bolts through you is sudden and total. Next thing you know you are running, and when you catch up you shove her as hard as you can. Her basket tumbles, mushrooms scattering in the grass.

"No!" Sabrina screams in a voice that you haven't heard since you were children: pure outrage. Then, her nails are in your skin, her face so close to yours that the ends of her hair tickle your shoulders. The two of you tumble to the ground, your body now heavier than hers for these past few months but Sabrina is more vicious, her fingers scrambling for your eyes, her hands at your throat. You land a hard kick to her shin, pull her hair until she yelps. For a second you can make out the smell of the mushrooms you've trampled, mineral and filthy, but even that passing thought is enough to put you at a disadvantage. Sabrina throws you off her and your head lands hard on the ground, your back teeth crashing together. The truth pulses between the two of you, both of you revealing just how much you want to hurt one another, in the way that only sisters can. Because in that rage, there is need. In that rage is its counterpoint—a wild, ineffable love.

Then, as quickly as she had attacked, Sabrina retreats.

"Annabelle," she says, and her voice sounds very far away, her breathing heavy. The sound of your name reminds you that you are separate: two brains, two throbbing hearts.

At first you don't know whose blood it is. Only that it is everywhere. Smears on Sabrina's cheek and wrist. A splatter on your shin. You both scan the ground, your eyes landing on it at the same time: a broken Ball jar, something your mother used to gather cut flowers in, half submerged next to what used to be her herb garden, the raised beds now disorderly with weeds. The rough edges of the pale blue glass shimmer with blood.

Once you see it, you feel it. The pulse drumming in your arm. Your shirt torn and the air on your skin where the fabric had been. The blood nearly black on the cotton.

"Stay here," Sabrina says, and bolts to the back door. The screen is wide open still from when the two of you first set out, now that your mother is no longer here to warn about flies. Now that there is never any fruit in the wooden bowl on the counter or baskets of scones to swarm. Only a freezer stacked with boxes of macaroni and cheese.

Wait, you want to say, though you know she is going to get help, to find a way to fix you. Please don't leave me.

You stare into the dark of the woods at the edge of the yard and wish you could stagger over and dip your body in the cool shade, but every time you move your cut surges with more blood. You lower yourself to the ground, not knowing if it is the heat or the bleeding that is making you lightheaded, making the world feel unfamiliar and indistinct. The blades of grass go fuzzy. The pines look like triangles, trees drawn by children.

Then, a sense of motion out of the corner of your eye. An animal, you think. But then you know the hands upon you as your sister's.

You are relieved enough to close your eyes, but then you open them to a flash of metal in the lazy summer light. With the blade of your father's pocketknife she cuts away the fabric of your sleeve, eyeing the wound evenly, without pity, without disgust or fear. She applies pressure, which makes you gasp, and the pain makes the world disappear for a moment, everything black. Sabrina's hands are steady as she wraps a dishcloth tight around your upper arm and she lifts the cloth every few minutes to check the bleeding, replaces one soaked rag with another.

She sighs. "I think you need stitches." Her voice is calm but she's started looking over her shoulder, as though she is searching for someone else who can help. "We could call an ambulance." What you both know but don't say: The hospital would be another bill. Another bill would be ruinous. Another bill would mean who knows how long without that cash appearing under the letter opener, both of you hungry, wearing sweaters that are too short this winter. The SAT registration fees you'll need to pay.

"I'll be right back."

She runs to the house and when she comes back she has a package of fishing line, 20-pound test, something she must have brought back from her job at the bait shop. But why? There's a glint in her teeth that you realize is a needle, something she probably had to scrounge out of your mother's sewing kit. She pulls a metal Zippo from her back pocket. Much nicer than the junky little Bic lighters your father uses to light up his Marlboros, or the long skinny matches your mother used for her beeswax candles. Where did you get that? You want to ask, but then you realize what she's about to do and the fear steals the thoughts from your head.

She flares the lighter and runs the needle through the flame.

You know you should feel something on your own behalf, but you can't. You are staring between the trunks of the trees, drifting somewhere else. Somewhere cooler, somewhere you are not encumbered by a body that can hurt and bleed. You have been able to do this since your mother left. Disappear from your body for long stretches of time. Leave your mind behind.

"Stay still," she says. She spills something over your wound, a chemical ammoniac stink to it, and it sizzles against your skin. You hear someone cry out, realize only when you see Sabrina wince that it is you.

She squints as she stitches, taking her time. Inhaling a little each time the needle pierces your skin.

"He told me he met you. Didn't say anything else. But he didn't have to."

"Oh," you manage to say. And you wonder how well you really know her. Wonder if she knew the glass was there, in wait, and she knew she just needed to get the angle right. Knew that if she was successful you'd be marked forever. And that there would be no risk of you thinking you could slip sideways into her life ever again.

"And I found those brochures under your bed."

The college brochures. Big cities and faraway places near the ocean. Schools Sabrina could never get into. Her voice cracks a little, but then she clears her throat. "Almost done," she says, soft, consoling.

You'll never know the truth. Whether she wanted to hurt you or heal you. Or maybe the truth is, she wanted to do both. Maybe that's what you both have wanted since you grew together in your mother's body, the two of you alone in the warmth and dark, competing for nourishment.

CALLIE

She and Devereaux walk along the edges of the trail in the waning light, Callie calling Jenna's name until she goes hoarse. She circles the place where the bag was left behind, but there are no signs of her mother anywhere. No footprints in the sandy soil. No trace of clothing. Not a strand of red hair tangled in the understory.

They get as far as the Buttonwood camp, where she shows a few hikers her mother's photo, but they only shake their heads over their tin-can dinners.

Callie stalks away from them, grinding her teeth. "Chief," Devereaux says tentatively, raising his eyes to the darkening sky.

He doesn't have to finish the rest of the sentence. They won't find her tonight if they haven't already. Worse, they'll end up lost in the woods themselves. The forest is dense and fickle and all these trails can go tricky. One step off them and you can walk for an hour thinking you're in a straight line when really you've been making a big circle, covering the same ground over and over again.

Back at the station she asks the troopers to send in K-9 units but they say they can't get out until the next day. If Jenna had been drunk or high, she couldn't have gotten far. It stands to reason that they would be able to track her down. Callie had been bracing for the worst out there. Jenna still and quiet among the trees. Lips blue, skin pale. The same way she found Layla. Except for Jenna it would be too late.

Next she calls hospitals and shelters on the off chance Jenna got dropped off somewhere by a civilian. She gets someone on the line in

Voorhees who reports a single Jane Doe heroin OD, but this woman is described as having tattoos on her arms. Not Jenna, then. Some other sorry soul.

Callie drives to Jenna's house again, this time not hesitating as she lets herself in. She searches through the drawers of Jenna's nightstand, in her dresser, rifles through the medicine cabinet in her bathroom—nothing stronger than Tylenol. She drops to the floor, crawling through the living room on her hands and knees to check underneath the furniture. No vial caps. No glassine baggies in any of the garbage cans. Not even booze in its usual hiding places—in the back of the linen closet, behind the extra sheets. In the cabinet above the refrigerator.

She drops onto Jenna's couch and plugs in the dead phone that had been found in the purse, taps her foot while she waits for the screen to chime to life. Almost all of the notifications that flood in are her own messages and calls. Most of Jenna's recent outgoing texts are to coworkers hoping to trade off shifts or bitching about the new back of house staff at the diner. But there's one person she seems to be in touch with daily: someone named Steve Wilkins. Their messages are sparse—*Can we talk in an hour? How are you doing today? See you tomorrow?*—but the call log tells another story. Sometimes they spoke for an entire hour. Jenna has saved his picture—an older man smiling through a bush of white beard, a red bandanna tied over his head. A boyfriend? Looks too nice to be Jenna's type, but Callie dials him and he picks up on the third ring.

"Jen? I'm glad to hear from you."

"I'm sorry, this isn't Jenna. It's her daughter."

"Callie?" A pause, and even over the phone she can hear this man choosing his words carefully, the way Deveraux had. "Is she—"

"She's missing. I hadn't heard from her in a few days and then her belongings were found abandoned off of a walking trail."

"Oh," Steve says, and in just that syllable the sorrow is unmistakable.

"It looks like she was in touch with you quite frequently. Can I ask what your relationship is to her?"

"We're friends."

"You talk an awful lot. It's not romantic?"

"No, no. I'm married."

"Does your wife know you spend hours on the phone speaking with my mother? Texting her?"

"That's not really—"

Callie cuts him off. "Mr. Wilkins, I have a sense you aren't telling me something. Let me impress upon you the seriousness of this call. This is a missing persons case. It's not looking so great that she spent hours on the phone with a married man every week and now is nowhere to be found."

Steve Wilkins clears his throat. "I'm her sponsor. AA."

Callie shuts her eyes. A sponsor. She was really doing it. Really trying.

"Did she tell you about her relapse? She was brought into the station the other night. DUI."

On the other end of the line Steve exhales heavily. "I didn't know that, no. I called her when she didn't make the meeting the other night. And then every day after that."

"Park police found her purse and there were drugs in it. Heroin. Do you know if she had used before?"

"We talked about it, when we first started working together. No drugs for her. Said it was only ever that one love, booze. I feel like she would have told me, if she were struggling with that. I . . . I don't really know what to make of it. But you see people make all kinds of choices in this life when they are hurting."

"Yeah. I was surprised too. Okay, well. I have her phone but if she calls you, could you call me down at the Pine Lakes station? Right away."

"I certainly will. I'll be praying for her." She doesn't believe in prayer or God—too close to superstition—but his kindness touches her all the same. "And, Callie?"

"Yes?"

"She's very proud of you." Callie fights off the prickle of tears, even as she wonders if he's telling the truth. The Jenna she brought in a few nights ago would beg to differ. Callie can't get that raw-throated cry out of her head. *The shame of my life.* The last thing her mother said to her.

"I'm glad she has you. Thank you, Steve. Please do let me know the second you hear anything. It seems like she trusts you."

The most recent number in Jenna's outgoing call log wasn't saved in her phone. Callie searches it on Google first—she doesn't like calling someone without knowing who she is taking to.

The first result is a business listing. William Fauver's Autobody shop. Dialed at 8:05 A.M. on Thursday morning. Not long after she had been released.

Looks like she knows her first task for the morning, then.

She rises at the first hint of daylight, scarfs a half-crushed granola bar from her bag. She spent the night on the lumpy couch in her office, up late printing off a stack of missing posters, a picture of Jenna from one of the women she worked with, from their holiday party last year. Callie uncovers a cheap plastic hairbrush in the bottom of her desk drawer and does her best not to look like a woman who slept with her face on her blotter. It rained in the night, a loud insistent pounding that woke her with a start. The kind of rain that will scour the woods clean, make it impossible for the dogs to find Jenna's scent today.

"What the hell have you done?" Callie asks the picture of Jenna on the flyer, her voice rising, breaking, her throat still raw from shouting in the woods the night before.

When Devereaux and Latour get in she hands them a stack of posters and tasks them with putting them up on every telephone pole and supermarket bulletin board they can find within a twenty-mile radius.

"Is this the best use of our time?" Latour asks. "Department resources on a missing person with a history of substance abuse? Who is probably trying to skip out on her court date?"

The anger that rears up in her is huge, total. "You seem to have a hard time grasping that you report to me. That your time is my time, Latour. From the second you walk in that door to when you leave at night, you're mine. Understand? And hey, you'll need this." She pulls a staple gun out of her pocket, whips it at him a little harder than she needs to so that he has to snap his hands up to keep it from clocking him in the jaw.

"Glad those reflexes are still good. You'll need that if you get bounced off the force and need to go back to breaking up bar fights at the Lodge, like you did when you failed your test at the academy the first time around. Don't think people don't know about that. I know plenty about all of you. How you got here. How you spend your free time. You probably want to register that second hunting rifle you've been taking out."

Next to him Devereux suppresses a smile while Latour's face goes white, his eyes narrow. But the last thing she's afraid of is a simple man's anger. Maybe it will mean more shit talk behind her back. Maybe it will mean more dead animals in her mailbox. But she won't hear one more person implying, one way or another, that Jenna's life means nothing.

She's still fuming as she walks out to her squad car, but when she sees someone on the ground stretched out it alongside it, she loses it.

"What the hell is this?"

Luke casts her a look over his shoulder. He's got the car up on a pair of jacks, the front left wheel on its side next to him. He's in a T-shirt, tools laid out on the back of a flannel shirt he must have just taken off.

"You said your brakes were loud. I'm replacing the brake pads. Totally shot."

"You came all the way over here to replace my brake pads?"

He shrugs. "And maybe I was delivering some new red bark cedars for a landscaping project nearby. But you mentioned at dinner the other night that it was getting on your nerves."

"If I didn't find you out here, were you going to come in and tell me? Or just let me think the brake fairy paid me a visit in the night?"

"Guess so." He wipes his hands on a grease-streaked cloth.

His eyes shift over her shoulder, to the doors of the station. Unlike Frank, Luke is a lone wolf, and she gets the sense that he's not eager to strike up small talk with the likes of Collins or Mac.

"What if I need my car right now? Like, right fucking now?"

"I just need to get this wheel back on and you're set."

She's raging. Every minute she has to wait is another minute she doesn't know what's going on with Jenna. She's done circling Fauver—now she has reason to head right to his front door. She paces the lot while he finishes up, puts the wheel on, tightens the lug nuts, removes the jacks.

Luke stands, rubs his hands on the front of his jeans. His tools are packed, his job is done, and yet he looms there like he's waiting for something else from her. Measuring something in her. Is it romantic, like Jane thought the other night?

"Something wrong?"

"My mom. She's missing." She doesn't want to go in to details. The bag. The drugs. Her worst nightmare from childhood unfolding: everyone seeing the true disorder of her life, the shame that she's never been truly able to shake off. Something to hold up against any mistake she makes and say *no wonder*. And her mother finally gone for good.

Luke gives her another one of those long stares. In his stillness she swears she can sense a thought pass over him. Probably same as Latour and everyone else. That whatever is going on with Jenna, she deserves it. That she brought it on herself. "I'm sorry to hear that," he says eventually.

"I've got to go." He steps aside so she can get in her car, and she slams the door hard, feeling his eyes on her again as she pulls out of the lot.

As she drives she runs through her theories. Maybe Sabrina Riley was just the first of many women on Fauver's bad side and who had paid the price for it. She's certainly come across so many like him, men who manage to strew the wreckage of women's lives behind them without any cost to themselves. And now Jenna got in his way somehow. Maybe Fauver sold to her and found out she was the mother of a cop. She's seen people offed for less.

According to Google the garage opens at 9:00 but when she gets there at 9:30 the battered doors of the two-car bay are shut. There's no light on in the office, or that she can see behind the glass panes plastered with old bumper stickers.

There's a house set back behind the shop, a rancher with sheets tacked to the windows, a filthy storm door leading to a sagging side porch. She figures she came all the way out here. She gets out of the car, steps over broken wooden storage palettes and empty soda cans, searches for a doorbell and can't find one, so knocks once on the doorframe, hard and quick.

At the second knock she hears a shout from inside the house. Footsteps, then silence. A creak from somewhere deep inside, more footsteps, retreating, silence again.

Then a voice, close, just over her shoulder, that makes her jump.

"What do you want?"

Callie pivots, finds herself standing just under Billy Fauver's chin. He's grinning, an ugly, snide smile. She takes a step back, stumbles a little. His grin gets even wider.

She expected him to look a fair bit older than in his mug shot, but even by her least generous assumptions, Billy Fauver is not a man who has aged well. He's still big, broad, but with a hard old-man's belly, the whites of his eyes crazed with veins. His hair both receding and greasy, stands up unbrushed and wild, and situated in the middle of that infuriating little smile is a gray tooth, dead at the root.

"Anyone with business at my house knows not to try the front door." He crosses his arms. A snake tattoo curls from underneath the edge of his T-shirt, the jaw opening near the bones of his wrist.

"Mr. Fauver, yes?" He doesn't say a word, doesn't budge. "You still running the garage? Online it says you're open nine to five."

"You here for an oil change or something?" Again, that hint of mirth in his voice. “Besides, everyone knows the internet is chock full of shit, right?”

He looks her up and down slowly, making sure she notices him studying her. A move she knows well by now, and still it makes her want to kick in the soft, rotten wood of his porch step.

“I’m Chief Callie Hauser and I was wondering if I could ask you a few questions.”

If the word *chief* gives him any pause he doesn’t show it. She needs it now, something she can hold between her and this man. Fauver says nothing, just clears his throat and hawks a plug of phlegm a few inches from her shoe.

“Have you seen this woman?” Callie holds up the missing poster.

“I don’t know her.”

“She called you. Three days ago. Did you speak with her?” According to Jenna’s call log Fauver had picked up and the call lasted a minute.

“I don’t know,” Fauver says, looking bored. He hands the picture back to Callie.

“Any guess why she called you?”

“Maybe she needed a car repair. I didn’t talk to her, though.” He smiles then, a smug little grin that makes Callie want to scream.

“Her car had recently been impounded. She hadn’t reclaimed it yet.”

“I’m not sure why you’re on my ass about this.”

“She’s missing, as you can see. You were the last person she had contact with before her phone died.”

“I said I didn’t talk to her.”

It is interesting that Jenna used his garage’s line. If he is involved with the drugs, surely he’s not stupid enough to give out that number to people buying from him. But if Jenna were just dabbling, maybe had only heard Fauver was in the game, she would have called him straight up.

“Does someone else work for you? Anyone else who would have answered the phone?”

“Nobody.” Fauver turns to go back inside.

She grinds her molars so hard it’s a wonder she doesn’t feel a tooth crack. She shouts to his back. "Wait. While I'm here I'd also like to ask you some questions about Sabrina Riley."

He stops and turns. "I don't know who that is either, lady." But there's the slightest shift in his bearing. His fingers tense. His shoulders rise.

"You were arrested after the two of you got into an altercation in front of Hines's Bait and Tackle in January, 1991. So you met her at least that once."

"I don't recall the incident."

"You have absolutely no memory of getting into an argument with a teenage girl that led to your arrest? I have some trouble believing that."

"What you believe isn't my problem."

"You must fight with a lot of women, then, if that particular day is so unremarkable. I noticed a few domestic charges on your record."

"If you're here about Angela you can tell her to go fuck herself. I haven't seen or heard from her in four years."

"Women who give you a hard time tend to go missing, it seems."

This gets to Fauver. She can practically feel it, heat coming off him now, the twitch of his muscles. She's hit a sore spot.

"What the hell is that supposed to mean? Angela ran off. I didn't do shit to her."

"No one has seen Sabrina Riley since '91. Not long after your argument with her. I have a theory that she might have been hiding a pregnancy, and there's word that the two of you were romantically involved." It's a leap, but she's leaning on the dumb talk from the guys at the station.

"No way. That skinny little bitch? Couldn't hide anything on her. She was all bones."

Callie has to surpass the urge to smirk. This is where she wants him. Scared, slipping up. "So you do remember her?"

The color rises in Fauver's cheeks. "She came after me, okay? I was minding my own business, forgot she even worked at that store, and she's there screaming at me, going absolutely apeshit, saying I ruined her life."

Callie makes another tally mark in the column for Fauver as the father. It makes sense, Sabrina would level that at him if he got her pregnant, left her without any help. Still, she wants to hear it from Fauver himself. "Why would she say you ruined her life?"

"She was crazy. I have no idea why she would say that." She's so tired of that word. *Crazy Sabrina. Crazy Jenna.* Crazy is a blank check men write themselves to deal with women however they want.

"What had your relationship been before that day? She wanted more from you and you broke it off? Let me guess, you were just trying to have fun and then she needed something from you and that pissed you off? What could have made you so mad, Fauver? That you went in the bait shop and broke that window? What did she do to you?"

Fauver opens his mouth, but then something over Callie's shoulder catches his attention. She turns in time to see a car in the parking lot of the garage. It cools him off, the presence of another person, and he comes back into himself, gathers his thoughts. A shrug of the shoulders, slight shake of his head. The heat goes out of the moment, which is both good and bad. He won't fly off the handle, and he won't let anything else loose. "I've got things to do. And I've got no obligation to talk to you. And for the record, she was the one who broke the window."

Fauver stalks away, ducks to speak to the driver in the lot. He looks once, over his shoulder at her as she walks back to her car, angling his body to block her view of whoever he's talking to. He's a big man, but still, she catches him accept an envelope from the driver and slip it into his pocket, the snake tattoo along his arm undulating with a smooth, unexpected grace.

Fauver disappears around the back of the house as she pulls away. She thinks of what he said about Sabrina Riley having been thin. How he didn't think she could hide a pregnancy. But some women, especially first-time mothers, don't show for a while. Jane had complained about it, sending Callie pictures when she was five, six months pregnant. *I thought I would look like a bountiful-mother-earth-goddess and I just look like I ate too many slices of pizza.*

The timing, three months before the baby was found, makes it a little more of a stretch, but not impossible. Sabrina could have worn loose clothing. And there was definitely something there, something he didn't want to tell her. How she had to back him into admitting any relationship with her. To even knowing her at all. Why deny it, unless all these years later there was something he was ashamed of, guilty about? Something he was eager to hide.

CALLIE

Her next stop is the tackle shop where Sabrina Riley worked. Inside Callie is greeted by dusty glass counters stocked with fishing reels and rod parts, and behind that, a burbling minnow tank and a yellowed fridge that looks older than she is. Tattered newspaper articles bragging about prize-winning pickerel catches taped along the freezer. Next to that, a sign written in black marker on a piece of posterboard. WORMS MAGGOTS MINNOWS FROGS.

An older man steps into the shop, tips the brim of his baseball cap with hands scarred from years of handling fishhooks and lures. "Help you? I'm Gary Hines, owner. I came in when I saw your patrol car out there."

"Callie Hauser."

"So, you're the new chief, huh? Frank Caputo is a good friend of mine. Jimmy, too, of course . . ."

Callie doesn't say anything to that. Hines is probably waiting for her to offer him some consolation, a crumb of self-deprecation. But if Jimmy had been good enough to get the job, he would have had it, and that's that.

"Anyways, I always give the guys in blue a free drink outta the cold case. Figured you mighta heard about that and stopped in. Please, help yourself."

"I'm okay, but thank you."

Gary Hines frowns, reaches around Callie and slides open a frost-coated freezer door, leans in and pulls out a root beer. "Here."

She doesn't want the drink but doesn't want to squander any

goodwill either, so she takes the can from him, pops the tab, swigs. So cold and sweet it makes her teeth hurt.

"Thanks. That's really nice of you. How long have you owned the place?"

"Came to me in '82 after my dad died."

"So you owned the store when a young woman named Sabrina Riley worked here."

"I did. It was good, you know? To have a young lady behind the counter. Not to be crass, but you know how it is. The guys liked the chance to come in and talk to a pretty girl."

A bolt of revulsion works its way through her. *You know how it is. One of those things.*

"Sure." Sabrina Riley installed at one of these counters, her own kind of bait. "What do you remember about her?"

"She was charming. Sweet. Nice smile. She didn't know anything about fishing but that didn't matter. Most of my guys come in here knowing what they want."

"How long did she work here?" She tries to decide if Hines is the type of man, who, on a slow day, might put his hand to the small back of his young female employee. Who might have been charming enough to convince her to sleep with him. Or the kind of man who could convince her that her job there was tenuous, take advantage of the fact she needed cash. Or who might lock the door, might not listen if she said no. Ugly thoughts, and yet. He can't even listen to a woman when she says she doesn't want a soda.

"About two years."

"Why'd she quit?"

"She never told me. Just stopped showing up. I called the number I had on file for her after two no-show shifts but the line had been cut off."

"Do you know anything about her home life? Her parents?"

"Eh, she was a teenage girl, I was in my forties then. We didn't exactly chat much. She kept to herself, that one."

"Any sense that there was violence or neglect going on? She ever show up with bruises or anything? Did she seem afraid to go home?" According to records, Terry Riley was killed after he crashed his car through a guardrail in Baton Rouge in March 1993. Two years after his daughter disappeared. His BAC was 0.2 percent. She couldn't help but feel a shiver of recognition when she read about the Riley father. Sabrina Riley was a girl not unlike Callie, fending for herself the best she could, trying to find a stay against the ugliness of her home life.

"Nothing that I ever noticed."

"Do you remember a time when she got into an altercation here? It resulted in her arrest along with a young man named Billy Fauver. Broke your front window, according to the report."

"Mean little bastard, Fauver. He was always coming around here to talk to her. Caught him a few times slipping a bobber or a package of sinkers into his pocket, just because he thought he could."

"Were you here the night the cops came?" From the report it seemed like it had been close to closing time. Fauver probably thought he could catch Riley alone, talk to her or threaten her or whatever he was up to. And then she fought back. Someone driving by saw them scuffling outside, pulled into the lot to see the gleaming glass.

"No. I had been up at my sister's in Tannersville. But Frank Caputo called me himself, told me there had been a little trouble. She never came back after that."

Callie slides the photograph out of the file she's kept pinned under her arm. "Does this bracelet look familiar to you? Something that perhaps belonged to Sabrina?"

Hines nods. "It was the one thing that pissed me off about her. I told her from day one, no rings or bracelets. Didn't want to risk it breaking, getting those little beads stuck in the filters of the tanks. But she'd wear it anyway."

Finally, some traction. This small inroad. Circumstantial still, but not nothing, either. She puts the photo away, braces herself for the next question. "Is there any reason to believe she was pregnant at that time?"

Hines's face hardens. "You're asking about those rumors. The baby. Why didn't you just come out and say that?"

The root beer is still so cold she has to switch hands, shakes condensation from her fingers. "Okay then. What can you tell me?"

"I can tell you that it was a damn abomination. You don't want a child, fine. Take it to be adopted. Let someone else care for it. But to do what that woman did is the ugliest thing I ever heard."

Callie nods, and of course after seeing the case files, she has to agree that yes, what happened was heartbreaking, brutal, but she feels herself gripping the can in her hand a little tighter. There's something else here, something that none of them are seeing. She waits a beat to point out that Gary Hines hadn't exactly answered her question.

"No, no, no. That girl was sweet. She didn't have it in her to do that horrible thing."

She can't help but feel impatient with Hines, senses she won't get anywhere else with him. But at least he's confirmed that the bracelet belonged to Sabrina, which isn't nothing.

"Okay, well, thank you for talking with me. If by chance you do think there's anything I should know, please leave a message with Della at the station."

She stands in the parking lot for a moment, surveys the morning. The air is cut through with a chill. The first leaves pinwheeling to the ground. In the quiet she picks up the trickle of water nearby and she scans the perimeter until she spots a narrow path between the trees. She can picture Sabrina Riley toeing her way along that path, taking a break away from the clutter of the shop, smoking a cigarette at the edge of the water, and so Callie follows it to see where it leads.

Gnats buzz around her incessantly as she walks, and no matter how many times she swats them away they find her, humming close in her ear, intimate. The path narrows to a pinch and even through the legs of her pants the underbrush scratches, claws at her shins. Finally, she emerges at the bank of a stream, wider and clearer than she would have expected, tree branches spanning across each side, connecting in a canopy overhead.

She sighs, puts her hands on the back of her head. Maybe Fauver had tried to hurt Sabrina that night, his temper boiling over, and she just got lucky that time, the bystander driving by who reported the broken window to the cops. A new picture of Sabrina Riley emerges, still hazy and uncertain: fighter, and possibly victim. At first she wanted to consider Jenna and Sabrina as opposite sides of the same coin. Jenna the innocent, Sabrina the evil one. But the more she learns, the more similar they become, two vulnerable teenagers whose lives went off course. Sabrina Riley, whom everyone was content to malign or turn away from and then forget about. Jenna, who saw something so brutal, something from a nightmare, and was sent back out into her life and expected to forget, deal with it, to move on.

A twig snaps to her right, brings her back into her surroundings. "Hello?" she calls, wary. She hopes it isn't Hines, poised to scold her some more, or lord around his so-called goodwill toward the cops. She's met with silence so she raises her voice, her mind throbbing with all of these stories and theories, about young women being touched in ways they don't want, about women finding some kind of ugly fate out here among the trees. "Police! Who's there?"

"Uh . . . Adrian," a voice says, and a man rises from behind a bush a little way upstream. He holds his hands in the air near his waist. There's a plastic test tube in one of them. "I'm just here collecting a sample. Is that okay?"

She's embarrassed by her zinging heart rate, by the beads of sweat that have sprung along the back of her neck. This place is fucking with me, she thinks. All these things she thought she escaped: that constant press of the woods from every angle. The way it always makes her feel small and conspicuous at the same time. Like something hunted.

The man is still staring at her, waiting for her answer. She casts about for an excuse but can't think of any. "Sorry," she says instead.

"That's okay. I'm used to slipping around through the woods but

I can get how that might make someone else on edge. I'm not used to running into people while I work either. So, all good if I collect some samples?"

The adrenaline drops away and she feels wrung out, and she can no longer ignore the tension headache that has pulsed across her forehead ever since she first laid eyes on Jenna's purse. "Sure, yeah. I'm just—" She looks over her shoulder at the narrow thread of the trail, her shins still stinging. "I'm just going to take another minute here, if you don't mind."

"Not at all. Are you . . . are you okay?"

"Bad day. Or maybe a bad year. I don't know."

"Sorry to hear that."

"What are you measuring?"

"I test for salt water intrusion. Or at least that's what I'm looking at today. The waterways here are fascinating."

"Sounds like it." A hurt look flashes across his face and she hates herself for it. He's young, her age, good-looking in an academic sort of way. Thick-framed glasses, ropy muscles, good posture. Another gnat tickles at her ear and she shakes her head, grunts. He smiles, reaches into one of the many pockets on his vest, tosses her something that she is almost too surprised to catch.

"Most people don't throw things at officers in uniform, you know."

"I think I'm doing you a favor."

She turns the bottle in her hand. Bug spray. "Thanks." She spritzes her wrists and rubs them together, relaxes a little at the idea of doing this one small thing that should bring her relief, even just for a few minutes.

"You're not from around here, are you?" she asks. The way he looks at the water, the woods, is too reverent.

"No. Or, I didn't grow up here. I'm from Lewisburg, Pennsylvania. My parents were professors at Bucknell. I teach down at Stockton. But I live in Mullica, right on the river."

"Nice." What must that be like, she wonders. A profession handed down. A legacy that wasn't trauma or dysfunction or pain.

"I like it well enough. It's good kayaking and the sunrises are something to behold."

"I've never been on a kayak."

"Well that's a crime. It's the best way to enjoy the woods, as far as I'm concerned."

"Yeah I've heard that before. My friend, Jane, she and her husband own Pines Adventure Company. She was always after me to go." It hits her a beat too late, that the way she's talking about Jane makes it sound like she's dead.

"You should take her up on it."

"She's—uh. Well. She had a bad accident a little ways back. She won't be out for a while." *Please*, she thinks. *Please don't make me explain.*

"I'm sorry to hear that. I've heard of her company. It seems like they do a lot of cool stuff. I don't want to overstep . . . maybe you want to go out for the first time with your friend when she's better. But if you ever felt like it, I've got two singles we could take out."

He reaches into his vest, finds a notebook, scribbles on a piece of paper that he tears out from a pad in another pocket. He walks down the bank and reaches over some brush to hand it to her, their fingertips touching for a second before coming away. Is this guy really asking her out? Out here in the woods? While she's wearing her uniform, swearing at the bugs? She's in no frame of mind to date. Her mother is missing. She works too many hours. She's chasing down a drug ring. She's taking care of Jane and Opal. And yet, she feels a little thrill taking the scrap of paper from him. Maybe there is one part of her life that should feel normal. One little pocket that isn't touched by the shadows of everything else.

"I'll check my calendar." She gestures at the uniform. "Work's been busy."

"I get it. But get in touch if you're up for it. I promise, I'm not as creepy as I seem when I'm sneaking around the woods."

She surprises herself by laughing. "Oh. Here." She holds up the bug spray.

"You hang on to that. So long as you tell me one more thing."

She frowns.

"Your name?"

"Callie. I'm Callie."

"Nice to meet you, Callie. Hope your day gets better."

"Yours too. Can't feel great to get shouted at by a cop in the middle of doing your job."

"I think it worked out okay."

She nods at him, a stupid grin on her face. She clutches the paper in one hand and the bottle of the bug spray as she follows the path back to Gary Hines's lot.

Later that night she's still on shift, backs up Collins on a call about a group of kids having a party in the woods. They arrive at the trail-head within minutes of one another, have to take the path on foot.

"They're probably in the factory," he says, nodding toward the sound of music, an occasional screech or whoop rising above the beat.

Callie knows the one he means. It used to be a brick baking factory, a whole little town. Schoolhouse, foreman's home, tiny cabins for the workers. Not much left of it but the foundation of the factory building, one wall. But its where kids have been doing this shit since she was in high school. The owner died before it could open and then the property's caretaker and his wife died on the site after they lit a fire without cleaning out the flue. Whole town went up in flames and now it's another ghost story people tell about what used to be.

They walk the trail without turning their flashlights on—don't want to give the kids a chance to spot them and scatter. The toe of her boot catches on something in the blackness—a railroad track, the rail line long defunct—and she hits the ground hard. Collins offers her a hand to help her up but she only shakes her head at him, her knees stinging and her face burning.

They approach the edge of the ruins, a bonfire in a trashcan lighting up the technicolor graffiti on the old factory structure. The kids have their backs to them, a few girls dancing around a speaker propped up on a boulder, two boys passing a joint between them a few feet from the girls, eyes locked on their swiveling hips, three others clustered in what looks like the mouth of a tunnel, taking turns insulting one another. Collins kicks an empty bottle of lighter fluid.

"Idiots." He steps ahead of Callie and cups his hand around his mouth. "Listen up. Everyone where I can see you. You run, you're screwed, you understand? We got guys on all sides here, you're bound to run from me and right into the arms of one of my colleagues, who will not be inclined to be gentle."

For the most part the kids don't look too alarmed at his bluff. No one shouts *cops* and makes a break for it, tries to hide. No one pours out their beers, and even the kid holding the joint is slow to pinch it out. Callie glares at Collins, unbelieving. He should have waited for instructions from her, followed her lead.

Collins is undeterred. "Any of you morons over twenty-one here?"

"Eat shit!" one of the boys yells from the other side of the trashcan.

A girl with a long braid hisses at him. "Shut up, Ryan." She crouches, sets her beer down at her feet. "Please take him in. He's so annoying."

"You love me, baby." Ryan wags his tongue at the girl. Callie catches a boy in a tie-dye shirt and a pair of mesh basketball shorts slide a hand into his pants pocket, a flash of green between his fingers.

She aims her flashlight on him. "You. What do you have there?"

"My inhaler," he says.

"Show me."

He stares at her, weighing his options, then shoves his hand into his pocket, draws out one of the little green glassine baggies, the pine bough stamped on it.

"What is it?" she asks, keeping her voice light.

The kid doesn't answer, just stares hard past her left ear.

Collins clears his throat. "I believe Chief Hauser asked you a question."

She wants to roll her eyes, to tell Collins that she's just fine on her own with this shrimp of a kid, who can't be more than seventeen. She doesn't need his Bad Cop act. She can practically sense him puffing up his chest.

She holds out her hand for the package and he gives her a hateful look as he places it in her palm.

"Where'd you get it?" She's still aiming for a tone that feels conversational. They need these kids to open up to them if they're going to learn anything about the drugs. Hollow scare tactics aren't going to cut it. She's got to toe the line between authentic yet firm. None of this cop caricature crap that Collins is pulling.

The kid cuts his eyes across the bonfire, then back to Callie. "I don't know."

Now, time to press a little. "Look. I'll level with you. I'm doing you a favor, here. Lots of dirty drugs circulating these days. But it sounds like you're not feeling too chatty out here among your friends. I could take you into the station, where we could talk properly? Or if you wanna help me out now, we can skip all the formalities. You let me know. We would have a lot to discuss if I take you in. Possession charges. Underage drinking. Would you like to do that?"

"Get some, Matty, she's hot!" She swivels to see which one of them said it, but her eyes fall on one of the girls. A petite blond sitting on a rock. Layla. The girl from the paintball field. The girl with the braid puts her hand on Layla's shoulder, leans in to whisper in her ear. Layla groans, shakes her head. The firelight shows the shine of her eyes. Sweat glistens across her collarbones. She's used recently. No surprise there, but Callie can't help but feel a pang. She turns back to the boy.

"Where'd you get it?" she asks him again.

"Usually I buy from a guy named Johnny."

"Where do I find Johnny? Can you tell me anything else about him?"

"He's older . . . he hangs out at the gas station on Route 12 sometimes. But someone else got this for me this time. Look. I mean it. I don't know." She doesn't believe the lie but he manages not to give himself away completely until his eyes dart across the fire, to Layla.

Ah.

Callie and Collins divide the kids up. She gives the girls a ride home, Layla and her friend Amanda. She drops Layla off first, at a tidy Colonial with a minivan parked in the driveway, the porch festooned with wind chimes that ting in the breeze.

"What was she on?" Callie asks Amanda, as they watch Layla fit her key into the lock.

"She snorted something. The green bag."

"Heroin?"

Amanda gives a little nod, turns her face to the window, but not before Callie catches a tear streaking down her cheek in the rearview.

"She's been in a lot of trouble this year. I'm pretty sure there's an older guy she works with who has her dealing, but she won't tell me. She knows I get mad when she takes this stuff. It's not like it was before."

"What do you mean?"

"People started buying the green bags back when they were just selling mushrooms. That was fun. But we haven't been able to get the mushrooms again since the end of the summer. A kid I know from Collingswood, though? He bought some stuff two weeks ago and overdosed. His shit was salted with fentanyl. He's fucking dead." The redhead had been trying so hard to sound older, in control, but her voice cracks on the word *dead.* A copycat, Callie thinks. She's seen it before. One guy starts making cash, another, less connected, less experienced, jumps in to grab a piece of the pie.

She feels for this girl. How helpless she must feel. Just like Callie, when she first saw Jane in the hospital, bruised and swollen, numbed out on morphine.

"Where does she work?" Callie asks

"A plant nursery. It's called Eden Grows"

"I know it," Callie says. She's never been there, but she's seen the logo plenty of times. On T-shirts she's washed at Damien and Jane's house. The bumper sticker on the back of Lorraine's car. Eden Grows is the name of the nursery Luke owns.

CALLIE

Frank comes into the station bright and early the next morning—she knows before she sees him by the bravado of the greetings. Shouts of *Chief* and *Hey, boss.* Even Della dips her head when she sees him, girlish and deferential.

He raps the doorframe of her office but doesn't wait for her response before he strides into the room, pulls out a chair. She's got a copy of her grant application on the desk and he reads it, raises his eyebrows.

"Drones? Interesting . . . lots of trouble with privacy violations though, right?"

"Not if they are used responsibly." She crosses her arms, finds herself wondering again why Frank doesn't use all this free time to help out more at Damien and Jane's. Drones could have been used to scan the woods for Jenna. If they had them. If they had been prepared.

Frank clears his throat. "Heard there was some trouble last night. More drugs? Were you able to get anything interesting out of those kids?" He must listen in on the scanners, must have heard the calls from the night before.

She had tossed and turned all night, wondering if she should stop by and talk to Luke herself. She thought about his truck, the cool arrogance with which he pulled out that spliff, told her about his pot plants. But what if he's got another game? Is that why he came by the station to change her brake pads? To cultivate some goodwill? To test what she knew?

But she's not about to tell Frank any of that. Not yet.

Instead she gives him the broad strokes: her theory about the copycat, Amanda's idea that this new guy was linked to the uptick in ODs.

"Sounds like this new guy is greedy, less scrupulous. It also sounds like the old dealer, whoever it was, wasn't really messing around with hard stuff. Just hallucinogenics. Now all these kids who were having a good time with that are ODing on fentanyl in the same packaging."

Frank sighs. "You gotta continue to get the messaging out there about all that. Maybe have Della update the social media with warnings about the fentanyl."

"Sure, I'll do that," Callie says, knowing it will be a waste of time. The department has Facebook and X pages, a few hundred followers each. Most of the engagement is people complaining about speed traps and parking tickets at the boat launch near the lake. Nothing young people will ever see. But what else can they do? Besides rooting out this dealer. Or dealers. More ghosts moving through the shadows of the woods.

"I'll have to contact some people I know, maybe get some cooperation from the DEA." She's heard enough of Frank's glory days stories to know there's tensions here, between the small-town guys who live through the day-to-day and the dickswingers at the state level, but it seems like a drug ring might warrant the extra manpower.

"We've tried that. DEA is overextended on another ring closer to Philly." Callie isn't totally surprised. The DEA likes cases that have tentacles, networks of dealers. Busting one or two small-town thugs won't get them those big headlines, no flashy cash and gun forfeitures to brag about.

She rises, a cue to Frank that she's got a lot to do.

"Well, you keep me posted on how I can help, okay? These guys treating you all right?"

"Sure," she says. She's not going to get into the animals—a dead duck in her mailbox when she finally got home yesterday. Probably not Collins, then, who was with her most of the night. But the others . . . could be any of them, more than one of them. Frank lingers in the door.

"How are you doing? This thing with your mother. It's tough."

Callie shrugs.

"I know it's hard. But you've got to stay focused. These guys, they need to see you as a leader. Not as a girl chasing after her mommy."

Callie stiffens. "I'd argue that a missing person falls under my job description. But I take your point." *What if it were one of your family?* She wants to ask Frank. What if it were your precious Lorraine who had wandered off the trail? What if it were someone *blameless*? He'd have razed these woods to the ground.

Frank grips his jaw with his hand, rubs his stubble. He must be close to eighty but doesn't look it: handsome, still as tall as his sons. But he does look tired today, Callie thinks. Like something is under his skin. "How's Damien seem to you these days?"

"He seems okay. Like he's hanging in there." Though the first thing she thinks of is the conversation between Damien and Luke, how she left them both in crackling, edgy silence. Maybe Damien knows Luke is dealing. She wonders if he would talk to her about it. "Stressed," she concedes. "But who wouldn't be, right?"

"Yeah, well. Our Janie is a trooper, that's for damn sure. And we'd all do anything in the world for Opal."

"One hundred percent." She has the sense that Frank is holding something back, or maybe trying to tell her something else while crutching along on platitudes. Does he know about Jane, about the way she had been poised to leave? Is he asking Callie something bigger? Or is he issuing a directive that she's meant to pass on to Jane? Stay the course. Do your duty to your family. Or else. We'll do anything for Opal. Anything to keep her close. Callie isn't sure if it's the lack of sleep, all the dark trails her mind has been following lately, but Frank's words fall on her ears with the ring of a warning.

She pulls up to Jane's house and something feels off. It takes her a moment to register what it is: Damien's car is gone. Did the three of them go somewhere? Has she gotten the time wrong? She had texted Jane when she woke to tell her when she was coming over, and Jane had responded with a thumbs up and a TikTok link. You should start doing this! Do a podcast like that guy who found the Golden State Killer!

No thank you, she texted back.

Though the mention of the case made her think about Healy, his team trying to pull a usable DNA sample. Fauver might be able to blow her off, but genetics wouldn't lie. And what a pleasure it would be to catch Fauver, the smug, woman-battering piece of shit, who could never have envisioned a world in which he didn't get away with everything he did wrong. All this blood and chaos on his hands. That's what she wants to tell Jane. These TikTok detectives want you to believe in conspiracies. In twists and turns. But so often, the guy who seems most likely to have done it, has done it. And it's just a matter of paperwork after that.

Callie tries the front door and it opens, finds Opal in a circle of blocks, something orange smeared around her mouth.

"Auntie Cal!"

"Hey Opes. Whatcha doing?"

"I'm building a city for unicorns."

Jane sits up on the couch.

"Where's Damien?"

"He went out to run an errand. He'll be right back." Callie can tell that she's trying to play it cool but that Jane feels caught out.

"He could have waited until I got here." She glances at her phone again to make sure she's not late. Noon, just like she said.

"We're fine, Cal. He just left like ten minutes ago."

Callie bends to pick up a container of hummus from the ground, searches around for the lid, finds it in the living room of Opal's dollhouse.

Jane sighs. "Opal can open the fridge on her own now. As you can see."

"Opes, can I clean your face?"

"I'm a dog! Woof woof!"

"Okay, can you be a good doggy and come here for your doggy

bath?" Opal runs to her on all fours and lets Callie swipe a wet paper towel around her mouth, over the hummus-streaked strands of hair that have fallen out of her ponytail, as Opal wriggles and pretends to wag her tail.

"He can't leave you alone with a three-year-old, Jane. Jesus. What if something happened to her? What if something happened to you? One of you could get hurt and then what?"

"Come on Cal, I don't need a lecture. He had to run out. It's quick."

"What couldn't wait until I showed up? What was the errand? You could have had me do it on the way."

They both turn at the sound of Damien pulling in the driveway.

"I can handle it," Jane says to Callie, a fierce glow to her eyes. Callie can't help but think of the hospital voicemail again. *I was going to leave him. I had a plan.*

Damien comes through the door empty-handed. So it wasn't a grocery run, a pharmacy trip. From where Callie's sitting she can't tell what about it was so urgent. He aims for nonchalance—"Hey Cal, good to see you"—but he can only meet her eye for a beat before looking away. "Janie, you almost ready?"

"I just want to put some makeup on. God knows physical therapy is the most I get out into the world these days. Gotta make it count."

"You've got to be the hottest patient they've got," Callie says. Now's not the time to push either of them. And not in front of Opal.

"I don't know, I think they've got some young athletes who've torn their ACLs, that kind of thing. I'm just a middle-aged lady hobbling through for an hour." Callie winces at the term *middle-aged.* They're both thirty.

"Jane, stop. You're still a babe and you know it."

"Second that," Damien calls from the kitchen.

Callie helps Jane to the bedroom, Jane's grip firm on her arm. Her friend, the former cross-country athlete, cowed by a walk down the hall. It makes her skin sizzle with rage and Jane must feel it, feel something, because she drums her fingertips lightly along Callie's forearm as she eases herself down on the end of the bed, telegraphing to Callie to stay calm. Callie gets Jane's makeup bag from the bathroom counter, among the clusters of bright-orange pharmacy bottles. One has Damien's name on it. Lexapro. She wonders if Frank knows, if that's what his question was about down at the station. *How's Damien seem to you?* Fuck Damien, Callie had thought, but realizes how ungenerous that is. How he's going through something too.

"Did you see that video I sent you?" Jane asks, as Callie steps back into the bedroom and hands the makeup bag to Jane, who swipes mascara over her eyelashes and frowns into a compact. "The cops didn't even investigate the half brother even though he was super shady."

"I did watch it. My money was he was involved but he didn't actually do it. Hired someone, probably. Hold on, you've got a smudge."

She licks the end of her finger and rubs the delicate skin under Jane's eye, wiping away a feather of mascara.

"Thanks. You should bring me to therapy one day. One of the trainers is a total babe."

"No setups, please, Janie."

"Not a setup. Just a chance for you to talk to a hot guy and see where it goes. I'm not asking you to wait for him at a café with a red rose on the table. Just come and hang around."

"I'm not really in a dating frame of mind right now." She doesn't tell Jane that she downloaded Tinder the other night, a little tipsy after her shift, swiped until she came across Collins's profile, then deleted the app. Or about the guy she met on the bank of the creek. Adrian, to whom she has written and deleted five texts already.

"If you're going to transplant your life to the sticks to help take care of us, you might as well get something out of it."

"I am getting something out of it. I get to hang with you guys all the time. So long as I'm not wearing out my welcome. If you ever need a little space, I hope you'll let me know."

Jane shifts her hands, winces, picks up a plastic pony that had been buried in the comforter. "You are the space, Callie." She holds the horse out like evidence. "I was drowning before. But this . . .

well, shit. Being here all the time. Everything a mess, not being able to do anything. This is something else."

Callie doesn't know what to say. She can't crutch along the same old platitudes about Jane needing to focus on herself, needing to recover. This feeling Jane is talking about is raw, deep. Despair.

Callie makes her voice low. "Can we please talk about it, Jane? The voicemail? Even if you don't remember it, I think you meant it. Come on, it's me, Janie. Tell me."

Jane raises her gaze to Callie's face. Her eyes brim with tears. She tries to speak and makes a sound that's not quite a word. Like someone choking. Callie takes her hand but before she can speak comes the patter of feet, fast on the hardwood.

"Mama!" Opal thrusts herself between Jane's legs, pulls back and looks up at Jane's kohl-rimmed eyes, penciled brows. "You look . . . weird."

Callie can't look at Jane again so she puts her hand on Opal's shoulder. "Your mama looks like a fox."

Jane clears her throat. "Opes, will you go find the necklace you made for Aunt Callie?"

Opal nods solemnly, runs out of the room again. Jane zips her makeup bag, her movements brisk and sure.

"Jane, come on . . ."

"How are you doing, by the way? What's the news? On your mom?"

"No real changes. The troopers brought dogs out but after all that rain they couldn't find any kind of trail. I keep calling hospitals and rehabs and shelters, keep driving by her house to see if she's come back."

"Why would she have started using now?"

"Beats me. Unless . . . I don't know. The whole thing at the station just sent her over the edge somehow. The Baby Doe case coming up again. The two of us at each other." The admission makes her breath feel shallow. She keeps thinking about what Steve said, that people make all kinds of choices when they are hurting. And

Callie had caused the hurt. She embarrassed her at the station, hadn't believed Jenna about being sober. She had been cruel and impatient. She hadn't listened at all.

"It's not your fault, Callie."

Callie sighs. "I just know there's something else going on here. Call it intuition, or whatever. But Sabrina's bracelet, the fact that no one has seen her, Fauver's record of being violent. It feels like it adds up to something bigger. Like maybe she didn't choose to leave the baby. What if someone made her? And maybe my mom knew that."

Jane opens her mouth to say something, closes it, looks down at her hands. Callie had been careful not to say the other thing, but maybe she edged too close to it anyway, the air in the room suddenly too warm. *What kind of person chooses to abandon a child?* Because who knows what Jane had intended, when she talked about leaving in that morphine-addled voicemail. Whether leaving would have included Opal or not.

Jane puts on a smile, raises her eyebrows. "Want me to see what the TikTok crime girlies have to say about it?"

"Please don't put any of this on the internet," Callie says, her voice harder than she intends.

"Joking! Joking, Chief Hauser. But maybe I can help you. I'm entering my *Rear Window* era. Invalid. Lots of spare time."

Damien raps on the doorframe. "Sorry to break up the girl talk but we've got to go now if we want to be on time."

Jane rolls her eyes. "He's right. Gotta run. Last week I calculated what these sessions costs by the minute. Not good."

Damien grimaces. She can't tell if it is the cost itself or if he doesn't like Jane talking about money in front of Callie. Jane leans her head to Callie's shoulder for a moment before taking Damien's hand and letting him help her up.

She meets the scientist—Adrian—on the bank of Rancocas Creek. He's got two kayaks in the water and raises a paddle in greeting as she pulls up.

She texts Jane before she gets out of the car. This Adrian seems normal, gentle—it had been Callie's aggression that characterized their first meeting—but she can't be too careful. Meeting a guy on a first date. Watersports. Call the cops if you don't hear from me in two hours.

Don't get too wet HAHAHA

You're gross

Sorry, invalid's gotta live a little 😁

But I'm glad you're letting yourself have some fun.

"What's that smirk about?" Adrian asks.

"I just can't believe I'm doing this."

He holds out a life jacket for her. She can't help but wonder who wore it before her. Whether it will hold the smell of some other woman the way a shirt or coat might. But when she shrugs it on all she can smell is lake water, clean, faintly metallic.

"Well, I'm excited. How are you feeling about your maiden voyage?"

"A ship has a maiden voyage, not a person, right?"

He laughs. "That's true. You'll have no problem. Not much that can set you off course when the water is as flat as this. Just nice, easy paddling. I thought we might go out and back for an hour or so, just get you used to things?"

"Sounds good," she says. How hard can it be? But the second she wades into the water she slips on slick rocks, ends up on her hands and knees in the shallows.

"Whoa there." He steadies her boat with one hand, holds out another to help her up.

"I think I hate kayaking," she says. She means it but he laughs, and she likes the sound of it, an easy, big laugh that sounds surprised at itself. It rings out across the water. She wants to hear it again.

She follows Adrian down the creek, through the bends, as he points out places turtles nest. She learns that he studied marine biology at a college by the sea. "All that farmland back home was pretty but after a certain point it just made me feel locked in. I always knew I wanted to be near water." He talks to his parents a few times a week—they still live in the house where he grew up. She feels a stab of envy, that Adrian and his family seem like the Caputos. All rallying around one another, main characters in one another's lives.

He asks her about her family, about where she grew up. She says what she always says about Jenna. Her beautiful voice, her love of music, her red hair.

"She's . . . missing." Callie says. She hadn't planned on mentioning it. Didn't want to saddle this man with her baggage, but the words end up tumbling out.

"Missing how?"

Callie sighs. "I brought her in for driving drunk. She slept it off in the station overnight but no one has seen her or heard from her since the morning she was released. And then they found her bag off the Batona Trail. Drugs inside."

"Wait. Those posters. That's her?"

"Yeah. Not that they're going to do any good. I've got a couple other departments looking out for her, as far as Philly, Atlantic City, but . . . nothing."

"I'm so sorry."

They're quiet for a while, that the only noises are the birds overhead and the sounds of their paddles sliding in and out of the water. The trees and the red of the understory are reflected in the lake's surface, the colors rich and sumptuous together, almost too vivid to be real, more like something assembled and composed, an oil painting. For a moment she gets it. The pull of the water. The austere, untouched beauty you find in pockets of the pines. Why someone might choose this place.

"Is it just you? Dealing with all this? Or do you have siblings?"

"Nah, only child. But I have a good friend who's like a sister to me. That's why I came back here in the first place. She needed me, and it's my turn to be there for her."

"That's noble of you. Not everyone would do that. Uproot their lives."

"She's got a kid, the funniest, sweetest three-year-old. Most of my help is watching her, and that's just—pleasure. I don't have anything else in my life like that. The pure innocence. That goofiness. It's good for me, too. Kids don't look at you and see all of your baggage, you know?"

"The dad still in the picture?"

"Yeah. I wasn't sure about him when they first met. He's a lot older than we are. She moved here after she made all these plans for her life, and supported his business, had a kid young."

"Their trips seem awesome."

"They do, but it was *his* dream, you know? She was a chemistry major in college. She had wanted to be an engineer. And then she fit herself around him. He's not a bad guy, a good dad, but I guess sometimes I wonder what would have happened if she hadn't met him. But then I realize, that would mean no Opal. And that kid is like pure sunlight." She blows out a sigh. "Shit. That's the first time I've said any of that out loud to anyone. Maybe that makes me sound like an asshole."

He shakes his head. "Not an asshole. Just at ease. It's the water. It relaxes you. See? Maybe you are a kayaker after all." She hadn't even noticed that they were almost back at the launch, until she caught sight of their cars parked side by side. She's surprised to realize she's disappointed. To get back to land. To say goodbye.

On her drive home she sees so many dead deer in the backs of trucks, hooves splayed, torsos strangely concave where the hunters removed the organs. She knows this from Jenna, who used to hunt deer along with Callie's grandfather when she was a girl, before her mom got sick. It helps cool the meat, taking away the insides that still pulse warm with blood. Jenna always described hunting as peaceful, as a way of being part of the land. But Callie can't see it that way. It makes her stare at the thick trees with even more apprehension, to think that there are coils of intestines, the wet bags of deer stomachs, livers, kidneys, hearts in wait in those woods.

* * *

She gets a text from Healey not long after she gets home. Got the file you're looking for. Transferred to our department in a big batch of old cases eight years ago. I'm working with a freelance genetic genealogist on a murder-rape from '82. She's good. Her team is working on the DNA sample, pulling a profile together.

Healey sends her a link to the woman's website next. Her name is Rebecca Nixon.

From Nixon's headshot alone, Callie already doesn't like her. A mouthful of big, white veneers, highlighted hair in barrel curls. Pictures of her on the homepage, hugging a frail woman with wooly white hair, a photo on the mantel behind them of a teenage girl in a cap and gown. Rebecca with her eyes closed, resting her chin on the woman's shoulder, self-satisfied, overly familiar.

Callie feels a jolt, territorial. Wants to text Healy back: *You should have run it by me.* But what ownership does she really have over this case? All the files were with Healy and the Cold Case guys all along. All she did was bring it to his attention. Hell, she asked him to do exactly this.

There's a media page on Rebecca Nixon's website. She clicks on the first video—an interview with ABC News. The correspondent asks Rebecca what it means to be working in her field at this particular time.

"What we do—it's the Wild West, really. There are no rules. We're inventing an entire discipline as we go. It's riveting. I mean, I used to do product marketing for a cosmetics company and I taught myself the skills to solve murder cases that even the cops, with all of their tools and resources, could never figure out."

Callie recoils at the barb, even as she knows it is true. Look at all of the missed opportunities and willful ignorance around the Baby Doe case. The rumors and hearsay and facts lost to time. DNA, on the other hand, is efficient. Can't lie or obscure. Below the media links, an invitation to follow Rebecca on TikTok. She wonders if Jane knows who she is.

Callie sets her phone down, rubs her temples. This is what she had wanted, but it feels different from how she thought it might. Out of her hands. Genetic genealogy is what got the Golden State Killer, and since then has led to the closing of hundreds of rape and murder cases that otherwise would never have been solved. This is a good thing, of course. But she's heard of cases in which medical DNA was accessed without permission—DNA from a woman's pap smear used to nab her father in an unsolved double homicide from before she was born. People using the internet to find relatives and build their family trees, only to have their DNA used to catch their favorite uncle for a thirty-year-old rape. Families torn apart over the revelation of a long-hidden love child.

No, she knows it isn't as simple as Nixon makes it out to be. DNA as saving grace. The more honest take is that DNA is something that connects and destroys in equal measure, and you never know which way things are going to swing. Except for in her case. Still just a blank space on the family tree, where her father's name should be.

ANNABELLE

Sabrina spends homeroom scribbling hard in a notebook you've never seen before. She says it is homework, but she never consults any books, just writes and writes, pausing to shake out her cramped fingers, her hand stained with smeared ink. *Look at me*, you will her, but you can only make out some of her features through the curtain of her hair. Even as the other girls hiss whispers about her, she doesn't lift the tip of her pen from the page. She writes like her life depends on it, and you can practically feel it in your own skin. Her urgency, a burning in her chest, and the pain of biting down on her lip to keep her expression even. To contain all the hurt in that one small place. The girls in the corner have gotten bored with their whispers and have escalated their tactics. Now they have chants.

> *Annabelle the good, Sabrina the bad. She made her mother run away and now they're both sad.*
>
> *Annabelle the prude, Sabrina the slut. One spreads her legs and one keeps them shut.*
>
> *Annabelle the wise, Sabrina the fool. Annabelle off to college, Sabrina will flunk school.*

"Those are the stupidest rhymes I've ever heard," you say, loud enough so Sabrina can't help but hear you, so that the girls in the back hear too.

It takes all of your nerve to speak up against them and you know Sabrina knows this. You expect her to look at you sheepish with gratitude. Instead she spits at you.

"Fuck you, Annabelle. And you know you are getting fat, right?"

The girls howl. Sabrina leaves in a huff, two spots of color high on her cheeks, with her notebook tucked under her arm while Mr. Pierce, the homeroom teacher, uselessly calls after her, telling her he will have to write her up if she doesn't return to her seat.

You look down at your middle, prod your thighs, pinch your upper arms.

It is true, that the sickness that plagued the end of summer is gone. That in its place is a hunger that wakes you in the middle of the night like a presence in your room. You eat only as much as you dare, having already been scolded by Sabrina for scarfing a box of macaroni and cheese at two in the morning when it was the last one left.

You're not getting fatter, you tell yourself. Sabrina's just lashing out, being mean. You heard her on the phone again this weekend, murmuring into the receiver. While she was talking to him, her voice small and high, you crept into her room and slid open her desk drawers. Your fingers came away dusted with purple iridescent eyeshadow. You rubbed them on the front of your sweatshirt, pushed yourself to think harder about where Sabrina might hide something. You wanted the notebook the most but you would settle for any clue. When you turned to her unmade bed you saw the glint of something metallic nestled in the sheets. A lighter, just like the one Sabrina used to sterilize the needle when she stitched you together, an S scratched into the back. You recognized it as the one the Coyote used to light his cigarette in the car that day. You've tried not to think of it but it takes you back, his eyes narrowed in some private delight, like he was pulling off a practical joke.

The bell rings, startling you. As the girls in the back file out of the room one of them reaches into her bag and drops a can of chocolate SlimFast on your desk.

You feel relieved to go to history class first period. It is barely October but Miss Hamilton already has the room decorated for

Halloween, paper moons silhouetted with black cats against the window. Bats swooping from the top of the blackboard. Diaphanous tissue paper ghosts hang from the ceiling above the heat registers, twirl on their strings.

Behind you Jessica Wolfson whispers to Anna Kempe. *Shit, do you have a tampon?*

You shiver, as though someone has put a cold hand on the back of your neck. Start to count.

You haven't had your period for over three months.

You pluck at your sweatshirt. Sabrina's voice in your head. *You're getting fat.* You try to remember what your mother told you, all those years ago, about periods and when and why they come. About what it means if it stops. But what you remember best is your mother talking about the moon, how women's bodies are tied to its pull. How women give life and how she summoned you and Sabrina from the darkness of the world's unconscious, the two of you glinting with stardust. You liked this idea so much—your baby limbs shimmering in her womb—that you never bothered to question it. To hold it to the light.

Miss Hamilton clears her throat to get everyone's attention, easy in this advanced class, smaller than the rest and populated by overachievers aching to get scholarships to Rutgers in a few years.

"Today we'll be doing something a little different. Holidays and celebrations are as much a part of our discussions of history and culture as battles and treaties, though the people writing your text books aren't exactly doing you a service in that sense. Folklore is an important part of any place's history," she tells them. "Now, this isn't exactly going to be on the AP exam in May but it is important to understand the stories a place can generate. So, every October in the seven years I've been teaching here I've set aside part of the lesson plan to talk about a fixture of local folklore: the Jersey Devil."

The other kids let out theatrical groans.

You feel a sense of dread. You know the story, or at least you think you know the story. But the departure from routine makes you nervous. Miss Hamilton has a wink of mischief in her eye and you don't like that either. You'd rather just continue yesterday's lesson about the Mayan civilization. You'd rather be bent over your notes, scribbling away. But you have no excuse not to look at her. There's a low gurgling in your guts that's been persistent for days. A bubbling sensation that won't go away no matter how many saltines or pieces of toast you eat. Today you've even tried no food at all, not giving your stomach anything to work away on in hope that it will go quiet. But this feels like a mistake too; your hunger pangs so loud that you know the kids sitting close to you can hear them. You cross your arms and hunch forward, waiting for Miss Hamilton to begin.

"There was a woman who lived in these woods long ago, before this territory was even a colony. Her name was Mother Leeds. Mother Leeds spent her days caring for her twelve children: washing clothes, heating food, filling up cups of water, scalding her hands as she scrubbed pots and pans. All this while her husband was off at the taverns drinking his wages away, almost never home to help, or when he was home he would take off his boots and pass out in his bed, leaving her to her endless work."

You think of your mother, in the days before she left. Counting cans in the pantry. Staring out the windows.

"When Mother Leeds found out she was expecting her thirteenth child she was distraught. She didn't know how they would afford to feed another mouth, how she could carry one more baby in her arms, how she would manage to wash even more diapers and cups and tend to more crying children in the night. She cried and cried and finally issued a curse. Let him be the devil!"

The other kids laugh at the way Miss Hamilton makes her voice solemn and deep for the curse, at the way she shakes her fist to the sky. But you feel your throat tighten. Your palms go hot and damp in your lap.

"Weeks and months passed. Mother Leeds grew larger, got more tired and worn out with the constant demands of her children, with dragging her husband out of the tavern or begging him for some of his wages so that they might eat that week. Even though she was pregnant she gave most of her food to her children, saving just a few spoonfuls of watery soup or porridge for herself a few times a day. She tallied up the days on a piece of wood and knew that soon, the baby would be here and her life would get even more difficult. The cabin they lived in more crowded. Her nights sleepless. She did so much cleaning and cooking that the skin on her hands was raw, the color of uncooked beef. Her feet swelled from the hours of standing at the stove or rocking babies so that she couldn't wear her shoes anymore. When she needed to go outside she wrapped her feet in cloth.

"She went into labor on a stormy night. She had her oldest child, a girl of twelve, run through the woods to tell the midwife in town that Mother Leeds needed help. The midwife came, and so did Mother Leeds's neighbors. Or the wives anyway. The women of the town the only ones who might ever drop off an extra loaf of bread or a pair of their children's mended pants that they had outgrown. The women formed a circle around Mother Leeds as she writhed in pain. All the while the rain is thrashing at the cabin. They can feel the thunder grumble through the floorboards, and every few moments a bright bolt of lightning illuminates the room. Mother Leeds contorts on the floor, begging one of her friends to save her, to spare her. The pain is worse than with any of her other children, searing through her. The women have lit candles and the light makes their faces look strange and unfamiliar to Mother Leeds, these people she has known her entire life. They sing and chant and pray. They give her a spoon to bite down on when the pain peaks. She grips their hands and squeezes tight enough so that they ache."

You bite the inside of your cheek, your breathing going shallow. You were right, you know this story, but have never heard it told like this before, so that you can see the women's faces ghoulish in the candlelight. So that it makes you feel cold all over, your body still except for the constant roiling in your guts.

"Finally, the baby is born, and at first it looks like a normal child. The midwife places it in the arms of Mother Leeds while another woman wipes the sweat from her brow. But moments later, Mother Leeds has her head tipped back and her eyes closed in exhaustion. And the child begins to move from its swaddling blanket. The women are dumbstruck, think it is a trick of the light. But the baby morphs in front of their eyes and it isn't a child after all, but a creature none of them had seen before. The head of a goat, bat's wings, horns and hooves. And a devil's forked tail. It screamed, a scream that made the women deaf to any sound that followed, and they clutched to one another as it began to fly around the small room. Finally it found its way up the chimney, out into the woods. The storm had gotten quiet by then, so they could hear the devil shrieking through the pines as it flew away.

"There have been dozens of sightings of the devil over the years. Including by Joseph Bonaparte, who settled nearby in Bordentown when his brother was defeated at Waterloo and exiled for a second time. He blamed the devil when his mansion burned to the ground. In 1909 the newspapers reported repeated sightings of the Jersey Devil and everyone was so fearful that they closed the schools and the mills. Mothers wouldn't let their children play outside. In the 1950s a group of boys playing in the woods swore they saw him. But no one has ever been able to capture it on film. So we're left to wonder. Is it a myth? Is the Jersey Devil real?"

"What happened to Mother Leeds?" Mindy Josephs asks from the back of the class. Miss Hamilton smiles, pleased by the question.

"Ah. That's a good point. What happened to her after her curse came true? Did she ever see the devil again? Some say she died not long after. That she lost too much blood in the difficult birth. Others say she went on with her life, relieved to be free of that thirteenth child, without another mouth to feed. That she felt a new lightness every time she did the family's laundry, with only twelve pairs of socks to match. But the legend doesn't tell us. We're only left with stories of the devil and the ways he's terrorized these woods."

You sit, still hunched, your arms digging into your stomach, clutching yourself tight. Miss Hamilton is smiling from underneath the brim of her witch hat. *You bitch*, you think, the words rising up in you before you have a chance to think about why, where they come from. But when her eyes land on you something in her face changes, and you know she has felt it. Your anger. Your fear.

She changes topics. For the last twenty minutes of class you are back with the Mayans, talking about their stories, their mythology, but in your head you are seeing flashes of lightning. You are imagining a floor covered in blood.

The bell rings and she comes to stand near your desk, holds a finger up to you asking you to wait. She doesn't speak until everyone has filtered out of the classroom.

"Annabelle. Did something about the story upset you? If so, I'm so—"

"No," you blurt out, cutting her off.

She looks at you a moment longer than you'd like.

"Are you coming to the yearbook committee meeting today?"

You had been looking forward to it all morning, then forgotten about it after the events of homeroom. "Yes," you say, because you can't think of anything else to do but to comply. To feel yourself guided along by other people's expectations and needs. Because the part of your brain that so wants to be good knows you have to stay on the yearbook committee, to keep up your extracurriculars, if you want to be a competitive applicant for college. If you want to get out.

"Great, I've got something that I'm excited for you to see."

There are six of you at the yearbook committee meeting, and as you gather around Miss Hamilton's desk she seems lit with that same sense of mischief you saw in her face during class.

"I didn't tell all of you about this because I didn't know how it would work out, but last spring I applied for a grant from the state and we got funding for a new camera. We're talking professional-grade equipment. Brand-new, state-of-the-art."

She produces a black bag from her drawer. Unzips it and with tender, careful fingers, she holds up a camera, but it bears little resemblance to the bulky old Canon you're used to using, with its frayed strap and scratched lens. The six of you gasp and Miss Hamilton laughs, delighted.

"Thirty-five-millimeter lens, titanium cover, crispest pictures on the market. I've had a chance to try it out and you will all be trained to use it."

The other committee members ooh and ah, trade glances of disbelief.

"Annabelle, why don't you take a walk with me and we can get some shots of the sports practices going on?"

You know why she's chosen you. You were the one most interested in photos, took most of the pictures of extracurriculars—school plays and sports and mock trial—that ended up in the yearbook the year before. You hate having your picture taken but you found that you like lifting the camera to your face, framing a shot, making the fleeting into something permanent.

You walk the school grounds and Miss Hamilton talks you through the intricacies of the dials on top of the camera, shutter speed and apertures, and when she hands it to you a tingle runs through you, of power, of possibility. You take aim at the girls' soccer team, and it doesn't matter that the girl taking a shot on goal is Kristen Hanover, one of the ones who laughed when Sabrina called you fat. You click the shutter, and you think *gotcha*. You are in control. She's as small as anyone else in the viewfinder. Captured.

"How does it feel?" Miss Hamilton asks, as you take photo after photo of the girls running their drills. "We have lots of film, so go to town."

"I love it," you say, a beat too late.

"I'm glad." A pause, and you can hear the question forming before she asks it.

"Annabelle, are you okay?"

"Yeah, fine," you say automatically.

"You just seem a little . . . distracted." You turn to the boys' soccer field, test out the zoom on the lens. "I want you to know that if applying to all of those colleges is too much pressure, we can change the plan. Try for community college, and I'll still help you in two years when you're ready to transfer, get a Bachelor's degree. I believe in you wholeheartedly, but I don't want you to feel overwhelmed."

"I'm not. I want to."

She says something else but you don't hear, because when you raise the camera's viewfinder to your face you catch sight of Sabrina beyond the chain-link fence that hems in the sports fields. Sabrina, getting into a black Camaro, a boy in the driver's seat. You zoom and zoom and before they pull away you can make out the texture of his buzzed head, a tattoo of a snake on his forearm, which is resting lazily out the window.

Billy Fauver. He graduated last year but you remember him in the halls, how he seemed too big for the small lockers, how with one lazy reach of his hand he could brush his fingers against the popcorn ceiling above your heads. He used to get into fights all the time—once you saw him bash another boy's face into the porcelain rim of the water fountain, his girlfriend pulling at his arm, crying, begging him to stop, blood on the floor, on the bulletin board, how it only made him angrier.

And there is Sabrina, getting into his car.

You lower the camera from your face, feeling revealed. The colors of the fields too bright, the whistles too loud, the motions of the players and the ball so fast they make you dizzy. And still. You find yourself promising to Miss Hamilton that everything is fine.

"Okay," she says. "Why don't you take that home? Mess around with it, bring it back next week."

"Really?" you ask, flushing with pride.

"Of course. I trust you. Shoot anything you want, and I'll develop the film for you so you can understand what you've done, how we might improve. You can use the rest of this roll and I'll give you a second one. I know how much you like photography."

"Thanks," you say, knowing your cheeks must be going crimson. That phrase rings through your body, your secret shadowing every exchange with a double meaning.

So you can understand what you've done.

ANNABELLE

You don't know what to photograph outside the buzz and bustle of school. Everything inside your house has the look of something forlorn and forgotten, so you walk out to the factory ruins, stepping ever so carefully on the path with the camera around your neck. You shoot the blank spaces where the windows used to be, which now frame slices of the sky. On impulse you stick your hand far into the gap in the wall where you and Sabrina would leave one another messages, trinkets, where your mother placed those flowers and wooden animal figurines the day she left. Nothing but cold air, cold stone.

You tell yourself you hadn't been hoping for anything and almost believe it.

Inside, you shoot the front hall and the last of the days' light coming through the fan window, to try to capture the lonely feeling that squeezes your ribs as the light hits the wide plank floors that carried your ancestors over the threshold, toward the warmth of the hearth. In her room Sabrina is playing music too loud with her door open, so you head up the stairs and pause in her doorway. She refuses to turn from where she stands in front of the mirror, so you inch to the left, raise the camera, and take a picture of the two of you framed that way, you in the background, Sabrina leaning in to the mirror in front of you, the glint of a necklace bright against her skin. She strokes the chain, flips her hair over her shoulder.

"Where'd you get the necklace?"

"The Coyote gave it to me," she says, angling her chest toward the mirror.

You raise the camera again.

"What the hell are you doing?" she asks.

"Practicing. For yearbook."

"Well go practice somewhere else. You're supposed to take pictures of people doing things. Not creeping around." Her voice is hard but still, you detect the begrudging kernel of admiration, maybe even envy, as she eyes you from the mirror. The necklace is pretty: gold and dainty and delicate, a star charm that sits in the hollow just below her throat.

Though you would never admit it to Sabrina, you agree that you need to find more people to practice on, so that weekend at the Cranberry Festival you bring the camera with you, walking three miles down the road toward the sound of music, notes of saxophone floating above the trees.

The festival takes place over two days, and every year since you and Sabrina were old enough to count change you would go with your mother and she would sell her tinctures from the garden, rub salves into people's hands. People would lean close and speak to her in confidential voices. *Do you have something for . . . My husband, he's having trouble with . . . My mother, her memory is going . . .* And she would produce a bottle or pot of something from underneath the table, send them on their way. They believed in her magic. You all did.

But where is she, and her magic, now that you need her more than ever before?

You had asked Sabrina if she wanted to come with you and she only sighed and looked down at her fingernails.

That constant hunger buzzes in you as you walk the fair, first past the hot rods and vintage trucks with their candy-colored paint jobs that glisten in the sun. *Snap, snap, snap* with the camera. You have never before been so alive to smells and sounds of food. The greasy sizzle of peppers and onions of the grill. Powdered sugar you swear you can taste in the air when you walk past the funnel cake stand. You walk the entire fair, partly convinced that you will see your mother as she always was, the cloth she dyed from beetroot spread over the card table, her hair long down her back, her sleeves rolled up and her hands glistening, greasy with poultices and salves. Root of wild indigo for slow metabolisms, poor immune systems. Pipsissewa leaves for skin ailments. The bark of wild cherry trees for sore muscles and bad lungs.

You're walking with the camera braced in your hands when you hear a familiar voice.

The Coyote.

You see him, so different from the way he was in his car. He's standing in a circle of other men, all of them with cups of beer in their hands. One of them is older and you recognize him as the chief of police. He had been to the school last spring to shake the hands of every student who complete their D.A.R.E. education. *You are doing your part to help keep our community safe and maintain your own bright future.* At the time it made you swell with pride, to hold the certificate bearing his signature.

"And this idiot, he takes this turn on his four-wheeler like you wouldn't believe, I swear, this close to flipping it . . ."

A man in a chambray shirt crosses his arms. "Fuck you, it wasn't that bad."

"It was, you moron. I saw your eyes under your helmet visor. About to pop out of your damn skull."

"Maybe if you hadn't been drunk off your ass . . ."

You watch the police chief for his reaction to this. You remember more lines from his address to the assembly. *Drinking is trouble. Drugs are trouble. Quickest route to an early grave.* But he only tips his head back with the rest of them, squeezes the shoulder of the man they are all teasing, the one who was supposedly careening through the woods drunk. There's a younger man with them standing next to him, taking smaller sips of his beer.

You raise the camera to your eye, frame the shot, snap.

You edge closer, just as the Coyote steps out of the circle and toward the woods, where other men are standing with their backs to the crowd, streams of piss between their legs.

While you watch him another voice calls in your direction. "Hey there, sweetheart."

You startle and the camera thumps against your body.

"Oh look, we've scared the poor thing. Would all of you shut up with your stories—we've got a lady present. Damien, look, she seems about your age. Say hi." The man on the boy's left slaps him on the back hard enough that he stumbles forward and some of the beer sloshes over the rim of his cup. The boy goes crimson.

All you can do is turn and run.

"Come back, sweetheart!" one of them calls after you. "He doesn't bite."

"Maybe she does," someone else says, and they all laugh again as you retreat. In your haste you bump into a woman carrying a tub of popcorn, who swears as it scatters at your feet. Sorry, you say. Sorry sorry. But you don't mean it—all you can think of is getting away from them, from the ugly, rough sounds of their laughter.

At the fortune teller's booth a red-haired woman eyes you with curiosity from between a pair of cheap gold curtains and you have the urge to duck away from her view. You walk until you find a bottle of cranberry wine abandoned against a tent stake, three-quarters full. You bring the bottle to your mouth and drink as much as you can in one go, closing your eyes and willing whatever people are chasing when they drink to come to you: relief, lightness, oblivion. But mostly, you want to forget the Coyote. Forget the men and their barbs. You want to forget the look on Miss Hamilton's face when she asked you if you were all right, and the sensation of bubbles rising in your guts. You want to forget Sabrina turning her back to you when you brought the camera home on the bus. No, maybe what you want to forget is Sabrina ever loving you, ever sharing your bed and whispering stories in your ear when you were afraid of the dark. If you could forget that, you'd be free.

The wine makes the world softer at the edges, the lights on the carnival rides ringed in halos as the sun sets. You stop at the funhouse mirror. Crimson stains at the edge of your mouth. You take another picture, this garbled version of yourself, proportions all wrong. Out of the corner of your vision you catch the whoosh of the tilt-o-whirl. Girls scream as they are jerked in circles, hair flying. You trudge back through the food stands. Someone must have overturned a crate of cranberries and you crush them under your feet, the pop and give of the fruit bursting from inside its skin making you feel sick.

You look into the dark of the woods and wonder what would happen if you just started walking. If you might just disappear entirely into the ink-black night.

You are sitting with your back against a ticket booth, your eyes closed, when there's a voice above you.

"Are you okay?"

It is the boy, the one who had been standing in the circle with the Coyote's friends. *He doesn't bite.*

You can only groan in response.

"I can give you a ride home, if you want. Sorry those guys were jerks."

You manage to nod. "Home," you say. He tells you his name and it's like your mind is a sieve. It slips through and is lost, the way the minutes leading up to this moment are lost, big black blots in your memory. The lights of the amusements glow prettily against the dark sky. You feel for the camera strap around your neck, think about taking a picture, but you can't get your hands to work right.

He helps you up and the two of you walk through the field, toward the parked cars.

In the car he gives you a bottle of water. You start to take long, greedy gulps but he puts his hand out, stops you.

"Slow," he says, "or else you'll be sick. Ask me how I know."

You like his smile, the easy sound of his voice. In another version of the world, you think, you would want to know him better. He's older than you, but by just a few years.

"Rough day?"

"He's such a . . . a . . . bastard," you say, deploying the word for the first time but it feels immediately right. Sabrina calls your father a bastard all the time. You try not to think about him, or at least as he is now. You still remember the years when he would lift you on his shoulders, hold your ankles tight and you would raise your head to the clouds, loving the sensation of being closer to the infinite sky.

"Who?"

"The guy you were with."

The look on the boy's face changes. "You . . . you too?"

You let yourself nod, though you wonder how he knows to ask. But his anger feels good, even secondhand. "My sister, too," you say.

The boy looks up to the ceiling. You think you see tears forming in his eyes.

"Your sister . . . you have a twin, right? I've seen you guys around."

You nod, wait for him to say something else, but he only drums his fingers against the steering wheel.

You fill the silence, suddenly protective of Sabrina. "She must be special though. He gave her a necklace. It's pretty. A star inside a circle."

"He did?" There's a note of concern in his voice that you can't parse, and then he sighs. "Let's just get you home, okay?"

You make it about a mile before you need to be sick. He pulls over and you lean out of the car, retch onto the road.

"I'm sorry," you say. He hands you a tissue for you to wipe your mouth with.

"You okay to get moving again?"

You don't know what makes you do this, but you move your hand to your stomach as he watches. You are tired. Tired of not thinking about it or talking about it. Tired of being the only one to know. "I hope I didn't hurt it," you whisper.

For a second, he looks as though he's been slapped, two spots of color on each cheek while the rest of his face goes white. Then, he throws the car into drive and takes the roads too fast, as though you are being chased.

The next morning you wake bleary, still nauseated, retch cranberry wine until you're empty of anything but bile. The memory of the car ride is hazy. You have the vague feeling of having said something you shouldn't have, but can't dredge it up from the swamp of your thoughts, the pressure on your skull too great.

You drink from the tap after getting sick and crawl back to bed. On your bedside table sits the camera out of its bag, the lens taking the mess of you in with its indifferent, one-eyed stare.

CALLIE

She makes a list of halfway houses, but they can be tricky—no one wants to give up residents' privacy, but sometimes she's able to drop words like *chief* and *missing person*, and they'll at least tell her Jenna's never been there. She drives from one halfway house to another, in between shifts babysitting Opal. The next on her list is a place called Ocean's Haven. She pulls up to a faded Victorian in Asbury Park on a Sunday afternoon expecting nothing, jittery with too much gas station coffee, and underneath that, a deep, abiding exhaustion that makes the bones of her face ache.

"I know you," a woman says from the porch, between hard draws on a vape pen. She's cross-legged on a rattan peacock chair, a faded streak of blue hair unspooling from under the pulled-up hood of her sweatshirt.

"Is that right?" Callie wonders if she arrested this woman once upon a time or if the lady is just bullshitting, bored in the late fall chill.

"You're Jenna's kid."

Her breath catches in her chest, the cold ocean air tingling in her lungs. "You know her?"

"Sure. She was here for a while. This summer. She was always showing people your picture."

Callie takes a big step closer, leans over the porch railing. "Have you heard from her lately?"

"Nah. She left in July. She doing okay? I liked her."

"She's missing," Callie says.

"Damn. Who did it?"

The woman's question hits like a hammer at the base of her spine. Sure, Callie hasn't mentioned the drugs, but this is the first person who hasn't assumed Jenna did this to herself. "What makes you ask that? Who did what?"

"She said she knew this was going to happen. She talked about someone who was going to hunt her down."

"She wasn't talking about the devil, right? That's always been her thing."

"Nope. Some guy from when she was a teenager. She said she was keeping some secrets for him."

"Did she say a name? What he looked like?"

"Nah."

"What secrets was she keeping?"

"Whatever they were, she sure as shit wasn't telling me. Something that was still hot to the touch, I'll tell you that much. She played tough but she was scared. You could tell. She'd pick her nails. Get this look on her face. Like she was far away."

Callie thinks the same thing. She felt the fear in the room that last time they saw one another. Underneath Jenna's obstinance, her bitterness, pulsed a worry she had been too scared to name, tender and vulnerable as her bare feet on the gravel-strewn road.

Callie leaves the woman from the halfway house—Dawn—her card and tells her to call, day or night, if she hears from Jenna or she remembers anything else that might be relevant.

The word she used sticks in Callie's mind all day. *Hunted.*

As she gets ready for her second date with Adrian, Jane sends her a link to a TikTok video that she watches to the end, realizing that all the young women remind her of Rebecca Nixon. That ladylike, perfectly polished makeup, and underneath their eyeliner and mascara that same bright-eyed eagerness for gore—considered okay in a woman so long as it is packaged right. Headbands and pearls and lipstick. Shiny hair and Pilates-toned arms.

I'm supposedly going on a date tonight. Don't fill my head with this shit.

The creeper from the woods???

The scientist. Yes.

He must be hot. Have fun. And tell me everything!!!

I'm this close to canceling. My head isn't in this. Too much going on.

Don't you dare! You need this, Calliope Hauser.

Callie sighs. Jane's right. And what Jane isn't saying, but she's surely thinking, is that this might be the rest of Callie's life: Jenna gone. Already the images on the missing posters are weather faded, the ink gray. There has to be some part of her that moves forward. Some kind of relief. Something that is hers.

She and Adrian have agreed to meet at the bar. Callie is glad they chose somewhere a little further afield than the tavern where the guys drink, even if it means a forty-minute ride each way. The last thing she needs is anyone from the squad listening over her shoulder as she struggles through second-date banter. In the car she puts on lipstick, wipes it off, puts it on again. It's different, going somewhere where they'll sit close to one another, without the water between them. She wonders if it will feel the same as it did the last time, both the conversation and the silence—easy, natural. The churn in her head, her thoughts of her mother, going still for just a little while.

He's there first, even though she's five minutes early, sitting on the wooden bench out front, head bent toward a book.

"Work or pleasure?"

He holds up the cover so she can see it. *The Left Hand of Darkness.* "I'm a big science fiction nerd."

"I gather. Shall we?"

They enter the bar and it's the same as any of the others in the Pines: stained glass chandeliers slung over the pool tables, a taxidermy deer head near the entry, a jukebox against the back wall. Men in hunting caps, men in leather biker vests. Heavy pours of dark liquor and cheap beer on cork coasters crumbling to bits.

"I hope you aren't a martini kind of gal."

"I mean, I can be. But I'm also a beer in a plastic pitcher kind of girl."

"That's very good news."

He orders for them and she watches him from the small table they've chosen. She likes the way he moves, an unhurried ease to his gait, all long legs and slim hips.

"Scare any other unsuspecting ladies this week?"

"Not this week, no. Not quite that lucky."

They're talking and things are going well, so well that she forgets her nerves, that she doesn't mind when he tells her about the plot of the book he's reading, that she feels herself smiling so much when he talks about his students and feels the tug of muscles she hasn't used in a while. Or she feels that way until he starts to go a little quiet, and she notices him looking over her shoulder, longer pauses between their exchanges. Maybe she misread the moment. Is he eyeing the door?

"Hey, so do you know those guys over there? They keep looking this way."

She turns and sees Collins and Reynolds, who raise their drinks from the bar.

"Oh god. Those are two of my esteemed colleagues. I'll go over and say hi. And by say hi, I mean, tell them to stop being creeps."

She crosses the bar and they watch her approach, grinning like a pair of tweens who have caught a glimpse of a teacher outside school.

"What are you two doing here? I thought the guys all favored the Pine Tavern close to the station."

"Mac is a dick," Reynolds says.

Collins rolls his eyes. "They got into a fight. Some hunting thing. I don't know."

"So now you're here."

"So now we're here. And so are you. You letting the ball drop? There's gotta be someone with a headlight out to bust, someone going forty in a thirty-five mph zone." A part of her is glad, that at least Collins and Reynolds are friendly enough now to joke. In the wake of Jenna's disappearance she's been even more regimented, more of a hard-ass. That same old compunction at work: When her personal life was messy, the other side of her life had to compensate. Some of the other guys on the squad are unhappy about it, but what are they actually complaining about? Doing their jobs?

"Har har har. More tickets, more funds. You guys want overtime back? We gotta get those citations up. Among our other issues."

"Could use that OT pay, that's for sure," Reynolds says.

"Yeah, you owe me a shit ton of money from our poker game last week."

"Not as much as Jimmy. And Frank." Callie's smile contracts. Maybe she was wrong about them warming up. Weekly poker games with the old guard. All of them talking to Frank all the time—no way she can ask any of them about Luke, about what might be going down at the nursery. But they can still be useful to her in this setting, loosened up and cheered by the drinks.

"What's the latest with Fauver? We needed probable cause on him, like, yesterday." She's tasked her guys with monitoring him. She doesn't have enough to get a warrant on the drugs, let alone anything relating to Jenna, but she's asked them all to do more drive-bys of his residence, keep their ears to the ground.

Reynolds sighs. "Well we'll never see him out this way. Pretty sure he's barred from every drinking establishment for fifty miles."

Callie watches two bikers make their way to the back of the bar, where there's another door leading to the dumpsters, and behind that, woods. Could be going to smoke, could be going to do a deal. Back in the day she would have had an undercover team who could have gotten close to them. Could have used all this time setting up stings and surveillance ops. Instead she's here, prodding two of her tipsy patrolmen to make sure they've been following up on her assignments.

"Reynolds, you would have gone to high school with him, right?" She hasn't talked to them about Jenna's phone call to Fauver's garage, about the connection with the Baby Doe case. How she's circling him like he's got the key to it all and all she needs is one slipup on his end before she can crucify the slimy bastard. For now, they only think she's on him for the drug rumors. She's keeping everything else close to her chest. "What was his deal then? Was he selling? Who did he hang out with?"

Reynolds groans. "Look, can we talk about this when we're on the clock? All I want to do is get wasted right now."

One of the bikers she had seen slip out back moves past them. There's a Pagan gang patch on the sleeve of his leather jacket and he gives Callie a stare that makes her go still. Even Collins and Reynolds are quiet until he slides back into a booth in the corner of the room.

Collins looks over her shoulder. "Who's your guy? Someone from Major Crimes? Skinny nerds up there wasting away behind their desks, huh?"

"Not a cop, thank you very much." Thank God, she thinks.

"No kidding," Reynolds mutters.

"I better get back there."

"All right, Hauser." Collins has a wink in his voice but for once it's not mocking.

Maybe it's the beer. Maybe it's that Collins and Reynolds have split from the other guys. But the question slides out before she can help herself. "Hey. Do either of you know who has been putting shit in my mailbox?"

Collins grins. "So Hauser, there are these nice people in blue. Not like us. They ride around in little trucks. They're called postal—"

"Shut up. And I don't get any mail except for the *Pine Barrens Gazette*." She thinks of the stacks of papers in her recycling, nothing more than a police blotter and listings for farmers' markets, classified ads filled with old boats and rusted out cars for sale. "You know what I mean. The animals."

"What animals?" Collins asks.

"Dead ones."

"You know? You gotta get off this man-hating, we're-all-against-you thing, Hauser. Okay, so some of the guys gave you a hard time or froze you out. But we're not barbarians. We're not putting dead fucking animals in your mailbox. Jesus."

He's a good liar. His outrage is believable, a pulse to it but doesn't feel too cooked up to be real. Callie will give him that. "Come on. Don't bullshit me. I let you guys have your fun or whatever. But really. Just tell whoever is doing it . . . enough."

Collins and Reynolds fix her with identical stone-faced looks. "I'm telling you, it's not one of ours. Come on, Reyn. Why don't we let the lady get back to her date?" Collins throws an arm around Reynolds and steers him away.

When she gets back to the table she apologizes to Adrian. "I knew I had to talk to them or else they'd keep staring. I'm sure they imagine me at home every night with my nose in a stack of duty logs and reports." She hesitates, wanting to be honest. "Though maybe that's not too far off from the truth." She looks over to see Collins racking up for a game of pool, Reynolds chalking the cue, and is relieved that they're distracted.

"Is that your usual type? Fellow cops?"

"Oh god, no. Not those guys. Well, the last guy I was with up north was a cop, but that was . . ." It sounds so feeble, so sad, to say it. It was about convenience. It was about understanding they were each too wrapped up in the job to give their personal lives a passing thought. It was about satisfying the animal need for a warm body next to yours every few weeks. "It was nothing, And now it's over."

"Glad to hear that."

And just like that, she sees something new in his eyes, in the fierceness of his stare. Desire. She has to suppress the urge to press the cool of her glass against her flushed chest.

"Okay then," he says. She likes his smile. The way the lines around his eyes are a little paler than the tan of his cheeks.

"Okay," she says, and slides her hand into his.

She has a second drink when she gets home, watches another one of the TikToks Jane has sent. A petite blond with crimson lipstick leans toward the camera. *Get a load of this. Number one on our look back at college murders that were never solved. Amber Fields, murdered in her dorm room bed on February 14—that's right, Valentine's Day.* The image cuts to a pale-pink rose on a white sheet, a smear of what is or is made to look like blood on the petals.

Maybe it's the drinks or maybe it's the stupid videos or maybe it's the sizzle of the goodbye kiss from Adrian—the hard press of his hand on her hip, hint of his tongue in her mouth—but when she lies down she tosses and turns, adrenaline zipping through her. She's finally fallen asleep when there's a pounding at her door, three urgent knocks. She checks her phone and it's 2:00 A.M.

Jane, she thinks. It can only be Jane. A fall. A blood clot. A seizure. Some ugly aftershock from the accident gripping her in the night.

She runs to the door and flings it open.

Billy Fauver is standing on her front porch.

"Nice place," he says, and his smile makes her gut drop, puts a metallic taste in her mouth. She calculates the time it would take to get her personal weapon from the safe, but that would mean turning her back on Fauver, and she doesn't like that. He's a big man, but surely he's out of shape. She could hold him off, unless he's got a weapon she can't see.

"What are you doing here?"

"And looking nice. Where were those legs the other day, Officer Hauser?"

"It's Chief Hauser. And you need to get off my porch. Now."

He puts his hands up. "I only came because I remember something. There's a name you should know."

"Humor me."

"Trent Brentwood."

"Who is that?"

"A little bitch."

"You drove here in the middle of the night to tell me this? Why do I need to know the name Trent Brentwood?" As she speaks she's doing another calculation in her head. If Fauver had something to do with Jenna's disappearance, would he really take the risk of showing up on her porch in the middle of the night?

"Let's just say I have friends keeping their eyes and ears out for me. I heard my name came up at the bar."

Callie stares at him. Does he mean Reynolds or Collins? Did one of them tell Fauver she was trying to put the screws in them, angling for probable cause? Is this what that look from the biker was about back at the bar? "Who do you mean?" she asks.

He smiles. "Someone pretty close to you."

Her stomach lurches. Is he talking about Jenna? Is he keeping her somewhere?

"My mother—" she starts, and he raises his hands.

"I don't have shit to do with that. Or this Riley thing. Look up Brentwood. Ask him what you asked me. Goodnight, Officer Hauser. Don't let the bedbugs bite." He steps off the porch, whistling into the night.

She follows him. The temperature has dipped into the forties, and her bare legs sting. Goose bumps rise on her arms. She winces as a rock stabs the sole of her bare foot. He's parked far down the lane. Wanted to scare her, or at least catch her off guard. Couldn't risk her seeing his headlights, hearing him pull up. And it also tells her he's capable of being strategic. Not just a puppet jerked around by his own impulses. Someone who could commit a crime and cover it up, or plan a crime and the cover up.

"Fauver. Why did you and Sabrina get into an altercation in front of the bait shop?"

"I told you, she was crazy. She was going on about me ratting her out for stealing something. A necklace some guy had meant for another girl, or something like that. That he was super pissed. But I didn't know anything about it. What would I give a shit about any necklaces for?"

"Did she say who she stole it from? Who was he?"

"I don't know. Brentwood was the only guy I know who she was fucking around with. Everyone thought he was such a charmer, but he dropped her fast. You wanna know about what happened back then? I have no idea. Go ask him."

"What makes you think he's the father and not you?"

"I never slept with her. She didn't want to."

The sting of rejection in his voice is clear even all these years later. She sure as hell doesn't buy this idea Fauver has of himself as righteous, good, just because he never forced a girl into sex—if he's even to be believed. "How do you know she slept with Brentwood?"

"She was always trying to make me jealous. All, *'Trent's going to take me to prom, Trent and I are hanging out Saturday . . .'*"

"Did it work? Were you jealous?" There's still a version of the story she can picture with Fauver at the center, jilted and taking revenge on the girl who taunted him, turned him down.

But Fauver only shakes his head and climbs into his car, leaves her shivering in the dark.

Trent Brentwood is easy enough to find in the system. He's got a few priors, arrested for possession, a little bit of weed. A DUI five years back. She's able to find him easily on social media too. He's a skinny white guy, blue-eyed with thick, fringed lashes. Posts lots of photos of the bay at sunset. Of himself on the back of a fishing boat. One in a blood-stained apron with the name of the fish market where he works. Geotags. Employer. A shot crouched by the tailgate of his truck, license plate in clear view. His whole life laid out for anyone to see.

Three days later Callie is off and not watching Opal until the afternoon. She decides to interview Brentwood, will try him at the fish market where he works down in Sea Isle. As she drives the thickness of the woods yields to a wide stretch of parkway, but still there are stands of pine along the side of the road even as she starts to smell salt in the air, sees signs for Cape May and Wildwood, the casinos of Atlantic City across the marsh. But sunlight—so much sunlight, compared to the Pine Barrens—riches of it, gilds everything. She arrives at a little tollbooth perched high on the middle of a bridge, and then just on the other side she's in Fish Alley, fishmongers and bait shops and seafood restaurants where people can tie their boat up while they enjoy a scampi and white wine.

She likes talking to people when they're at work. They're less inclined to make a fuss, don't want to draw the boss's attention, whereas at home, on their way to their cars, they have doors to slam. Places to recede. Another one of the reasons it's been hard to press Billy Fauver—he only seems to answer to himself, has no appearances to keep up.

There's a clatter of bells when she walks into the market, which is charmingly old-school. Trent Brentwood stands behind the display case where whole striped bass, silver and shimmering, laid out on snowy beds of chipped ice. Blue claw crabs in rows, metal buckets filled with rings of cleaned squid, a doormat of a flounder with its flat, dead eye fixed skyward. In a freezer behind her, quarts of fish stock. A tank of lobsters, all in one lethargic pile. Homemade red sauce. Piles of lemons in wire baskets and tins of Old Bay stacked in a pyramid.

Brentwood has tattooed forearms: several women's names in script, a picture of Jesus looking mournful, his hands pressed together in prayer. She knows before she sees it that somewhere on his body it says *Mother*, and as he wraps a fillet of tuna in brown paper she spots it, curling out from underneath his gloved hand. He hands the fish to a wooly-haired woman who drops it right into her handbag.

"What are you cooking tonight, Mrs. Wentzel?"

"I'll sear this and make a side of potatoes and green beans, some good bread from the market—they bake fresh on Tuesdays, you know—and for dessert some banana pudding."

"Okay then. What time should I come over?" He bats his eyelashes at her.

"Oh, Trent, you come over any old time, okay?"

"You're sweet, Mrs. W. You're the best. You enjoy your dinner, okay? And one of these days I'm gonna take you up on that."

Mrs. Wentzel moves toward the door and his eyes fall on Callie. "What can I get for you, Miss? We got bluefin, just caught this morning. If I were you I'd snatch that up while it's fresh." Ah, he's one of those, she thinks. The kind of man who can make anything about sex. Mrs. Wentzel felt it. Callie feels it now. Something indecent about the most banal of questions, how he cut a glance at Callie when he said *snatch*. This is her guy.

"You're Trent Brentwood, right?"

At the sound of the last name he understands this is serious. The smile that crinkled his eyes contracts. His flirtation revoked. "That's me."

"I'm Chief Callie Hauser, Pine Lakes. Do you have a minute to talk?"

Brentwood calls out to a coworker she can't see over his shoulders and she can tell he's wary by the way his shoulders rise. "Hey Doug, can you come cover me up here for a bit? I gotta go down to the docks." He doesn't take his eyes off Callie even while he pulls his gloves off and even in this, she sees it, the proximity to sex. The snap and slide of the rubber reminding her of the way some men pull off a condom. Watching you watch them do it.

"You gotta stop smoking so much, dude," comes a voice from the back.

"Quitting next week, brother, quitting next week."

Callie follows Trent out of the shop, across a parking lot littered with crushed clamshells, and down to a bench near the docks. She feels something too, replacing the flirtatiousness. Fury. Brentwood is skinny but she can see him being the kind of guy who gets into bar brawls. Who has a surprising strength coiled tight in him. Can see those white teeth gritted into a grimace. Interesting. Fauver isn't cleared in her mind, but she can see Brentwood for Sabrina's disappearance, too.

He's agitated, ready to blow his lid without her doing much at all. She crosses her arms and he paces back and forth. She counts backward in her head from ten, knows he'll talk first.

"Look," he says. "If this is about child support, I'm doing the best I can, okay? I told Jenny, I told her, that things are a little rough right now. That it was going to be late."

"I'm not here about Trisha."

"Amanda?" He kicks at some of the clamshells. "Shit. She's never asked me for a thing since that kid's been born. She's gonna start now?"

"I'm not here about Amanda either."

He looks up, confused and intrigued.

"How many children do you have, Mr. Brentwood?"

"Four." He pulls a packet of cigarettes out of his apron, shakes one loose, lights it, takes a long draw. "At least that I know of." A flash of it again. That charm, the wink-wink of it.

"Well, as it happens, I'm here because your name came up in regard to Sabrina Riley, who was believed to be pregnant in 1991 before she went missing."

"Are you serious? Who is putting my name in when it comes to that shit?"

"Does it matter?"

"Yes, it matters! I got a lot of enemies, Officer Hauser. Lots of people trying to drag my name through the dirt, and look. You see me. I'm just trying to make an honest living, pay my bills. Who was it? Pete Turner? That guy is a prick. Why you think I got outta those woods the second I graduated high school? Because people there talk too much shit. They got nothing else to do."

"On the contrary, in this instance I can't get anyone to talk enough shit. I'm finding it difficult to get anyone to tell me about Sabrina Riley. Maybe you could describe your relationship with her."

Brentwood rolls his eyes. "We hooked up a few times. She was fun. Until she wasn't, you know? Broads like that need to come with a warning label. It's going to be all fun and games and a little Malibu Rum in the Wawa parking lot and then all of the sudden you're getting bitch-slapped at school on Monday morning because she hears you took another girl out on the back of your four-wheeler."

"So you dated? Or it was just casual?"

"Casual. Not my fault she wanted something more."

"Did she ever tell you she was pregnant?"

"It is not mine. I always bagged it up with that girl. She got around too much. There were rumors she was with an older dude. Or more than one older dude."

"Tell me about that." Callie feels her impatience rearing up. *Rumors rumors rumors. Crazy crazy crazy.* Never anything concrete.

"Look, I don't know. Someone told me she was with someone older. Married or something."

"Married?" Not Fauver then. He didn't get married until his midtwenties. Maybe someone from the bait shop? A teacher? Brentwood looks pleased at the sound of surprise in Callie's voice.

"Yeah. Take a look at the real suspects before you go chasing me down for more child support." She wants to interrupt him, remind him he's not a suspect in anything, nor is she interested in his issues with child support. But he is on a roll. "I'm bleeding, here. I've got nothing. Fucking backpacks and crayons and rollerblades and soccer uniforms and all that shit. I'm trying to invest in my own thing right now! I'm going in on this charter boat with my cousin. We're gonna take people out to catch flounder in the summer."

"That sounds nice."

"It will be nice! That is if these bitches don't stop bleeding me dry. How's a man supposed to do anything he wants to do with people always showing up and asking him to fork over his hard-earned cash." He takes another long draw on his cigarette. Seagulls wheel and shriek overhead, then land at the end of the dock. Callie grits her teeth, wonders about these women doing the endless work of raising Brentwood's kids. A shadow of a thought at the edge of her mind, of her own father, whoever he was. Released from ever having to wonder if Callie was sick or sleeping well or had enough to eat.

"There's another thing. The baby. It didn't survive. It was found in the woods."

For the first time since she's met him it seems that Trent Brentwood doesn't know what to say. The silence thickens between them for a moment. She lets him stare out at the horizon, waits for him to talk first.

"Oh shit. I heard about that," he says, finally. He looks at Callie, and there's a flicker of sadness in his eyes. "I don't think it was Sabrina's. I mean, I saw her. Sometime that winter. She didn't look pregnant to me."

Callie isn't going to get into it with him, the same way she didn't feel like going there with Fauver. How some women might not show, especially not a first child, until pretty far along. How futile it is to explain the complexities of a woman's body to a man, how it is possible to not know she was pregnant right away, particularly a girl with no access to the internet, who couldn't pull up a thousand forums and websites telling her to take a test, analyzing her every symptom, finding lists of places she could go for help.

"What about her sister? You looking into her? Now she was a little . . . I don't know. Weird. Kept to herself."

At first, Callie thinks she's misheard. "Sister?"

"Sure. Sabrina Riley had a twin. Her name was Annabelle."

Callie can't seem to focus, stares hard at the gulls picking at the scraps of cleaned fish at the end of the dock. "You—You're positive about this?"

"Yeah. I was her partner for a biology project sophomore year. I remember thinking I hit it big. She was smart as hell and did the whole thing on her own, I just showed up and collected my A plus. Only one I ever got. You know I'm gonna remember that."

"Tell me about her. The sister. Anything you remember."

"Umm . . . like I said. Quiet. She had a scar on her arm."

"A scar?"

"Yeah, she was always tugging her sleeve down to cover it. Like three inches long. But messy looking, like it didn't heal right."

"You know how she got it?"

"We didn't exactly make small talk." Trent moves as though he's about to say something else, but then his phone buzzes in his pocket. He glances at the screen and his face changes. "You know, this has nothing to do with me. Okay? I gotta get back to my shift."

He leaves Callie at the dock, the gulls still wheeling overhead, shrieking, diving, relentless.

A sister. A twin. An entire girl lost in the history of all this mess.

It takes every ounce of will not to shove her fist in her mouth and bite down on her knuckles until she bleeds.

CALLIE

She babysits Opal during another PT session, flips through the Baby Doe file for the thousandth time while Opal naps, pauses over Jenna's statement. That girlish signature, the penmanship you can see the strain in. How scared she must have been, down in the station in an interview room. She is relieved that at least it was Frank Caputo who questioned her and took the statement. Frank would have been gentle, would have been delicate. Would not have pushed her more than he had to.

Jane is quiet in that drained way she is when she gets back from PT, so they don't chat much before Callie says goodbye. Callie hugs her hard, though, and Jane squeezes her arm once, twice, as if to say, *I'm still here, somewhere.*

She marches through the facts again. Sabrina Riley disappeared right around the time the baby was found. Her father died two years later. Annabelle gone too, though who knows the timeline on that. So what's happened to the house? She's still on Jane and Damien's Wi-Fi so she pulls up directions. A half hour the opposite direction from home, but what's that matter? It's technically her day off. Adrian is away for a conference in Wyoming. She's got nothing to do besides stare at cobwebbed corners of her cabin, listen to the low drone of her neighbor's radio.

It's only 3:30 but feels later, in the dim of the trees, that thin November light draining away earlier every day. She misses the Riley house but doesn't know it, didn't even register a driveway, until the GPS tells her it is recalculating then unable to connect again. She swears, pulls a U-turn, gasps when a deer leaps across the road, lets her foot off the brake just in time—another pair of eyes, startled wide. That old warning about deer in the street: Where there's one, there are usually two. She waits a moment, her heart thumping in her ears, and then the other bolts in front of her, tail high.

She slows to a creep after she misses the house for a second time and makes another hasty U-turn. Not a single car on the road, no noise beyond a blue jay issuing a warning call from the trees. She knows that between the woods that border the Riley property, to the east and a little bit north, she'd find the house where Jenna grew up, the one she sold when Callie was a toddler and Jenna's father passed away. Where Jenna had been young once, building forts in the yard, mastering the acoustic guitar, blissfully unaware of the blunt way she was about to be cut off from her girlhood forever. Callie grew up early, had to, but so did Jenna. Overnight.

She can't see the house until she's nearly upon it, the driveway hook-shaped so the house doesn't come into view right away. It is bigger than she thought it would be, a Colonial that must have been beautiful once. Dormered windows, a wide wooden front door, a portico above it—most of the windows broken, the paint peeling and weathered away, but graceful lines to it. The lawn is covered in a jumble of debris: a busted lawnmower and a stack of car tires, a sofa with a shovel laid across the cushions. A boat engine but no boat in sight. Along the lower roofline the places where the gutters should be are bare—the originals were probably copper, pried off and sold for scrap.

She gets the Maglite out of her trunk, takes a breath, approaches the front door. She doesn't think there will be anyone there—the house too far gone, too remote, even for squatters, but still she can't help but wish she had her personal weapon on her instead of locked up back at the cabin.

The porch is soft with rot, the wood giving under her boots. The lock has been forced years ago, the front door open a quarter inch already. She nudges the door open with her toe and is hit with a wave of cat piss, catches the flick of a tail around a doorway as she steps over the threshold.

She's right—squatters once, as far she can tell by the ancient sleeping bag slouched over a camelback sofa, a litter of Dinty Moore cans in the middle of the room, clothes strewn across the floor.

"Police," she calls, putting the word out in front of her like a shield, the way she has so many times before. Waits for a groan of the floorboards, a door creaking closed: nothing. "Police!" she yells again, her voice echoing through the rooms.

Inside, that same juxtaposition of elegance and rot. Wainscotting on the walls, a pendant in the center of the ceiling, rococo with flowers and boughs of fruit, from which a chandelier must have hung once. The smell of cat piss so strong it makes her eyes sting. The elegant turn of the banister, the stairs furred with dust and grime a quarter inch high.

She takes a lap around the lower floor, the kitchen like a time capsule. Mouse shit scattered on the shelves of the pantry. A few half-empty bottles of spices. Off the kitchen a narrow set of stairs, the kind that had been used by servants once. Or for a girl sneaking out the back of her house. The stairs creak, announcing her every move. Perhaps Sabrina Riley had known exactly where to place her foot, how to calibrate her weight, so she could move through the house unheard. Though it would have gotten harder as her pregnancy progressed. As her stomach pushed her center of gravity off balance, as her feet and ankles swelled, as her body became unfamiliar to her.

Wallpaper along the upstairs hall, water-stained and faded with age, patterned with vines that twist together and come apart again. The landing is thick with dust, a scrim of footprints through it like someone danced or fought a long time ago. The smell from the bathroom is so putrid that she has to pull her shirt up over her nose to keep from gagging, and even from outside the doorway she can make out dark sludge around the base of the toilet, the shower curtain ripped from its rings and bunched over the rim of the tub.

She closes her hand around the delicate brass knob of the first door to her right, turns it and finds what must have been the primary bedroom, a wood sleigh bed, the headboard carved with pine boughs, the bedsheets stained yellow with time. Terry Riley is not of much interest to Callie. Some teenage pregnancies are hidden because of incest, but Callie doesn't get those cues from this case. Riley was probably gone too long, too checked out, to mess with his daughter. Daughters, rather. Probably, if Callie had to guess, he never had any idea of the pregnancy.

She crosses the hall so she's on the other side of the stairs. The next room is so clearly a teenage girl's room. A four-poster bed with finials carved into pine cones. A little painted nightstand with an alarm clock on it. A collage of faded pictures on the wall above the bed. Supermodels with their big hair and high-waist jeans, teenagers who look ravaged by hard drugs: all stark bones and wan, miserable faces, their eyes protruding from their starved flesh. It seems like it hurts, to exist in those bodies. She thinks about Opal, wonders when there will be a time when girls aren't told how to look, won't be forced to contort themselves into one thing only for the fad to pass and then they're handed the next template. Curvy and womanly, big hair and lashes and all-American smiles, a girl who would eat a burger, lick her fingers, wash it down with a Cherry Coke. Or waifish and impossible to please, a ladder of rib bones protruding through their chests.

"Fuck that," Callie says to herself. She tries to imagine Annabelle and Sabrina Riley's teenage years. No internet, no cell phones. Just two girls trapped in this house with the magazines they thought could tell them the rules of being women in this world.

She opens the doors to a hulking wardrobe, which is empty save for a few metal hangers and improbably, a single dress pressed to the side. Pink, sweetheart neckline, with a frothy bundle of fabric flowers at each shoulder. Callie can't help but touch the bodice, which is stiff with wires and scratchy tulle.

Under the bed, a cardboard box. *Iris*, it says, written in marker on the side. She nudges it into the light with the toe of her boot, lifts the lid. Inside, a doll. Mice have made its hair into a nest so it is mussed and matted, woven with scraps of paper. There's a second box under the bed labeled *Hannah* but she doesn't open it. The dead, unblinking eyes of Iris are enough to give her the creeps.

She moves on to the next bedroom. Annabelle's.

They are mirror images on each side of the wall. The same twin bed and wooden nightstand in ballet-slipper pink. Another wardrobe like Sabrina's, with its carvings of fairies and vines. The same hooked rug on the floor. The desk in this room is tidy and when Callie opens a drawer she finds notebooks. Stacks of yellow Post-it notes. And in the bottom drawer, an SAT prep book. She flips it open, each test problem solved in delicate but deliberate pencil strokes.

On the shelf above the desk there's stacks of textbooks, piles of spiral-bound notebooks. A yearbook, green cover with gold foil accents. 1989–1990.

Callie cracks it open, scans the rows of black-and-white pictures of kids that still have baby fat in their cheeks, mouths crammed with braces. She finds Sabrina Riley first, looking not much happier than she did in her mug shot, a little softer, rounder in the cheeks, the same hungry gleam to her eyes and point to her left incisor. That foxlike face. A tangle of necklaces against her chest, above the lacy edge of a push up bra. Next to her, a girl with slightly darker hair smiling with her mouth closed. Her face is wider than Sabrina's, and their expressions set them apart, but the similarity is striking, as though there was a printing glitch and two photos of the same student appeared in a row.

"There you are," she whispers.

Callie flips to the back of the book, where there's an insert of creamy blank pages. They are pristine, save for a single note written on the third one.

Annabelle,

Thank you for all of your hard work on the yearbook committee this year. I hope you are pleased to see your work on these pages. Where would we be without your layout skills? You are a star and I'm so excited for all of the things in your future.

Enjoy your summer, Miss Hamilton

She doesn't know what makes her do it, but she finds Jenna among the freshman. She's skinny, with narrow shoulders and a big, guileless smile that makes Callie's chest ache.

She snaps the yearbook shut and tucks it under her arm.

Callie closes her eyes. For a second she can almost see it. Two girls, racing down the grand staircase, too young to notice the rot seeping in, the mold along the walls and the stains on the ceiling, the disorder coming for them. Two girls, playing games in the woods. One another's worlds. She hears their laughter, their shrieks of fear and outrage and delight. Making dolls out of pine cones. Turning stones into jewels in the palms of their hands. Shrouded in their girlhoods for a little while longer.

Then, two girls just a few years out of playing games, of imagining things in the woods and winding through the trees. They learn what it feels like to be touched by someone: sometimes transcendent, sometimes a kind of theft. Girls trying to decide who they might want to be, aiming themselves toward the futures they want, or think they should want. All those gaunt-cheeked models on Sabrina Riley's wall. Annabelle and her fastidiousness, trying so hard to be good.

When she opens her eyes they go to the edge of the desk, the yellowed blotter, the cup of pens. And then she sees it. A little row of ridges along the top slat of the desk chair. Callie traces her finger just below the marks. But she knows what they are the second she lays eyes on them.

Teeth marks.

Three overlapping rows, wavelike frills where the blue-painted wood gives way to the raw stuff at its center. The yellow pine exposed where someone bit down on it again and again.

In a room this orderly, this controlled, it stands out. Practically gives off a vibration, the way the photo of that broken amber bracelet does. A story there, and with it comes a shiver, the sensation of information passing through her skin.

Back in the car she has to steady herself with a few deep breaths before she can drive away. The disorder of the house has shaken her, the idea of the girls living there, doing what they had to do to survive their teenage years. Sabrina, working, then acting out, stirring up trouble, playing boys off of one another to feel something, not love, but connection, need. Maybe it helped mask the trouble all around her, the kind she had no control over. Callie had been the Annabelle type. The one who thought that if you can be really good you can make the bad in your life right.

She turns out of the Riley driveway and loops around to the street that backs up to their house so she will pass Jenna's childhood home on her way back to her cabin. Someone has written out a Bible verse in black spray paint on a big piece of plywood and propped it up in the front yard. The person Callie wants to tell most about it is Jenna, who liked to recount the various ways she got kicked out of Sunday school when she was a kid. Chewing bubble gum, singing "Wild Horses" at the top of her lungs, draping her coat over her head and pretending it was a habit. Jenna had always had a rebellious streak, a disdain for authority—blamed it on her ancestors, who came to the Pines in the 1700s from the Philadelphia Quaker sect they abandoned when they couldn't stick to the Friends' code. It wasn't until later though, that it seemed to alchemize into self-destruction. That the pride in her rebellious nature shifted into something more like shame.

At home Callie starts to make dinner—a grilled cheese and a can of tomato soup heated up on her hot plate—when her phone rings.

Healy.

"Please tell me you have a match for me," she says, dumping the soup into a pot, splattering some of it on the front of her shirt.

"Where are you right now? Is it a good time to talk?"

"Why do you sound like you're about to tell me someone died?" She instantly regrets her phrasing. Isn't that what a part of her has been waiting for, dreading, since Jenna's bag was turned in? "I'm at home, if that's what you mean."

"We do have a match on the Baby Doe case."

"Hell yes." Callie feels herself stand straighter, all of her muscles and ligaments going taut with anticipation. Fauver, she thinks. If she can get him on the DNA, then maybe she can get a warrant to search his place.

"Hauser. I don't know how to tell you this."

"Just tell me. This is good news, isn't it? It's the first real evidence in this case in thirty years."

"We have a match. A half sibling of Baby Doe. I didn't believe it at first. Like wondered if you were playing some kind of joke here or something—"

Callie's excitement shifts into annoyance quickly. "You're killing me, Healy. Enough with the suspense, please. Who is it?"

He exhales through the line. "You, Hauser. The match we have for Baby Doe? It's you."

Callie stands still, at first convinced she heard him wrong. The soup starts to boil but she doesn't move to turn down the heat, just listens to it bubble angrily.

"Callie?" He says, and that's how she knows he's not messing with her, how she knows she heard it right the first time. Her first name, tender and tentative.

Still, she doesn't answer him right away.

She closes her eyes and counts back the years. The DNA test she submitted, tipsy and bored on a Friday after her last attempt at Thanksgiving with Jenna. 2017. The tube she spat in and then forgot about until the email came six weeks later heralding her results. Nothing but a few distant relatives whom she had to pay a higher membership fee to view or message. Everything else, she already knew. She was predisposed to think cilantro tasted like soap. She can't roll her tongue. Nothing about the father Jenna claimed had been a one-night stand before he moved out West to be a roadie for Pearl Jam—a story that always seemed provisional, sure, but Callie figured it was because Jenna was embarrassed about who Callie's father was, or wasn't exactly sure. And that had been that. Or so she thought.

And suddenly, the mysteries of the past few months resolve into meaning. This must be why Jenna ran. Why she picked up the drugs. She knew Callie would look into the case. Knew that she would be exposed as the mother of Baby Doe. But how? How did Frank bring Jenna into the station for questioning without realizing? Could he have been so oblivious? Or was it willful? A form of mercy? Why had Sabrina Riley's name been in the mix? Was it just coincidence that her bracelet was found nearby?

She aches in a new way for sixteen-year-old Jenna, who, in her statement, claims she ran back to her house as quickly as she could after finding the child so she could call the police. Maybe she always knew she would be found out. Maybe she had wanted to be punished back then. Maybe she's spent the rest of her life crushed under the guilt that was never, for whatever reason, discovered. Jenna abandoned Baby Doe.

Callie fumbles to explain all this to Healy. "My mother gave a statement. She said she found the baby. She said—"

He cuts her off. "Listen to me. I don't know anything about your mother. You're related on the father's side."

"What?"

"You are a genetic relative on the paternal side. There's no match linking anyone to the child's mother, or anyone she's related to."

Healy gives her a moment to process, and when he speaks again his voice is softer, padded with pity. "You really didn't have any clue?"

A chill moves through her. Her father. A figure she can't picture more than the avatar in one of those profiles online. A shadow, a generic outline of a man.

And Baby Doe. A half sibling. Someone else in this world who might have stood alongside her. Might have helped edge away the loneliness and shame of her girlhood. Someone else who, like Jane, could have said, *I'm here.*

The soup is burning on the hot plate. And still, Callie can't move to turn the heat down.

She forces herself to ask, "Can you see who the father is? I never knew him. My mother . . . my mother never even told me his name."

"You're the closest genetic match we've got. Listen, I know this will be sensitive to bring up with your mom but—"

"My mother is missing. She's an alcoholic. And an addict, apparently. And she disappeared a few days after the last time I saw her."

Healy says something on the other side of the line but Callie doesn't hear, can't take in anything else. She tells Healy she will have to call him back tomorrow, unplugs the hot plate, and walks outside into the bracing night air.

She needs to move, to work off some of this unruly energy prickling along her nerves. She paces around the outside of her cabin once, twice, then walks down to the shore of the lake, crouches into a squat, drops her head into her hands.

There used to be nothing she couldn't make sense of in her work. And by cutting ties with her mother she had created an existence that felt tidy, clean. For a few years her place in the world felt clear and solid. She knew who she was and what she was doing.

And now? The whole story of her life feels rewritten. Who would she have been if she could have defined herself in relation to this sister? To have known she wasn't always alone? And look at what has been taken from her. The hurt is sharp and personal now.

Part II

BLAIR

September 2023

Blair's phone chimes.

I miss you, Henry says.

Lol. It's only been two hours.

Send me a picture.

She snaps a selfie, grinning in her soccer uniform, her hair loose around her face, her cheeks still flushed. She thinks she looks pretty. Herself.

That's cute . . . but I was thinking more of a Hailey Delman picture.

Blair has a feeling like a stone dropping in her gut. Everyone knows what a Hailey Delman picture is because last year Hailey Delman got into a fight with her boyfriend and he sent the pictures she shared with him to the entire lacrosse team, who in turn sent them to the whole school, spreading them like a virus. Blair laughed at Hailey like the rest of them, but the truth was, she was awed. By Hailey's lips outlined with dark liner, filled in with shiny gloss. Her legs crossed, a thong that tied in black satin ribbon at each hip. No bra, just one skinny arm drawn across her chest. It was her eyes that shocked Blair the most. The steady stare at the camera. The eyes that seemed, in the half second it took for the camera to capture her face, to say *devour me.*

And that's what everyone did.

She wonders how Hailey Delman is doing. If she's found new friends or if the photo made it to her new school, too. If everyone calls her the same names there. If a fresh start is ever even possible, when *delete* never actually means *gone*.

I hope your silence means you're
getting undressed for me 😃

She is standing in her kitchen, a half-eaten banana on the island, the last bite she took glutted thick in her throat, shivering from the combination of her cooling sweat and the air conditioning. She and Henry have been hooking up for the past six weeks, ever since they made out in the backyard at Avery Huang's pool party. So far they've only kissed and groped, grinding their hips into each other in Henry's room, or Blair's on the rare occasion Blair is home alone. But things are getting more intense. Last week Henry moved Blair's hand to where he was hard, underneath his jeans, and she guided his hand under her shirt, let his finger graze her nipple. She likes him, likes experimenting together, likes the tingle of anticipation she gets whenever she knows she's going to see him. But she doesn't know about this. Giving him a piece of her that she can no longer control.

She could take the picture just to have it and then see how she feels. File it away in the Hidden album on her phone until she decides what to do. No harm in that.

She has half an hour before her mother will be home with her two brothers after pickup over at the middle school. Half an hour could be enough to strip down, arrange herself. She doesn't have any satin-trimmed underwear like Hailey, but she does have a black cotton thong that could do. Maybe her mother has something she could borrow. Not lingerie, not anything weird, but something to make it more grown-up. High heels. A necklace that will disappear into her cleavage.

* * *

Her mother's closet is a study in contrasts: the stiff, bright scrubs she keeps around from when she worked as a home health aide, way back before Blair was born. And the things she wears for the PTA lunches, the date nights with Blair's father. Silky camisoles and soft, thin knits. She examines a pair of black pumps but they seem so brisk, businesslike, the heel too low to be sexy. Her mother favors them for library fundraisers, the holiday party for her father's work. She opens another shoebox to find a pair of brown suede loafers, scoffs, and puts the lid back onto the box. She knows it is a paradox—that she derides her mother's ordinariness, and yet, how she would hate it even more if her mother were unordinary. If Blair had opened the box to find a pair of stilettos studded with rhinestones, or boots that went over the knee.

She's about to give up when something else catches her eye. A duffel bag in the corner that had been hidden underneath an old blanket, the hint of weathered brown leather peeking out from beneath orange-and-white crochet squares. Though she has no reason to, Blair pushes the blanket aside and tugs on the zipper pull.

Inside she finds three pairs of black cotton underwear, one nude bra. A pair of jeans and a pair of sweatpants. A white T-shirt and a pale-blue button down. A small cloth toiletry bag containing a travel toothbrush, travel toothpaste, dental floss, a comb. In one of the side pockets there are three small envelopes, her initials and her brothers' in her mother's handwriting. Inside the one marked *BER* she finds a single curl of her baby hair and the tiny, hollow pebbles of her first lost teeth. Flat against the bottom of the bag is a manilla envelope containing three black-and-white snapshots of Blair and her brothers, Blair's front tooth missing and the boys' cheeks padded with baby fat, that her mother took with the first DSLR camera her father bought her when Blair was small.

There's another side pocket, a smaller one, but now she's curious, wonders what pieces of herself she might find. Her fingers graze something cool and smooth and hard.

It's a lighter. Not the long, thin kind that she's seen her mother use to light taper candles on the dining table when they've had guests over for dinner or that her father uses to start the firepit in the yard. This is heavy, metal, a lighter designed to slip into a pocket, to be concealed. She turns it over in her palm. On one side, an S scratched into the surface, rough and crude.

Oh my god, she thinks. *Does my mom smoke pot?* The thought can't help but make her laugh out loud, picturing her tidy, order-obsessed mother sparking a joint or bending over a bong. But the sound of her own laughter in the quiet house, holding this unexplainable object in her hand, soon leaves her feeling unsettled.

She runs her hand along the seams of the inside of the suitcase and uncovers a small film canister, black, that rattles when she shakes it. There's another, smaller envelope underneath of that, the size someone would use for a letter. Inside there are two sheets of waxed paper, and when she peels them apart she finds a single pressed flower that might have been bright yellow once but has aged into a brownish-gold hue. There's a scrap of paper folded in half also stuck in the envelope, and when she handles it, it feels worn to softness, like fabric. On it, a note in unfamiliar handwriting.

I love you. Forgive me.

She stares at the words until the sound of a car door slamming startles her. Her mother already back with her two brothers, Kyle thumping a basketball up the drive, Jake asking if he has time to play a video game before they eat. She takes another second to weigh the heft of the lighter in her hand before putting it back in the pocket of the bag, drawing the blanket over it again, closing the door, tiptoeing her way out of the room.

Over dinner she tries to tell herself it is nothing to worry about. The bag. This lighter. The note. So what if her mother allows herself one secret cigarette a month? So what if she occasionally lights up a spliff when everyone is asleep? But she doesn't think that's the story. Blair doesn't like it, this side of her mother that she senses but can't see. Like the dark side of the moon.

Throughout the meal Blair finds herself staring at her mother the second she's not looking—when she rises to get more meatballs for the boys, or to fetch another stack of napkins because Kyle keeps getting sauce on the ends of his sleeves. And maybe because Blair has Henry, has her own secrets now, she can see it. Not the secret itself, but the halo of something untold.

"So, looks like they're moving the construction date up for the condos," Blair's father says, making his voice gentle. He and Blair watch Iris. The condos are a difficult subject in their house. Iris had attended zoning meetings, written letters to the local paper on the value of protecting the woods alongside the river.

"Moving the date up?" Iris asks. "When?"

"They break ground next week. They want to be able to lease to people by the start of the school year next year. I'm sorry, sweetheart. I thought you might have heard already."

"Oh," Iris says, turning to look out the bay window at the end of their dining table. Blair looks at Iris's reflection, the pale oval of her face, her mother's features blurry and indistinct.

BLAIR

She goes over to Henry's house on Tuesday after soccer practice. His mom is on the PTA with Iris, and the parents are getting together to decorate the gym for tomorrow's homecoming carnival fundraiser. Blair's brothers and dad are home, while Henry is an only child whose father is in San Francisco for work.

In Henry's bedroom they kiss and kiss, until he asks if he can unbutton her jeans. She is nervous and excited and afraid, and she says yes. He asks if he can touch her, and she says yes to that too, and guides his hands in the way she's learned she likes when she's experimented, alone in her room, when everyone else has gone to bed, or sometimes in the bath, the rush of the water into the tub filling her ears, the pressure building and building in her body until there's a catch sprung somewhere within her, then the helpless, glorious release. At first it's strange, dreamlike, having someone else touch her in places only her own fingers have known. After a little while, he seems to understand what she likes, the pressure, the direction, and she lets her hand fall to the bed, lets her eyes close and her head fall back, lets herself feel everything until she gets hot all over, and the sensation spreads throughout her body, and she has no choice but to let go.

She rides her bike home in the chill of the autumn air, tender against the seat, little aftershocks traveling up her spine as she shifts and pedals, the feeling alternating between pleasant and nearly unbearable. There's a smell of the first fires in the air, woody and sweet. She had felt so self-conscious saying goodbye to Henry's mom in the driveway, her cheeks flushed and hair mussed. She had hoped to leave before Diana was back, but she and Henry couldn't stop kissing goodbye. So there she was, in the driveway, sticky and slick between her legs, Henry's mom telling her how she had just been with Iris, how they had filled all the balloons for the fall homecoming carnival together and how beautifully Iris had planned everything.

The day after she spends the afternoon with Henry, Blair is eating breakfast when Iris asks her if she wouldn't mind driving separately to the carnival. Her dad is with her brothers at a soccer tournament two towns over. "I've got to go early. We need to blow up all those balloons."

She almost calls her mother out—*Diana said you did it last night*—but then she realizes what she has. Iris is lying. She wouldn't normally think much of it, but since finding those things in her mother's closet last week she's got a question fizzling in her mind. The note in a stranger's writing lit up in her head like a neon sign. It feels absurd to think it, yet she can't help it: Is Iris having an affair?

Following Iris is easy enough. They each have location sharing enabled on their phones. They did it last year when they went to Disney World as a family so they could find one another easily in the parks. Blair hardly ever thinks about it, because she knows Iris doesn't use it. Unlike some of her friends' parents, who track their kids' every step home from school, Iris seems to forget that she can find Blair whenever she wants to.

Blair watches the little dot that represents her mother move down their block, turn left on Oak, then right on Elm, the way she would if she were heading to school. Blair feels both disappointed and relieved, until her mother makes a left on Lafayette Drive. If she were on the way to the high school Iris would have stayed straight for another two miles. She watches the dot progress toward the outer limits of town.

What's out there? Blair wonders. She pulls up street view but all she can see are trees. But then she remembers. The new housing development going in. How it was a source of endless debate. Luxury condos that meant tearing down so many trees close to the creek so the owners could have good views. All these town meetings, her mother involved in some of them. She liked to walk along the dirt paths out that way, was always saying how sad it was that they would build there. It was so peaceful. But if she were going for a walk, why not just say so?

The dot is still for a long time, her mother parked. Blair feels a bolt of panic, dials Iris's phone, but Iris doesn't pick up.

Blair gets in her car, still in her pajamas, and drives there. It only takes ten minutes. If her mother catches her she can make up some excuse. *You didn't answer. I was worried. The carbon monoxide detector went off.*

She parks just behind Iris's crossover and sets off on the trail she knows her mother favors. She is surprised to see how many construction vehicles line the road, at how loudly the machinery booms as they take down trees, lines of orange caution tape marking the perimeter of the site.

The path slopes downward, and Blair takes the hill, looking out for her mother's pink sweater between the trees. She's lost in thought until she hears a snap of a branch. She slides behind a trunk and peers downhill. Her mother is alone, carrying something. Blair squints. Iris has three big stones in her hands. She's bringing them from the direction of the construction site, walking downstream. There's an old stone wall that runs through the woods, remnants from the town's Revolutionary War days, and Iris steps over the wall and disappears from Blair's view.

When Iris steps over the wall again she's empty-handed. She walks back in the direction she came from, returns in a few minutes with another armful of stones. A third time, Iris disappears, then comes back, this time the stones smaller, and she has to cradle them close to her body to keep from dropping any. She looks blank but determined, and Blair can't help but wonder if she's watching her mother have some sort of psychotic break. The small stones seem to be the last, and across the distance Blair can hear the clink of them together, her mother hidden but busy underneath the boughs of the tree, arranging the rocks. Then it's quiet for a long time.

She waits for five minutes, ten, fifteen, but her mother doesn't come back up the path. There are shouts from the construction site, the sounds of saws and stump grinders working away at the woods. Blair waits another five minutes before she tiptoes her way back up the path to her car. On the way home she wonders if she should call her father, call Aunt Margot, call someone who can help her understand, or even just marvel at, the insanity she's just seen. Her mother saving a bunch of rocks from demolition? It doesn't make any sense.

At the carnival Iris looks tidy as ever. Not even a crumb of dirt on her pink sweater. A bright smile for each person she sells a ticket to. The other mothers on the PTA compliment her on a job well done.

"How'd it go with the balloons?" Blair asks her.

"Oh, easy with the helium tank."

Blair stares at her, in wonder and awe. How easy it is for Iris to lie to her. As the carnival winds down, Iris tells Blair to order takeout at home—she'll have to stay here and help clean up, but Blair should go enjoy her Saturday with her friends. Normally Blair would relish the time alone, but she's uneasy. She doesn't leave until she watches Iris absorbed in the task of collecting paper plates, boxing up extra food which she'll donate to the homeless shelter.

Instead of heading home, Blair drives back to the construction site. It's dark now and she only has her phone as a flashlight, but she makes her way down the path, this time descending all the way to the creek, to where the stone wall bisects the woods.

She pushes the pine bough aside to see the place where her mother had been hidden from her earlier that day. She stands before the two tidy piles of rocks, nearly identical in size, the largest ones arranged at the base, the smaller ones piled on top.

Cairns, she remembers, a word from her history class. Monuments. Memorials. Used across cultures, an ancient practice. Her teacher, Mr. Corrigan, sweeping his arms to indicate the vastness of distance and time.

In front of the cairns there's a patch of dirt that's rougher than the rest, as though it had been dug up. Her mother had a trowel with her. Had she buried something here? Blair hasn't brought any tools, so she breaks a branch from a nearby tree and begins to scrape at the earth. She digs until she's sweating and her fingers ache. The night has gotten cold and it creeps into her lungs. But she keeps working until she hits something hard, then finds a rock to scrape through the rest of the way.

With numb, swollen fingers she gets her phone from her pocket and shines the flashlight on what looks to be the top of a small metal box. Blair digs some more until finally she can pry the box loose with her fingers. She stares at it for a moment before she springs the latch, her fingers and nails caked in filth and throbbing with the strain.

Inside is an envelope. Blair handles it tenderly and still muddies it with her fingerprints.

Unlike the note in the duffel bag, she recognizes the handwriting as Iris's immediately.

She sits and reads in the light of her phone flashlight. When she is finished she feels dizzy, out of breath.

The wind picks up and rattles the orange tape marking the perimeter of the construction zone. She places the message back in the box and with shaking hands buries it best she can as the cold of the descending night seeps through her sweatshirt, sinks into her skin.

ANNABELLE

Miss Hamilton drives a blue Toyota. When she guides it down the long, dirt driveway you hear your father's voice in your head. *Damn imports ruining the economy. My great-grandaddy's business run into the ground because no one is putting America first.* The other morning you woke to the sound of him retching in the bathroom. You hadn't seen him in a month, other than his boots in a heap by the door, had started to think he might have evaporated right out of them, like some kind of fairytale.

You're standing at the front window, tucked behind the curtain, trying to imagine the house and the yard as a stranger might see them. Yesterday you had done your best to cover some of the metal scrap with a mildew-flecked tarp you found in the shed, pulled the weeds that had burst up around the front walkway, but there is no covering up the essential mess of the house.

Sabrina comes behind you while you are watching, her necklaces jangling, her perfume heady. A chemical-laced vanilla, which always gives you a headache.

"Who's that?"

"Miss Hamilton." Your stomach is doing flips. Nerves, you tell yourself. All week the bubbling sensation you had felt before has become stronger, more insistent and demanding. When the test is over it will go away, you think. You just have to get through this day. You pluck at the waistband of your sweatpants. The only pair that still fits and still the elastic leaves angry red marks in your skin.

"What is she doing here? You one of her pity cases now?"

"She's just giving me a ride."

"Where?"

"To the SATs." A jolt from below your belly button makes you move your hand to your shirt.

Sabrina purses her lips. "Something is going on with you."

"Nothing. I just have to take this test. It's really important. If you score well enough you are eligible for more scholarships, even at private schools."

Sabrina is ruffled by the mention of college and scholarships. You can tell by the way her shoulders rise toward her ears. For a moment you feel powerful, in control. But still, she won't let you go so easily. "Where have you been getting tampons? You haven't used any of the ones in the upstairs bathroom. That box has lasted since the summer."

You thought about it. Taking a few tampons out by the fistful, throwing them away in a trashcan at school. You and Sabrina have complained before, about how tampons and pads are the most expensive things on your grocery list. So you didn't. At the time, you wished she would ask. Now, you're sorry you didn't cover your tracks.

You stare past her, watch Miss Hamilton get out of her car and tiptoe her way across the cracked paving stones that lead to the porch. Even though you are terrified, a part of you is treasuring this moment. It is the most interest Sabrina has taken in you in months. You open your mouth to say—what?—but as soon as you do the doorbell sounds throughout the house, a tinny three-note chime.

"I have to go. The test."

"Annabelle. Are you—" You can't let her get the question out, no matter what you do. Another part of you begs her to say it. Just say it, so that she can help you. Sabrina always knows what to do.

"Later," you say. "I can talk later." Later later later. That same refrain that's been running through your mind for weeks.

The doorbell sounds again. You want to stay and tell Sabrina everything. Want to throw yourself at her feet. But instead you look past her, your face burning. She grabs your wrist.

"Annabelle. This is serious." Her perfume so intense close up, you feel the ache already collecting at your temples. You can't risk it, can't show up to the test not feeling good. You need this, need to concentrate. You've paid the fee, you've studied, and now it's time to measure your worth.

You pull yourself free, with such force that Sabrina stumbles backward.

"Leave me alone!" you scream. Sabrina's eyes go wide but you ignore her, grab your bag—number 2 pencils sharpened to fine points, a granola bar, scrap paper—and run for the door.

"How are you doing?" Miss Hamilton asks brightly, as you walk to the car.

"Good," you say. You turn back toward the house. There's no one in the window but you can feel Sabrina's eyes on you, that she was watching just a moment ago.

"Don't be nervous. You've worked so hard. I've seen your workbooks. You've done all the practice tests. Now it's time to trust yourself."

Her car smells like peppermint. There's a Kate Bush cassette case in the center console. You wonder what it is like to be an adult. To have the freedom and the means to put together a life, any life you want. Who would you be, given the choice? College seemed like a way of answering that question, once. But now it hurts to ask.

You've been assigned a test room at random and you file into the gym behind the proctor, an honors English teacher for the eleventh grade who has a habit of rubbing his thumb and pointer finger together, like he's pinching something you can't see. Rows of desks have been arranged in the middle of the floor and as you settle in there are some kids you recognize and others from neighboring schools who you don't know, who are just here to take the test. It feels like a relief, to be around people who don't know you, who haven't heard the cheers that the girls in homeroom continue to chant whenever they see you. *Annabelle the prude, Sabrina the slut . . .*

You think of Sabrina waiting for you back at home. About the questions in her face. Because as much as you can hide from yourself, you can't hide it from your sister. And so you begin to count.

The proctor instructs all of you to break the seal on the first section of your test booklet. Faced with the first question—What is the closest synonym to the word *abysmal*?—you make hatch marks on the edge of your test book. The last time you remember bleeding was in June. It's November now, the halls of the school lined with Thanksgiving decorations. You make a small line for every month that has passed since then. Five tally marks. Now it's no longer about counting back, but counting toward, in the direction of a future that makes your mind go black.

You let your pencil fall to your desk. It rolls off the ledge, across the freshly waxed basketball court. You recall standing on the free-throw line during gym class last year, your classmates pressed on either side of you, the gym teacher, Mr. Barrington, yelling. *Shoot the damn ball, Riley! Now! Come on, Riley!* You knew the only way out of the moment was to do what he told you. To go through the drill just as everyone else in class had. But still you couldn't bring yourself to do it. To raise the ball and push it through the air. Mr. Barrington was yelling so hard by then a clot of spittle collected at the corner of his mouth.

In the end, the bell rang and saved you, broke the tension, broke everyone's stares. And you realize that is what you have been waiting for now. For a bell to ring somewhere. To be rescued. But no one can help you. Not anymore.

You don't answer any more questions, even though you have an extra pencil on your desk. You feel the tumbling in your stomach and a sudden thrust so insistent you have to bite your lip to keep from crying out. You watch the big circle of the clock on the wall, its twitchy second hand, and still you don't know how much time passes before the proctor tells everyone to put their pencils down.

* * *

You wait until everyone else filters out of the room, eyes on the free-throw line the whole time. Not meeting the proctor's gaze when he collects your test booklet. When you feel his stare on you. "You'll have another chance," he says, softly, so softly, so that none of the other kids can hear. Tears burn behind your eyes. You are so desperate for kindness and yet when you receive it, it feels so much like pain.

Miss Hamilton told you to wait for her in the front of the school by the flagpole after the test let out. She's there when you leave the school building, bright patches of color in her cheeks that make her look cheerful and young. Younger even, than you feel, when you think about all that she doesn't know about you, all that's right there that she can't see. Her eyes catch on you and you know she is measuring something in you, the way she did after she told that Halloween story about Mother Leeds and the devil, the child screaming through the woods.

"Let's get in the car, it's freezing as hell out here!"

You can tell she's used the word *hell* to soften you, relax you, and maybe before it would have worked. This paling around, but now it only feels insulting. "We could stop at Wawa for some hot chocolates. What do you think?"

You shrug. You feel exhausted, as though you've expended a great amount of concentration, the way you sometimes would after working through one of the three-hour practice tests. Empty.

She waits to ask about it until after she's pulled out of the parking lot. Technically, she doesn't ask at all. Only says a single word. "So."

You shake your head.

"I'm sure you didn't do as badly as you think. You're hard on yourself, Annabelle."

"I screwed up," you say. It feels surprisingly good to say it. To release a little bit of this huge, hidden feeling you've been holding on to. *I screwed up, I screwed up, I screwed up.*

"Well, even if that's true, you'll have another opportunity to take the test, once you get your scores back and you understand where your strengths are and where you need to do some more work. If you really aren't happy with your scores, we'll get you registered for another test in March. You have time to figure it out."

"I don't think I do," you say.

"Look. I've asked if you're okay several times, and you blow me off every time. So now I'm not going to give you that chance. I know there's some stuff at home, and that your dad isn't there a lot. That your sister has dropped out."

"What?"

It's the first time you've heard it put that way. You have thought of it as a break. As Sabrina staying home, not going. All of it temporary. Something that can still be fixed.

"She's missed over three weeks in a row, and with her absences scattered throughout the first weeks of school even before all that, there's no way she'll pass any of her courses. She's welcome to come back, naturally. Though she would have to repeat the eleventh grade. And statistically most dropouts don't."

You stare at the tassel hanging from the rearview mirror. The Coyote. This is his fault. If she hadn't met him none of this would have happened. You can't believe it ever aroused you, the idea of being with him. *Aroused*, a word next to one of the bubbles you didn't fill in, that you now realized is the answer. Aroused suspicion. Aroused by the sound of a knock on the door. An easy one. A gimme. And still you stared at the letters like you had never even learned the alphabet.

"I know that must be upsetting. She's your sister. You care about her. And she must be going through something. But Annabelle, you have to think about yourself right now too. You have to think about what you want." Miss Hamilton pauses. You worry she is going to try to comfort you, take your hand, feel the clamminess of your skin, the worried stutter of your pulse. Could she feel anything else? That second heartbeat within you, hammering from somewhere deep inside.

"If there's enough trouble at home that you think the authorities should get involved, or if you want to talk to a counselor at school, I can help you with that. But I'm also aware that that can set into motion a lot of other processes and reviews that . . . well, while they are well-meaning, might be more disruptive than helpful. Social services. Other legal authorities, depending on what is going on. Do you understand what I'm asking you?"

You want to tell her, so, so bad, but then you hear Sabrina's voice in your head. *Another one of her pity cases.* And you think of the Coyote with the police chief the night of the Cranberry Festival. That tight circle of men. That's who she means by *the authorities.* That's who would come and pore over your lives, your home, your body. That's who would decide where you and Sabrina would go.

"We don't need help," you say.

Miss Hamilton sighs. "Okay, Annabelle. I'm going to run in and get us those hot chocolates, okay?"

You nod. While she's gone you stare out the window, watching cars pass. Your eyes catch on something. A poster on a telephone pole. For a second you think you've imagined it.

PREGNANT?

The text is too small for you to read from that distance, so you slip out of the car and walk toward it.

PREGNANT?

We can help. Get compassionate counseling and learn about your options.

Free care for those in need.

There's an address and a telephone number at the bottom. You could memorize it, wait until you get home to call, but then there's Sabrina, who could be listening on the other end of the line or from another room. Sabrina, whose questions you would have to bear while she won't ever answer any of yours. No, this is your chance to handle this, the flyer appearing in your life like an omen. Maybe something sent from your mother. You've avoided that kind of thinking and yet, it seems too lucky, too fated, to be anything else.

You chant the number as you walk across the parking lot to the payphone in front of the store. You dial the number and a woman answers on the third ring while you keep an eye out for Miss Hamilton and hope that the line to checkout is long with the lunch rush.

"Women's Crisis Center. My name is Brenda, how can I help you today?" Her voice is soft and calm, no hint of the scorn or scolding you might deserve.

"I need . . . I'm . . ."

"Sweetheart, it's okay. I'm here to help you. Now tell me, are you pregnant?" Remarkable, how easy it is for this stranger to simply ask you the thing you needed to be asked, to see your problem more clearly than anyone else. Even more clearly than Sabrina, whose thoughts you can see but who couldn't manage to get the words out.

"Yes."

"Okay. That's all right. We can assist you with a test and anything else you need. I'm glad you found us. When would you like to come in?"

"Soon. Tomorrow?"

"Well tomorrow is Sunday, sweetheart."

"When . . . when else?" You can make out Miss Hamilton's green coat as she steps into the vestibule.

"Monday, would that be okay? Let's see. Perhaps Monday morning?"

"Monday," you say. You'll have to skip school, but you think about Sabrina, and how all the rules you thought governed your world are actually false and hollow. Sabrina, who simply decided not to go at all anymore. What's a single day? Especially when the rest of your life depends on it. You've heard whispers about this, other girls saying their cousins have done it, had a pregnancy undone, taken away. You don't know the mechanics of it, but you don't care. All you want is to be free.

"And now, sweetheart, do you need a ride? Where are you?"

You rattle off your address and Brenda hums. "We have a volunteer who lives out that way, someone who can assist you. She drives a white minivan. Her name is Tammy. She'll pick you up at 9:00, okay?"

"Yes, okay, thank you so much, thank you." Miss Hamilton has spotted you, her brow furrows. You hold up a finger.

"You're so welcome, darling. You have a wonderful day, okay, and we'll see you soon."

Miss Hamilton approaches you bearing the two paper cups.

"Making a phone call?"

"I was calling my dad. To tell him about the test."

"What did he say?"

"He didn't pick up."

"I thought I heard you saying thank you to someone."

"I—It was his secretary." The lie is so blatant and absurd that Miss Hamilton is caught off guard. Something you've cribbed from TV.

"Here," she says finally, holding out the steaming cup. You follow her to the car and a few times you can feel her deciding to say something and then changing her mind. The quiet has a choked air about it. Kate Bush sings about her broken heart. But as you sip your drink, the sugar and milk oversweet, then chalky on your tongue, you feel a thrill of hope. You don't need Miss Hamilton. You don't need Sabrina. Help has come just in time and you found it all on your own. Monday. You hold the word close in your mind, a mantra. Everything will be right again after Monday. And what had sounded so false moments ago now feels true: You'll take the test again. You'll fix your mistakes. You'll get everything right the next time around. Everything will go according to plan.

CALLIE

As Thanksgiving approaches, she finds herself in a low mood, worse this year after Healy's revelation. Mid-November is always hard for her, the descent into the darkest part of the year. Every radio commercial, every supermarket display, every conversation she overhears about family gatherings and dinner plans feels mocking, cruel.

Solve the Baby Doe case and she solves the mystery of who she is. But, she's running out of road on the Riley girls. She feels a heaviness in her body and she thinks it must be because Jenna is really gone this time. Jenna, who could unlock so many answers. Who took the truth with her, wherever she went.

Callie can't say she's not angry. It hits her out of nowhere, little frustrations—a hasty incident report, the heat in her Jeep acting up—tipping her into a teeth-clenching fury. She overhears Keegan joke to Deveraux that Chief must be raging with PMS.

Still, despite this roiling anger she stops by her mother's house once a week, sometimes more. She opens drawers and flicks on the lights. She waters the flowers on the step until the first frost kills them off. And most of all, Callie chastises herself. She's been in this work long enough to know that people can hide whole universes of secrets inside their daily lives. Drug habits, trafficking rings, escort work. She mistook proximity for closeness, but Jenna had been right, the night Callie brought her into the station. When was the last time Callie asked Jenna a question about her life? She thought that she saw all of the woman who raised her. But there were so many questions that she hadn't asked, so many avenues unexplored. And now she will probably never get the chance.

She's angry at herself, too. No way around that.

Fauver had been with Sabrina Riley. Fauver had been her mother's last phone call before she disappeared. He's the one person that links the two of them. She feels nauseated whenever she considers the possibility of Fauver's DNA making up half of who she is. He had claimed he never slept with Sabrina but he's not exactly a man she takes at his word. Maybe there's a reason Jenna kept the secret of her father's identity from her: The truth was too ugly, too hard, to reveal. Callie considers a new side to her mother—protective—and realizes that she was wrong about who her father was, but also wrong about who Jenna was. And if she ever gets the chance, it's the first thing she'll say to her. That she's sorry about everything she didn't, couldn't, see.

Aside from the Baby Doe case her work at the station churns on. Meetings with local administrators, more grant applications, calls to the local lab to rush the testing on the drugs she's confiscated, paperwork paperwork paperwork. The guys seem to have settled into a grudging kind of respect for her, or so she thinks until she pulls into her driveway after the end of a long day to find a tail hanging out of her mailbox. Dark, with a white stripe down it.

Fucking bastards. She pounds her fist against the steering wheel. *A skunk?*

She has half a mind to drive straight to the tavern, toss the animal remains in the middle of the table where she knows she'll find Collins and Latour and Reynolds three drinks deep, red-faced, Miller Lite on their breath.

She can't bear the thought of dealing with it anymore. She stomps out of her car, shaking, and her eyes catch on her neighbor's wood pile. The axe rested against the side.

"I'm borrowing this!" she shouts, not waiting for an answer. Her first swing is wild, misses, so that the weight of the axe pulls on her arm, aches.

She connects on the second attempt, lets out a grunt, furious and satisfied. Two more swings and the mailbox is severed from its post. She's sweating all over, her nostrils sting, her eyes water, but she wishes she had thought of this weeks ago. She picks up the splintered post and carries the whole thing to the end of her driveway, tosses it in her empty trash can.

She can feel it on her body, the smell in her hair, all over her skin. The skunk, the sweat from the effort of taking out the mailbox, the staleness of the station, all of it combines to feel like the smell of failure, of something ruined that can't be saved. In the bathroom she scrubs herself head to toe, working a loofah over her skin until it is raw. She thinks of Jane's shower chair and scrubs harder, eyes watering.

After she showers she makes herself a pot of pasta that she eats standing up, pours a glass of wine. She hasn't really eaten all day and the food and the shower return her to herself. She flips through Annabelle's yearbook again, looking for any kind of notes, the scrim of a teenage girl with a secret to hide, with a grudge, a boy whose eyes she blacked out in pen. Nothing but Lynne Hamilton's inscription in the back.

She scans again, looking for a boy with features like her own, lingers over a senior whose left canine tooth that is pointed like hers, before scoffing at herself, this foolish line of thinking. Mostly she takes after Jenna, or did before Jenna's drinking warped her looks, with the same red hair and upturned nose that makes her look younger than she is. She flips past Jenna's page quickly. It hurts to see her, those round eyes and tidy pearls of white teeth.

In the faculty pages, Lynne Hamilton has a canny smile, a short, sporty haircut, and the set of her narrow shoulders telegraphs an easygoing confidence. She looks like the kind of woman who is all movement, all metabolism, and as soon as the shutter snapped she bolted off to do something else. In addition to being a faculty yearbook adviser, the yearbook mentions she was also an assistant field hockey coach.

She googles Lynne Hamilton. *Lynne Hamilton New Jersey teacher* yields a faculty profile page at a private day school in Princeton. The school has a motto in Latin, a crest featuring some kind of bird of prey. Lynne Hamilton is the head field hockey coach and has won several state awards for her distinguished teaching. The school tuition is $60,000 a year.

There is an email address listed on the page, so Callie takes another swig of wine and writes her a note, asking if she might have some time to talk. After that she buys three security cameras online and springs for express shipping. She can mount one in the corner of the porch, another to one of the trees on the drive, and a third out back. Between the dead animals and Fauver's late-night visit, she wants a little insurance. Anyone who steps foot on her property, she'll know, and from now on, she'll have proof.

Adrian texts her on the last day of his conference out West and they make plans to kayak again. *I swear I do other things*, he says, *but it's just really good to get out there before the weather turns.* She tells him she's looking forward to it, seeing him and being out on the water, and finds she's telling the truth about both. It was good to use her body that way, to do something slow and meditative. She hadn't realized she needed the release. And of course she feels it too, the creep of winter. Frost silvering the ground more mornings than not. Even the woods seem stiller, austere, with the animals starting to go into hiding, hoarding their sustenance away.

She has driven by Luke's nursery three times in the past week, nothing suspicious that she can make out from her car, just a woman loading an armful of potted mini cedars into her back seat and a man tenderly carrying a wooden birdfeeder across the lot. There's a shop in what used to be an old barn and the farmhouse where Luke lives behind it, but she doesn't want him to know she's watching him—not yet. Then, the day before she meets Adrian, she stops by again, but this time she decides to park, gets out of her car, and paces the perimeter of the property. She pauses in front of two greenhouses, padlocks on the doors. She's not there for more than a minute before she hears footsteps behind her.

"Chief Hauser. To what do I owe the pleasure?"

Shit. She knew this was a possibility. That he'd find her here, and she'd be forced to come up with a convincing lie.

"I'm thinking of sprucing up my place."

"Bullshit," Luke says, crossing his arms.

"I'm worried about Damien. And Jane." She realizes she's taking Luke's advice from the night of the dinner. Tell a lie as close to the truth as you can get. "They seem like they're struggling. With money. With everything."

"You talk to my dad about it? I'm not Damien's keeper."

"Between you and me, I think your dad is more invested in reprising his role as good old Chief Caputo, in having a hand in this drug case, than anything going on with his family." It's the truth, but Callie also wants to see what he will do, with a mention of the drugs. Whether it makes him nervous to think of Frank circling.

Luke raises his eyebrows, amused. "Damien doesn't always make good choices. He tries, but he doesn't always think things through. I'm sure he's dealing with some regrets right now."

"Like?"

"Guy's got a wife who needs a lot of medical care, a kid at home, his little pet business isn't going to cut it, it wasn't before all of this either."

"Too bad he isn't as enterprising as his brother." Callie nods at the greenhouses. "Whatcha growing in there?"

Luke narrows his eyes. "Kale. Swiss chard. Though it's about the end of the season for them, would cost me an arm and a leg to keep the heat on through the winter. You can take a look if you'd like."

"Why the padlocks?"

"Someone kept stealing my tools."

"You report that?"

"Wasn't worth the hassle. Didn't want to waste the time of those good men in blue."

Callie scoffs. "You know as well as I do that those good men waste their own time. But you change your mind, you know where to find me."

"I won't give you one more mystery to sleuth out."

Callie feels a rush of anger. She gets what he's implying. Girl detective, playing games. And that she's not good at what she does.

"I've gotta go, but I'll see if Damien wants to help out a little over here. I might have some work for him once we get Christmas trees in."

Callie watches him retreat around the back of the shop building. When she's sure he's gone she steps up on the running board of his truck and looks into the cab. She knows he would be smarter than to keep anything out in the open, but she can't resist. The truck is clean, save for a takeout coffee cup, the rim marked with red lipstick.

This time, she's meeting Adrian at his house on the Mullica River. On her way out the door she kicks over the pile of unread copies of the *Pine Barrens Gazette* that the newspaper carrier now leaves to the left of her doormat since she axed the mailbox. She swears, pushes them back into an unsteady heap. It's been a week since she installed the cameras and so far nothing on them but footage of deer tiptoeing across the driveway.

She's not over this way much, by the river, and she's struck by how open it feels, the horizon all water, the Atlantic in the distance. She pulls up to his house, an 1800s cedar shingle with a big wraparound porch. As she approaches the door she studies the porch furniture, red chairs covered in navy-striped cushions, and tries to decide whether she thinks they were picked out by a woman. Yes, she thinks, and then she tries to guess how old they are. They look pretty new to her.

Adrian opens the door before she has a chance to knock. He stands back so she can come in, kisses her on the cheek, lets a hand linger on her hip. *Stay there*, she thinks. He pulls away with a smile, like he's read her mind.

Inside there are wide plank-wood floors, a fireplace in the living room with a framed map over the mantel.

"It's a survey of this area dating back to 1899."

"You really are a dork for waterways," she says, but leans in closer to take a look. "It's cool." She recognizes Atsion Lake, finds the creek behind the bait shop where Sabrina worked, the little cedar lake where her cabin sits. "What are those dots that are darker than the others?"

"Sinkholes. You ever been out to Blue Hole?"

"A few times. Was smart enough to keep my distance." Looking at the map, it makes sense: The Pines is riddled with sinkholes, Blue Hole the most notorious. Seventy to eighty feet deep. A kid drowns every other year up there, drunk or high or just doing something dumb on a dare.

He flashes her a smile. "Don't worry. We'll stick to the rivers. You need anything before we go? I've got a few beers and packed some sandwiches. Marinated beets, avocado, hummus, Irish cheddar, toasted the bread so it won't get soggy."

"That sounds perfect." She's charmed by the extent of his planning. She never ate around any of the men she used to hook up with back up North. Fellow detectives always meeting up at odd hours, having a quickie. It seems like an essential thing to know about a person, how they eat, what comforts and sates them.

As they make their way to the dock she tells him she likes his porch furniture. Can't help herself. If she's walking into what had recently been another woman's home, another woman's relationship, she needs to know about it, needs to get her disappointment out of the way.

"Oh yeah?"

"Who picked it out for you?"

"Oh come on, you don't think I have good taste?" He hands her a lifejacket. "My sister helped with a few things when I moved in."

"Ah." She unclenches a little.

"You'd like her. She's an ER nurse in Philadelphia. Sort of has the same no bullshit vibes as you. I would have been fine sitting on my ten-year-old camp chairs, but she told me to be a grownup and buy some real stuff once I had a mortgage."

“Well I’m not really one to judge. I live in a one-bedroom cabin meant for seasonal visitors.”

“How’s the insulation? You get cold there during winter?”

“I haven’t been here long enough to know. I guess I’ll find out.” She doesn’t want to admit that she’s been wearing two pairs of socks and a jacket inside and technically it’s not even winter yet.

“I’ve got two fireplaces. Just saying.”

“I’ll keep that in mind.” He turns toward the boats and she finds herself blushing, and bubbling with panic on the inside. She’s not good at this. It feels overwhelming, how direct he is, how he wants to lay claim, and part of her wants to turn and run but she talks herself down. This is what people do, she reminds herself. They make room. They stay.

They paddle out toward the place where the river meets the ocean. They don’t talk much, but the silence is easy, just the two of them and the rhythm of their paddles. He points out where an eagle made its nest last spring, where in the summer, orchids bloom along an unassuming bank. She watches his smooth, assured movements with the paddle, lets her eyes travel upward, thinks about what it would be like to press her mouth to the skin at the back of his neck.

Her arms and back are aching and she’s relieved when Adrian asks her if she’s ready to make a lunch stop. They find a sandy stretch of riverbank, drag the boats onto land. He takes a blanket from his pack, spreads it on the ground, cracks open a beer for her first, then his own. They clink the bottles together and she savors the fizz, her whole body alive with sensation, her muscles humming with the work of paddling, the late fall sun warm on her face. She feels his eyes on her when she takes off the lifejacket, and unlike all the other men who size her up—Fauver, the guys at the station, anyone she pulls over for a traffic stop—he makes it feel good to be looked at, studied.

She gestures to the blanket, to the spread he’s brought. “You certainly come prepared. Thanks for planning all this.”

"This is one of my favorite spots. I like to come out here when I've got something on my mind, usually a work thing that I can't figure out."

"Does it help?"

"A little change of scene usually does. Moving around. Something happens when you're not thinking about the work, banging your head against the wall for an answer. Another part of your brain takes over. And then, not always, but a lot of the time, you find a little break. A way in."

"I should come out here. That case is still making me crazy." She hasn't told him yet about Healy's news about Baby Doe or how she wakes up at night, drenched in sweat, thinking about the possibility of being Billy Fauver's daughter. She will, but for now she just wants to be in this moment, savor the beer, the fall sunlight warm on her face.

"My kayaks are always tied up at the dock. You're welcome to come any time."

"What's the last problem you came out here to think about?"

"Well, right now I'm trying to figure out whether this woman I've been seeing will think it is forward if I invite her to stay the night. She's pretty cool, and I don't want to blow it. But also . . . I would like to . . . well, I'll be a gentleman."

"Don't," she says.

"Don't invite her?" His look is amused, playful.

"Don't be a gentleman." She presses her beer bottle into the sand and straddles him. His hands are calloused from gripping the paddles but it feels good, the friction of his palms along her back, under her shirt. They kiss like that for a long time, until the air becomes cool and the sun shifts above them, arcing back down to the west, and the contrast of their body heat against the cold air is addictive, sustaining.

Back at his dock they've barely tied up the boats before he takes her hand and pulls her toward the house. They peel off their shirts, trip out of their pants, and fall onto the living room couch. Their hands and cheeks are cold from the exposure to the wind. His fingers taste like the river when she takes them into her mouth and his neck smells slightly of salt. She straddles him again and he pulls back, laughs.

"I'm trying to kiss you but you keep smiling."

"I'll stop," she says, smiling again. "Sorry."

"Don't. I'll find something else to do with my mouth."

As he kisses her ribs, and then the tender place just below her navel, her left inner thigh, then her right, she shivers, wonders why this feels so different. She's had good sex but it was never like this. Hot, but also . . . easy. After, when they lie together, the leather couch sticking to their skin, she realizes she doesn't remember the last time she slept with someone in a room filled with daylight.

The next morning she has to leave as the sun comes up even though she wants nothing more than to stay—an early shift, then to Jane's so Damien can lead a canoe trip. Her hair smells like woodsmoke from the fire he built after dinner.

She kisses him goodbye, flush with sex and affection. He takes her by the wrist, puts his lips to the ends of each of her fingers. "Don't go scaring the crap out of any more scientists, okay?"

"I only scare the hot ones."

"That's bad news, we're a good-looking profession. Once you get over the glasses and hunchbacks."

She kisses him again, putting her hands through his hair. "That's true. But believe it or not, I've only got eyes for one of them."

She gets her uniform on at home, brushes her teeth, pockets a granola bar, stops on her way to the station for a second cup of coffee. She's still feeling bleary from the lack of sleep, but catches herself smiling in her rearview mirror like a fool.

At Wawa she gets a sixteen-ounce dark roast and is in line to pay when the cashier tells the girl in front of her that they can't sell her cigarettes.

"Layla, I know your mother. I know you're only fifteen."

Layla. Layla Hart.

"Come on. I'll just get them somewhere else anyway." It's early and she's in cutoff jean shorts despite the cold, a sweatshirt thrown on top that nearly covers them, and a pair of work boots, the rubber treads worn down.

The cashier clears her throat and makes a point to cut her eyes to Callie standing there in her uniform so the girl turns too.

"Fuck it," she says, narrowing her eyes on Callie. "Fine."

When she turns, Callie notices the logo on her sweatshirt. *Eden Grows.* A picture of a tree, an apple, a rake in the foreground.

Callie reaches in with her card. "You know what? I'll take a pack," Callie says. Layla pauses and looks at her, wary.

The cashier just shrugs, blows out a puff of air that ruffles her bangs.

Layla leaves, but walks slowly, and Callie catches up outside the store.

"Hey. I'm glad you're doing better. Last few times I saw you, you were in rough shape."

"So what? You're gonna act like I owe you something now?"

"No," Callie says. She feels clumsy and awkward with the cigarettes in her hand. She holds them out. "But I was hoping I could ask you a few questions about where you get your stuff." She gestures to the sweatshirt. "You work for Luke?"

"He's got nothing to do with it," Layla says. "He hates it when I'm high. Unless it's the stuff he grows."

"Your boss gets high with you?" She's seen it in kids of cops, that same arrogance that Luke has. They think they're untouchable. But Luke, a guy in his mid-fifties, getting stoned with his teenage employees? She hadn't seen that coming.

Layla gives her a look that Callie can only classify as pitying. "There's something you're not telling me," Callie says.

She takes the cigarettes from Callie. "The rest isn't your business.

I'm not in the game anymore but I know better than to talk to you. I've been warned."

"Warned by who?"

Layla bites the inside of her cheek. For a second, her bravado falters. "Let's just say there's some vipers in these woods."

Vipers. Snakes. A dark, undulating creature running down an arm. "Fauver? Is that who you work for?" She does her best to ignore the chill that overtakes her when she says his name.

"I don't sell for anyone anymore, remember?"

Callie reaches into her bag for the folded missing poster with Jenna's face on it, now creased into softness. "Did you ever sell to this woman?"

Layla studies the photograph. "I've seen her before. She bought me a six-pack at the gas station once."

Of course she did, Callie thinks. "But you've never sold to her?"

"Nah. Never sold to her. Look, lady, I've said plenty. I gotta go now. Thanks for the smokes." Layla starts to walk away and Callie can't help herself.

"I hope you'll get help. It's not a way you want to live, what you're doing. I've seen enough to know that using, if you keep up with that stuff . . . it's going to become the only thing you'll ever want. What else do you want, Layla? I'm sure there's something. Probably a lot of things. And you deserve a shot at them."

Layla has gone still, turns slowly to face Callie again. She braces for another one of those furious, withering stares, but that's not what she sees this time. For a second Layla's lower lip betrays her. Trembles like the child she still is.

"Please, take care of yourself, okay? If not for yourself, then at least for your family, your friends. I only spent a little bit of time with Amanda but it's so clear how much she loves you. I'm sure she's not the only one."

The look fades and Layla sets her jaw, hardens before Callie's eyes. "My life and the people in it are absolutely none of your business."

She stomps away and climbs into the passenger seat of a black Honda Accord, which reverses out of their spot and peels out of the lot like they're being pursued. Callie catches one last glimpse of Layla from the passenger-side window, as she traces her mouth in lipstick, smacks them together to admire the color in the rearview. The color so bright as to be a warning, like the red of a poisoned apple in a fairy tale.

ANNABELLE

Sabrina is still asleep when the volunteer—Tammy—guides the white minivan into your driveway. You realize you are shaking as you stare through the window next to the door. In your bag, all of the money you've saved from this summer, which was meant for so many other things. College application fees. Books. But you'll deal with all that later. You'll make more money somehow. You have heard about other girls who had to pay for the whole thing themselves, girls who have had to ask the boy to contribute and come away with nothing. You are glad for all of those long, empty hours at the ice cream stand, though now you'll have to find another job to pay for the SAT registration, for more study books because you don't want to mess it up twice. But you'll figure all that out once you sort this out. Once you are on the other side of whatever is going to happen today, this thing you have only heard the faintest whispers about.

You wonder if you'll bleed a lot. You wonder if it will hurt. If they will have to cut you open. You run a finger over your scar. It wouldn't be the first time, at least. That you have a part of yourself split apart and sewn back together again. It won't be like Sabrina's ministrations, the way she sucked in the breath between her teeth every time she pierced your skin with the needle, as though she felt it too. But maybe it's better that way.

Tammy waves at you through the windshield, rolls her window down, calls to you. "Come on in, honey."

You open the door. The car smells like cinnamon and underneath that, a sour smell, like old milk. A wooden cross dangles from the rearview mirror, swings as she backs out of your driveway. A lanyard strung with plastic beads hangs with it. Tammy sees you eyeing it.

"My daughter made that one." She touches the beads and smiles to herself. "What's your name, sweetheart?"

"Anna," you say, your throat too clogged with worry to get the rest of it out.

"Anna, nice to meet you. Sorry the car is such a mess; hard to keep up with the little ones, you know."

She gestures behind her and it is only then that you register the two car seats, the plastic rattles and dinosaur figurines on the floor, the fine orange crumbs that maybe were Cheez-Its or Goldfish crackers before getting pulverized in tiny fists, under tiny feet.

Tammy is nothing like you thought she'd be. You realized you expected someone younger, hipper, more like Miss Hamilton. Even now speeding along with Tammy in her minivan you feel the urge to call Miss Hamilton, to tell her the truth. To be with her instead.

"You're quiet. It's okay. Most of the girls are when I pick them up. But you'll feel so much better once you meet with Brenda and Fran down at the center. Believe me, swear to Jesus I've seen it so many times myself. Girls just like you, desperate and without anybody in the world to talk to, to help them, and don't they just walk out of there whistling—whistling!—like new women, seeing the world in brighter colors."

You smile, surprised at the cheer with which she's talking about it, this thing. Talking more openly than anyone you've ever heard, really. This mother with crushed crackers and a sticky film of spilled juice covering her car. "That will be good. I haven't told . . . I haven't talked to anyone. No one knows."

Even describing how the secret is a secret makes you feel unburdened, without having to even use the words you've been afraid of, the ones you've been avoiding, kept in a dark box in your mind for all these months.

After twenty-five minutes in the car Tammy pulls up to a ranch house painted a faded blue gray. There's two other cars parked in the yard, a maroon Oldsmobile and a station wagon with wood paneling along the sides.

"Here we are!"

By the door there is a name, Preston, and underneath the name a paper label edged with masking tape: *Women-First Pregnancy Crisis Center*. It is written in faded marker, black turned navy blue.

Tammy lets herself in. "Fran? Brenda? I'm here with Miss Anna."

They step into a living room with crocheted blankets thrown over the back of the sofa in lumpy piles, hooked rugs on the floor, another cross on the wall—this one white, with a mournful Jesus draped across it. Little bowls of potpourri on the end tables. How can they do everything here, you wonder. You had expected a doctor's office like the one your mother took you to when you needed shots as a child. White walls and fluorescent lights, padded tables covered with paper that crackled when you moved. A thought rises up that you try to quiet. *They can't help you here.* You concentrate on the potpourri, the sickle of a dried orange nestled among the flower buds and cinnamon sticks until you feel someone else enter the room.

"Hello there, I'm Fran. Please, make yourself comfortable. Brenda will be right out too."

Fran is older than Tammy, with woolly hair cropped close to her head and deep wrinkles around her mouth. She wears a crewneck sweatshirt with a turtleneck underneath, and still rubs her hands together and complains of the cold. "Brenda is my daughter," she confides.

"Is she a doctor?" you ask.

Fran looks at Tammy for a moment, something passing between them, before looking back at you. "Brenda, please come meet Anna."

You expect Brenda to greet you in the bright scrubs you remember from those visits all those years ago, the rubber gloves that the doctor snapped on her wrists, but instead she's just another woman like Tammy and Fran, wearing sweatpants and a T-shirt that says *HARRAHS CASINO RESORT* across the front.

"Anna, can I get you anything? Tea? Water?" You smell something new, now that you've gotten used to the potpourri, and then a glance to the kitchen floors helps you make sense of it. A litter box, one that has not been cleaned in a while.

"No thank you."

"We're here to take care of you, Anna. Maybe you'll change your mind about a drink. Whatever it is you need, you just let us know, okay? This is a precarious and special time for you. We're here to look after you."

Even though you sense something is essentially off about the situation, you feel relieved, the way you did on the phone. You try to relax, to let their reassurances wash over you. They are here to take care of you. When was the last time someone offered to get you a drink? Not since your mother.

"Tell us a little about what brought you here," Tammy says, tilting her head.

When you speak, the words come out so quietly that they are nothing more than a whisper. "I just want it to be over. I just want to go back to how it was. I want—I want my life back."

The women exchange looks again. Let your words hang in the air for a long time, long enough that you start to wonder if you are allowed to want those things. But if they don't agree with you, why would they say they can help you in the first place?

Fran puts a hand on your knee. "Anna, there are things in life that we can't take back. I know it doesn't seem right. But we can't go back in time. We can't turn our backs on blessings we are given. Even if those blessings come to us in ways we aren't expecting. And it would be a shame to waste those blessings. To think of them as burdens."

Brenda takes up next, not long after Fran, as though she is impatient to speak her part. "It is part of being a woman, Anna. We have certain responsibilities, but if you can come to think of them as special, as a privilege, then you will be on your way to living an enlightened and happy life."

Tammy leans in. "My children, Anna, are the best thing that ever happened to me. And my goodness, seeing their faces for the first time? These gifts from God, that kind of pure love? It might seem scary now, but I promise you, you will fall in love with this child."

Child, that word like an anvil being struck inside of you.

"Is the father in the picture?" Brenda asks.

You stumble over the word *father*. First you wonder if they are asking about your father. It is only after you shake your head that you realize they mean the Coyote. The Coyote who knows nothing of any of this. Who is still meeting your sister, who comes home with bruises on her wrists, hickeys splotching her neck.

"Raising a child is the best thing a woman can do with her life, Anna."

You would do anything, anything, to not hear anyone use the word *child* again. A child is what you just were. You just put your dolls in their boxes a few years ago. Maybe they need convincing. This is a test to make sure you are going to be okay with the decision. With going back to some secret room filled with all the right instruments and tools and medicine, or whatever it is they need, to undo what has been done to you. You need to make them see that you are serious, that you know your mind, that the decision is right.

"I can pay," you say, taking the money out from your purse.

They pause. The mention of money works for a moment, makes them quiet. Makes them stop using those words like blessing and baby. Like this is all something you can do, something you can allow to happen.

You fan the cash out so they can see how much it is. Everything. Everything you have. The women are still silent, and you think they must be deciding something. Whether or not you are worthy. The cat meows from deep inside the house, a needy warble.

Fran reaches for the money and before you can say anything else, folds the bills and sinks them into her sweatpants pockets. "We'll take this and hold on to it. Because you need more time to think about this decision. I think you may end up seeing what we mean. And in that case, I would hate for you to squander this money. You will need things, after all, and we can help with that. Diapers and bottles, clothes and blankets. All of these things require support."

She disappears into the next room and you object. "I would like that back. I still want to get the thing done."

Fran clears her throat, her tone different. Not as honeyed as before. "Anna, when was your last period?"

You close your eyes. "June." You are still trying to go back to that last moment, wonder what you could have said to convince them that you were worth the kind of help you wanted.

"Even if we were to help you in that way, which to be clear, is a sin, it is far too late for that. There are some people who think nothing of snuffing out an unborn life at any point, for any reason, but we are not those women." Next to Fran, Tammy nods in agreement, closes her eyes as if the thoughts cause her pain. "We are saving you, Anna. It might not feel like it right now. But we are saving something more important than your plans for the next few years—going to the mall with your friends, weekends at the Shore, all these things that don't actually matter. What we are saving is your very soul."

"Hell is a brutal place, you know. And you've committed one sin already, Anna, by joining with a man who was not your husband. Don't make the mistake of committing a second, more grievous sin by murdering the fruit of that union."

"And murder, Anna, isn't just a sin. It is illegal in the eyes of God and in the law," Tammy says. "It is the cruelest, most base thing you can do to another human. Do you want to be a murderer? Is that what you think will solve everything?"

That word, *murder*, sets off an alarm bell inside of you. All of the sudden the potpourri is overpowering, a choking sweetness and spice that irritates the back of your throat. The cat that you haven't gotten a glimpse of is making your eyes water. These women are still staring intently at you, strangers speaking of your soul. You want to argue with them. It isn't fair. *I can't do this.* You feel this thing thumping and kicking inside of you, thrusting up toward your lungs, crowding out the air. *My father will kill me. My sister . . .* Sweat forms under your arms, along your back, in all the places where your flesh touches other flesh.

"No one will help me," you say. Your words just little mouse squeaks. It is not a question, but the women take it as one. Tammy leans over and grasps your hand in hers.

"Of course that's not true. We're here to help you. You found us. You've already taken the first step." You pull your hand away.

"I want to go home." There are tears leaking from your eyes even though you have tried so hard to keep them away. Of all the people you could cry in front of, you do not want to cry in front of these women, and realizing that, you realize that you knew—knew the second that Tammy pulled up in the driveway, or maybe before, when the hope was too sweet and pure to be true, that no one can help you anymore.

On the drive home Tammy makes a comment here and there about songs that come on the radio, about shows she watches when her kids go to bed. You don't say anything, just feel the emptiness of your bag in your lap without the weight of your savings inside and watch the swing of the cross from the rearview, listen to it clack against the plastic beads of the lanyard.

CALLIE

She's playing with Opal in her bedroom, an invented game that involves a princess and a troll and the crossing of a river, lines of dialogue that get assigned to Callie then revised, rules that seem to change by the second.

"What kind of money should I use to pay the toll?" Callie asks. Opal frowns, then lights up.

"Oh, I have something! It looks just like real money. Green and everything." She rushes to the corner of her room, where there's a low shelf, shifts some books and plastic stacking cups around. Callie remembers when it was neatly arranged with toys, before Jane's accident, and now it is crowded with pine cones, sticks, stray puzzle pieces. She makes a note to tidy it up next time she's here.

Opal is beaming when she turns around. "Here's your money to pay the toll!"

There's a green glassine bag in her tiny palm.

Callie tries to swallow her shock, blinks a few times, wondering if her brain is short-circuiting. Too little sleep, distracted, worlds merging. But no.

"Opal, where did you get this?"

Opal shrugs, the pride on her face a moment ago already gone.

"I need you to think really hard, Opal, and tell me where that's from."

"Am I in trouble?"

"No, no, nothing like that. But I need to know. Please tell me?"

"Daddy."

"Daddy gave this to you?"

"It was in his truck."

The thud of her heart reverberates against her ribs. "And you picked it up when he wasn't looking? Was it empty when you found it?"

"Empty. I thought . . . I thought it would be good for money. To play." Her voice cracks on the word *play*, her lip wobbles, and then her face crumbles. Tears streak down her cheeks.

"Oh, Opal, I'm so sorry. Come here." She pats Opal's back as she sniffles into her shirt. "You didn't do anything wrong, okay? I'm so sorry if I scared you. You know I'm not mad, right?"

Opal nods, her face still pressed to Callie's chest.

"Everything okay?" Jane calls from down the hall.

"We good?" she whispers to Opal.

Opal musters a little smile, nods again.

"Yeah, all good in here! I think my bridge troll was a little too convincing."

"Ha."

Callie slips the baggie into the pocket of her jeans.

Does Jane know? Is this what Frank meant, when he asked if Damien seemed okay? When Luke said that Damien was dealing with some regrets? Is he on drugs? Is that what he's really doing when she's here babysitting? Getting high out in the woods alone? It would explain a lot. His moodiness. The day Callie showed up and he had been out on his mysterious errand, left Jane and Opal alone.

A buzz from her pocket. Jane. Bridge Troll, you also have to tell me about your man. You've been way too tight-lipped.

Later? Story is rated NC-17.

Oh hell YES. Get some, Callie Hauser.

You getting any, Jefferies? She's started calling Jane Jefferies, like Jimmy Stewart's character in *Rear Window*. Jane's still TikTok and Reddit obsessed, always scrolling through old cases, calling out facts to Callie and asking for her thoughts.

She knows her question isn't subtle, but maybe it's the way in to talking about whatever is going on with Damien. Her mind reels.

Maybe this is what Luke was hinting around, when he asked Damien the last thing he lied about. Maybe he had a habit and is trying to get clean, was at a meeting that time Callie came over and Jane and Opal were here alone.

ha HA ha, Jane writes back.

Opal tugs at the hem of her shirt. "Can I watch Peppa Pig on your phone, Aunt Cal?"

"Uh, sure. A little bit." Opal's squeal of glee when Callie hands over her phone quells the queasy guilt she still feels at making her cry.

She steps out of Opal's room once Opal is completely absorbed, her mouth slightly open, the colors of the video flashing against the pale skin of her face. Jane is on the couch reading. She looks so peaceful, more like herself, than she has in weeks. She's been walking, with Damien and Callie's help, up and down the driveway. The fresh air seems to do her good. The circles under her eyes don't look as dark. Her smiles don't have that sardonic crook at the corners quite as often.

"Opal let you free? How'd you pull that off?"

"Had to sacrifice my phone. Peppa Pig."

"Ah. Praise be to Peppa. So wait, tell me about the guy. All the dirty details. Like I said. Not getting any over here. The doctors say it's fine but . . . I don't know. Hard to feel sexy when your husband has had to walk you to the toilet every time you need to take a shit."

"You'll get back to normal."

"Normal wasn't all that often, either."

Her hand moves to the outside of her pocket. She can feel the outline of the green bag through the fabric. "Look, I realize that I really wasn't around a lot before. So there might be stuff I don't know. I was checked out. Too absorbed by my job. I should have been paying closer attention. Should have been a better friend to you. But I get the feeling you meant what you said in that voicemail—"

Jane opens her mouth to interrupt, stops when Callie holds up a finger. "I get the feeling you meant what you said, even if you really don't remember calling me."

Jane sighs, picks her fingernails, looks like she is deliberating.

"Sometimes I think that the whole world runs smoothly because women don't ever say what they really think. The world would implode if we all threw up our hands, called bullshit at once."

What truth is so dangerous for her to tell? She thinks of Jenna, how Callie had no idea about the Baby Doe case, that Jenna had kept that secret wrapped up as though it were something dangerous, sharp. Though Callie understands now. She has also been keeping her own secrets from Jane, hasn't yet told her—or anyone else—about her relation to Baby Doe. Hasn't wanted to say it out loud, as though that might make it go away. Instead, she feels it festering, pictures this secret filling her body, a black rot between her ribs, closing in on her lungs, her heart.

Callie clears her throat. "So, tell me."

Jane takes a long breath, and Callie can feel her clenching, angry and exhausted and trying to decide which feeling should win out.

A crash from down the hall and Opal lets out a high, outraged howl.

"I'm on it," Callie says. Jane gives her a weak smile. So much for that, she thinks, as she rounds the corner and finds Opal holding out the phone, her face pink with fury at an ad that's interrupted her show.

Lynne Hamilton doesn't respond to Callie's messages—the original email, another to check in, and a voicemail—so on her next day off, a Tuesday, Callie gets in the car in the afternoon and drives north and west, out of the Pines. The roads twist and turn and spit her out in a stretch of farmland, bales of hay stacked near the road, cows at pasture. Then with a few miles to go the spaciousness constricts: low stone walls that look hundreds of years old. Ivy-strewn Tudor houses, estates hidden behind meticulously sculpted topiaries. And then, the school itself, Gothic architecture mimicking an Ivy League campus, she guesses, as if to say this is not so far off from that.

Callie parks in the back of a student lot, her Jeep looking dull and clunky among the sleek BMWs and Volvos. It's 2:30, school should let out soon, and Callie is hoping to catch Lynne Hamilton before she heads out to the hockey fields.

A bell chimes from somewhere deep in the school, low and resonant—not the shrill scream of her high school bells, more like a grandfather clock. The heavy oak door bursts open and a group of boys in navy crewneck sweaters and rumpled khakis bursts out. They don't even look twice at Callie leaning against the stair rail. A thirty-something woman who isn't a teacher? She's meaningless to them. Better for her, but depressing nonetheless.

A directory in the foyer tells her the history department is on the second floor. She sticks tight to the railing, moving against the tide of students draining out of the halls. Mahogany paneling along the walls, gilt-framed portraits. She peers into doorways of classrooms, sees a man in corduroys wiping equations from a chalkboard. A woman in pinched-looking boots arranging a pile of papers at her desk. On the second floor the air still compared to the rush of the first floor, just a pair of girls giggling together in the halls, their shoulders touching. One dark haired, one light haired. She thinks of Annabelle and Sabrina. Wonders if they ever moved together through the halls that way, allies, speaking in code.

Finally she sees Lynne Hamilton, her head bent over an essay, a boy in front of her biting his lip. She still has the same haircut she had in the '90s, a short shag, though the blond has faded a little. "Here, this is where you summarize the argument from Hallfield's paper, but you still need to cite it. Does that make sense?" She must sense Callie shadowing the door, looks up, and straight in her eyes, but then turns back to the boy just as quickly. "I'd like to give you a chance to address this. Could you have it rewritten by Monday?"

He murmurs an assent, and thanks her. Lynne Hamilton does not immediately turn back to Callie once the boy leaves, but instead opens a desk drawer, deposits her red pen. She must know Callie is not a parent of a student, in her flannel and jeans.

"Can I help you?"

"Lynne Hamilton, yes?"

"That's me."

"I'm Callie Hauser, Chief of Police, Pine Lakes. I've tried to get in touch with you a few times."

Callie waits to see Lynne Hamilton's reaction. Sometimes with interview subjects that are hard to track down or avoidant, she gets a flicker of guilt. Worry. Some kind of concession. Something that tips her mind to the way the conversation will go, what kind of power she might have over them. But in Lynne Hamilton the flicker is too quick. Callie can't catch it.

"I didn't respond to your messages because I don't have anything to tell you. I left that district nineteen years ago. I don't know what I could possibly help you with when it comes to a case in the Pine Barrens."

Callie clears her throat. "I would think you cared about justice. And about your students. Even the ones who weren't paying tuition at a fancy private school."

The effect is exactly what she intended: Hamilton starts at Callie's bluntness, then casts an eye to the hallway, where another faculty member—a gray-haired man in a polka-dotted bow tie—passes by, lifting a hand.

When she responds her voice is as soft as Callie's was forceful. "Please, let's go to my office."

Callie can't help but marvel as she follows Lynne Hamilton across the hall. Her office is filled with books and field hockey trophies, with two casement windows that look out onto the rolling green of the school grounds. A far cry from the high school she taught at in the Pines, whose records Callie has been trying to access for background on the Rileys, only to be told the shed that held them was flooded ten years ago, everything too moldy to hang on to.

"I have ten minutes before I have to be out on the field for practice."

"Do you remember a student named Annabelle Riley?" Callie asks, and as she says Annabelle's name she catches it again: another flicker of something in Lynne Hamilton—not so much in her eyes, but a change in her bearing. She's hit something. The Riley girls are a sore spot. The question is, why?

She clears her throat and whatever indecision or worry she had just witnessed in the woman is already gone. "Annabelle was in my Advanced Placement History class. I also oversaw her work on the yearbook committee as the committee's faculty adviser."

"Do you know what happened to her? It appears she left the area around 1991. Dropped out of school, along with her sister, Sabrina."

"Annabelle left school that winter and never came back."

"So did Sabrina."

"Sabrina, I believe, dropped out earlier. In the fall. Those girls did not have much in the way of parental supervision, as you've possibly gathered. Their mother was MIA and their father was always doing gig work, or at a bar. And my god, that house. It was probably unsafe for them to be living there."

"The faculty knew this? The school was aware that they were on their own?"

Lynne Hamilton sighs. "You have to understand. The school took care of those girls as much as we could. Free breakfast and lunch. They were bused to and from the building. And they seemed to be doing okay. It seemed like the order and routine and support was good for them. Rather than risking a call to social services, having them separated, displaced. It would have been difficult to place two teenage girls in one foster home. They didn't need a lot, but they did need one another. Their relationship was very . . . symbiotic. It took a lot to convince Annabelle to apply to colleges, even though she worked so hard, had great grades. It felt safer, better for them, to be there. To do what it took to keep them together. At the time."

"And now?"

She sighs. "Well, they both left, didn't they?"

"You must have been surprised that Annabelle would drop out, if she were so involved with her academics. If she was as determined to go to college as you thought."

"She only would have left school if she had to."

"Why do you think she had to?"

Lynne Hamilton takes a breath. It is a moment Callie recognizes from other interviews. A subject shoring something up. Deciding something. The cost of telling a difficult truth.

"I think once Sabrina left, Annabelle couldn't get through the days without her. Her schoolwork suffered. She was more distractable. Still a good student, still perfectly behaved. But she was off, you know? I think she just couldn't stand the separation from Sabrina."

Callie has to hand it to her. She didn't think she had it in her. But Callie knows that Lynne Hamilton is lying. The story has the well-worn feeling of a justification you run over again and again at night when you can't sleep. It means that something happened and Lynne Hamilton has long expected to have to answer for it. But what?

"So, where do you think they went? Did they ever talk about going anywhere together?"

"God, who knows? Annabelle had really wanted to apply to NYU. We were working together so she might apply to colleges and scholarships the following fall. They could have gone to New York. They could have gone to the shore. They might have gone twenty miles or two hundred. People underestimate teenagers. They are capable of a lot, and they let their emotions rule them. Everything that happens to them feels huge, feels black and white. There is an honesty in that, but it also drives them to dramatic decisions. Maybe Sabrina convinced Annabelle to leave. Who knows where they ended up."

"Do you think Annabelle would have listened?"

"Annabelle was smart, but she wasn't fully confident in her abilities all of the time. I can see a version of events in which Sabrina persuades Annabelle to leave. And Annabelle listens, because what she needs more than NYU or good SAT scores or great grades is her sister. At least in her mind. I was less convinced that the relationship was healthy for Annabelle. But it was what it was." For a second Lynne Hamilton looks contrite, and Callie wonders if she is going to cry before she cuts her eyes to her phone. "Look, I'm late for practice. The girls will be out there starting warm-ups. It's the last week of our season. Playoffs. Every second counts."

"Sure, just one more thing before you go."

"What's that?" Callie can feel the woman biting back annoyance.

"Well, I find it a little odd that you have yet to ask me what I am investigating."

"What do you mean?"

"Dropping out of school after the age of sixteen isn't a crime. Both girls were seventeen that fall. Why do you think I'm here?"

By now Callie knows that Lynne Hamilton isn't going to bring up the baby. That she's shielding something, or someone. But it can be worth it to press someone who you know is going to lie. To see what they come up with. To see what they give away when they're trying to hide something else.

Lynne Hamilton sighs. "Sabrina was involved with an older man. Or at least that's what the rumors were at school. That he was a cop. I figured this was some sort of internal investigation."

Callie is both shocked and not. It doesn't feel like a lie. It could make sense of everything. The sloppy investigation. Why Sabrina would feel like she had nowhere else to go, no other choices. But she hates how everywhere she turns she feels flatfooted. How Trent, now Lynne, have caught her off guard.

"And . . . another question. I know, your practice, your girls are out there. But did you hear about the child they found? The baby? That winter, 1991. The same one the girls disappeared."

"That was a very sad thing," Miss Hamilton says, rising from her chair, sliding a backpack on her shoulders. "But I don't know anything about that. Now excuse me, I need to be running drills right now."

"Did you know Jenna Barry?" The question slips out and Callie hears the desperation in her voice. She can't stop looking at the yearbook photo of Jenna. The girl she was before she became the joke down at the station, the woman with the crazed hair and glassy, dead-to-the-world eyes.

"I did."

"She's my mother. She's the one who found the child."

For the first time this afternoon Hamilton doesn't have a polished answer at the ready. She studies Callie's face, and Callie guesses she can see the resemblance now that she knows to look. "I'm very sorry. She was a sweet girl."

Callie nods. She's never heard that descriptor for Jenna. Hundreds of other words come up for Jenna before she'd think to call her sweet. Troubled. Lonely. Messy. Lost. But Jenna had been a girl once, just like Annabelle and Sabrina. A girl brimming with her own desires and hopes. Who had been something else other than the names everyone slung at her, all the labels everyone stuck to her back.

ANNABELLE

You walk to the supermarket, the day mild enough that the snow from earlier in the week drips from the trees, and underneath everything you hear water rushing groundward. You can smell the sunlight and mineral melt of ice, like a superpower, but the sounds of liquid everywhere call attention to your bladder, the way you have to piss every thirty minutes. The urge undeniable and the store still twenty minutes away.

Your feet punch through the wet snow as you make your way through the underbrush, squat against a tree. The relief turns to panic when you see a flash of color at the edge of the road, a red coat and orange hat, bright, the kind favored by hunters.

"What are you doing?"

Jenna. Your neighbor, who used to circle the perimeter of the factory when you and Sabrina were girls, asking if the two of you would play. Sometimes you would let her, but the triangle always felt lopsided. It was such a burden to have to explain the long-established rules of your games, your code words and shorthand. At the bus stop for school she was always nudging, peering, desperate to be let in.

She cuts a look to your middle, the coat your father left behind that you've taken to wearing because it zips over your sweater. Because it helps you feel hidden, even as you recoil at the smell of him on it. Skoal and spilled liquor.

You haven't seen Jenna in a few weeks and it is like seeing her anew. You notice the way the cold puts patches of pink on her cheeks, the bright whites of her eyes, that she has become pretty, even, under her cap.

"Nothing. What are you doing?"

She turns to show you a sack on her shoulder, the canvas strap. "Delivering papers. This road is on my route."

It should bind you together, both of you out there in your fathers' clothes, but it only fills you with repulsion. You have been so busy in the storm of your mind that you forgot that other people want and need, and something about seeing Jenna in that hat hurts. Makes you feel it more keenly. How much both of you lack.

"You know, I've been wanting to ask you about something . . ." You remember now about Jenna's dead mother, and instead of pity you feel rage. How much easier it would be, to have a mother who left you involuntarily. To have a diagnosis and a reason. To have a father who chopped wood for the woodstove in the kitchen, where you could at least warm your hands.

"I've got to go," you say, brushing past her.

"Annabelle!" she shouts. "It's about him!" she says, her voice coming apart in a desperate split that makes you stand still. When she speaks again her voice is somber. "I know what happened. I guess I want . . . I want to make sure you're okay."

"You don't know anything," you say, surprised by the low growl of your voice. An animal with its haunches up. "You have no idea."

It comes back to you as you walk away, that it was Jenna who first told you the story of Mother Leeds and the Jersey Devil. How you and Sabrina swore you didn't believe her, but the next time you found yourself alone in the trees and heard a noise—a pine cone skittering to the ground, a squirrel scrabbling through the branches—you screamed and ran for the safety of the factory, pressed yourself against one of the stone walls, your breath heaving in and out of your chest.

You stomp the rest of the way to the store, indignant, jealous of Jenna's future, unblemished like the clear, snowmelt-scoured road ahead of her as she finishes her paper route and returns home. You grab a basket at the front of the shop and it bangs empty against your knee as you walk the aisles, find the runtiest, cheapest bunch of bananas you can, a box of cereal, the smallest container of milk. You stand in front of the meat refrigerator and eye bloody cubes of beef like the kind your mother would add to stew, simmering it to tenderness, with bay leaf and barley, sweetened with carrots and onion. You step away, your veins practically humming with desire, to feel the warm stuff of that stew, to feel the ways it would fortify you, fill you.

You head to the checkout, the shelves next to you bright with shampoos and conditioners. Before you can reach the end, where the registers are, you are accosted by a wall of baby formula to your right, a blue-eyed child with a feathery tuft of brown hair staring out at you from a canister promising *Only the Best.* The prices underneath the formula canisters are staggering, so much more than the milk you have in your basket. You let your eyes drift to the packages of diapers, add the cost of one box to one canister of formula and find that its more than you budget for a week's worth of food. A display of teething rings and pacifiers catches your eye, all of that pastel plastic. Before you can think about it, you grab one and shove it underneath your coat.

"Annabelle?"

You startle, drop the pacifier on the ground, look up to see Della, a friend of your mother's from when you were a girl. Della and her husband, Keith, would come over for bonfires in the yard, your father building the flames higher and higher, roasting marshmallows to a golden brown for you and Sabrina, two at a time so that neither of you had to wait. Your mother cooked and you all ate outside under the stars, paper plates in your laps. Della and her husband could both play the fiddle, but she was better. You could see it even then in the way she let herself get lost in the music, the way her eyes closed like she was savoring it, while Keith often looked around to see who was admiring him play.

Della looks to the pacifier, then to your face. Behind her, there's a little girl in the cart, maybe two or three years old. Your mother told you once that Della and her husband were having trouble conceiving a child, and she would drop pouches of crushed herbs on their porch that were meant to help. *Looks like she didn't need you*, you think, with a treasonous thrill.

"How . . . how are you?"

"Fine," you say, the response so automatic by now it is like a punchline. You think of Della and your mother, their mouths wine-stained, leaning together, laughing, reaching out for one another's wrists. You and Sabrina desperate to be let in on the jokes, while the men rolled their eyes and flicked beer tabs into the fire.

"That's good. I haven't seen your dad around in a while."

"He's busy. Work."

She narrows her eyes at you. "Right." Silence between you. Even the child is quiet. She sighs. "I'm sorry. I'm sorry we stopped coming around."

There had been a fight, before your mother left. Your father had started drinking more, losing himself, shouting, all impulse and ego. He broke the bow of Della's husband's fiddle in an argument, tossed it into the flames on the bonfire like it was kindling.

"Well, she's not here."

Della sighs. "I wanted her to leave him. But I thought she'd take you."

"Do . . . do you know where she is?" you ask, your throat gone to sandpaper.

Della shakes her head. "I don't know. I'm so sorry, Annabelle. I miss her though, and I know you must miss her too. I still think of her every spring, when the heather blooms."

The little girl starts to fuss. She doesn't like this talk, you think, of mothers disappearing.

"And Sabrina? I heard some rumors. She shouldn't be hanging around with—"

"Sabrina is fine."

"It's just that, I've started working at the police station. They had to bring her in the other night. Something about a fight."

This is news to you. "She was arrested?"

"I don't know the whole story, but there was property damage, a broken window. Down at the bait shop. There had been an argument.

It was late. I wasn't there. I only answer phones during the day. But I'm worried about her. About both of you."

A shriek from the little girl in the cart. Della turns to her, pats her head.

"This is Wren. She's three."

You nod. You can't look at her anymore without thinking of Della and your mother, both of them with their big laughs and quick-moving hands, and who, from across the yard, were nearly indistinguishable with their heads bent together whispering secrets, plotting, the ends of their hair touching and making a curtain in front of their faces.

Della bends to pick up the pacifier on the ground, holds it out to you. Her eyes glitter with questions.

"Why would you take this, Annabelle? You had it under your coat."

You shrug.

Ask me again, you think, the same way you did with Miss Hamilton. *Ask me again who this is for and I'll split like a ripe fruit, like the pods of seeds my mother dried for you to prime your womb for a child, like the firewood underneath my father's axe, like the thin skin of a roasted marshmallow before you pressed it between two graham crackers.*

Della opens her mouth and you can almost taste the relief of telling her. This woman who may be the closest thing to a mother you've got left. Squint and it's her. Close your eyes and remember the feeling of her fingers along your scalp while she braided your hair and your mother worked on Sabrina's. But then the child screams again, ear-splittingly shrill, and Della remembers that she already has a daughter, a daughter who is calling her back, territorial in her fury, her small face red and clenched in outrage.

"Don't be like her, Annabelle. Don't go getting into trouble like Sabrina. Finish school and get away. Start your life."

That's the story everyone wants for you. Your mother, Miss Hamilton, Della. The good sister, the one who did everything right. You shove the pacifier back on the display rack.

"Good girl. Call me if you need anything, Annabelle." She opens her purse, unfolds her wallet, hands you two twenty-dollar bills. "Promise me you'll only use this for you. To get away. You have to think of yourself. You have to take care of you first."

You nod, taking the cash. The little girl scowls at you from the cart as they walk away.

CALLIE

That Saturday she's working late at the station—reviewing resumes of new job candidates, more admin, another grant application, this time for a K-9 unit and handler. Under everything she does the questions still hum: Who was Baby Doe's mother? Who is the father they share? When, how, will she ever learn what happened to Jenna? She forces herself to concentrate, even as she feels this sticky mess of secrets sucking her backward. The last thing she needs is anyone on the squad to think she's slipping: after all, they've still got all these overdoses on their hands. Another just last week, a father of two. Callie found a picture of his family online, posted along with his obituary. She can't get the round cheeks of his smiling sons out of her mind.

As she's wrapping up Jane texts to ask if they can go for a drive somewhere in the morning. Damien, Callie thinks. Maybe she's finally ready to talk about the drugs. Maybe Jane will give her what she needs to go after Luke.

You got it. Where to?

Anywhere. I just need to get out of this house. And I need to be ALONE.

Uh, I can drop you off somewhere and come back for you? Or we can go to a park and sit on different benches?

You know what I mean. You don't count. I love my family but today I hate my family.

Sure. What time?

We ride at dawn.

8?

Fine. But know that with a small child at home I'll have lived half a day by then and may already be cranky.

You're cranky now . . .

Too much TikTok. Btw, is this your girl?

Callie doesn't know what she's expecting, but not Rebecca Nixon. Callie had told Jane about her before the DNA results came back, about Nixon's obvious disdain for the cops she's helping, about her self-congratulatory air that she tries to pass off as empathy. And there she is when Callie clicks on the link, all false lashes and contoured cheekbones. She's wearing a suit not unlike the one she has on for her website photos, but this one is purple and her top is cut a little lower. She brushes a barrel curl over her shoulder and tilts her head. *I wanted to share what is so important to me about solving cold cases.*

"Oh what the fuck?" Callie says. There are only three other videos on Rebecca's profile and she's far from the number of views that Jane's usual roster of crime girlies can rack up. The second video on her profile is centered on a cold case, the kidnapping and murder of six-year-old Laura Munch.

Authorities were stymied for two decades. When Laura's older sister, Amanda, came to me, I knew there was a way to help them. I knew there was more that could be done. Watch my next video to see how I cracked the decades-old case.

That's her, she texts Jane. She can't bring herself to say anything else.

Def gunning for a podcast. Or maybe she wants to go primetime? There's a guy like her who just landed a network deal.

I can't even talk about it. I'll see you tomorrow AM. She closes her eyes, pictures Rebecca spinning Callie's story for the rest of the world to consume between makeup tutorials and dance videos. Straitlaced cop finds her own life at the center of the cold case she's investigating . . .

She turns her phone off and has to will herself not to smash it as hard as she can against her desk.

The next morning she rings the doorbell at Jane and Damien's and Opal answers, dressed in pajamas with rain boots and a blue tutu.

"Hey Callie," Damien says. He smiles, but it looks forced. She looks at him a beat longer than is polite. Do his eyes look bloodshot? His pupils dilated? His arms—are there track marks? Would he, desperate, cross over from pills or powder to shooting up? Jane had mentioned that he was picking up some shifts at Luke's selling Christmas trees and ropes of pine garland now that hiking and canoeing has slowed for the winter. Luke made good on his word. Money still tight, worse if he's got a habit to support.

She only looks away when Opal tugs at her shirt. "You're taking mama away. I want you both to stay here."

"We'll be back before you know it, Miss Opal. And before I go back to my house today I'll talk to your mommy and daddy about the next time we can hang out. Maybe Wednesday? That's my off day this week."

"My folks will be here," Damien says.

Jane's eyes narrow. "Well Callie can still come over. She and Frank can talk shop."

"Sure, yeah. You probably see my dad more than we do, Cal. God knows he can't give up the job."

Callie doesn't know what to say. Frank dropped by the station again this week, talking shit with the guys, leaving during shift change for beers at the tavern. But not before popping into Callie's office to give her a few pointers on where to best set up drunk driving checkpoints during the holidays, even after she told him she had it all sorted out.

"He's been helping a lot," she says, but can't look at Jane, who surely knows she's lying. "But I don't want to impose on your family time. I'm off on Friday too. Maybe that will work."

"Let's hit the road," Jane says, inching toward the door. Both Callie and Damien move to help her.

"I got her," Callie says.

Damien frowns. "It's just the porch is hard, there's a certain way . . ."

"Dame, we're good. Go find Opal and make sure she's not flushing her socks down the toilet again."

"Have fun," Damien says. From down the hall there's the sound of a toilet flushing. Damien strides off to take a look and they hear him protesting, "Oh, Opal, no, come on, we can't do that . . ."

Jane raises her eyebrows at Callie. "Let's go before we find out what she did."

She helps Jane in the car, still not used to the new thinness to her arms.

They back out of the driveway and Callie tosses a paper bag of donuts into Jane's lap.

"Oh, hell yes. Thank you for not making me share these with my child."

"So maybe it's because I'm an incredibly observant police officer but I'm picking up on some . . . vibes. What's going on?"

Jane breaks a donut in half. "We're fine. We're all just sick of one another. I'm sick of being a burden on everyone. There were days when I thought I was losing my mind in that house with just a little kid and my husband during COVID and even after, when things started opening up again, and then it was like . . . the universe heard me think that, decided to really show me what an ungrateful bitch I was."

"You're not an ungrateful bitch. You've done so much for them. And your recovery, not being able to do anything on your own. Shit. I would be crazy too."

"Thank god you are here. Maybe I'm really better. Just faking it a little bit so that you feel sorry for me and stay. I don't want you to ever go." She's surprised at Jane's tone—the bitterness that has seeped into her voice when she talks about being home. Had she really been going crazy before the accident, and Callie hadn't noticed? From the photos and texts and calls, Jane had always sounded so happy. Pictures of Opal covered in flour after baking a batch of cookies. Damien with Opal in a pack on his back under a canopy of trees. Maybe Callie hadn't been paying close enough attention, caught up as she was in her eighty-hour workweeks, making sure she went to every happy hour with the guys, every target practice session, brought cases home on the weekend. She should have visited. She should have gone on one of Jane's foraging tours. She should have asked her friend some simple but crucial questions: Are you happy? Are you okay? What else do you need? Had Damien had a problem even then? It was a story she heard more and more, ordinary people cracking under the weight of the pandemic. Affairs, drinking too much, online gambling. Habits that pushed them into pits they couldn't climb back out of as the world began to right itself.

"I'll stay as long as you need me to. You know that. Just me, or did your husband not seem too happy to see me?"

"Don't worry about him. He's been weird around *me* lately." Callie waits for the conversation to turn, the way it was about to the last time she was with Jane. Tell me, Callie wills her. Just tell me and I'll help. She's brought the baggie, keeps it in her wallet, waiting for the right time to bring it up.

Jane claps her hands together, brushes the sugar from her fingers. "Enough about me. What's the latest on your case?"

"I drove up to Princeton to see that teacher who signed Annabelle's yearbook."

"How'd that go?"

"She was super evasive. She knows more than she's letting on, I think. It seems like she suspected there was something weird going on with the sisters and she should have had CPS involved but doesn't want to catch flack for it now."

"Can't blame her."

"She's suggested that Sabrina Riley was in a relationship with a cop."

"You think she was?"

"It's possible. I need to dig up a roster from the '90s, see who was on the squad that would fit the bill. Maybe ask Frank what he thinks about that."

"Frank won't tell you shit about any of his guys. I'll tell you that right now."

"What's their deal? Frank and Lorraine? Why don't they help you more instead of—"

"Instead of butting in down at the station? Yeah, no wonder the last guy at your job had a heart attack." Jane sighs. "They're helping us plenty."

"Money?"

"We'd have lost our house if it weren't for them. Don't get me wrong, they've got some expenses of their own. I think they took out equity on their house during the recession, so there's that. The rest is Luke."

"Luke's helping too?" Weed must be doing well, even better than she thought. Or, something else is filling his coffers. Getting all these kids high, getting them hooked. Even his own brother.

"Yup."

The theory feels reasonable to her, but she hesitates mentioning it to Jane—Layla had seemed adamant that Luke wasn't dealing, but maybe he's not doing anything directly. He could be letting other people sell stuff at the nursery, taking a cut. And then there was that coffee cup in his car. Could be coincidence, but the shade of the lipstick print looked the same as Layla's. Maybe they drive around together, meeting with buyers. Would Jane tell her, if Damien was buying drugs from Luke? Or someone who worked with him?

"You don't like him. I didn't notice it until I moved here. I guess I was never around the two of you together, aside from the wedding." But now she hears it in Jane's voice, the disdain unmistakable.

Jane looks out the window again. "You can almost smell the ocean."

"You're avoiding my question."

"I didn't hear a question."

"Why don't you like Luke?"

"He's a bully, to Damien. Not like Damien cares, though. He's one hundred percent the little brother, devoted even though Luke is a total asshole."

"Is he? A total asshole?"

"The only reason he's loaning us money is so he can lord it over us. That's his whole motivation, no matter what he does. Control. Making other people feel small."

Callie doesn't know what to make of Jane's tone. Whether her bitterness about Luke is related to whatever mood she's in this week, or if there's something deeper there. But Callie senses it's not the time to push. Jane rolls the window down. There's saltwater on the air, bay in the distance, white triangles of sailboats. A seagull shrieks and wheels above the marsh.

"Christ. It's so good to smell something new." Jane picks at another piece of donut. "Thanks for letting me vent."

"Vent away."

They make their way to a sandy turnoff just past a marina, where Callie used to go as a teenager. There's a bench at the end of the stretch, close to the water, solitary and weather-beaten. Callie offers

Jane her arm to help her out of the car and Jane takes it at first but lets go after Callie closes the passenger-side door behind her. She takes a few slow, shuffling steps on her own, Callie tight by her side, and then, because Callie understands the look on her face, she hangs back and lets Jane go ahead without her. Jane's left foot drags, and Callie registers the effort it takes for her to lift it, to make herself take each slow step, but she doesn't move to help, doesn't move closer even when she wobbles and her arms rise from her sides for balance. If Jane falls, Damien is going to kill Callie. If she falls, she's going to get scraped up. But she knows she is going to let her, knows that Jane needs this. Step by step, inch by inch, she gets to the bench.

When Callie gets close she hears how hard Jane is breathing. She also sees her smile lit up wide. The first real smile from her in months.

When they sit, Jane pulls a flask from her pocket. "To celebrate."

Callie takes a small pull—"I'm your DD"—but the burn of bourbon down her throat, the sunshine on her face, feels good. Ahead of them, sparkling water as far as the eye can see. She feels the openness in her chest. Swells with it.

"Tell me about the guy," Jane says.

"I don't know. We're having fun."

Fun is the wrong word. It is fun, but it's more than that. Fun is Callie's way of describing it to herself, in case she gets hurt.

Jane gives her a knowing look. "It's okay to love someone, Callie. A good thing."

"Yeah . . . I know." She doesn't say what she's long thought, that she feels like she and Jane came out of their tumultuous girlhoods two sides of the same coin. Jane throwing herself into a relationship to feel safe, while Callie's form of self-protecting meant avoiding anything deeper than casual sex.

"What do you do?"

"Kayak. Cook." Two nights ago she had gone over and she and Adrian had sex in the kitchen before they could even sit down for dinner, then stood next to the stove, naked, forking pasta straight from the pot, her earlobes tingling where he bit them. "Fuck."

"You kayak?" Jane elbows her. "You wouldn't kayak with me, ever, when I invited you down here."

"I'm sorry. I was an asshole."

Jane stares out at the horizon. "You were. But you're here now. How are you doing?"

Callie looks out to the water too. Easier to say the next part when she's not looking at Jane. "I think she's gone."

Jane reaches for Callie's hand. "Why do you think that? She could have gone to stay with someone, maybe she's in treatment . . ."

"She missed her court date. Even she knows better than that. I feel like she wanted to disappear. She was so restless my whole life. Always wanting to be somewhere other than the room she was in. Even when the room had her kid in it." She had been a fool to hope when she saw that chip from AA on Jenna's table. The article on the fridge. To think Jenna might have tried, one last time, to save herself.

"Maybe you should go easy on her. I wish in the end I was easier on my parents. I don't forgive them for everything. My dad was sick, just like your mom was sick. My mom couldn't leave him because she was always holding out hope that he would get better. I was always just as pissed at her as I was at him. But I don't know, after having Opal I guess I understand her a little more. She was just a person. One person against all the fucking expectations around moms? Work and be progressive; stay home, they're only small for such a short time. Cherish it. Don't lose your identity. Shit. It's impossible. They each probably wanted to be better. I feel that. *I* want to be better. But I'm still just me. Day in, day out, doing this thing that tries your patience and makes you laugh and is so boring and tedious and then shot through with these moments of like, wildly transcendent joy, all before 11:00 A.M. It's enough to make anybody crazy."

"So you're saying I need to have a kid to heal my mommy issues?" Callie aims for lightness, but the mention of having a child feels hot to the touch, tender. A little spark of interest, of possibility, whereas before it had always felt hypothetical, far-off.

"I'm saying, you know all this. All that work you do with the Narcan and trying to help people around here. You know it's a disease, you know she can't help it. You're capable of extending kindness and empathy to strangers—why not to the woman who raised you?"

Callie kicks her sneaker through the sand. "Because we're hardest on them. Because they have to be perfect."

"You have to be perfect," Jane echoes, her voice a whisper. Callie throws an arm around her and they sit for an hour before getting back in the car without needing to say anything else.

When they get back Opal is coloring at the kitchen table, alone.

"Where's your daddy?" Jane asks her.

Opal shrugs. Jane looks down the hall, where the bedroom is dark. "I'll be right back," she tells Callie. "Can you . . ." she nods at Opal.

Callie pulls out the chair next to her, starts matching opened markers to their caps. "Opes, tell me what you are coloring."

"The snake man," she says, her tongue poking from her mouth as she concentrates.

Callie makes out the circle of a head, the stick of a body, two arms and two legs. Opal grabs for the black marker and makes a fat scribble along the man's arm.

"He came to the house today. Daddy is afraid of him."

"He sounds pretty scary." Raised voices from the bedroom. Callie can't make anything out—Jane must have closed the door behind her. Opal looks up at Callie and Callie has to resist the urge to clap her hands over the girl's ears.

"Want to go look for magic rocks outside?" Callie asks. Opals nods and puts her hand in Callie's. It's warm and small and she still has indents at her knuckles.

Outside Opal is still quiet, serious, as she turns over rocks, brushes dirt from their undersides. "They fight when the snake man comes."

Callie wonders if the snake man is one of those childish projections, someone to blame for whatever scares them. Bogeyman, ghosts.

She crouches. "Hey, Opal. Check this one out." She picks the first rock she sees, a little tan pebble veined with gray.

"That one isn't special. It isn't even pretty."

"No, but it is magic. You want to hold it?"

Opal looks skeptical. "What kind of magic does it have?"

"It makes you brave. All you have to do is give it a squeeze when you need a little extra courage."

The girl takes the stone so solemnly, squeezes it so hard in her palm that Callie wants to tell her the truth. That she made it all up. But then Opal looks up at her with such delight on her face, a smile that looks so much like Jane that it makes her chest ache.

"It's working!" Opal says. "Let's find more magic ones." She turns and races along the edge of the driveway, comparing every pebble to the one in her hand.

She holds the stones Opal hands her, runs her fingers over them, turns back to the house, sees movement behind the glass. A moment later Damien comes out. He makes no pretense of exchanging pleasantries. Does not thank Callie for taking Jane out, for watching Opal.

"She's laying down."

"She okay?"

"Just tired. I think today was a lot for her."

Callie ignores the dig. "I'll get going then, unless you need me to stay."

"I've got it under control."

Do you? Callie wants to ask. *Because from where I'm standing, it looks like you're falling apart.* She fights the urge to rip the green baggie out of her wallet, shove it into his chest.

"Opes, I'm going to hit the road."

"No! I want you to stay, to find more stones with me. We didn't get all the magic ones yet."

"Next time I come back we will find more. And you've got the most important one of all. Take good care of it, okay?"

Opal nods. Callie crouches in front of her, wraps her in a hug. Smells her little-girl smell of dirt and shampoo and applesauce. She counts to three before she forces herself to let go.

"See you soon," she says to Damien.

His lips are tight and he only nods at her in way of goodbye.

She's halfway home when she thinks of Billy Fauver's snake tattoo. How the man that Opal drew looks a little bit like him, the thick black rope of it writhing up his arm.

ANNABELLE

You force yourself to get dressed in the morning. To wait for the bus at the end of the driveway, your breath rising in a hot cloud in front of you. You experiment by holding it as long as you can. Convince yourself you can just disappear. That would solve everything, wouldn't it? The problem of your body, of its horrible mutiny.

You had thought that the long holiday break might give the kids at school a chance to forget. To drop their torments about Sabrina, their interests reset with the new year. But the girls on the bus rally for a few chants when you board, ask in mock-innocence where in the world Sabrina has gone.

Has she moved in with her creepy old boyfriend?

Which one?

They're playing house, how cute.

Maybe she's pregnant! one of them shrieks.

Oh my god, the others say. *Annabelle, is she going to have a baby? Is that why she can't come to school anymore? Annabelle, tell us the truth! You can tell us.*

God Annabelle, you're the smart one! Didn't you tell her she's gotta make those guys bag it up!

Your face burns and your ears ring, which they take as confirmation.

Oh my god, look at her! You guys, look!

You turn toward the window, your face as close to the cold glass as you dare, and study the trees as they blur past you, your breath a shallow pant. Now you know how people would treat you if they knew. Like a joke. Like a fool. Like a disease they might catch.

* * *

At the end of the day, after suffering the endless whispers and taunts about Sabrina and her supposed baby, you relish the chance to go to the yearbook meeting where you can hide your face behind the camera. You photograph the boys' basketball team practice but you are distracted, clicking the shutter without pausing to frame your shots or make sure you are getting the best angle. Between drills you see Henry Hicks tap Victor Donohue on the arm and nod in your direction. You can't make out what he says but you don't have to hear. A new feeling wells up in you. Rage. You are so angry that this is happening to you, angry about the women you met with who stole from you, angry about the ways people whisper, angry at Miss Hamilton for not being able to see. The anger crests like a wave, huge and total and so much bigger than you.

You don't know what you are doing until you've already done it. Heaved the camera up above your head and bashed it down on the floor.

John Hall had been in the middle of a drive toward the net but stops, holds the ball in his hands. Coach Wentz bleats his whistle. It stretches on and on. It is the perfect sound. High and clear, outraged. It rings in your ears for a moment and you try to hold it in you. You think if you could just find the words for that sound you would be able to tell everyone exactly what you need to say.

"I don't know what you think you're up to young lady, but it is unacceptable. Men, back to your drills."

The basketball thumps across the floor, a steady beat like a heart pounding. Henry Turnbull kicks the camera's lens toward you. There's a crack through the glass. When you press the shutter it makes an ugly grinding sound. You hear one of the boys muttering to another. *She's acting crazy because of her sister. Did you hear? Sabrina is knocked up.*

In the hallway outside the gym everything seems to tilt. You are cold from the burst of sweat already cooling to a chill on your back. How can you face everyone with the broken camera? Even if it can be fixed it will probably need to be sent away for repairs. They will probably cost a lot of money, money the committee doesn't have. You can't walk back into that room. You imagine the way they will all look at you. It will be clear that you've ruined this one special thing with which you were trusted.

You hang the camera by the strap on the door of Miss Hamilton's classroom and creep away. It's still a half hour before the late buses will take kids home from sports practices and after-school meetings but you can't bear the thought of waiting around to be caught. It is seven miles from school to your house. It's cold and there's a thick layer of slush on the ground from the last snowfall, but you decide to walk anyway. Your coat is in the classroom, your bookbag, anything you might need, but you cannot make yourself go back inside and answer for what you've done.

The first mile isn't so bad. Your body still holds some of the heat from being inside. But by the second your toes feel frozen in your shoes and the wind knives through your sweater, the only one that is big enough to cover you anymore. A few cars slow but you keep your arms crossed and do not turn to them. A man yells something from a passing truck but you can't make it out. For the most part, there is silence, just the sounds of the woods. Fallen branches breaking under tiptoeing deer. The flutter of birds squabbling over the last of the berries in the trees.

By the third mile your feet feel like hooves. You can't wiggle your toes in your sneakers. Darkness seeps into the spaces between the trees and the cars are few and far between, but when they come their headlights bore into you, the harsh white light making you see spots. Snowmelt soaks your sweatpants.

Finally the house comes into view, the roofline over the tops of the trees. You would run down the driveway if you thought you could get your body to cooperate. If you could make your limbs move any faster, if your now-numb feet could be trusted to carry you any quicker. The first few times you try the knob it slips in your frozen fingers. You grip your right hand in your left to warm it up and only then can you make the right shape, your fingers formed into a raw, red claw.

You run the water in the kitchen as hot as it will go, stick your hands under, scream and pull them back. Sabrina enters the room, reaches past you, turns the water off.

"What the hell happened to you?"

"I walked."

"From school? Annabelle, for someone who is so smart, you can be so stupid sometimes. Come on."

She pulls you up the stairs and runs the bath. You take your sweatshirt off, revealing your stomach, hard and taut, still not as round as the women you've seen around town, running their hands over the dome of their bellies, smiling, accepting well-wishes from strangers. But undeniably changed. Even you will admit that now. You are too tired to hide anymore. You hear Sabrina take a breath, sharp, as though she's been punched.

"Jesus Christ," Sabrina says. "Annabelle."

It feels good, to bare your body to her in the way you did as girls, when everything about the two of you was still the same. No scars, no difference in your shapes, no self-consciousness about being naked together. When you thought you were interchangeable and that felt like reassurance. If one of you ceased to exist, there was another one of you ready to take her place.

BLAIR

It's the stones, the box, the letter, that make Blair decide to develop the photos. She takes the film from the bag while her father is in the shower and Iris cooks eggs for her and her brothers downstairs.

She stares at her mother's back while Iris stirs the eggs in the pan. She sings a little as she works, turns over her shoulder with a bright smile for Blair. How to reconcile this woman with that letter she found? That crazed, confusing ramble of *I'm sorry*'s and *forgive me* and *I think of you every day*. But there was no name at the top, no clear recipient, and even after reading the pages three times over Blair had no idea what Iris was apologizing for. Only that she was sure she had caused some kind of horrible hurt.

The clerk at the film store is a thin, pale guy in his thirties. Blair feels his eyes sweep over her. It is something she is learning, a difference between men and women. The girls she knows are always calibrating themselves in relation to boys, trying to temper their desires, to assess whether they are hot enough to want someone, usually selling themselves short. Men just want, bluntly, openly, without any of that painful self-assessment. Want like a dragnet cast wide, ready to catch whatever gets tangled within.

"Can I help you?"

"I want to develop this."

"Cool." He palms the canister. "Vintage." She nods, pretends to study the cameras and lenses on display in a glass case to her right. "What's your name?"

"Jamie." The lie slips out of her mouth, but she doesn't like the way the guy is looking at her. Doesn't want to give him any part of herself. He scribbles it onto a yellow pad on the countertop, rips a sheet off and hands it to her.

"I'll call you in a few days."

She hopes her mother won't be there when she gets home but Iris's car is in the driveway. She's in the kitchen when Blair steps into the hall. She can hear her stirring something, the clang of the wooden spoon against a pan, onions simmering.

"Blair? Come in here! I have something for you."

Iris has her apron on, gestures at Blair to sit at the island. Her mother beams at her. It's a feeling Blair has had before, that it can be painful, to be so loved, just for existing. On a day like today, when she knows she hasn't acted her best, it can feel like a kind of burden. She wonders what it would be like to have grown up the way her mother did—or at least what she's been able to piece together from her father. Unsupervised, unloved, untethered. Her father always says how hard Iris had it, but Blair wonders if there must have been some freedom in that.

"We had some extras of these from the library bake sale fundraiser. I thought you'd want some." She tosses Blair a cellophane bag stamped with snowflakes. Inside, chocolate cherry cookies. Iris's specialty. Blair's favorite.

"Thanks," Blair says. She doesn't take one out yet. She is torn between flares of guilt and anger. *I don't deserve this. I'm a traitor.* And: *Who are you, and what have you done?*

"Of course." Iris turns to the stove, turns down the heat, walks to the island and puts a hand on Blair's shoulder. "You okay?"

"Yeah, fine."

"You're so busy lately, with soccer and school. I feel like we hardly got to talk this week. Nothing's on your mind? You look like you have the weight of the world on your shoulders."

She wants to crumble before Iris. Beg her to explain what she's found, what she's seen. But she can't form her mouth into the shape of the words. The possibilities she's come up with seem wild and silly out loud. Are you having an affair? Are you leaving us? Instead she leans into her mother, her warmth. The material of Iris's blouse is thin and Blair can feel the scar underneath her sleeve, where her mother was bit by a dog as a girl. When Blair was young she used to trace her fingers over the ridged, raised skin. She didn't understand what a scar was, confused by an injury that didn't heal completely but also didn't hurt anymore.

"I'm fine. Just tired."

"Okay. Everything good with your friends? With Henry?"

"Yeah."

"You promise nothing is wrong?" Iris holds her gaze.

"I promise I'm going to do some homework. Calculus."

"Okay. Dinner at seven."

Blair turns the corner when she hears her mother call out for her again. She turns around, expecting her mother to proffer a box of tissues to restock the upstairs powder room, a laundry basket to heave up.

"Listen to your gut, okay? With Henry. If it doesn't feel right . . . it probably isn't right for you. If it makes you happy . . . well. Happy is a good sign. I know you have a good head on your shoulders. But I just wish someone had told me that when I was younger. To trust myself and to ask for help if I needed it."

"Okay," Blair says, a little taken aback. Iris never talks about being a teenager. The timeline of her mother's stories, references, memories, all seem to start after she met Blair's dad.

Henry is the easy thing in her life right now. What feels murky and confusing is Iris, and whatever secret she is tending to just beyond Blair's view.

A voicemail, Thursday, in the middle of AP World History. She checks it in the bathroom—the photo guy. *Um, yeah. I'm looking for Jamie? This is the number I have for you. Your pictures are ready.*

She listens three times, trying to discern some kind of reaction in his voice. Is he titillated? Disgusted? But his affect gives nothing away. Most of all he sounds confused that the name on her voicemail doesn't match the one she gave. Rookie mistake. But who even leaves voicemails anyway?

She texts her parents that she has to run an errand for a group project she is doing and will be thirty minutes late. At the photo place she sits in the car for a few minutes, wondering if these will be the last moments before everything changes. But the shop closes at six, so she doesn't have a ton of time. She cuts the ignition and goes inside.

The same clerk is at the counter. He doesn't try to suppress a laugh when he sees her, or ogle her, or raise an eyebrow.

"Hey. Jamie, right?"

"Yeah." He's got the envelope on the counter.

"Twenty bucks."

She pays him, peeling the cash out of her wallet hastily.

"Very *Virgin Suicides*," he says.

"Excuse me?" She thinks he's making a joke about her being a virgin still. She knows eighteen is a little old, a lot of her friends have done it, but who the hell is this guy to make a crack at her? Perv.

"The movie? I mean, book first. But the vibes. Sophia Coppola?"

"Oh." She still doesn't understand what that has to do with anything.

"Never mind. Just . . . cool pics. They reminded me of the film. The colors. Interesting framing. You get these at a garage sale or something? You know, Vivian Maier was discovered when someone bought a bunch of her negatives at a garage sale. You got more of these?"

She has no idea who Vivian Maier is either. This whole conversation is mortifying, just in a different way than she thought it would be. "Uh. No. At least I don't think so."

"Bummer."

"Yeah." She takes the envelope and leaves, her face hot.

She drives around the corner and parks on the side of a residential street she's never been down before, so she might have a chance to look at the pictures away from the clerk, away from her parents.

The first photo is of her mother, but her features are sharper, more pointed. She's wearing a crop top and Blair can see the arcs of her hip bones, the shadows they create on her skin in the end-of-day light. Her mother is scowling, angry to be caught this way. It's not an expression she's ever seen Iris make. Behind her, trees, a dirt path. She feels a rush through her body, her heart beating faster. Is this where her mother grew up? Is this who she used to be? Blair stares at the girl's expression, the hardness of it. How did this girl become her mother, who folds notes into Iris's backpack and braids her hair before soccer games?

The second picture is an interior shot. The photographer must be crouching down low, looking up at a window gray with grime, letting in a filtered, tempered sunlight.

The third is of her mother again, standing in front of a mirror. That same scowl, those same skinny forearms. But as she is about to shuffle the picture to the back of the stack, Blair notices something. The starburst of a flash, and the shadow of a figure behind it. Arms and legs. The arm is unmistakable: her mother's scar.

And so she's presented with a riddle. Her mother is the subject of the photo, her arm unblemished. Her mother is taking the photo. She is here and she is there. Right in front of Blair's eyes, and hidden in the corner of the shot.

There are two Irises. Is it some kind of editing technique? Did her mother do this? Or the guy at the photo shop?

Or, are there really two people in the picture?

If her mother is holding the camera, then who the hell is standing in front of the mirror?

A ghost, she thinks, before she can tell herself how foolish she sounds. The word rising unbidden from her mind.

There are three more images of the girl with her mother's face. None of the other pictures are head-on, but the harder she looks the more Blair can see the differences between them. A small freckle below her bottom lip, where her mother's skin is unmarked. The jut of her chin more defined. And something else, something Blair can't name, or not without sounding woo-woo. An energy. This girl does not have her mother's softness. She is all nerve, all angles, all I-fucking-dare-you.

There's the girl in profile. She must have turned away fast, just before the shutter clicked, because the image captures the blurred lace trim of her nightgown, her hair a fan concealing her features. Another, of her seated at a table, the picture taken from behind. The girl's foot is tucked up underneath her and she's leaning with an elbow on the table, her head resting in her palm. A daydreaming pose. She can tell it's not her mother because the girl is wearing a tank top again, even though goosebumps prickle her arms, and from this angle you would be able to see the scar.

And then there's one shot from above, maybe out an open window. The girl walking down the driveway, a long dirt path aside a yard heaped with metal odds and ends. Her shoulders are squared, eyes fixed ahead, as though she's telling the house—or telling Iris—to fuck off. Her hair is long down her back, shiny and straight and bright against the darkness of her surroundings: the woods creeping in at the edge of the picture, her dark clothes, the dirt underneath her feet.

The photo of a group of men surprises her, feels like an intrusion, a stark counterpoint to the dreamy and strange pictures of the girls. All those boots and thick, hairy, crossed arms, the stubble and weighty jaws. None of them notice the camera, save a teenage boy, maybe Blair's age. Light brown hair, smooth, baby-faced cheeks. He stares out of the side of his eyes, the corner of his mouth pulled down.

None of the other pictures feature people. A creepy abandoned building without a roof, crumbling walls of gray stone. A broken Ball jar in the dirt, the glass a pretty aquamarine with a jagged edge. Bunches of dried herbs hung from twine against another dirty windowpane. Two dolls resting in boxes, their hair mussed and wild. A hand, maybe Iris's, next to a pressed flower that looks a lot like the delicate, crumbling one she found in her mother's closet. A pair of men's boots by the door. A chandelier furred with dust. A wallpapered hallway, stained in places, darker in others where pictures must have hung once.

The girl with the hard stare would have been her aunt. She has to get used to the idea, run it over in her mind, like learning a word in another language. When she was small she always thought her mother and her father's sister, Margot, were the ones who were related. Margot and her mother laughing and whispering over coffee at the kitchen island. Margot banging through the front door without knocking, a bottle of wine under her arm, scolding Blair's cousins to take off their shoes, right away busying herself with making coffee as though she were in her own kitchen. Aunt Margot stayed with Blair when each of her brothers were born, lavished her with breakfasts of chocolate chip pancakes. Iris going over to Margot's house the time she lost the unborn baby who was almost fully grown—until then, Blair hadn't even known that such a thing could happen—bringing soups and doing the laundry. One day that spring Blair came downstairs to hear hushed voices in the living room, Margot and her mother sitting close to one another on the sofa.

I just want someone else to know she was real, Margot was saying. *These are hers.*

The women had their backs to Blair, so Blair watched as Margot took a folder from her lap, opened it to a piece of paper bearing two black, inky commas.

Footprints.

Iris didn't say anything, just sighed and wrapped her arm around Margot. They sat that way for a long time, until Margot rose to go.

After, Iris pulled a throw pillow into her chest and wailed into it, ugly bleating sounds that filled the empty room.

Blair had never seen her mother cry like that and she stood paralyzed on the steps, wondering if she should go to her. Even though her mother and Margot were close, she was shocked at her mother's grief, terrified of it.

Does Margot know her mother's secrets? Does her father? Or is it just Blair? Her burden to carry, to decide what to do with it.

The idea comes to her in the middle of calculus. She doesn't know why she hadn't thought of this before. Her mother didn't come from no one, from nowhere, even if she doesn't like to talk about it. The photos are one kind of proof, but she can find another.

In between classes she pulls up the website for the genetic testing company. Her friend Allegra's mom did it, and she found this second cousin on her dad's side who she met once before at a family barbecue when they were four. But there was some falling out between the parents so they hadn't seen each other since, and turns out they live twenty minutes away from one another so now they meet for coffee all the time.

Genes are a story, the website says. *The most powerful story on Earth.*

It gives Blair the shivers to read that. To think of unlocking the promise of something so basic, so elemental and taken for granted, this narrative she's carried around in her body for every minute of her life.

Her mother has always found a way to bat away her questions about her childhood. Her father always took her mother's side. *There's a lot of pain there, Blair Bear. Your mom prefers to focus on how lucky she is now, how much she loves you and your brothers.* A spike of anger in Blair. How can her mother keep all of this hidden? This story is Blair's story too.

In study hall she orders the kit using her Dad's credit card, which is saved on her phone. Her mother is more meticulous about checking the statements, more careful with money in general, while she can get away with slipping some things on her dad's bill without him noticing; or if he notices, he doesn't ask. And if he asks, she will just tell him the truth. She wants to—deserves to—understand where she comes from.

And, she could end up doing some good. What if she finds her mother's lost sister? What if she changes the story for the better? She can picture it now, her mother and aunt hugging, their mannerisms so similar across all these years, their faces still the same, aged in the same ways, that it is like a woman looking in the mirror at herself. They will laugh and cry and wonder at the thought they were never going to see one another again, if it hadn't been for Blair. Blair will have another aunt blowing through the front door like a brisk wind; she'll get to listen to them talk about their fights and their school days and what they liked to do for fun. Another aunt who will take her out for pedicures, let her have sips of champagne on New Year's while her parents are in the other room. Another aunt who will stand shoulder to shoulder with her and show her how to be a woman in this world.

The box is delivered on a day when her mom leads her volunteer group at the library—she's relieved that she sees it come off the back of the UPS truck, recognizes the branding right away, the blue tree against the white background, branches reaching to the sky. She'll even have time to do the test and ship it back in town before anyone gets home—her father works late in the city on Wednesdays. And after her volunteer session with the senior citizens, her mother drives a few of them home with foil-wrapped single-serve dinners that she and Blair make together the night before. Eggplant parm or macaroni and cheese—simple, dense foods that are easy to reheat. Blair likes to do this alongside her mother—besides it being good for her college applications, she likes to watch her mother's hands work, the quick, sure motions of her chopping and stirring and cinching foil around the containers, even likes to clean up and compost their scraps. It makes her feel like everything in the world can be put in order, every mess resolved.

Blair opens the package in the dining room, reads through the test instructions twice to make sure she understands. She spits in the tube, adds the vial of stabilizer fluid, screws the cap on tight, seals it up in a bag that she'll slip into the return envelope. The biohazard symbol on the plastic bag gives her pause for a moment—it is dangerous-looking, menacing—before she reminds herself that this is only spit.

A thrill runs through her as she walks the package down the street, to the blue mailbox at the corner of Elm Court and Rodham Road. George Bingham found out he was related to some British king. Maybe her mother's family was exiled royals who had to cut all ties if they wanted to live. Maybe one of them has turned out to be a movie star. Most of all, she pictures her mother's face when she tells her about the results. How grateful she'll be, hugging Blair in close.

The brochure promises she'll get an email with the results in four to six weeks. Blair has the feeling that once she gets these results back, a story will fill itself in behind her mother, behind her, like the scenery of a play slowly lit up.

CALLIE

Christmas Eve. She takes the eight to four patrol shift so she can give one of the guys off. Handful of DUIs, reckless driving. Paperwork. The station is decorated with garlands of pine laced with antique sleigh bells in a weighty cast bronze—Della's handiwork. On her patrol route some of the seasonal décor struck a grimmer note, one guardrail wrapped in pale-blue tinsel where there had been a fatal crash three years ago. A road sign with a wreath zip-tied to the post, a plywood sign underneath it, RIP MARK WE MISS YOU, scrawled with spray paint. The missing posters that Callie put up all those months ago are gone or tattered beyond recognition, damp with rain and snow. In the ones that remain Jenna's face is reduced to a featureless white oval.

On the way home she detours to the Stop and Shop to pick up some food—Adrian is out of town visiting his family and her pantry is empty. She's restless. The drug trade has quieted down a little bit, the weather forcing everyone out of sight, into their houses or in the back rooms of bars or wherever her shadowy dealer is going to conduct their business. Still, a paramedic she's gotten to know texts her to say there's been two OD calls in the last week. Luckily they got to these ones in time.

She's been working more lately, end of the year budget forecasts, preparing employee reviews, getting ready to tell the guys that bonuses will be light this year. She hasn't been around to watch Opal or help with errands as much. The last two times she offered to do a grocery run for Damien he told her not to worry about it. She texts Jane:

How are you doing?

Fine, Jane says. An ellipses to indicate she was typing, then nothing more after that.

Tell me, J, she thinks at her phone. But whatever Jane had been about to say, she's decided to keep to herself. Callie still hasn't worked out what Fauver might have been doing at their place—or really, if he was even there at all. She thinks back to that conversation she had with Damien and Luke outside after dinner back in the fall. *Opal's started to lie.* Maybe the snake man was another one of her stories, something she imagined into the world. It would probably be a relief, as a little kid, to have your own version of the bogeyman who comes and makes your parents fight. Better than the more likely reality: that her parents fight because there's trouble. Because there's something broken that might be hard to fix. Maybe her childhood is careening toward the kind of girlhoods Jane and Callie endured: unpredictable, characterized by want and chaos. History repeating itself.

She'll confront Jane about it next time. That vow they made when they were still teenagers to take care of each other, be there for each other, has another party to it now: Opal. Before she goes to bed at night she sees the heart of Opal's face, her gray-blue eyes the same as Jane's, full of wonder and trust.

She's studying packages of shredded cheese when someone says her name.

It's Wren, Della's daughter. She's older than Callie but Callie remembers seeing Wren around when Callie was in high school and Wren was home from college working as a lifeguard at the lake. Callie always liked her, even though the two couldn't be more different. Wren's got a sleeve of tattoos, flowers twisting on their vines, a split-open pomegranate, quotes from poems and novels Callie's never read. She works for an arts organization in New York, writes for magazines, and publishes short stories—Della keeps a file of everything she's done at her desk and is always eager to brag about Wren's latest publication or byline.

"Hey, Wren. You in town for the holiday?"

"Yeah. Mom and Dad sent me out to pick up a few things." Wren rolls her eyes at her cart, which is nearly full: cartons of eggnog and bottles of rum, two dozen eggs, frozen puff pastry, packages of butter, a sack of oranges.

"Your mom goes all out, that's for sure." The kind of holiday Callie would have killed for once. She went through a phase of cutting tablescapes from magazines in the fourth grade: candles glowing on the table, a centerpiece of pine and red berries, red-and-green glazed plates.

"What are your plans?" Wren asks.

"Oh. I'll be working."

"You should come by. I mean, when you're done. We've got enough to feed an army and it's just the four of us."

Callie musters a smile. She knows Wren's heart is in the right place but the offer makes her squirm. It's just like when she was a kid. A pity case. "I appreciate it, but I don't know if I'll have time."

"Mom said you were working on a cold case. The thing with the baby."

"You know about that?" Callie had approached Della after she gave her Sabrina Riley's name and asked her if she knew anything else, but Della only told her that was what the rumors were. Everyone at the high school had heard she was pregnant, that she was getting in a lot of trouble that year, and that she dropped out.

"We used to go drink out by the old factory near where she was found. Tell ghost stories. That was part of it . . . that story. I'm not proud of this but Mom told me about that case when I was a teenager and I used to try to scare the other kids with it. Used it as evidence there was like, a serial killer in the woods. I guess it's no wonder I tell stories for a living now. Writers are always taking from someone, right? We're thieves."

Callie starts to feel uneasy. She feels a shift in Wren's attention.

Something grasping in it. Like she's waiting for Callie to divulge details on the case that she can polish up, spin into one more tale. "What old factory?" Callie asks.

"I guess it's technically private property, behind an abandoned old house. You can't see it from the road but it must have been gorgeous, once upon a time."

The Riley house.

"Mom said she knew the people who lived there, a long time ago."

Callie's attention snaps back to Wren. "Excuse me?"

"Yeah, she was like, friends with the mom. There were two girls. The ones who disappeared. We found a sweater out there once, this faded pink-knitted thing. Creepy as hell. And the shoe for a doll. Patent leather, covered in dirt."

Callie doesn't have to ask. She's sure Wren and her friends made ghost stories out of them, too. Della hadn't mentioned anything about knowing the Riley girls or their family. Why would she have lied to Callie? Why wouldn't she have said anything? She excuses herself with a hasty "Merry Christmas" to Wren and rushes through checkout with half the things she meant to buy.

As Callie speeds away from the supermarket, her whole body is taut with anger. She lets out a scream, and then another. All these stories circulating, stories and rumors and whispers, none of them close to the truth. The frustration gathers in her gut, a hard knot. She wants to do all the things she's never allowed herself, things she's always associated with Jenna; smash something, to park at the nearest bar and drink herself stupid, wants to pick up a stranger who will be rough with her, leave her body aching and wrung out and used. She pulls the car over to the shoulder, gets out and paces in the cold, her hands on her head like a sprinter who is trying to get their first deep breath after an all-out effort. She's got to get herself under control, hem herself in.

Take stock, she tells herself. Inventory the facts.

What does she know about the Riley sisters?

Annabelle had a scar on her arm. Annabelle was the one everyone looked away from, who could get away with something because everyone else was busy watching Sabrina.

And this factory. The doll's shoe that Wren's friends uncovered. Would the girls play out there? She can picture it, the way she was always looking for places to call her own as a child, places where she could be in control, make the rules. She'll go, because she needs something to do that doesn't engage with this appetite for destruction, with this unruliness she's spent her whole life tamping down. She wants to understand what it was like to be these girls, to know where they hid from the world, where they found refuge, where they felt safe.

She climbs back into the Jeep, and at the next intersection she takes the road that will cut through the woods to the Riley house.

It's already dusk when she pulls up, 5:30 and the blackness seeming to seep up from the ground, joining with the shadows of the trees. She doesn't have her Maglite on her, so the flashlight on her phone will have to do. Luckily there's a three-quarter moon and no clouds, enough so she can make things out a few steps at a time. In the moonlight the heaps of trash in the yard throw strange-shaped shadows, and the house looms behind it all, looking bigger but shabbier than it did during the day.

She looks to her right for a break in the trees, a glimpse of a wall, but finds nothing. Then she tries to find a trail, some kind of marker. She paces the line where the yard meets the woods twice, three times, a fourth, before her toe connects with a boulder. She's only got sneakers on so she swears at the pain of it, the smarting of her shin.

When she looks down again she sees it, another boulder in line with the one that tripped her, framing the path—or what used to be a path—like a gateway.

She aims her phone past the boulder and finds a line where the understory is less thick, not as tangled. She can only make out the ground a few feet ahead at a time but she starts to walk, high, plodding steps. The ground is level, at least—everything in the Pines is flat—but it doesn't mean she doesn't have to stop and backtrack, find her line through the trees to the place where she thinks she senses a gap.

A cloud passes over the moon and shifts away, and there it is: the line of the stone foundation, a gap where a door once hung. She steps through the doorway and there's more of a drop to the ground on the other side than she realizes, lands hard on her right ankle, which starts to throb right away.

She limps to the center of the structure, not knowing what she's looking for. The stone seems to hold the chill of the night close. She shivers, thinks of two girls climbing the walls and whooping as they jump, two girls pointing broken branches at one another like swords. Two girls laughing together and speaking in code as teenagers, hands quick in one another's hair, tight French braids that look perfect and make their scalps ache, shins beaded with blood from trudging through the understory, though by then they hardly feel the sting. Their own world out here, the abandoned factory a place they could invent and explore, unlike their own home, with its bare cupboards and filthy windows.

"What happened?" she whispers, shrugging up at the place where the factory roof should be. What made everything go so wrong?

She paces the perimeter of the factory walls once, twice, a third time, learning now where she can place her feet, where the ground is uneven, ignoring the throb in her ankle. By the fourth lap her body knows how to keep her steady and she runs one hand along the cool stone of the wall, her phone in the other.

She thinks she is imagining it, her eyes playing tricks on her, when she catches the flash of white on the short northern wall of the ruins. A spot of it, just below the window. She steps closer, tripping once on the way, too eager to be careful.

In between one of the stones, a ziplock bag, damp and blooming with mold, with a piece of paper inside.

Iris Owens
57 Cleveland Lane
Cortlandt, New York 10567

There's a phone number below the address, too. Callie's breath catches in her chest. It's the handwriting from the SAT workbooks. Careful, deliberate, exacting.

Annabelle.

And the name. The same as a doll under Sabrina's bed. The name a girl would pick for herself if she had to invent herself anew. A name she had practice pretending with. A proxy self she was used to creating stories for.

"You were a fucking kid," she whispers.

Annabelle has been here. Annabelle has been trying to tell Sabrina where she's gone.

She knows more now, but she's also back at her original questions. Who was the mother of Baby Doe? Where did Sabrina go?

Except this time, she has someone to ask. She'll go to Annabelle.

ANNABELLE

Sabrina brings books from the library. *Guide to Home Birth. Birthing Better. What to Expect for Baby's First Year.*

You flip open the guide to home birth and even the illustrations make you queasy. The organs crammed around the fetus, floating in its watery sack.

"I can't," you say, shutting the book.

Sabrina rolls her eyes. "Fine, I'll read them first and tell you what you have to know." She pulls a book from the top of the stack and studies it with the concentration she had reserved for the notebook she was always scribbling in back when she was still in school. With the concentration you recognize when she stitched your arm back together. You remember something she said last year. *Too bad I'm not like you, good at school. Or else I'd study to be a nurse.*

She bites her lip, takes a pencil from her backpack and circles one word, another. The old habit from when you were in elementary school. Circling words to look up in the dictionary when you went back to the library. You look at the ceiling but you can still hear it, the drag of her pencil around one word, then another, then another. There is so much the two of you do not know.

You cannot imagine life beyond this thing that is waiting for you, the thing you have heard stories of but cannot picture. Mother Leeds in the circle of chanting women, cursing and writhing with pain. Blood. The dark coil of a cord. It is like how you have known, a fact crouching in the back of your mind, that you will die one day. It is coming for you, but impossible to imagine your way into the moment, to prepare.

"It's going to be okay, Annabelle."

"Tell me again, about the plan," you say to Sabrina, as she stands over the stove stirring a seasoning packet into a pot of ramen. You've lost track of how many days you've been out of school, though you still refer to it that way in your head. As though you've only been sick. As though you'll return.

"We'll get our own place. An apartment somewhere. Maybe by the ocean. We can take her for walks on the boardwalk." You close your eyes and for a second you savor it. Your mother used to take you to see the ocean. Not in summer when it was hot and crowded, but in the shoulder season, when the sand was cold on your bare feet and you had the beaches to yourselves, save for a few dog walkers and old men with their metal detectors. You picture you and Sabrina, together, the salt in the air making your hair go wavy. Taking turns pushing a carriage along the shoreline.

Sometimes you listen, the way you'd listen to your mother tell fantastical bedtime stories when you were girls. Today, with your back aching and your body feeling so heavy and tired, you push her.

"Where are we going to get the money for that?" Your father left last month, and you find yourself hoping it is for good. Something about an oil rig, more money than he could ever make in this backward town. He said he'd send some back, but you all know that's not true.

"I told you, I'm working on that. We'll get you to a doctor soon. It will be okay."

"Don't ask him. The Coyote," you say. There's still a complicit agreement between you two, to not use his real name—not that you even know it. You don't want to make him more real, more a part of this, than he has to be. Only you and Sabrina matter now.

Sabrina doesn't say anything, only gets up from the table. "Where are you going?" you ask her, but she doesn't turn. You hear the front door slam.

You flip open another one of the books. *How to know labor has started.* Even the phrases make you queasy. *Bloody show. Mucus plug.* You snap it shut and vow not to look at them again. Sabrina says she'll do it. Sabrina says she'll learn. And even with all that has passed between you, you trust her more than anyone else in the world.

Your breath has started to get short and shallow. The thing in you tumbles and punches and kicks. You piss every twenty minutes, even in the night. You wait, for someone from school to show up and yank you back into your life. To ask you what you are doing. Miss Hamilton, Principal Kohley. All they would need to do is knock on the door, a single look to understand. The house seems smaller as you get bigger. As you think about another person nestled inside of you. Sabrina stays up late reading the books, making notes in her notebook.

Sometimes you catch Sabrina looking at you like you are a riddle. Once when you leave the bathroom she reaches under your shirt, her hands brisk and cold, feels the hardness of your belly, where you don't even let your own hands stray anymore.

"What are you doing?"

"They say you can feel where the baby's head is. If it's breech that will be a more complicated delivery."

"Breech?"

"Feet first. I can't tell like this, come lay down."

She guides you onto your back on her bed, lifts your shirt, and presses into you. You watch her face as she tenses her fingertips along your stomach, pressing, pressing.

"I think it's normal. I think this is the head."

"That's good," you say. Normal. But the phrase *the head* sends a wave of sickness through you.

She turns away and counts off the days on her calendar, running backward through the pages, backward through time.

"I think it will be any week now. But first babies tend to come late."

Maybe it will never come, you think. It will stay locked between your pelvis, your body won't do what the books say it is made to do. Instead, it will bend to your will. It will make sure that nothing ever changes, not before you are ready. Not until Sabrina finishes looking up all those words she's circled and written down.

Your eyes catch on a basket in the corner. Stacks of clean sheets. Tiny clothes that you have to look away from, the pink tags from the thrift store still attached.

One day she tapes the end of a paper towel tube closed, fills it with dried black beans, and tapes the other end shut, gives it a shake, adds more tape, shakes it again, smiles to herself.

A rattle. Her sleeve slips as she hands it to you to try and you see the black-blue of a fresh bruise around her wrist.

"What are you doing with him still?" you ask.

"I'll fix it, Annabelle. He's going to pay for this. He's going to help."

"I don't want his help."

"Money, Annabelle. We're going to need money."

"Why would he give us money?"

"He has some secrets worth protecting. A job worth protecting. And we aren't the only ones."

"The only ones what?"

"The only girls. He likes to brag about it. To get me to do what he wants. The others do this. The others like that."

For a second her voice breaks and she looks away from you. You put a hand on her arm and her skin feels fever-hot. You realize you still have no idea, really, what Sabrina has gone through. That the Coyote has remade you both in different ways, and it makes you so sorrowful that you want to lie down and cry, the way the two of you did together when your mother first left.

But it still gives you a bad feeling. Bringing him into this. The idea of revenge. Yes, of course, since the night at the Cranberry Festival a part of you has been simmering with rage. That he moves through the world so unencumbered, while you have been sick, exhausted, colonized, exiled from your own life. But that doesn't mean you want anything from him. Sabrina, on the other hand, wants to draw blood. You feel her thirst for it. All that energy you felt coming off her as she curled her hair or put on another coat of mascara or filed her nails, now it is in service of something else. Of you, of some plan. And that scares you. Drop it, you tell her. Let it go.

"It will be fine," Sabrina says, but she keeps her eyes on the rattle, turns it in her hands.

CALLIE

She has to drive all the way home before she gets good enough cell service to google Iris Owens and the address on the paper. Even without Google she recognizes the number as a New York City area code. Callie wonders if that means she made it, after all. Maybe not to NYU but to the city. To something like the life she imagined for herself there.

She practically sprints inside her house, pounds the name *IRIS OWENS CORTLANDT* into her computer. She'll look at property records, at LinkedIn profiles, at social media, in time. But for now the first thing she does is click on the Images tab. She has to see for herself, who Annabelle has made herself into. What she has become.

Annabelle has highlighted her hair to a sunny blond, similar to the color in Sabrina's mug shot photo. She's thinner, and underneath the rounded face of her yearbook photos are some of the canny, sharp angles of Sabrina's features. It is like she's looking at both of them at once, layered together in the form of a middle-aged woman. She looks for the scar Trent Brentwood told her about but the woman in the photo is wearing long sleeves.

She clicks on the article affiliated with the photo. IRIS OWENS RECOGNIZED FOR VOLUNTEER COMMITMENTS

Iris Owens, mother of three, spends her afternoons volunteering at a soup kitchen—

Annabelle, the good one. But then . . . Why had she felt the need to reinvent herself? Why would she have run away and taken on a new name?

There's another photo of Annabelle with her husband, taken at a school fundraiser that ran in a local paper. Ben Owens is not much taller than his wife, has a big, easy smile, a slightly receding hairline, and a crinkle to his eyes that to Callie indicates a jovial air. She googles him in another tab and finds that he works as a CPA in a two-man firm in town. His bio on the company's page is folksy, sweet. Mentions his love of cooking, fishing, and camping, his beautiful wife, his three children. Property records indicate that Ben and Iris Owens purchased their home twelve years ago. On Google Maps she zooms in to see a well-kept Colonial with a basketball net fixed above the garage door.

Callie's whirring with feelings: relief, that Annabelle found herself a new life, that it seems to be solid and steady, that she hasn't been lost, destroyed by the world. Confusion: How did she pull it off? Forged documents? A new birth certificate? Does the husband know that she had spent the first part of her life as someone else? And most importantly: Why? Why would Annabelle rename herself, take on all of the risk and effort?

Unless she couldn't afford to be who she had been. The girl who abandoned Baby Doe to the elements. The one who had run away, aching and alone and afraid.

Iris Owens doesn't maintain any kind of social media. Even in the photos Callie's found online, she looks reluctant, uneasy, her eyes cutting to the left in both images as though she wants to slip out of the frame.

The only thing to do is to go see her. Not on Christmas, not the days after, but in January, when everyone is back in school, when the world starts up again. This woman who not only could unlock the case, but could tell Callie once and for all who she comes from.

On January 3 she's meant to meet with a middle school principal to discuss the D.A.R.E. program schedule for the following year, but she tells him she has the flu and can't make it. Instead, she leaves at 6:00 A.M. and drives to Westchester while it's still dark out, the first of the day's light coming through the trees just as she leaves the Pines behind.

Iris and Ben Owens live on a curved street that slopes toward a little creek. The houses are all tidy, with wide, green lawns and neat bristles of hedges, and a low stone wall runs the length of the block. It's still early when she arrives, the neighborhood just beginning to stir. Newspapers at the ends of driveways in blue-and-green plastic bags. A jogger making quick progress on the opposite side of the road lifts her hand to Callie in a wave. She parks in front of the house across the street from the Owens's and slouches low in her seat.

Half an hour passes before there's a flicker of movement behind the glass. A teenage girl emerges wearing jeans and a gray zip-up hoodie, with a bag slung on one shoulder, a thick blond ponytail swinging between her shoulder blades.

Callie sucks in her breath.

Iris steps onto the porch wearing black tailored pants and a fitted sweater in an icy blue that Callie knows must pick up the blue in her eyes. She reaches up to her daughter and tucks a strand of the daughter's hair behind an ear. The daughter says something that makes Iris laugh. Two boys tumble out after them, younger, nearly the same height, probably just a year apart, with Ben's curly brown hair, and they load hockey sticks and black duffel bags into the trunk.

They get into their car, a Volvo hatchback, a few years old, a bumper sticker with the name of the high school on the back. She thinks about the months she's spent on this case, the time she's stolen, the way the guys in the room laughed. About her mother and the answers she took with her when she disappeared, Fauver and his hulking shadow. All the time she's spent feeling frustrated and confused and adrift. And so before she can argue with herself she's following them. Her compulsion for answers drumming along her veins like a second pulse.

Iris takes her sons to school first. Callie parks and watches from across the street. The boys raise their hockey sticks in a form of goodbye and walk shoulder to shoulder into the building, one of them waving to a group of girls nearby, the other bending to pick up a shiny food wrapper that the wind blew against his shins.

The daughter is next, at the high school a few minutes away. After she gets out of the car the girl turns to wave to her mother instead of slumping off without a second glance the way some of the other teenagers do. What Callie knows about Iris—Annabelle—she can't decide which name to call her in her head—makes everything about this routine crackle with intrigue. How often does Iris think about who she used to be? When did she come back to leave the note for Sabrina?

Callie follows Iris again, this time to the town library. The houses along the road still bear holiday wreaths draped with velvet bows, swags of pine along porticos and railings. The library's sign is traced in tinsel. Iris parks up close while Callie finds a spot in the back of the lot.

The building is quaint, redbrick. Callie waits for Iris to step out of her car and through the vestibule; it shouldn't be hard to find her inside, the building small, and she'd rather not raise suspicion by tailing her right through the door. She counts to fifty before getting out of her car, kills time by glancing at the app she uses to check her home security cameras. A whole lot of nothing, just the occasional squirrel streaking across the driveway.

Inside the library is quiet, empty. She scans left, right, can't see Iris anywhere. She studies the spines of a few books on the New and Noteworthy Fiction shelf. Grabs one at random, scans the jacket copy. Something about a plucky female detective solving a string of brutal murders in Wyoming.

She and Jane used to joke about lady detective stories like this. How you had to be damaged to want this job as a woman. Had to drink hard liquor with the boys and have had a shitty childhood to wade through the gore of it. Had to be broken in some essential way. But, underneath the jokes she knew there was some truth to the cliché. That the disorder of her childhood had pointed her to this life, with its laws and rules and uniforms. Where the unpredictable could be managed, solved, contained.

She hears a murmur of voices toward the back of the building, follows them. Stops, grabs another book from the shelf. A cedar shingle house on the cover, a green lawn livid with hydrangea.

She rounds the last shelf in the fiction section to find a small circle of chairs set up near the windows. Each chair is occupied by a senior citizen with a ball of yarn and knitting needles in her lap. One woolly-haired woman looks up, asks what time Robert is going to pick her up.

Iris answers her, "Your son brought you today, Mrs. Clifford. Your son George. He'll be back in forty-five minutes."

"Is Robert in the office?"

"I'm not sure what he's up to. But look at the progress you've made."

Callie catches the neck of a sweater, a sleeve halfway done.

"It is looking good, isn't it?" the older woman says, sits herself up a little straighter.

Neither of the other two women look up, but their hands work the needles and Callie finds herself soothed by the soft click of them. Lulled. Her grandmother used to knit. Somewhere in her mother's attic are the baby blankets and little cardigans she made when Jenna was born, stacks of them in sweet, candy-colored pastels.

She is so locked in to the rhythm of the knitting that she is mesmerized. She is surprised to hear a voice at her side.

"Do you knit?"

Iris.

She stands close enough so Callie can make out little flecks of green in her blue eyes. The little lines like commas around her mouth. It's jarring to see the years on her face, though she is still fairly young. Almost fifty. Just no longer a girl in the woods.

"No," Callie manages, fighting off a flush. She could not have been more off guard if Iris had walked up to her and shoved her. She had been too lulled by the knitting, too absorbed watching the quick work of the women's needles that she had lost herself for a moment. Thinking of those baby cardigans knit by her grandmother made her recall how, at least by Jenna's account, her drinking seemed to tip from habit to crisis in the years after her own mother died.

"What are they doing?" she asks. She wants to do anything to keep Iris talking. She cuts a quick glance to her arm. Long sleeves, again. She must keep the scar covered. She wonders if she tells people the truth of how she got it. Wonders what the truth is.

"It's a group for seniors with dementia. They come from a local home twice a week. Studies show that the socialization is good for them, even if they don't really engage in conversations. Greta and Teresa are mostly nonverbal now. But it gives them purpose, to work on something like this. And a lot of times their hands remember how to use the needles. Not as well as they used to. But it comes back."

She has to force herself to focus on the conversation, to try to keep things easy and light. "And you lead the group?"

"I facilitate it. Lead is a strong word. Mostly they don't need me. Their bodies take over and they're doing all the work. Do you know someone who might be a good fit?"

"Me? Oh, no. I mean, maybe. I'd have to think about it. How did you learn to knit?"

"My mother," Iris says. She turns away from Callie, watches the women working. "I learned when I was a girl."

"Are you close?" Callie regrets it as soon as she asks. It's a nudge too far. Too personal, too pointed. Not the question of an impartial stranger.

Iris shakes her head.

"She died a long time ago." An interesting lie. As far as Callie could tell from the records, Vera Riley was alive—no death certificate on file. Vera is another cipher, another woman who disappeared herself without a trace. Callie expects Iris to make an excuse, to look away again. So she is startled to find Iris has turned toward her instead. Her whole body a question. Her face neutral save for the eyes, narrowed, in a way the reminds Callie of Sabrina's yearbook photo. For a second, Callie feels as though Iris sees right through her. That she must.

Then one of the women mewls for help. She has to go to the bathroom.

Callie uses this as an opportunity to leave. She's flustered, hot under her coat. An alarm blares on her way out, makes her jump, and she realizes she still has the book under her arm, the one whose jacket she was reading as a prop.

"Shit," she swears, lunges to the nearest shelf, shoves it between two doorstop fantasy novels.

She sits in her car for a moment after she starts it. That wasn't how it was supposed to go. She didn't have a precise plan for this day when she came here to watch Iris, but she's fumbled it. She can't help but feel dirty, dirtier than she used to after going undercover to buy drugs, or pretend to solicit a man for sex. What is she doing, trailing this woman through her life? There are ways to go about interviewing Iris about Sabrina, but this isn't it. Her head feels cloudy, her body wrung out.

The body remembers, Iris had said. Her body is feeling all of it: Jane, Damien, Jenna, Wren, the mess of this case.

A tap at the window makes her jump.

Iris again.

She rolls it down, waits for Iris to speak first. She looks different than she had in the library, among the knitters.

She looks afraid.

It takes her a minute to speak, and the silence is charged. Something has been laid bare between them.

"Did she send you?" Iris asks finally, her words slow and measured. Nothing of the amiable tone she took with Callie among the stacks of books.

"Who?" Callie says, finding she means it two ways. Who are you talking about, and who are you?

She takes a breath, as though it pains her, like someone whose ribs are bruised. "Sabrina. Please tell me Sabrina sent you." Callie feels her mouth gape open a little bit. Iris continues. "You're a PI, right? She's hired you?"

Iris has been holding out. Hoping. All this time. Callie can see it in her face, in the tight clench of her fists. What she's suspected, what she's worried about and the stories she's been telling herself, over the many long years she must have been waiting. That Sabrina would find a way back to her. That they'd be together again.

"Let's go somewhere we can talk more openly," Callie says.

Iris nods. "My house. No one is home. You can follow me. Or do you . . . you might already know the address?"

Callie nods, flushing hot with shame.

ANNABELLE

It's perfect," Sabrina says, holding up the note the Coyote pinned to the front door, a time and a place scrawled in blocky print. "I'll meet him, like I always do. But then I'll tell him he's got to pay up."

"It seems . . . weird," you say. Sabrina had started leaving him voicemails from the payphone in front of the convenience store, cryptic and bitter. Your phone lines had been cut off, finally, after months of the phone company sending increasingly strident warnings. Envelopes marked *URGENT* in red ink.

"Stop worrying," she says, putting her coat on, zipping it to her chin. She's wearing the gold star charm after keeping it on her dresser all these weeks. You wonder what it means.

At the window you watch her pale hair recede into the dark. To your surprise, she turns once at the end of the driveway, gives you a smile and a wave, turns back again. Sets her shoulders and disappears from view.

Night falls, no Sabrina. You consider walking to the payphone, but who would you call? It wouldn't help you find her, and you'd freeze. After a short thaw, winter came back, swift and hard and bitter.

You don't know what to do with yourself. You pace the hallways, open the same cabinets over and over again, jump at every creak in the old house, thinking it's her.

You lie down to sleep but can't rest. You have no way of calling her. You have no one who can help. You think for a moment of calling the cops, but then you remember the Cranberry Festival, how the Coyote had stood in the circle of men with the police chief. His friends.

You try to calm yourself, tell yourself she will come back with a reason it took so long. She'll return and tell you a convoluted story about where she'd gone and what she had to do and why, her face flushed with victory. She'll show you her purse, a wallet fat with cash, and then the two of you will turn toward the future, toward the rest of your lives. But that only works for so long. You check the clock every few minutes. You search out some coins from between the couch cushions, resolve to walk to the payphone at the market. You will call the police after all. You get as far as putting on your coat, but a moment later you are taking it off again. What if she's hurt and comes back while you are gone? Every step you'd take down the road could be a step in the wrong direction. You feel her close by, you know she wouldn't leave you, not now, if she could help it.

In the end, you walk in circles in the yard calling her name. Calling and calling and calling. Once, you think you hear her calling to you from far off, but realize it is only your own voice thrown back to you. You don't know whether it is the cold or the fear that makes you start to tremble, but you stay out until your teeth clack against one another, until your knees begin to falter and buckle underneath you like the untested legs of a fawn.

"Come back, help, help, help," you plead, to the sky, the cold, indifferent stars, one last time. "Sabrina!" you shout, your heart pounding, your limbs weak. "Sabrina!"

Inside, you collapse against the door, exhausted and crazed with worry. You can't get up and yet you feel a strange electricity running through you.

You have to make it nice for her, you decide. Then she will come. You have to keep moving, because when you are still you feel dread radiating from every nerve, every muscle and bone.

So you force yourself off the ground and put the kettle on for tea, though your hand shakes as you pull the cup and saucer from the cabinet. You pour her a pitcher of milk and a bowl of cereal, clean a spoon to a high shine and lay it on a napkin. Your eye lands on the fireplace and you think *yes!* And haul chopped wood in from the side porch. But, the wood is damp and old and the only lighter you can find takes try after try to spark, the wheel leaving a groove in your thumb from pressing so hard.

You're on your third try with the fire when you feel a familiar pain low in your belly. You straighten, wait a few minutes, feel it again. *Oh*, you think. You've had it all wrong. It gets you giddy, those low cramps, the squeeze and release you know from your period. You even laugh. Imagine, that you thought . . . All this time . . . wait until you tell Sabrina.

You go to the bathroom, get a pad out, put it in your underwear in anticipation. You leave the wrapper next to the sink, as though you forgot to toss it out, a thin slip of pink, so that Sabrina will see. A little flag: All is well here. Your mind whirs. You can go back to school. You can tell Miss Hamilton you were wrong. You can still go away one day. You can still . . .

But then, a cramp like a vise around you. A pang that makes you bite your lip. This worries you, but you tell herself it is your body storing up months of its usual wash of blood. It is normal. It must be normal. To be expected. And Sabrina will be back soon.

Your brain is buzzing, with hope, with plans. You ignore the dark fault line of worry running through you, ignore the fist opening and closing low in your pelvis. You walk. Walk the upstairs hallway, grazing your fingers along the spindles that support the banister, rub dust from your fingerprints. You go downstairs and walk from room to room, trying to keep up the story that everything is about to improve, while that same worry is caught in your mind like a burr. Sabrina should be back by now.

You pace and pace and pace until it is midnight and there is still no sign of your sister.

You lie down but can't get comfortable, shove a pillow between your knees. The ache is radiating across your lower back, through your hips, down the outsides of your thighs. You reach a hand between your legs to check for the blood that is surely about to come, your period releasing you, but nothing, just a milky white film that you wipe away on your sheets.

Another hour passes and you can't call the pain cramps anymore, the word doesn't match. Cramp, an inconvenience. A charley horse you bite your lip through. Sabrina, you think, between the waves of pain. Sabrina, where are you? Sabrina, come.

You are the only one home but even so, when you scream, you scream into your pillow. Smother the sound.

You get up, straddle your desk chair, and when the next pain comes you hug your arms around the back, squeeze, squeeze harder, but it is not enough. Not enough to bring you relief, to pull you up and out of the vise crushing you tighter, tighter, tighter still. When the next pain comes you bite the top slat of the chair as hard as you can, a scream coming from the back of your throat, the taste of paint and resin and pine in your mouth.

Everything you are wearing is soaked through with sweat. Your mother's old nightgown is sticking to you and you hate the feeling of the fake lace at the neck. You claw it away, claw and claw until it rips. You are half girl, half animal. When you look out the window you see the woods, and you can't articulate it, but it feels like a kind of answer to a question your body has been asking. Sabrina is waiting for you out by the old factory. Your old meeting place. Of course she is, of course.

Getting down the stairs feels impossible, but you must. Your survival depends on it. Just get to Sabrina and everything else will be fine.

You wait until the next pain comes and goes before you start down the stairs. You grip the banister like a person trying to stay steady on the deck of a ship in a storm.

The woods, the woods, the voice in your head says. In your delirium you decide it is your mother's voice. It seems perfectly reasonable, in this moment when your body wants to destroy itself from the inside out, that your mother would counsel you. That when you find yourself alone, with death crouched in the corners of the room, that your mother would return to you. Sabrina will be there, waiting in the ruins of the old factory. Her voice comes to you too. *You must be confused, Annabelle. Did you forget I said to meet here?*

As you cross the foyer there is a gush from between your legs. You haven't turned on the light but can feel it over your thighs. For a moment you have the presence of mind to be mortified. Have you peed yourself? But this liquid doesn't have the sharp acrid tang of piss, Instead, the liquid smells slightly sweet. You imagine an organ within you bursting, releasing its contents, something you need now just draining away.

You hobble down the hall. Another pain in the kitchen, and in its grip everything goes unfamiliar. The copper pot that's been on the stove your whole life, the crock full of wooden spoons, the old farm table that your grandfather built, all of it alien to you, threatening and strange in the darkness. You stop, decide you need water, something to replace whatever is spilling from you, this liquid your body is wringing out. You drink from the tap, huge gulps that dribble down your cheeks, splash across your chest. There's a little moonlight coming in through the back window, putting a shine on the spigot. It will have to be enough to guide you, there's no time to find the flashlight.

The rush of cold air from the back door feels good against your fever-hot skin, but with the next pain the water you drank comes back up, mixed with a stream of bile. Your body is at fault. Nothing can touch you, enter you, without being tainted. You transform the normal into the wrong.

You stagger to the woods, the moon enough to catch the white sand of the walking path. The pain has been seizing the muscles of your outer thighs so you feel as though you've run a tremendous distance, but you know you must push on. You make it to the first line of trees when another pain takes you. You bend, hug yourself, scream into the dark.

It takes you longer than ever before, longer than when you were a little girl making your way here the first time behind your mother. Your mother talking easily as you walked. You and Sabrina behind her with your fists stuffed with wildflowers and kindling, pine cones and stones rattling in your pockets.

Another belt of pain that drives any thought from your mind. You squat, bite down on a stick and it cracks between your teeth.

Clouds. There must be clouds because the moonlight is gone. You can't make out the stones of the factory walls. You can't see your feet or even your own hands held out in front of your face. The world has shrunk down so that it holds nothing but pain and darkness, pain and darkness.

You whimper, tears hot on your cheeks. Sabrina, please. PLEASE.

Something shrieks from the woods as pressure builds low in your guts, a feeling that, you think with indignity, is not unlike the urge to shit.

The sound is unlike any woods animal you know, not a fox, not an owl seizing its prey. It must be the devil taunting you, shrieking louder, longer. Please just make it stop, you think, please please please. Spare me.

You crouch low, the pressure now building to a fierce, fiery burn, and as you set your jaw you realize that all along the noise has been coming from within you, and you let out the loudest shriek yet, filling the woods with your furious, savage screams.

CALLIE

Annabelle is waiting for Callie on her front step when Callie pulls up.

Callie doesn't notice when it happened. Sometime between the library parking lot and pulling up to the house, she's stopped thinking of her as *Iris*. Because it was Annabelle who stood before her, the girl from the yearbook, the girl with the tidy room—with that plea in her eyes.

"Please, come in," Annabelle tells her, and whatever traces of emotion that Callie had witnessed back in the library parking lot are gone. Callie can see it now, the glimmer of the Annabelle who had been flinty and ruthless enough to get herself here. To remake herself.

Annabelle makes them each a cup of tea. The cups rattle in their saucers as Annabelle carries them from the kitchen. The porcelain is thin, thin enough that you could probably bite through it.

Annabelle smiles weakly as she sets the cup and saucer down in front of Callie. The living room gets a bath of natural light and it picks up the colors in the rugs and throws. Annabelle—or whoever decorated the room—has good taste. On the walls, framed snapshots of the kids.

"I took those," Annabelle says, when she sees Callie looking. "Every summer we spend a week in the Finger Lakes. Ben's parents have a place there."

"Yearbook committee."

Annabelle frowns. "Excuse me?"

"You liked photography when you were younger, right?"

Annabelle's mouth hangs open a moment before she remembers herself. "That's right."

Callie clears her throat. "I should make this clear right off the bat. I'm not a private investigator. My name is Callie Hauser. I've spent many years working as a narcotics detective but as of August of last year I'm Chief of Police in Pine Lakes."

"Right," Annabelle says, and is quiet for a moment. Callie presses on.

"Back in the parking lot you asked if Sabrina had sent me. She didn't. No one in the area has seen her since the 1990s. But I've been trying to figure out what happened to her. What happened to both of you."

Annabelle raises her hands, spreads them to indicate the contents of the room. A facetious gesture that makes them both smile awkwardly, shift in their seats.

"Could I ask you some questions about Sabrina?"

Callie swipes through her phone, finds the crime scene picture of the broken bracelet. "Does this look familiar to you? It was found not far from your former home. In late winter 1991."

Annabelle presses her lips together. "It was Sabrina's. It had been our mother's. We had compromised, said we would share it. But Sabrina made it hers. She had a way of doing that."

"When was the last time you heard from Sabrina or saw her?"

Annabelle sucks in a breath between her teeth. "It would have been March 1, 1991."

Callie notes the date. One day before Baby Doe was found.

"Was she wearing the bracelet then?"

"I'm not sure. I'd think so. She almost never took it off. We fought over it. She didn't want me to have a chance to take it back."

"Can you tell me a little bit about that? The last time you saw or spoke to her?"

"She said she was going to talk to him and never came back."

Callie gets the feeling Annabelle is slipping into a code. That she is sliding into the middle of a conversation Annabelle has been having with someone else for a long time. "Who is this *him*? Can you give me a name, here?" She braces herself, a second away from learning the truth, Annabelle's and Sabrina's and her own.

Annabelle shakes her head. "I don't know his name."

Callie can't help herself, incredulous. "You don't . . . You don't know?"

"She only ever called him . . ." Annabelle looks to the ceiling, swallows. "She called him the Coyote."

It takes her a moment to understand what she's feeling. Crestfallen, and strangely relieved. "Do you know why?"

"No. Only that . . . no. I don't."

Callie's mind teems with questions. Why didn't Annabelle go to the police when Sabrina didn't come back? When did she stop looking and leave the Pines? Slow down, she wills herself. Don't scare her off. "Okay. Can you tell me more about that? What were the circumstances around this conversation? Did she say he seemed angry or upset with her—I'm assuming we are talking about the man she was seeing, yes?"

"Someone she had been sleeping with."

Callie takes a sip of her tea. It scalds the back of her throat. "I heard a rumor that Sabrina had been with an older man. Was he older?"

"Yes. Probably in his midtwenties."

"Did she ever mention his job? Or where he lived?"

"No. She became very private once she started up with him. We used to share everything, and then . . . she wouldn't tell me anything." Again, that closed-off look on Annabelle's face.

"He drove a silver sedan. He would pick her up sometimes."

"Did you ever see him? Could you describe him for me?"

"He had brown hair, brown eyes. Medium height, maybe five eight, five nine. He smoked cigarettes."

"Did this man have any tattoos or birthmarks, any scars or piercings that would stand out?" She thinks of Fauver. She can't be sure when he got the snake tattoo but the ink is pretty faded, the image weathered with his skin.

"I don't think so. I only saw him twice. Once in his car and once at the Cranberry Festival. He was there with the chief of the police department, a bunch of other men. He was from the area, I think. He knew the roads."

Callie sits up. Frank was named chief in 1989. "But you don't know if he was a cop?"

Annabelle shakes her head. Callie thinks of Jane's warning. Frank would never turn on one of his guys. Did Frank *know* who the father of Baby Doe is? Is he protecting someone?

"Was he with anyone else you recognized?"

"No, I didn't know them."

She ticks through the roster in her head. Could be Keegan. Maybe that's why he pretended to forget Sabrina's name when she asked him, that day they sprung the muskrats. It gives her a pang to think of him as this Coyote, but she's been doing this long enough to know. Takes all kinds. And Keegan had been so awkward when Callie asked if he knew Jenna. Keegan, who had been easier on her than everyone else.

"I have to ask you a sensitive question. Had Sabrina been pregnant? I heard some rumors to that effect as well . . . Her name came up in connection with another case from around the same time and as far as motives for her disappearance go—"

Annabelle shakes her head quickly, cuts Callie off. "She wasn't."

The atmosphere in the room has changed, become stifled and charged. She knows the answer, but still, she has to ask.

Callie leans forward, tries to make her voice as gentle as she can. "Annabelle. Were you pregnant?"

"Please!" Annabelle bangs a fist on the coffee table, then covers her face with her hands. Callie's undrunk tea sloshes over the rim of the pretty little cup. Annabelle's sleeve has ridden up and she can see a part of the scar Trent Brentwood described. Messy. Something that came back together all wrong. Annabelle swallows, her eyes watering, her chin trembling so hard Callie wonders how she's going to get the words out. "Please. Do not call me that name."

Callie waits a beat. Stares at the splotch of spilled tea on the table.

"You tapped on my car window. I was going to go home. Leave you to your knitting. You invited me here. Why?"

"She was supposed to help me! She promised. Said she would be there for all of it. She would find a doctor and be by my side and help me. And after . . . after we would raise the baby together. I wouldn't have to do any of it alone. It was going to bring us back together. Things were going to be all right again."

Tears leak down Annabelle's face. She wipes them away with the heels of her hand. Callie watches Annabelle—Iris, whoever she wants to call herself—cry. She turns to the portraits on the wall again. The boys with their salt-tousled hair and athletic shoulders. Blair with her bright-blue eyes and easy grin.

When Annabelle speaks again, her voice is a hoarse whisper. "They don't know. No one knows."

It makes sense now. Why she couldn't have gone to the police when Sabrina didn't come home. Why she ran. She must have been terrified.

"She was going to see him, he wanted to meet. And she was going to blackmail him. Demand money."

"Blackmail?"

"He was the only person I had ever been with. But apparently he used to brag to her about others. She said she would go to the police and tell them about all the underage girls he had been with."

Callie is confused for a moment, until she's not.

Annabelle seems to understand. "I just did it. Once. I got in to the car with him and that was it. I don't know why. I guess I wanted to know what she was abandoning me for. Our mother had left a few years before. Our father was . . . checked out. She was all I had. And then, I didn't even have her."

Annabelle slept with her sister's older lover out of spite? Loneliness? Curiosity? She supposed it doesn't matter now. Her own head throbs thinking about the mental gymnastics. The claustrophobia of keeping a secret for this long. And this man, this man who was juggling girls, playing them against one another. This man was Callie's father too. She has to push the fact out of her mind while she's sitting here with Annabelle, or else she's afraid she won't be able to do it, won't be able to ask the things she needs to know. She can't be the daughter and the cop, can't hold those two halves of herself together while she's in this room.

"Why did you leave the note? In the factory?"

"After . . . after I had Blair. I knew it was far-fetched, that she probably wouldn't ever see it. But I guess I just thought, I had so much. I had to try. If she was out there, I wanted to share with her. I wanted her to know I was okay. That I could take care of her."

"I see," she says. But Callie doesn't ask which *she* Annabelle means. Either answer too unbearable, too sad.

A dull pressure forms at her temples. She doesn't know what to do with this information. It had been what she wanted, but now? Now what does she do? Destroy this woman's life? Hurt her children and her husband? Or let her keep lying? How much choice does she have? Healy and Nixon hadn't been able to find a DNA match linking her to the crime, maybe they never will. Callie is the only one who knows everything. And she knows better than anyone what it means to have a secret—for years no one knew the extent of Jenna's problem, so long as Callie showed up to school with her hair brushed, her homework done, her pencils sharpened. A secret can feel like a form of control, but the secret is controlling you. And the magnitude of this secret she's uncovered here makes her head spin.

She takes a deep breath. "I want to find out what happened to Sabrina. I'd like to find a way to do that without implicating you in any way." She doesn't know if this is a promise she can keep. But she'll try to find the answers. And she won't sacrifice Annabelle to do it. She's already been through so much. Whatever she keeps from Ben and her children is her own burden to bear. None of this conversation would be admissible in court. It hasn't been recorded. She hadn't read Annabelle her rights. She doesn't have any corroborating evidence. But now she knows one half of the story, which is so much more than she had before.

Annabelle is quiet for a long time. When she speaks again her voice is barely above a whisper. "How did they find . . . who . . ."

Callie hears the words she can't make herself say, *Who found the baby?* She weighs her options. At the beginning of this case she would have told the truth, would have savored the chance at righteousness. That is was Jenna, her mother, who found the child. Jenna whose life was marred by what Annabelle did. But she knows it isn't that simple. That Annabelle, and in her own way, Jenna, were both the same. Two women doing what they felt they needed to in order to survive. And Jenna somehow finding her way to the same man, this Coyote, after all of that.

"Someone out walking," Callie says.

Annabelle watches her carefully. Another question in her eyes. Someone who keeps secrets recognizes withholding when they see it.

Callie relents. "Jenna. Your neighbor. She was out delivering papers." She won't tell Annabelle that she's Jenna's daughter. She doesn't want this visit to take on the air of a vendetta. Because even if it started that way, things have shifted now.

"Have you asked her about him?" Annabelle asks. "The Coyote. She knew him too. She tried to talk to me about it once. I couldn't do it. Maybe if I had everything would have been different. Maybe if I had let myself hear the truth . . . I don't know."

"You mean she tried to warn you about him?"

"Maybe. Maybe she did. I wasn't able to listen. I blew her off."

It makes no sense. Why would Jenna have warned Annabelle about this man, then gotten pregnant with Callie a year later?

Unless Jenna hadn't had a choice.

She hates this man, the Coyote, with every cell in her body. Realizes, with a wave of nausea, that to hate him is to hate a part of herself.

ANNABELLE

You didn't die, like you thought you would.

Instead, you rose up on shaking legs and walked through the woods. You took what you needed from the house when you knew you had to leave. Hitchhiked to the bus depot, hoping the rags in your pants would be enough to stanch the blood for the time being. Used the cash from Della to buy a ticket that trembled in your hand.

But the driver didn't even glance at you or your ticket. You could have been holding a McDonald's receipt for all he knew. He only looked at you when you hesitated too long, eyeing the empty seats, unable to choose one. Were they assigned?

Everything okay, miss? His voice snide. You managed a nod and sat, were dismayed when you looked up and saw his eyes on you in the huge panorama of the rearview mirror. You slid down in your seat—winced at the pain—and still, you were caught in that reflection. Violet rings under your eyes, the blue of a vein standing out along your neck.

You rested your head against the window, banged your skull when the bus hit a pothole. Sleep came eventually, a deep, dreamless sleep like falling into a pit.

Figuring out how to survive in your body was one matter. To find food and money and a place to sleep, all the mechanics of keeping the machinery of yourself humming. Your was mind another. For a long time, you survived on inventing stories. The ones you clung to were the ones in which everyone was okay.

Sabrina came back, heard the baby's cries, swaddled it—her—tight in a soft cloth. She had done it. Gotten the money, the apartment by the sea, the stroller. She shook the rattle and the baby laughed at the clatter of dried beans in the tube. The ocean crashed and hissed along the shore while the baby slept. Sabrina's hair salt-tangled, her face a little rounder, the hollows of her body filled up with slices of boardwalk pizza and soft serve, a sprinkle of freckles across her cheeks. More beautiful than she'd ever been. Happy.

Miss Hamilton finally put everything together, sped up the drive in her Toyota, and she knew everything there was to know, knew where to find the baby in the woods. She took it home and it became hers and the baby could name the treaties that created the map of Europe and the dates they were ratified. The baby learned about feminism and the lyrics of all of Kate Bush's songs. She could cook vegan meals and marched at protests and shopped for her clothes at vintage stores, patched the sprung knees of her jeans with leopard print fabric. The baby became so much wiser than you had ever been.

Your mother came back, lingering between the trees in her white nightgown like a ghost. Your mother wanted another start. A daughter who would heed her. Who would remain faithfully hers. They sped across the country seeking out sunlight. New Mexico, Arizona, California. Anywhere they could turn their faces up to the sky and feel warmth reaching down for them. The baby was covered in freckles. Even the soles of her feet were tan. They laid crystals in one another's palms. Had their auras read. The baby's was yellow, the color of sunshine.

The baby grew wings, like the devil, and flew away. The baby knew better than all of them how ugly life could be and decided to become the ugliest thing it could. To rule the woods as a monster. Because once you become a monster, you have nothing left in the world to be afraid of.

Or so you thought, until you built your family. Until a man smiled at you from across a café and you felt a zip of joy shiver through you, and let yourself think *more.* Until you had an orgasm for the first time. Until you heard each of your children laugh for the first time. Until a child held their arms to you from the safety of their crib and smiled up at you like you were the sun. Until you sent each one of them to kindergarten, wearing backpacks that looked too big on their small bodies. Until you woke to construction paper Valentine's cards slipped under your bedroom door, signed in Magic Marker with shaky, crooked handwriting. Until your husband cried on your shoulder when his grandmother died, because he could trust you with his pain. They all did. You kissed hurt fingers and bandaged knees. You tracked homework and nursed every hurt. It meant something, all this caring, this joy that you grew in your body and protected within the four walls of your home. A counterweight against the past, the harm you have done. All this love you created and tried to give and give and give. And that is what shocked you the most—that you never ran out, that the well always refilled itself. That you never reached the end of your feelings for this family, this world, you have made for yourself. Love wasn't scarce or conditional, as you were made to believe.

And yet. You never could tell them. You could not tell them who you had been, and how you learned exactly how precious a life was.

That night, after the police chief leaves, you cook dinner for your family and remind your son to study for his math test and fill out a form for your daughter's upcoming field trip and scour all the dishes and rub lemon along the knives to mediate the smell of garlic on the blade. You pair all the clean socks in the laundry basket and put them away, sweep the mudroom and the kitchen and the living room, take out the garbage, reline the bin. And when there is nothing left to busy yourself with, to clean or organize or dust, you sneak into each of your children's rooms to watch them sleep, the way you used to when they were small, to observe them in the perfect safety of their warm beds. After Ben climbs into bed and reads three pages of his new biography of John Adams before falling asleep, you stand in front of your bathroom mirror and take off your jewelry. The earrings he gave you after Blair was born, sapphire for her birthstone. Your wedding band and engagement ring, which leave indents in your skin. The watch for your tenth anniversary, with the mother-of-pearl face. The bracelet Kyle saved up for at the school fair last spring, little red-and-yellow seed beads in the pattern of daisies.

You need to know how it would feel, to get used to your hands bare. Bare as when everything is taken away. Bare as when you are taken away. Bare as when you are first born, as when the stories you told yourself in order to survive don't work anymore. The bag you packed one sleepless night years ago is one more fiction: You couldn't leave any of them if you tried. But you might be taken. And that is a feeling you need to make room for.

It sits uneasily, makes you jittery, restless. You feel the fabric of your world pulled taut, about to split. After you slid the notebook from under a stack of sweaters you checked the suitcase pocket for the lighter—how it still gave you a shiver to touch it after all these years, bile rising in the back of your throat—the other for the canister of film. You ran your hand along the lining of the bag once, twice, a third time, checked every crevice but it was no use. The film was gone.

Ben? But no, your husband is not the type to snoop. Your sons? You doubt they have the guile to take something of yours and not ask you about it. Blair? Would she even recognize what it is? When, though? When was the last time you even dared to open this bag, dared to acknowledge its existence? A year, at least. Who knows how long these pieces of your past have been taken or lost?

All those pictures of Sabrina you snuck while you were practicing for yearbook committee. The picture of the Coyote and his friends. You have held on to these things for so many years, the promise of evidence, the promise of seeing Sabrina's face again. And it was that possibility that kept you from developing it. You were waiting for a time when it would not hurt so much to see her, not how you used to, but as an adult, from a place of safety. You would not be able to bear the anger in her face. The hurt. She, like you, had been a girl who had seen and been through more than most at her age, and yet had so much to learn.

You hadn't promised a photo to the detective, and you felt relief in that, as you handed over the notebook and lighter. You would have sounded insane. More insane. And you hadn't told her the truth about the last time you saw the bracelet. Broken. That in your jewelry box you keep a single amber bead. It would have brought you close, too close. To the moment everything changed.

The detective had said she was not here for punishment, not here to investigate you. That she wanted to help. Even if that is true you feel it, the woods, the ever-present mineral cool, creeping into your body. The woods, the long shadows of the trees, coming for you again.

CALLIE

She heads from Annabelle's to Jane's, needs to go straight there in order to arrive on time to help while Damien leads an evening snowshoeing group for a few hours. She keeps the music off out of habit, though here she would get enough service to play anything on her phone or scan through more than three stations on the radio. In the silence she hears the clicking of the knitting needles, the unlikely perfect shapes emerging in the laps of those milky-eyed women. The bodies that remembered what their past selves had done.

She looks over to her passenger seat. Before she left, Annabelle had handed her a notebook. On the front, a jagged imperative. *SABRINA'S. KEEP OUT!!!*

"Where did you get this?" Callie had asked her.

"I took it before I left."

Callie hadn't known what to say. Annabelle shifting before her eyes. Callie had been ready to peg her as a victim, driven desperate and senseless by pain and shock. But then there's this version of Annabelle too: the Annabelle who had her wits about her enough to take this notebook, to hoard it away as evidence. The Annabelle who understood consequences. Who held on to reason.

"Is there something in here in particular I should see?" Callie had asked, avoiding all the other, thornier questions crowding her mind. *How did you do it? How did you get away, and how did you disappear?*

"The star drawing shows up twice. It's the necklace he gave her."

"Do you know why she and Billy Fauver fought about it? He said she yelled at him, that she claimed he ruined her life over a necklace."

Annabelle had blinked. "Sorry. That name. I—"

"He's still in the Pines. Runs an autobody shop." Relief surges through her. Fauver is not the Coyote. Not her father. One small mercy.

"No, I don't know why he would have said that. Sabrina said the Coyote gave it to her, but she was always taking things from him, too."

"Like what?"

"The lighter, money . . . little things. She was a magpie like that."

It makes Callie sad, the idea of this teenage girl so eager for someone's scraps. Taking whatever she could get, maybe even with the idea of provoking him. It reminds her of something Jane told her about raising toddlers when Opal was acting up one day. That they think any attention is good attention, that they don't always care about the difference between annoyance and affection so long as they've got a hold on you. And there had been other girls, according to Annabelle. "Maybe the necklace was meant for someone else?"

"Probably," Annabelle said. "I don't think they had that kind of . . . that kind of thing." Callie watched her bring a hand to her chest, where a tangle of gold necklaces, each one bearing the first initial of one of her children, lay against her skin.

Callie slid the notebook under her arm, the lighter in her pocket. It seemed like nothing, but she wasn't going to say that then. She simply promised she'd make copies and mail the original back as soon as she could.

She gets to Jane's and the house is a mess. Bowls of congealed macaroni and cheese on the kitchen island, flies buzzing over spots of spilled juice. A splatter of what might be yogurt on the floor near the dishwasher, days' worth of dishes in an unsteady pile in the sink. She files this away as more evidence: that Damien isn't able to pull his weight, that he's getting out of control. She's got the little green bag in her pocket, is waiting for the right time to show Jane that she knows, test out her theory that Luke's in on the drug game and that's why Jane hates him. Callie practices her script, knows that she has to come from a place of concern without Jane feeling like she's being condescending.

He needs help. He can't take care of you like this. You and Opal deserve him at his best. He needs to go away somewhere, needs to get better. His parents can help you. I'll move in. Whatever you need.

She can hear them all in the back bedroom, the cacophony of some tinny, musical song from one of Opal's toys, Opal pleading for something—*Mom, Mom, Mom*—Jane trying to tell Damien that they need peanut butter from the store.

"Hello!" she calls, and Opal comes running, followed by Damien. She stares at him openly. Studies his pupils. Cuts her eyes to the mess in the kitchen.

"Sorry it's a wreck," he mumbles. "I gotta run."

He slides by her and Opal tugs on her arm. Her dress is stained all over. In the hall there's a heap of dirty clothes in front of the washer.

Jane steps out of the bedroom. Callie wastes no time asking her what's going on.

"He's super busy at work, between our stuff and working for Luke. And I'm up more but just . . . the headaches have been bad this week."

Callie doesn't bother calling the lie. That Christmas is over and the nursery is dead quiet. That no one is going on many hikes in January. "Call me next time, okay? That's why I'm here."

Usually Jane would roll her eyes, come back with something snarky, but she only nods. *He's wearing you out*, Callie wants to say, feels the anger in the tightening of her jaw. "Go lie down. I've got this."

Jane doesn't argue, just lays a head on Callie's shoulder before retreating down the hall again, her fingertips grazing the walls for balance, her left foot dragging.

Callie does her best to make a game of it. She and Opal conquer Laundry Mountain, vanquish the Evil Dish Pile, and scrub the floor by sliding paper towels with their toes, dance with the Swiffer sweeper. She has to go over all of Opal's work but it keeps her busy, tires her out, and by 2:00 P.M. she's down for nap after a single bedtime story. Callie tiptoes out, shuts the door as quietly as she can. She's brought her backpack in with her, slides Sabrina's notebook onto her lap.

More than a writer, Sabrina is a doodler. She's drawn the shores of a lake. A raccoon. The doorknocker from the Riley house. The star in its circle takes up half a page.

Some pages are drawings only, without any kind of text, and she can still feel the way the pen pressed hard into the paper. Sabrina filling the white space so urgently, the indents still there thirty years later. Near the end of the notebook she finds a list, written in what must have been Sabrina's best handwriting. Not as neat as Annabelle's, but deliberate and clear.

Gentle pressure near perineum to help head pass
Push slowly
Guide shoulders
Clean airways (nose and mouth)
Slip cord over neck if wrapped around
Wrap baby in clean towel or blanket
Put baby on skin for warmth
Deliver placenta
Cut cord
Massage belly below navel (mothers)
*If not breathing, rub back or tap feet. If still not breathing do mouth to mouth (*look up mouth to mouth instructions!!!)*

Callie looks up to the ceiling, feels a lump in her throat.

Kids. They were lonely, neglected kids. Kids who couldn't google anything. She thinks of that panicky feeling she gets when she passes through the densest parts of the woods and her cell service disappears. That was their lives. It would have been the exception to be able to call for help, not the rule. And here was Sabrina, dutiful, trying to help Annabelle the best she could. She had so wanted to do this one thing right. Maybe she thought it would redeem her. Maybe she thought the baby's love, her sister's love, were the only kinds she might be able to count on.

She turns the page and finds another picture of a shoreline—the same one from the second page, the crook of a tree branch reaching toward the water from the right-hand side. Once in an entry from October and another from December. Did it mean something to her? There was no water for miles from the Riley property—she checks the map to be sure. Maybe Callie could text Annabelle a picture of the drawing and ask her if she knew what it meant.

"What's that?" She had been so absorbed she hadn't heard Jane's door open, hadn't heard her creep down the hall.

"It's Sabrina Riley's notebook."

"Holy shit. How did you get that?"

"I found Annabelle."

"You weren't going to tell me that?" Jane leans over to get a closer look at the pages. "Can't I see?"

Callie doesn't feel right letting Jane see the notebook, wonders if it is a breach of Annabelle's trust. An active investigation. But, she does need to soften Jane for what she needs to say to her before she goes. Opal asleep, Damien gone. They might not have a chance to have this conversation for a long time, if she doesn't do it now.

She hands the notebook to Jane, who flips through the pages, frowns once, flips back between the two images of the shoreline.

"Not quite the confession you might hope for, huh?"

"No, not really. Annabelle had been the one who was pregnant. She is sure Sabrina was murdered. That she was supposed to be there when Annabelle gave birth but disappeared before it happened. Apparently she was off to threaten the guy. Demand he give her money. She said he was with other young girls. Teenagers. That he used to talk about them to Sabrina, taunt her."

"She sure could pick 'em," Jane says. She gets to the page with the picture of the star, traces her fingers around the points.

"A necklace that Sabrina took from the Coyote—that's what she calls the father. They were both with him, apparently. But Annabelle doesn't even know his real name. Sabrina was always nabbing stuff from him, trinkets and whatnot."

Jane hums. "Taking whatever she could get."

Callie looks down the hall toward Opal's room. It's now or never, she thinks. "Janie. There's something we have to talk about." Callie reaches into her wallet, puts the green glassine bag on the coffee table.

"What's that?" Jane asks, but Callie can tell by her voice that she already knows.

"Opal gave it to me. She was keeping it in her room. It's the packaging that the dealers use. For drugs. But I think you know that."

"I don't know where she got that. Must have picked it up outside. That's fucked up. Here, I'll throw it away." Jane moves to pick up the bag but Callie slaps her hand over it.

"Jane."

"Callie."

"It's Damien's, isn't it?"

"No. It isn't, Cal."

"Come on, you can be straight with me. I'm not here to get him in trouble. But he needs help. If he's on this stuff . . ."

"He is *not* on anything, Callie."

"How can you be so sure? Why would your kid have this? And what business does he have with Billy Fauver, then? We're looking at him for dealing, and Opal said the snake man came to your house—he's got that black rat snake tattoo up his arm, right? She said that you and Damien fight when he shows up here. You yourself have said things are rocky between you. So now, don't play dumb with me, Jane, please. You know how this story goes. You can't have Opal growing up the way we did. He needs help."

"You're going to listen to a three-year-old? Yesterday she had a tantrum because I flushed the toilet before she could look. Callie. Please. I'm telling you. He doesn't have a drug problem."

"He does, Jane, and he can't take care of you and Opal if he's . . ."

Jane stares at Callie, her expression both irate and anguished. "It's mine! Jesus Christ, Callie! The bag is mine! You are so smart but you can be so fucking stupid sometimes."

No, Callie thinks. *Oh no.* She takes a long inhale. How did she miss it? It was something they talked about often in college. How they vowed to make their lives different from their parents', but they knew that their genes could tilt them that way. "Okay, Jane. Here's what we'll do. We'll get you help. You've been through so much. It's understandable that you'd be trying to cope—"

"You don't need to pull this therapist shit with me. I wasn't using. I'm not using."

"Then what—"

And then it snaps into clarity, and Callie has to put her head in her hands. Jane the track star. Jane the chemistry whiz. Jane isn't using. She's hardly touched the painkillers from the doctors, even on her worst days.

Jane is dealing.

"I would have told you, if you weren't the damn police chief. And I don't know. I didn't want to know what you'd think about it. I didn't want to put you in a bad position at work, with Frank . . ."

"Does Frank know?"

"No. No one but Fauver."

"Fauver? No wonder he talks to me like I'm the biggest moron he's ever met. I am! So Fauver knows, and isn't he just a paragon of trustworthiness."

"I know, he's scum. But he was working for us, in the beginning. He had the connections who could really sell. I didn't mean for it to become this big thing. I just . . . there are these mushrooms that grow here. And I had read somewhere that the Lenape used to use them as a hallucinogenic. We weren't making ends meet. Someone stole our kayaks out of the shed. Costs were going up. Opal was six months old. Covid hit. We needed something else. Something reliable. I turned the mushrooms into powder, which made them easier to store and distribute, put into baked goods. And so, I started offering what we liked to call off-the-books hikes. They became popular. Bachelor parties. Even unofficial corporate retreats, finance guys coming down from the city in these big black Range Rovers looking for this magical trip that only we could give them, eager for stories about the Jersey Devil. Then, I don't know how it happened, but some local kids got their hands on our stuff. We started dealing to people here. And demand got crazy. Everyone wanted in. People were coming by before weekends at the shore, driving here from Philly. We finally had some money. And Fauver could connect us to more people, so we cut him in. We could even save a little. I was doing something, Callie. Jesus Christ, I had some way to spend my time that wasn't wiping someone's ass or singing some dumb song or pureeing peaches or looking for the cheapest organic diaper cream online. I was dying, and then all of the sudden, I wasn't. I had this thing that everyone wanted, that I created. I felt like I belonged in my own life. I didn't feel like this . . . stranger to myself anymore."

"You're not still doing it, are you?"

Jane shakes her head. "Fauver is, but we're out."

"So the hard stuff—that's all him? Not you guys?" Jenna. Layla Hart. All these people hurt by what was in those little green bags. If Jane has had anything to do with all that . . . Callie can only feel the edge of her anger, but knows it would be enough to make her whole life split in two.

"Yeah. But I don't know who else he's working with, or where it's coming from. I promise I have nothing to do with it. I've been out since the accident. He made sure of that."

"What are you talking about?" Callie's voice is high, light, the way it gets before she starts to cry.

"Things got messy when Fauver started in on the heroin and whatever else. We didn't want to be involved, wanted to part ways with him. He wasn't ready for that."

"So Fauver ran you down? That was your accident?"

Jane shakes her head. "No. One of his guys, we think. He's not that stupid. But, I should have known something was up. He had someone pose as a buyer and I went out to meet them. And then, the next thing I know, I hear the car, and it's right there . . ."

"I'm such an idiot." Callie's head throbs. "I've been out there stopping every fucking silver and white car that I can, sending pictures up to people I know at forensics, interrogating people, and you knew? You knew! And you didn't tell me that? You said you were picking flowers. My god, Jane."

"How could I, Cal? Not without telling you everything. And shit, I wanted to. I got close. That day we went for a drive."

Callie rubs her palms into her eye sockets. So she had been right. There had been something Jane was about to say, that crackle of it in the air. It just wasn't what she thought. She is so tired of this place, of its inscrutable woods, of the wrong turns she's making at every moment, the way she feels like she's never going to get a handle on any of it: Baby Doe, Annabelle, Jenna, the squad and their hazing, and now this, with Jane and Damien and the drugs. She doesn't know who anyone is anymore. Not even herself.

Jane rubs her temples. Callie wants to wrap her in a hug, and she wants to scream. She doesn't know which impulse will win out. She stands, paces around the room while Jane watches her.

"What am I supposed to do, Janie? With my work? This is my job, finding this dealer. I go for Fauver on the heroin, he's for sure going to implicate you for the mushrooms and we can't just sweep that under the rug. It's not the same as selling narcotics but sure as shit still illegal. And both you and Damien wrapped up in this? What happens to Opal? Maybe there would be some kind of deal for turning him in but I can't guarantee that. I can't protect you and I can't know this and stay in my position, Jane. I'm totally, completely, fucked."

Jane stares straight ahead, still and grave. She whispers, "I'm so sorry, Callie."

"You asked me to come here. You must have known there was a chance I'd find out. Why did you let me take this job? Why would you bring me into all of this?"

"I needed you. I still need you."

A creak of a door from down the hall. Opal, rubbing sleep from her eyes, hair tousled, a fistful of blanket in her right hand. Like a little girl in a storybook.

"I had a bad dream," she says.

Callie is grateful for the interruption, even as it hurts to lay eyes on Opal right now. She checks her watch. "Damien should be back in forty-five minutes. As soon as he pulls up, I'm out."

She gets Opal a snack and plays with her on the living room floor, before walking her back to her bedroom. Callie can feel Jane watching her but won't look up to meet her eye. And as soon as she hears Damien in the driveway she gives Opal a hug, tucks her favorite stuffed dog under her arm, kisses her on the forehead, and leaves without saying goodbye to Jane. She glares at Damien in the driveway as he gets out of his truck and raises a hand to her, thinks of telling him off but is so overtaken by rage—at him, at Jane, at herself—that the words won't come.

She drives to Adrian's house that night. They drink wine on the porch underneath plaid blankets, watch the sun set over the water.

"I got you some new gloves for the trip. Neoprene. The good stuff."

Callie sighs, sets down her glass. "I don't know if I should go. Work just got . . . complicated."

He turns toward her but she can't meet his gaze. This was what she had been worried about, starting a relationship. She couldn't have predicted this thing with Jane and the drugs, but something else would have interfered. Some other baggage she'd drag with her. Some other way she'd let this good man down.

"Do you not want to? Or—"

"No. No, I really do. But something came up today and it's going to be . . . it's going to mean I need to shift a lot around." Jane wasn't dealing hard drugs, but in a way didn't she open the door for all of these other things to happen? Fauver seizing his opportunity to spread dirty heroin around. To kids like Layla. To people struggling, like Jenna. But, look what happened when she was merciless with Jenna the night she pulled her over. Callie had thought she was doing what was right, imposing order. But what followed was turmoil, devastation. Can she be the cop she pledged to be and turn in her best friend? Can she bear to be the one who brings Jane to disgrace, ruin? And not just Jane. There's Opal, who nearly lost her mother once already. Is Callie going to be the one who sends her away now?

Adrian sighs. "Okay. Well we're meant to leave in two days. I guess just let me know if you're going to be available." He swallows the last of his wine and heads inside without saying anything else.

She hates the way she feels alone on the porch in the fading light. Maybe that's its own kind of answer. Maybe this trip is exactly what she needs right now. Off the grid, no phones. Time in which she doesn't have to make a decision about Jane or Annabelle, doesn't have to stare at the same four walls inside her cabin, doesn't have to go through this roster of horrible deeds committed by this person who is supposedly her father. Just being with Adrian, the two of them their own little world. S'mores and sex and instant coffee, the pleasant exhaustion in her arms after an afternoon spent paddling on the river, the cathartic click and fizz of popping the cap off a beer bottle after a long day. She will empty herself, reset, come back into her life in a few days. It might be exactly what she needs to see everything straight.

When she gets home she sees it from the base of her driveway: the lump on her porch. A heap of fur. She can't see the blood yet but knows it is there. Leaking onto the floorboards. Soaking her doormat. Before she even gets out of the car she pulls up the camera app and checks the feed from today.

Even after what she just learned, she's surprised.

Surprised to see Damien sliding a tarp from the bed of his truck. Surprised to see him ease the animal onto the doormat with the same graceful patience he uses to carry a sleeping Opal from her car seat into the house. Surprised at the grim set of his mouth as he uses his knife to cut a line through the creature's belly, releasing a tide of blood.

CALLIE

The campsite is only reachable by kayak. They leave at dawn, Adrian's Subaru packed with wetsuits and wicking layers, kayaking booties, wool hats, whistles, food, headlamps, dry bags stuffed with extra clothes. She finds she likes the ritual of it all, the preparation. It feels good, applying her mind to a practical task with a clear goal, versus the mess of Jane and the drugs, of Annabelle and her confession. It strikes her, as they pack, that she's never really had a hobby as an adult. As a child there had been piano, but she gave it up when Jenna stopped showing up at her recitals, and by then keeping the house up and making sure Jenna didn't pass out with the stove on more or less edged out any hobbies anyway.

And then college, work, all about getting ahead, about being the best and the sharpest, edging free time, pleasure, out of her life. She had been so focused on survival, on keeping everything together from such a young age, she never learned: Life didn't have to be a grim, gray slog. It didn't all have to be so hard all the time.

She looks over as he drives. He got up before she did to make them breakfast sandwiches and wrap them in tin foil, eggs on English muffins with melted cheese and a generous spread of pesto. A thermos full of French press coffee. She teases him about this, how particular he can be, but really she loves the way he cooks with care, with joy.

Or maybe what she loves is him, she realizes. And even though it scares the shit out of her, she can't help but smile. He is the one solid thing in her life.

"What? What's that look for?" But he slides a hand over her thigh, squeezes, like he knows. Like he's thinking the same thing.

Just say it, Hauser, she tells herself. *Tell him.*

She's distracted by a buzz from her pocket. Jane. Callie, we need to talk. Please, please call me back.

Jane had called her twice before 6:00 A.M. Callie let it go to voicemail both times, even as she felt that tick of worry, same as the night she heard Fauver knock on her door. Something is wrong. But she can't talk to Jane. Not until she sorts out what she's going to do.

She turns her phone off and shuts it in Adrian's glove compartment as they pull up to the boat launch. He looks at her with approval. "Look at you, committing to a weekend in nature."

"I need the break." She hasn't told him the details about Jane, or anything about Baby Doe—only that she's been looking into a cold case, that it's been getting under her skin. He asked her how the drug case was going and she only shook her head. "And who says anything about committing to nature. I'm committing to being shacked up with a hot guy all weekend. Nature be damned."

He smiles, leans over, and plants a kiss on her neck, precise and firm and that she feels between her legs.

"You're really gonna make me kayak for two hours to get more of that?"

"Yup."

"Ah, fuck you."

"Eventually."

She reaches a hand underneath his jacket, under his shirt, to the bare skin and taut muscles of his stomach, desire crackling through her.

They get the boats in the water, and as they push off a shiver runs through Callie, despite all the gear. The cold radiates off the river, presses against the place where her neck meets her hair. Adrian told her the rule for winter paddling was dress to swim. The surface is flat and easy, but still, she can't help but taste the cold in her mouth, imagine the plunge.

She warms up as they get moving, and the work of paddling feels good, the freedom of pulling out and navigating the bend, the car disappearing behind them. She looks around at the winter-stilled forest and thinks that there is a part of her that likes this place. But since the fight with Jane she's also been thinking about what it would be like to leave. She only rents her cabin on a monthly basis. She could try to get her old job back. Get a new apartment, finally get all of her boxes out of storage. Jane is getting better, maybe as good as she'll ever be.

And she would forget about the Baby Doe case. Forget her own connection to it, allow the question of her paternity to go dormant again, the way it was for so long. Let Annabelle live her life. Tell her she's sorry, but she doesn't know what happened to Sabrina, that they don't have enough to go on. A broken bracelet, an old lighter, a hunch. Especially not without the resources she's used to. Sometimes it is impossible to find the end of a story like that. Some cases just go that way, even though it hurts to admit as much. She won't look for her father, this faceless man who cast such a shadow over so many lives. For once in her life, she doesn't want the answers. Doesn't want to know what she might have inherited from him, if they share any mannerisms, if she would look into his eyes and see her own staring back at her. Maybe it was never Jenna's unruly nature she was reacting to, with her obsession with order, but something uglier and more primal, a cruel strain encoded in her DNA, something about herself she can never run away from or change.

Adrian is the only loose end. It feels dangerous to shape her life around him. And she couldn't possibly live here in the Pines if she and Jane were—what?—not friends anymore. And if she stays here, will she be compelled to study every man of a certain age at the supermarket, wondering if perhaps his hands are the same shape as her own? If there isn't something familiar about the turn of his jaw? She'd never stop torturing herself. Adrian could come see her in North Jersey. But even as she thinks it, she knows he wouldn't. His life is here. The house on the river. His boats. Maybe he would make the trek up to see her a few times, but it would get old, the tug between two places. It wouldn't work. Though the thought of ending things feels unbearable. She's already lost too much.

As though he can feel her thinking about him, he turns and smiles at her, the laugh lines around his eyes fanning out in that way that makes him look mischievous. She paddles faster to catch up, to move her body so that she might make her thoughts go still.

The tent is humid with the heat they've created—since dinner they've already fucked twice. He laughed after she reached for him the second time—"I've barely had time to catch my breath"—but she's eager for oblivion, the way only sex can smother her ticking brain, all her thoughts pressed flat to the back of her skull.

After, she lies against him. He traces a finger around her ear.

"So, Callie Hauser, is it time we had a conversation?"

"We've had lots of conversations."

"I think you know the one I mean. The conversation about what we're doing here."

"We're having lots of sex in the woods." It isn't what she wanted to say. She wants to tell him about the feeling she had in the car on the way here. That this is the real thing. Tell him what she loves about him and have the courage to be honest and just hope he feels the same way. The snark is a habit, ugly and cowardly, the way she is with the guys at the station. Always has her hackles up.

He takes a breath. She's gone a step to far and she knows it. "Okay. I'll go first. I really like you. But I can't gauge whether this is a serious thing for you or a diversion. If I had it my way, you'd be my girlfriend. You'd keep a toothbrush in my bathroom. I'd make some space in my dresser for you to keep some things to wear so you didn't have to leave early all the time. You'd meet my friends. My sister. And we'd see how that feels. You know what? No. I know how that would feel. It would be awesome. But I get the feeling that you're not ready for that."

"Is this why you brought me out here? So I couldn't avoid your questions?" *Stop, Callie,* she thinks. *Just talk to him.* But her mouth is a step ahead of her mind. She's not going to drag this good man into her messy life, into the dark morass of her heritage. He deserves better than that.

"I'd say you're doing a pretty good job avoiding them now. Which I suppose is its own kind of answer." He shifts onto his side, and a little bit away from her.

She moves closer to him, closes the space. Takes a deep breath. "I want this. I do. But things are complicated. I don't know if I'll be able to stay at my job. Jane and I had a fight. And I don't know how to stay here without one of those two things. Jane, or a job. Because right now it's not looking like I'll have either. I . . . like . . . you too." Coward, she chastises herself. The word *like* so small. "I'm happy being with you. But I can't pin my whole life on one person."

"I'm here. I'm all in on this. I'll tell you as many times as you need to hear it."

"I know . . . but that's scary for me. Too scary."

His hand had been on her stomach. He takes it back and she can only feel the cool air rush over where his warmth had been. "So you're leaving, is what you are saying."

"No. I'm thinking about leaving. It's different."

"When were you going to tell me?"

"I've had a lot on my mind. I just wanted to enjoy this trip, to be with you."

"A last hurrah."

"No! It's not like that."

"Sure feels like it to me." He sighs, sits up. *How did you screw all that up so fast?* she thinks. He cocks his head like he's going to say something else. *Please*, she wills him. *I can't speak anymore. I only make everything worse.*

"I've gotta get some air," he says.

There's a blast of frigid night air as he unzips the tent. She watches the zipper work all the way around the edge. How careful he is to close it up completely, not let any more cold in.

When he comes back he says that he's tired, wishes her a good-night but does not touch her. She spends the next hour, two, on her back listening to the noises of the woods. She's finally about to drift off when she hears a howl, high and clear. A coyote. She puts her hand on Adrian's arm but he doesn't stir. The animal howls again, louder, and the noise makes her shiver from within the sleeping bag.

The next morning things have thawed a little. He kisses her on her cheek when she wakes, a chaste peck, tells her he's made coffee. They sit in camp chairs by the edge of the water and the silence, if a little fraught, doesn't feel awkward, or punishing, the way it had the night before. He tells her about the kayak route he has planned. That the last time he took it he saw an eagle's nest. She tells him that sounds good, but finds herself distracted. She's thinking of Sabrina's notebook, wishing she had brought it with her, but she had left it at Jane's when she stormed out after Jane's confession, and she can't bring herself to ask for it back, to talk to Jane just yet. The star drawing had looked so familiar to her, but she can't place it. A logo? A symbol from a band? Where would she have seen it before?

"Hey," he says. "You with me?"

"I—no. Sorry. It's this case." He turns from her, looks at the river with his hands on his hips. She waits for him to tell her to go. That she knows the way. She can leave the kayak with the car, find a way home.

"Tell me about it."

"It's—It's pretty upsetting. A baby was found dead in the woods. It's been unsolved for thirty years. Are you sure you want to know?"

"You can give me the basics. If it's on your mind this much maybe you need to talk about it." He sets himself in the camp chair again. "So. Let's talk."

So she does. She tells him about Jenna disappearing. About the DNA results linking her to Baby Doe. She describes finding Annabelle. The tap on her window. All the things she didn't get to tell Jane, has been holding close. She's so tired of secrets, her own and everyone else's. If he wants to be in her life he deserves to make an honest choice, to know every ugly detail.

"I don't know how to move forward with this one, how to find Sabrina, without offering up Annabelle. Without blowing her cover. And I don't want to do that. I thought I did, at first. When she was still an abstraction to me. But now? She's made a life. Has three kids. What good would come of her being punished? What does justice look like for someone like her? Even if she's tried and not convicted of anything, the disgrace, the shame . . . it would ruin her. But I also get the sense that there's something I'm not seeing about Sabrina. Something glaring and big and I just need a little more time and I could do it all—spare Annabelle, find out what happened to her sister. She's convinced he killed her. And if he did. . . . then, I'm the daughter of a murderer. The daughter of a lost mother and a very bad man."

Adrian is quiet for a long time, and she feels it coming. The same conclusion Jenna's men always made. That there is too much drama, too much damage, for them to contend with.

Adrian clears his throat. "Shit, Callie. I'm so sorry. And to think you're letting me sit here going on about eagles."

"I like hearing about the eagles. I just . . . I've never had this feeling before. Like I don't know how to do my job. That it's my job to keep people from finding out the truth. That I don't want to know the truth."

"Well, you have time to figure that out, right? It's not like you need to track someone down before they do it again, some crazy serial killer on the loose. Like you said. She's a mother. She's got a life. And as far as finding the father goes . . . Whoever he is, he's got nothing to do with you."

"Aside from fifty percent of my DNA. And I was wrong about my mom. I mean yeah, she suffered, and because of that, I suffered too. But she also survived so much and I never saw that. She had been sober and I just . . . drove her off the rails. I can't get away from this idea that I'm like *him*, whoever he is. I ruin people."

"You're not responsible for what happened to your mom. It's awful, but it's not your fault. You don't ruin things. Listen to how much you care about all of these people. You're loyal and generous to your core. You aren't bad. You can't tell yourself that."

She exhales, leans her head against his chest. He's right. There's time. What's happened to Annabelle has happened. She can try to work out Sabrina's end of the story. Time to figure out how she's going to handle this situation with Jane. Time to figure out if she can stay here, knowing what she knows, what her future might look like if she has to resign from the department. Who she might be if she doesn't have a gun and a badge and a bad guy to chase down.

They paddle all afternoon. They don't see any eagles, but the river is beautiful, placid and austere. They pass by stands of Atlantic white cedars, ghostly and ethereal, their pale bark silvery in the light, visit a place where the stream pools into a pond shaped by beavers, have the lunch he packed on the sandy banks.

That afternoon they pack up the tent. "Can't we stay?" she asks Adrian.

"Live off of the land?"

"We'd figure out the logistics."

He takes her by the shoulders. "We'll figure them out back home, too. I'm not trying to pressure you. I know your situation is complicated. Me, my work—I'm tied to the water. Tied here. My house. The university a half hour away. Sometimes it's hard for me to see outside of that, that other people have choices in their life that are still up in the air, or things that are evolving. You're the only thing that is up in the air for me. It's exciting and it's scary. And I love you."

"I'm not up in the air," she says, leans in and kisses him. In the clarity of the light it does all feel so simple.

They paddle back down the river slowly, taking in the sounds of the woods, to the flutter of birds in the trees. She feels peaceful but knows that the peace belongs to the woods, that the closer they get to the truck the more she'll feel the weight of all that's waiting for her on shore. *You have time*, she tells herself, a mantra, and tries to concentrate on the sounds of the paddles dipping into the water.

You have time, she tells herself, after they've loaded up the equipment and secured the boats, as she starts to feel the tug of her phone in the glove compartment. She bargains with herself, that she'll wait until they hit a paved road to check it.

But she breaks her promise and Adrian laughs as she releases the latch on the glove compartment. She powers her phone on and for a second it seems as though nothing has happened in her absence. No one has called her, no one has sent her a message. But then, she gets a second bar of service and the notifications flood in. She can't keep up, names flashing before her as they load—a missed call and voicemail from Healy. Four texts from Jane, three missed calls, two voicemails. She steers her attention to Jane first, because even though Callie is still furious with her, she can't help but worry.

The first text: Look, I know you're still pissed but I really need to talk to you about something. Can't be over text. Can you come by? D is out.

The second: Cal, please. I wouldn't get in touch unless it was important. It's about the case.

The third: I just realized you might be on your camping trip. But fuck, Cal. Something else came up. There's something you need to see.

The fourth message is from Healy.

We got a match on your cold case.
Making an arrest tomorrow.

Tomorrow. The message was sent yesterday. It's 3:00. Which means Annabelle was probably already arrested today.

She can barely hit send on the call, her fingers are trembling.

Healy picks up with a sing-song hello. "I was wondering when I was going to hear from you."

"Why didn't you tell me before . . . Why didn't you warn me you had DNA evidence?" She would never had made that promise to Annabelle if she had known. That promise to protect her.

His tone shifts. "Why would I need to warn you? This is good news, Hauser."

"I thought you said you didn't find any matches."

"Things change. That's why DNA works. The databases are always growing."

"I—she . . . It was my case, Healy." She knows she sounds ridiculous, petulant.

"I believe the files were with my department, had been with my department for some time now. And once her kid submitted the sample for genetic testing. . . . well, it was a slam dunk. Kid didn't opt out of anything, naturally. No one does, who has time for all that fine print? So it went into all the other public databases. And Rebecca made the match."

Callie closes her eyes, sees the photographs on Annabelle's wall. It must have been the daughter. Eighteen years old. A legal adult, she could submit her sample without needing permission from her parents.

She scrambles. "You really think you'll get a conviction? I mean, do you have enough evidence? Isn't this all a bit . . . rash?"

"Hauser, why do I feel like we have a problem here? We have conclusive DNA evidence linking Annabelle Riley to the child. She's also got a fake passport and fake birth certificate, has been going by a different name for thirty-some-odd years. We can ding her on a bunch of other charges if we feel like it. And look, my department is under a lot of pressure. We need to close cases. We need all the straight-up solves we can get. You want us to be able to go after the murderers and rapists? We need a budget for that. For a budget, we need good numbers. I won't pretend that I don't feel a little bad for the family here, okay? But she's a criminal, and what I do is put away criminals. You know how this goes."

A new idea occurs to Callie. "The DNA. Wouldn't her profile be similar to Sabrina's? How can you tell which sister gave birth to the child if a mother has an identical twin? That has to affect your case."

Healy sighs. "She already told us the baby was hers. She talked before her lawyer even showed up."

She thinks of her morning with Annabelle. How she had seemed torn: desperate to tell someone the truth, and desperate to keep her secret. Had a part of her been relieved to feel the cuffs cinch around her wrists? Been relieved to just say it? *The baby was mine.*

She can't think of anything else to say. She has no right to tell him that he's not allowed to do his job. She's the one who asked him to look into this case in the first place. But that was before . . . before she had sat in Annabelle's living room. Before she knew there had been a second sister. When she thought she was chasing down a double homicide, when she thought she would emerge from the whole process triumphant and self-righteous, carrying the banner for justice. Redeemed.

And now. Now she's ruined a woman's life. Her children's lives.

Another text from Jane when she hangs up:

I guess you've been busy. I just saw this. Another link to TikTok. *For real, Jane?* she thinks. *This, now?* But then her eyes focus on the title of the video. *Cold Case, Mother Abandoned Infant: SOLVED!*

The user is Rebecca Nixon.

She didn't, she wouldn't. "No," she says out loud. "No no no no no."

"What's wrong?" Adrian asks. He pulls over, leans across the console. She hits play on the video, a wave of nausea already rising from her gut, sweat prickling at her hairline.

Rebecca claps her hands together. She's got her nails done to match her lipstick. Crimson. The video has already gotten over 500,000 views.

Do I have one for you all today. A monster was walking free among us. A monster who murdered her newborn child. I have conclusive DNA evidence that a woman abandoned her baby to the elements and has been living as the perfect mother up in Westchester, New York.

This case has gone unsolved for over thirty years. And now, with the power of technology, I've blown it wide open. The authorities made their arrest of the suspect this morning. I will be cooperating in any way I can to bring justice to this life lost too soon.

By the time she finishes watching the video it has ten thousand more views. Callie watches it again, and it's got fifteen thousand more. Nixon didn't give Annabelle's name, but it's been leaked in the comments. Callie had promised discretion and now the whole world knows.

The commenters are feverish, dogs snapping at the smell of blood.

One of them posts Annabelle's address. Another, a link to a local news article about her volunteer work. Even her daughter's name, her husband's bowling league, the daughter's Instagram handle tagged in the comments. Callie hits *report* on the comments as fast as she can, even as she feels how futile it is. None of it can be undone.

She can't breathe. She's vaguely aware of Adrian's hand on her back. A pack of motorcycles blow by them and she's relieved for the noise, the way the sound outside the car feels exactly like the roar inside her head.

There's nothing she can do. And everything is her fault. She should know better than anyone that control is always just an illusion. That the truth always seeps out, no matter what you do to keep it close.

Part III

BLAIR

Aunt Margot drives her to school. She hadn't come over all week but Blair had been too afraid to ask her father where she was, what she had said. Was too afraid that it would mean this was their life now, that they would need to sever ties with anyone they had once loved.

And then she came down for breakfast and Margot was there in the kitchen, hugged her hard enough Blair felt it in her bones. She made Blair eat a bowl of cereal, toast for her father. Her hands were as fast and as busy as ever but there were purple circles under her eyes.

Blair's phone chimes and she winces. An email. Someone put her email address on a Reddit forum. It was taken down but not before it was screenshotted, shared, pinged from inbox to inbox, reposted on new threads, in Instagram stories, in Reels and TikToks. The true-crimers send her inquiries, thinking nothing of asking her the most personal of questions: *I read that it was your DNA profile that linked your mom to the baby. Is that true?? Hi! I'm interested in your mom's case, how is she doing? Did any of you know?? Are your parents going to get divorced?? Will you maintain a relationship with her? Did you know her real name?* And because she's eighteen, even journalists are reaching out to her. No one has to ask her father for permission to speak to her, to try to get her on the record. Their inquiries are phrased a little more delicately—*I want to understand this story from your perspective. It must be so difficult. I'd love to arrange a time to speak at your convenience.*—but the essential thrust is the same. Turn yourself inside out for us. We're all owed the truth. Hand it over.

Her family's address has been posted and in the night someone wrote the words *BABY KILLER* in red paint on their driveway. Her father has covered it with a tarp until they can get it repaved. Blair has never seen anything like the look on his face when he came in. A little shake of his head at Blair and her brothers, which they understood—don't tell her. When he sat at the kitchen table to swallow down the coffee and toast Aunt Margot forced on him, Blair was taken aback by the shock of gray hair that came through his brown overnight.

If she were to talk to any of these people, she would tell them the things that actually matter. How Blair's youngest brother, Jake, came home yesterday with his left eye swollen shut. He hadn't wanted to talk about it at first, but apparently some kid shot off his mouth about his mom going to jail and Jake shoved him against a wall. Things escalated from there. He's been suspended for the rest of the week. Her other brother, Kyle isn't eating, twelve years old and new hollows in his cheeks. None of them know how to talk to one another anymore, just pass one another silently like ghosts. Her father is on the phone all the time—with lawyers, friends, who knows who else—holding the phone in one hand, his other raking hard at his hair. She hears scraps of conversation that scare her. *Temporary insanity? Postpartum psychosis? No? Would she be tried as a minor because— You really think she should take a plea? But she says—No. I don't . . . I don't know what to believe.*

In the car with Margot she sifts through the emails as they wait at the light on Main. Some are angry, the subject lines in all caps, expletive-laden, urgent. Delete, delete, delete. It doesn't matter how fast she makes them disappear, they pop back up in a new form an hour later. The tags and the DMs and the texts. It makes her heart race, makes her ribs feel too tight in her chest.

Margot shifts next to her, her winter coat rustling. "Give me that. I'll be out front to get you at 2:45. If you need me before then borrow someone's phone or have the office call me, and I'll come get you. But take a break from these people. They don't know you, they don't know her. What they think doesn't matter."

Blair holds her phone out to Margot. She doesn't think about how she will be cut off from her friends, or how she won't be able to get in touch with Henry. She doesn't worry about checking her email to see if her early application to Columbia was accepted, or whether Sephora is having a sale she wants to know about. Those questions belong to the Before times. She just passes the little brick of steel and glass and feels the lightness when Margot takes it from her.

"There are the facts of what happened and what the internet thinks about it, which in most cases, are very different. Let's focus on the facts."

"I just want to know what's going to happen to us. To her." The words come up hard and aching, and Blair starts to cry. The tears turn into open-mouthed sobs, ugly, wracking, closer to vomiting than crying. Her body at war with itself trying to get the toxic thing out of her. Margot pulls over to the side of the road.

"Oh Blair," Margot says, wiping her eyes. "This is so hard. I'm sure it is especially for you and your brothers, your dad. We all love her so much."

"You didn't come over. I thought you were gone from us."

Margot inhales. "No. No I didn't. I needed time."

The footprints. Those little crescents of ink. "But you came back?"

"Yes," Margot says. "I . . . yes. I'm here now."

For the first time Blair is able to put words to this feeling she has. Her mother did something terrible. Everyone on the internet is saying how evil she is, how cruel. She is angry at her mother, but there's something bigger than the anger, something taken away from her.

"I don't feel like I'm allowed to love her anymore."

Margot unbuckles her seatbelt, leans over, wraps Blair in a hug that smells like orange juice and toaster waffles. But that only makes Blair cry harder. Being touched. The smells of the ordinary breakfast Margot fed Blair's cousins at her house this morning before coming over. "Listen to me. She's your mother. You are always allowed to love her. No matter what anyone says."

"But she's . . . It's so awful."

"I know we are all still sorting out the facts here, and trying to understand what happened all those years ago. But I think . . . I think the thing is, it is something that she did, but also something that happened to her. A tragedy she made, and one that she's a victim of. Does that make sense? I don't think anyone feels more pain over this than she does. She's not a monster. She was practically a kid herself."

Blair nods, looks into her lap. That's not what people on the forums say. *I don't care how old you are, you know the meaning of human life. Unless you're just sick. Unless you're broken.*

When she gets home from school Blair climbs the stairs—slowly, slowly—and makes her way down the hall to her parents' bedroom. Her mother was released today after her bond hearing, is able to be home with them until the trial. She knocks on the door but doesn't get an answer. When she creaks the door open, the room is dark, and she makes out the shape of her mother in the bed. Blair tiptoes over, lifts the covers and settles in, the way she used to as a little girl still in the grip of a bad dream. Her leg brushes against something hard: her mother's GPS ankle monitor.

She doesn't know if her mother is awake or not. "It's my fault," Blair whispers. "It's all my fault." Her mother has deep purple circles under her eyes. She looks older and smaller than she did just a few days before.

Iris's hand finds Blair's wrist, circles it. Warm and firmer than Blair could have thought.

"No," Iris says.

"I just wanted to know her. Know who she was."

"Know who?"

"The girl from the pictures." She doesn't want to go any further, to talk about the day she watched Iris moving the cairns. Not now, that it all makes such terrible, horrifying sense.

Iris pushes up onto an elbow. "The film. You have it?"

"I developed it. I'm sorry. I . . . I was worried. It scared me. Because I couldn't explain it."

"But you have the pictures?" Iris's voice sounds different. Unused. Or maybe this is what she really sounds like. Blair doesn't know what's true anymore.

"I can bring them to you?"

Iris waits a long time to respond. "Yes. Can you?"

Blair slips out of the room and takes the packet of pictures from the desk drawer where she's been hiding them. When she comes back into her parents' room, Iris inhales like she's been hit. She sits up against the pillows, pats the space next to her to indicate Blair do the same. The first photo is the one of the two girls. One in the mirror, Iris holding the camera behind.

Iris runs a tender finger along the edge of the photograph. "This is Sabrina. Until I had you, I loved her more than anyone else in the world."

Late that night, when the house is dark and silent, Blair drives back to the cairns in the woods. Her neighbors have left their Christmas lights up and they cast an uncanny glow on the street as she slips in to the car.

The construction site is quiet in the dark, all the machinery gone still. This time, she's come prepared with a trowel, the same one her mother used from their garden, and digs until she finds the metal box. She lifts the letter out, walks to the river's edge. She tears the letter into so many small pieces before dropping them into the water. She stands over them until every last pale dot of her mother's confession has disappeared.

CALLIE

Annabelle's mug shot makes Callie wince. A woman curled into herself. Lips pressed together. Eyes narrowed, glazed over with fear. This is not the woman who bent over the senior citizens and their knitting, or who presided over the PTA bake sale. Quotes from neighbors vary: *She's a good woman, I can't believe this*, to *I always knew there was something off about her*. Commenters on the articles, the forums, are more ruthless. *How could someone do this? I've been trying to conceive for five years with no luck. It makes me SICK that someone like this gets to have children. Life is not fair. The only fair thing is if she's given a lethal injection!!! UGLY BITCH, UGLY INSIDE AND OUT!!!*

Adrian makes her stop reading when she spirals this way. He can tell by the look on her face when she's been lost to the articles, the Reddit pages, the TikTok videos for too long. The internet thrives on the ugly, the lurid, the least-nuanced understanding of any given situation. She knows that, and yet. She needs to measure it, needs to know exactly how cruel the world will be, a kind of penance for what she did.

Frank stops into the office the day after the arrest.

He claps his hands. "Look at you, cracking the impossible case. Good work, Hauser. I knew you'd do well here."

"Yeah, well. I really didn't do much. Healy and his team made the solve. But Frank . . ." She figures she'll run it by him. The theories on Sabrina, now that everything is out in the open. She wants to test Jane's statement, that Frank would never rat on one of his own guys, test her theory that Frank nudged the case aside to protect one of his friends. "There's more to the story. Annabelle's sister, Sabrina. I think she was murdered. Annabelle hasn't seen or heard from her since the day before she gave birth. I went to see Annabelle. Before . . . before her arrest. She confirmed that the bracelet that was photographed in the files belonged to her sister, not to her, and Sabrina Riley had been wearing it before she disappeared."

She finds it strange that Frank doesn't react to the news, that Callie found Annabelle before Healy's team did. Just shakes his head, shrugs. "So the girl lost it. By all accounts, she was careless. Reckless. It's a coincidence, not evidence. I'd think you would know that difference better than anyone." In the bullpen a phone rings. Frank cocks his head.

"Third call since I've walked in. Press?"

"Yeah." Healy has promised Callie that there's no need at this point to release her name as a relative of Baby Doe, and yet she's been living in fear of a leak. She pushes the thought aside. "Della's telling them that we'll make a statement once we have more information, that they can call Healy's people if they want more info. Reporters, and also assholes pretending to be reporters trying to dig up some details to post on their YouTube or whatever. But back to Sabrina . . . This bracelet was precious to them. They fought about it. It had belonged to their mother . . . I just don't think she'd lose it."

"Another head case, that one."

Callie grits her teeth. She hasn't seen this side of Frank before, blithe and dismissive. The phrase *head case* rankles her and it takes effort to keep her tone measured. "I don't think we can just call them all crazy, Frank. I think Sabrina Riley was murdered. I have a notebook of hers, new evidence . . ."

Frank slaps his hands against her desk.

"Hauser. You've got to focus. We have real problems to solve in this department. The ongoing drug crisis in this community. People need you to lead. Not chase down some high-flying fantasy about a thirty-year-old supposed murder case that you'll never be able to solve. But this drug thing? It is affecting real people. Right now."

A few weeks ago Callie might have felt mortified. The dressing down, the office door open, anyone able to hear. Instead, she feels angry. This is her office, her job, her case.

"Frank, I appreciate all of the guidance you've been giving me, and your passion for what you do. But with all due respect, I have a lot of work right now, so if you'll excuse me, I'm going to do this job the way I see fit. Maybe you should check in with your family. See what help you can offer them. God knows they need it." She hadn't meant to raise her voice, doesn't realize how loud she's spoken until she notices the way everyone out in the bullpen has gone still, listening.

"Yes Chief," Frank says, his voice low, blue eyes bright with anger.

Callie punts the reporters over to Healy's office, but that doesn't stop them from contacting Frank, who is more than happy to go on the record. *This one has been needling me for a long time. When you're in this job as long as I've been, there are cases you just can't get out of your mind. I'm very glad that we've gotten to the bottom of this one, that justice will finally be served, and that woman appropriately punished for what she's done. This has haunted my community for decades and this isn't who we are.* But he doesn't say anything about the drugs, doesn't text her with questions or advice, doesn't stop into the station unannounced.

Callie can't beat the sickening, constant pull of dread. Adrian makes sure she eats. Talks her into going for long walks without her phone. It's about bearing witness, she tries to tell him. She has to suffer along with Annabelle. It helps with the guilt that makes her breath go shallow, that wakes her in the night like an ache.

All the while, Jane keeps calling, leaving voicemails. Her messages are low, hushed, strained. Callie wonders if she's not lying about being on drugs—there's a hunted, paranoid tilt to her voice. It's always the same thing. *We need to talk. Call me please.* Callie's glad to be staying at Adrian's, glad for his cooking, his arm around her at the end of the day. And glad Jane doesn't know his last name, where he lives, so that Callie doesn't have to face her. And Jane wouldn't dare come talk to Callie in the station. Because in a way that she can't understand, underneath her anger toward Jane burns a hot, bright shame. They vowed to always stick together, and she wonders what those vows mean. They aren't codified in front of a group of people, made official by certificates and legal documents, like a marriage, but surely they matter, scaffold a life in some of the same ways. And now Callie has broken it. Or maybe Jane did. She's not sure.

Three weeks after their confrontation, Frank breaks his silence, calls her on her day off. She's at Adrian's, reading a book on the sofa, trying to distract herself while he's doing a site visit with a group of his students. She lets the phone ring twice, three times, before she picks it up. At first it had been a relief to have Frank off her back, but the more she thinks about it, the more she needs him. Not with her job, but with Jane and Damien and Opal. Callie needs to find a way to get each of them the help they need, and she doesn't feel like she can do it alone.

"We've got a scene out here. Pine bough bags. There's something else you should see." He describes where to park and how to take the trail into the woods. Callie looks at the map, wishes she could get him to drop a pin, but Frank says she's breaking up—bad service, as usual—and that she'll find him if she follows his instructions. It's not far from Jane and Damien's base camp, the land that's been in Frank's family for centuries. Maybe half a mile from the little cabin where they keep their paperwork and safety kits for their trips.

It could be a coincidence, but she thinks not. Jane might have been telling the truth about being out of the game, but there are factors outside her control. Even if she wouldn't have wanted to get involved in the narcotics it could have been more complicated than that. Fauver blackmailing them. Or all those hospital bills to pay.

She grits her teeth, gets hot all over. Before she can change her mind she writes a text and sends it to Jane. Frank just called me out to a scene, right near your cabin. You said you were done. Is that the truth?

She's surprised that Frank would call her after she dressed him down, but it occurs to her that maybe he's found something linking the drugs to Jane and Damien. That's why he wouldn't call it in to anyone at the station, why he's getting in touch with her directly. Of course he doesn't want to text her—sensitive information. They'll want to step lightly. Maybe he has a hunch and wants to know what she knows. She'll come clean, tell him everything that Jane confessed to. Then they can make a plan for how to help Opal, make sure she's safe. They'll figure out how to handle Fauver, get Jane to turn herself in, make sure she has a good lawyer, get Damien clean if he's using.

And then she'll resign. Just like all the guys said. *Won't even make it a year.*

She feels a heaviness at the base of her spine. So many parts of her life ending. She doesn't know who she will be on the other side of what she's about to do. But that will be a project for the next year, two, three. Figuring out who she is without Jane. Without her badge and gun.

She spots Frank's car at the turnoff. He warned her she would have to go the rest of the way on foot, take a narrow, sandy trail through the trees, that she might lose the trail in some spots where the understory was choked with huckleberry but to look for the water. It's out by a sinkhole—the blue water bright between the trees. She pictures Adrian's map, all those blue dots in the woods, shivers. *And those are only the ones we know about.*

She hears him before she sees him, twigs snapping underneath his feet and he shifts his stance. A nervous pace. The water ahead the most beautiful, beckoning blue.

"Hey, Frank," she calls out.

But it's Damien who steps out from behind the cedar.

Her heartbeat goes loud in her ears. *This isn't right.*

"Where's your dad? He called me out here."

"He's going to be a minute."

Damien looks edgy, hair mussed, shoulders high. She doesn't understand what's going on, why he would be here instead of Frank, but she's so tired of subterfuge, of secrets. Better to just get everything out in the open. "Look, Damien. I know everything. Jane must have told you that. I know about the drugs. I was going to come here, talk to your dad, tell him what I know, find a way to get you guys some help. So if he's not here, I'm leaving. I'm going to find him, and we'll figure out what to do. For Opal. For the sake of your little girl."

Damien goes still, anger flaring in his eyes. "Don't you dare come here and judge us, judge me. You think you know what's best for Opal? For Jane? For me? That's your problem, you know? You think you are smarter than everyone. You know I would do, will do, anything for my family, right? And look at you. Look who's talking."

"What about me?"

"You push everyone away. You have no relationship with your family. No partner, no kids. None of the guys in the department can stand you. And now you've lost Jane."

Her fury crests, gets the better of her. "Oh, fuck you, Damien. She was going to leave you, before the accident, you know that? And besides, you think I'm going to take criticism from a sociopath who has been leaving dead animals on my porch?"

It gives her a hit of pleasure, to see him look taken aback.

"I don't know what you're talking about," he says.

"I have it on video. Luke was right. He was ribbing you about the drugs, wasn't he? He was baiting you in front of me that night at your house. That's what he meant when he asked about the last lie you told."

Damien shoves his hands in his pockets, kicks at a rock, smiles a private little smile to himself that puts Callie on edge. "Did you know that Luke was a cop? Did you find that out too, in your little investigations? I know you've been keeping Janie in the loop. But even she doesn't know that one. Good old family secret."

Her mind falters for a second before she catches up. Luke? A cop?

An internal investigation, Lynne Hamilton had said. *There were rumors that Sabrina was with an officer.* It all snaps into clarity: the lighter in the glove compartment of her car, the one Annabelle gave her. Same heft and shine as the one he used to smoke in the driveway all those months ago. But she makes the split-second decision to feign ignorance. Wants to see what Damien will say, waits for him to fill in the blanks. "What's that got to do with anything?"

"It didn't last long. He was always fucking up people a little too much when he'd arrest them. There was a lawsuit. Or he'd use it as a way to meet girls."

He gives her a meaningful look.

What else had Annabelle said about the Coyote? Brown eyes, dark hair.

And Layla. *He's not dealing. He hates it when I'm high.*

Luke was the Coyote. And Damien has known all along.

Luke is her father.

The woods around them are so very still, none of the creatures she's learned to listen for making any sounds. She looks to the water to her left. That tree. Crooked, pointing like a finger out to the water.

She knows that tree. It's Sabrina Riley's drawing.

A shiver works its way through her. She takes a step backward toward the trail, hoping he won't register it, and slides her hand to her hip out of habit, to where her gun usually sits when she's on duty. But he catches it, her hand landing uselessly against her jeans.

Why has he brought her out here? Why now? It's never a good thing when a man with secrets suddenly decides to start being honest. She doesn't waste any more time. She pivots hard, breaks into a run.

She gets a good head start, screams through the trees. She's never screamed like this before, Callie Hauser who can keep her cool in any kind of chaos. Who's been on the chase in dark alleys, who's stared down drug runners in investigation rooms, cuffed men more than twice her weight and shoved them into the back of a police cruiser, all adrenaline and righteousness. But now, she's screaming like a woman in trouble. Screaming like a victim.

He's breathing hard behind her, feet pounding. Closer, closer, too close. She's fast, but he gets near enough to catch the sleeve of her coat, wraps his fingers are around her forearm. She growls like an animal, primal and furious, gets a punch in with her free hand, straight to the bridge of his nose. The crack of bone rings out through the woods and for a second she feels like that might be it, his grip loosening on her. But he jerks her wrist, pulls her in, and manages to get his right arm around her chest so that her back is pressed against him. The blood from his nose drips against the slick fabric of her down coat. *Tap tap tap.*

She has to keep him talking. If Annabelle and Jane have been forced to give up all their secrets, she's not going to let Damien get away with keeping his. "We're related," she spits. "Do you know that?"

"Maybe. But you don't belong to us. We don't *owe* you anything."

"Your dad agree? He helped me get this job. Why did he do that?"

"He never thought you'd go digging all this shit up. I thought he was out of his mind. But that's what happens when you get sentimental. You don't do the things that need to be done."

She takes a deep breath, forces herself to be steady, even as her stomach bottoms out. "Damien, please. We will figure it out. All of it. We can work this out together but you need to let me go."

He's considering it, she feels it, something gathering in his silence.

"Be your own person. You don't have to do what they want you to do. Frank, Luke. They don't own you. And how will you look your wife in the eye if you do this?"

She had figured an appeal about Jane would soften him, but she knows this is the wrong thing as soon as she senses the slight shift in his weight and tightening of his muscles. His arm rears back.

"No!" she screams, right before his fist connects with her temple.

The hit makes the trees blur into a dark mass. Darkness crowds the edges of her vision. The sky goes sideways and she can't hear anything over the ringing of her ears.

She comes to on the ground, cold and damp seeping through her jacket. He's standing over her, something clutched in his palm. A rock. She touches a finger to her face to assess the damage and even the slightest pressure makes her cry out. Her fingers come away slicked with blood.

She tries to stand but everything goes dim. He grabs her as she staggers, binds her hands behind her back, her ankles, and at the knees with the bungee cords she's seen him use to load their kayaks on the van, lets her fall to the ground again.

The trees multiply and blur before her eyes, the woods becoming infinite. She screams again, and the effort makes her feel like a firework has gone off inside her skull.

Once she's bound, Damien pauses to take a packet of tissues from his pocket, the same ones she's seen him use for his daughter's runny noses, and stanches the blood from her one good punch. Her mouth feels like it's filled with pebbles, she's nauseous, and the pain in her head rings through her whole body, but she wants to keep him talking for as long as possible. Wants to buy herself time, even as she feels the chill coming off the water. Tendrils of it creeping along her hairline, down her neck. Even as she feels the truth in her bones: There is no way out.

It takes a long time to put the words in order, to gather the strength to get the sentences out. "So . . . you're going to kill me? Is that really a smart move?"

"Are you kidding? Do you know how easily we can explain this? Dad is going to tell everyone you told him the job was getting to you, that you couldn't take the pressure. You were underperforming on the drug issues here, your attitude rubbed everyone the wrong way. You weren't able to come to grips with the disappearance of your mother. It was all too much." He pats her side, takes her cell phone, her car keys, tosses them into the water, where they disappear with a quickness that makes her throat tighten. "No one will even know to look for you here. Jenna got away, but she knows better than to show her face here again."

Her stomach drops. "What do you mean, she *got away*?"

"Doesn't matter. She won't dare come back now."

Jenna, alive? The thought helps her blink away the pain for a moment. Jenna is out there somewhere, free.

He crouches behind her, heaves her upright. She struggles against him, but her vision is still off, black circles dancing in front of her eyes. She tries to drive an elbow into his abdomen and the effort sends a bolt of pain through her skull.

"Why are you doing this? Why are you covering for Luke? I've watched your child. Washed your wife's hair when she was too weak to do it herself. You're going to kill me? Tell me the truth."

"Some of us wouldn't arrest our own family. Some of us have more loyalty than that. You might not like what they do, but you belong to each other."

"You knew about Annabelle's pregnancy. The baby—"

"I have nothing to do with what happened to that baby. That's all just proof that the Riley girls were fucked up without any help from us. But she was after Luke. Sabrina was. Making all kinds of threats, trying to blackmail him. Luke was worried."

He goes quiet for a moment, stares into the water.

"You know my dad never said anything about me joining him in the department. Right? Always Luke. The firstborn son, all that shit. I was too soft. I liked to be alone in the woods, liked to read. No one cared what happened to me. So I wanted to show them I could look out for the family. Luke was the screwup. Not me."

"Where is she, Damien? Where is Sabrina? What did you do to her?"

His voice is calm, cool, the same tone he might use across the dinner table or in his living room, and it's more frightening than if he were angry. "This is where they used to meet. Wasn't hard to get her out here again, when she thought he wanted to see her. Well, at least it wasn't once I got her in the truck."

The broken bracelet. She must have fought with everything she had. Had he hit her too, the way he did Callie? Was she bound? Is that why Damien's movements feel so practiced, so sure? And all the while Sabrina must have been thinking about Annabelle waiting in the house, needing her.

He brings Callie to the water, stands her at the edge. His hands are tight on her shoulders and she grimaces at the thought that he will be the last person to touch her. She looks past him, into that unlikely, beautiful, depthless blue, and knows that's where they'll find Sabrina. If anyone ever knows to search. How long does it take to drown, in water this cold, limbs bound? She could hold her breath a minute at most. Then her burning lungs would be forced to inhale water. Another minute before the airways would close up, the body trying to protect itself, a last-ditch instinct. Then, nothing. The brain, heart, and lungs all going still.

Above them a pair of birds startles from a tree, the dark arrows of their bodies reflected across the surface of the sinkhole. Damien turns his head upward, follows their path.

She has one more chance. "Don't do this. Don't do it to your wife. To your daughter."

She hears him swallow. She presses on. "Things can still be different, Damien," she says, as softly as she can.

"There's no other way. I told them about the notebook. Jane left it out one day. I recognized the charm, the tree, the water. I said there was nothing tying any of that to me, to Luke, but they said it was only a matter of time before you caught on."

They meaning Frank and Luke. The family she thought she always wanted.

She's getting woozier by the minute and her eyes are getting heavy. Each blink lasts a little longer, and she feels the pull of darkness, of rest. She lets her eyes sit closed for a second when a voice reaches her. *Let her go.*

She's sure she's imagining it in her delirium, summoned it from her mind: Jane's voice coming through the trees.

But then she hears it again, closer. Real.

"Let her go."

When she opens her eyes Jane is standing on the other side of the clearing. Her face shimmers with sweat. The hands she holds up to her husband are dirty, bleeding. She must have fallen on her way out. Still unsteady on her feet. She's got a rifle strapped to her chest. The one they kept in case of wolves, bears. Coyotes.

"Janie. Oh Christ. I'll explain. Go back to the car. Go, and I'll tell you everything later." His voice is high and panicked. "Please, Janie. Now."

Jane doesn't waver. "I said let her go, Damien." She raises the gun to her shoulder. Callie lets herself exhale. She had been holding her breath, preparing for the shock of the cold water.

"I can't—I can't do that, Janie. Now please, please, I'm begging you. Go back. Go back and I'll explain. She's going to ruin our lives."

Jane's voice is low, measured. "I know what you did. The charm. The picture in the notebook. It was all right there. And I called the state police to tell them. They'll be here in a few minutes. For now, it's just the three of us, and you need to let Callie go."

Damien takes a step backward, bringing Callie with him.

Jane's finger tightens on the trigger.

Jane's a good shot.

Used to be.

Damien's grip around her tightens. He's going to do it—push her in the water and let her body sink. Jane won't be able to save her. Or—Callie nearly vomits at the thought—he'll overpower Jane even with the gun. And she'll end up in the water too. Jane's eyes meet Callie's for a second, and Callie gives her the smallest of nods before closing her eyes.

I trust you.

The sound of gunfire cuts through the silence.

She falls to the ground and the second impact to her tender, aching skull makes everything go black.

She blinks her eyes open to the sound of screaming.

Damien is a foot away from her, grabbing at his leg. Blood soaking his pants just above the knee. She closes her eyes again until she hears Jane come closer, the ragged pull of air through her lungs. Jane still has her gun trained on Damien, relents only to unhook the bungee cord around Callie's wrists so Callie can release her bound knees and ankles.

She stands unsteadily, and she and Jane fall into one another. Callie presses her face into Jane's shoulder.

In the distance, the long, mournful wail of sirens.

"I called the state police," Jane says. "Before I started down the trail. But I knew I'd get here first. And I sure as hell didn't want to call this into the station, to Frank's cronies."

As if on cue, from the edge of the woods there's the squawk of radios. Footsteps. Shouting. Uniforms swarm them. She and Jane hold hands as they put Damien on a gurney while an officer reads him his rights. An EMT eyes the wounds on Callie's head, on Jane's shins and palms, though she shakes them off.

"I just need help getting back to the car. Now. My daughter."

Opal. Oh god. "I'll go with you," Callie says.

"We're going to need statements. From both of you. When you can, the sooner the better." The statey dips his head to Callie. "Well, you know the drill."

The cop walks with them. He offers his arm to Jane but she shakes her head, reaches for Callie.

"I'm sorry," Callie says. "I'm so, so sorry."

"Me too."

"How did you know?"

"When you texted me this morning. I was telling the truth when I said we hadn't been dealing. I thought Frank was up to something. But then Damien had said he was doing a hike that wasn't on the calendar, a private group he'd forgotten to tell me about. He wouldn't have forgotten that—in winter? When we need the cash? He said his mom was coming over and that she'd help with Opal. I left a few minutes later, strapped Opal in the car and gunned it out of there. For all I know Lorraine is sitting in my living room, wondering where the hell everyone is."

Callie wonders how much Jane knows about the other stuff. About Sabrina Riley, Luke. And whatever happened that night, to Baby Doe.

"And I had been looking at the notebook. The picture of the star finally clicked."

"What is it?" Callie asks.

"It's a charm—Sabrina must have worn it to meet Damien. He must have taken it back from her."

"Holy shit. Lorraine's bracelet." That first dinner. Callie had asked Lorraine about her charm bracelet, an attempt at making conversation. *This one is from Damien, my sweet boy. He was just a teenager. I almost fell off my chair when he gave it to me. Gold fill!*

The look between him and Luke across the table. And the tension outside.

It was all right there at the beginning.

Callie groans. "You knew he must have hurt Sabrina. You were trying to call me. You couldn't talk with him around."

"And he was always around. Or Frank, or Lorraine. You know how that family is. And he was watching me, God, like he knew something. I couldn't find a minute."

That family. *Her* family. "Jesus, Jane. I'm so sorry."

"It's not your fault. I think Lorraine is the only one who doesn't know. It's going to kill her."

"You think she's oblivious?"

"I mean, I was. It's really hard to see who your family is sometimes. Like standing too close to a painting."

"Amen."

They get to Jane's car—only then does Callie notice that they've walked the opposite way she came.

"There's an access road from one of the old cranberry bogs, so the trucks could get in. But most people don't know about it. It's not on the map. It's why I figured I'd beat the cops here. Even a gimp like me."

Opal is strapped in her car seat, her mouth open in sleep. Her hand is wrapped around a magic wand, pink with a star at the top. She knows without either of them having to say it that they are both struck by how tightly her fingers are curled around it. For a moment Callie lets herself miss her own innocence. The time when she believed the world was hers to put in order, by magic, or more recently, by the law, by her own arbitrary code of rules.

"What will I tell her, Callie? What am I going to tell my kid about this?" Jane's face goes blotchy, the way it always does when she cries. Callie hugs her as close as she can. Jane's ribs heave under her palms and Callie grips her tighter.

What would have happened had Jenna told Callie the hard truths of her life years ago? It would have hurt, and it would have spared them all so much more pain down the line.

But, if Callie had known the truth, or some of the truth, she would have warned Jane about the Caputos. There wouldn't have been Opal. Callie lets her eyes settle on Opal's cheeks, still curved with baby fat. And she's never loved anyone like she loves that little girl.

Her cousin, she realizes, with a start.

"It's going to be hard. Probably for a long time. But you'll tell her the truth. And she'll know that her mother is the strongest woman in the world."

ANNABELLE

Ben sits on the edge of the bed. He's been sleeping downstairs in the study, though by his puffy face you know *sleeping* isn't the right word.

"Iris—I mean—God. I don't even know what name to call you."

You don't know either. The name Annabelle you had gotten rid of had felt like a stain you couldn't wash off. You had tried to proceed through life with it, in the weeks after. But you couldn't bear it. Couldn't bear to be the girl that all those things happened to. If you hadn't been Annabelle, you hadn't walked away from your child. You hadn't had a twin and then lost her.

"Tell me everything," Ben says. "Please. Just tell me." You hear in his voice that you might break something so finally and irrevocably in this man you did love so much, and who had loved you so well, if you did not tell the truth.

So you do.

How you carried the child to the side of the road, waiting for headlights to find you.

The baby had stopped moving. She looked too small.

You walked and walked, dizzy and disoriented in the night.

And then, the clouds blew past the moon for a second, and just enough light came back into the sky. Enough so that you could see the bracelet a few steps in front of you. As if Sabrina was trying to warn you, take care of you, one last time.

Your mother's precious beads scattered in the dirt, the string broken.

And you knew then that Sabrina wouldn't be here in time to help you, to tell you what to do now. You stared at the beads like they might spell out a message. There was no meaning in it that you could make out, though as you stared you could feel it, her desire to help you, to be with you, the faintest tingle along your nerves. But still, the feeling didn't change anything, and she would not be there to guide you like she promised she would. You had to act, completely on your own.

This realization freed you to take stock of your situation with more clarity, the kind of inventorying of your circumstances that you had been avoiding for so long. No cars were going to come. It was the middle of the night. You were getting dizzy, lightheaded. Every inch of your body ached, your very bones ringing with pain and cold.

You were both so cold.

Her weak, mewling cries had gone quiet.

She had never opened her eyes.

You set her down, gently, gently, in the grass.

In the darkness, looking at that bracelet, aware for that moment of all that had been destroyed in your life, you felt something in you like a match struck and held up against the night. Small and subtle, but undeniable.

You picked up a single bead, held it tight in your fist, to remind you that you were real, you were still here.

Your body hurt in so many ways, and yet what you felt when you turned your back to her made you double over, made you see white stars behind your eyes. You clutched the bead harder in your palm, feeling it press against the bone.

She was already gone, you told yourself. There was nothing anyone could do. It was the only thing that let you lift your foot off the ground and take that first step in the opposite direction. She was already gone and one of you had to survive. Your gait was heavy but lit with grim purpose as you walked back to the house. Faster, and faster the closer you got, even as each step made you want to cry out. Even as you felt every cell in your body straining back toward that place in the grass.

It was like everyone kept telling you. One of you had to get out. Had to live.

Ben wraps his arms around you. Hugs you hard, as though he is trying to save you from some immediate physical danger.

"Maybe I could go by Anna," you whisper. Because your life has broken open yet again. Because you will need to answer for who you had been and what you have done. Because here you are, starting over once more.

CALLIE

Callie is released from the hospital with a concussion diagnosis and a few stitches. Adrian picks her up. Brings her soup in bed. Cancels his classes to sit with her while she sleeps. She dreams of Jenna calling her name. Calling and calling and calling, but Callie never finds her. Just hears the echo of her voice.

Jane visits and Callie tells her everything else she knows while they sit together on the front porch. Tells her that she is a half sibling to Baby Doe.

Jane stares at her for a long time. "Maybe that's why I liked Damien. He reminded me of you."

Callie raises her eyebrows.

"Joking. You're nothing like any of them." Her smile drops. "Thank god."

Frank was arrested the day before, charged for accessory to murder for his role in the attempt on Callie. Nothing, though, on Luke. For all Callie knows he's still ranging through the woods with girls like Layla. Girls like the one Jenna had been. Callie has taken a leave of absence from the station. Jimmy Nichols has been named interim chief of police. *Job's all yours,* Callie thought, when she heard the news.

Jane turns and looks toward the river, which sparkles in the winter light. "So where did your last name come from? It's not Jenna's last name. She said she gave you your dad's name, right? But obviously that's not true."

"I don't know. She was so young. It could have been anything. Someone in a band she liked. Plucked out of a hat."

"I'm going to google it," Jane proclaims. "Google knows everything."

"Hauser Pine Barrens," Jane says as she types, and Callie rolls her eyes. Jane scrolls and scrolls, her brow furrowed. She looks at Callie, her cheeks sucked in.

"What? Are there other criminals I'm related to? Please don't tell me."

Jane hands Callie her phone without a word. Her browser is open to a blog post from a hiker about a route through a place called Hauser Hollow.

Rumor has it Hauser Hollow was once home to Quakers who fled the strict rules of their communities and came out to the Pines to live their own way. There used to be settlements here, but they're gone now. What stands in its place is an old hunting cabin, restored and kept up. There's a sign claiming it is private property but I've never seen anyone here, though a buddy of mine said he has seen buck skins stretched for scraping outside.

She sits up. "It's real?" Callie asks.

"What do you mean?"

"My mom used to talk about this hunting cabin she'd spend time in when she was a kid. Her family used to keep a watch out for the Jersey Devil a hundred years ago. I always figured it was BS."

Callie stands up.

"Cal. What are you doing? I know that look. I don't like this look on your face. I'm supposed to be taking care of you."

"I'm going. I'll be back."

She leans over and kisses Jane on top of her head and takes the front steps in a leap.

The hiker's blog post gives instructions on where to park, warns about the difficulty of finding the hollow and how easy it is to lose the trail. *Don't mess with the woods out there. You'll never find your way out if you wander off.*

She takes a long breath in when she pulls into the little clearing alongside the road where the trail starts. Callie's brought her water bottle and a granola bar that had been in her glove compartment, takes screenshots of the hiker's instructions for finding Hauser Hollow in case she loses service.

The sugar sand trail had once been a carriage route through the pines, but now it's choked with understory, dense and inhospitable. It's only five miles to the cabin from where she parked her Jeep, but progress is slow, despite feeling like a furnace is blazing in her chest.

She stops to look for her first landmark, the hull of a wooden boat that had been hauled out of the river, dragged here for who knows what reason. It feels like it's taking too long, that she should have passed it by now. She starts to feel dizzy, panicked. Would she know the way back if she wanted to? She spins in a circle and can't remember if the fallen tree had been on her left or her right when she came out. She turns back slowly, squinting until—there!—she finds the blurred shape that she hopes is the hull. Her feet are aching and blistered, her mouth feels dry despite the water she drank, and yet she plunges forward, because that's all there's left to do. She needs to keep moving or else the sweat against her skin will start to go cold.

She marches most of the way with her head down, looking for roots or rocks that could trip her, but when she lifts her face to the sky now she sees a slight widening of the trees. Open space ahead. And then she smells it: chimney smoke, cutting through the scent of wind-chilled pine.

One of the reasons Callie never believed the stories about this place was that it seemed too lovely to be true. Too much like a fairytale. A secret house tucked deep into the woods.

The hunting cabin looks more weathered in person than it did in the photos, the logs battered and bleached, but the door is painted a bright, glossy red that looks fresh—the same color as the front door to Jenna's house. She stands on the porch and inhales. Knocks once, softly, worried all of the sudden that she is wrong. That someone is here but it isn't her mother.

But then the door swings open and Jenna stands in front of her, wearing an old wool sweater. Her eyes are clear and bright and alert, her pupils normal. Not the dark holes of someone lost to drugs. Not the bleary look of someone on a bender.

"You don't have to knock. This is yours, too." Jenna's voice is wry but Callie sees something tender, gentle, in her face. "Come on. If you've found me here it probably means we've got a lot of shit to work through."

The door swings open wide and Callie follows her mother in.

Inside the cabin is tidy and spare, with a single stone fireplace and worn but comfortable-looking armchairs, a sofa, a sliver of a kitchenette.

"I started coming out here when I first got sober. Walk like that makes it pretty hard to get booze out here."

"Does Steve know that?" Seems like he would have mentioned it to Callie if he did.

"You talked to Steve? I owe him a call. Poor guy probably thinks I fell off the wagon."

"Well . . ."

Jenna waves her hand. "I haven't touched anything since that night, I want you to know."

"What is this place?"

"It's been in our family a long time. My mother used to take me out here, before she got sick. Almost every weekend. This land has been ours for hundreds of years, on her side."

"I know. But I didn't believe you until today."

"Looks like you figured it out okay."

"I figured out a few things. A little late."

Jenna watches her, and when Callie realizes she's not going to say anything she continues.

"Your bag was found on the Batona Trail. That's twenty miles from here."

"Well I probably walked twenty miles here, but not from there. Damien knocking on my door, saying he wanted to talk to me about something. I know what that means in that family. Nothing good ever came from a Caputo telling you they wanted a talk."

"How did you get away from him?" Callie can't picture it. Jenna fresh off a bender outpacing Damien the woodsman? Doesn't make sense.

"That boy thinks he knows the woods. Maybe he does. But not like me. I knew as long as I was here I was safe from them."

"So the drugs in your bag . . ."

"Drugs?" Jenna snorts. "That's a nice touch. No, you know me. Only ever had one true love."

So that had been Damien too. Planted the drugs, placed the call to Fauver, knowing the assumptions Callie would make.

"I found your chip. From AA. I'm sorry I didn't believe you, about being sober."

"Well, hard to believe a drunk person about that."

"What made you relapse? Did something happen?"

Jenna sighs. "I ran into Lorraine at the store. Clickety clacking her big bracelet, hair perfectly done. She told me you were having dinner with them. Made a big show of pointing out the mascarpone for the tiramisu she was making. Said she knew how much you liked it. And I realized . . . I didn't know that about you. That there was just a lot I didn't know."

It's the shame of my life that you've become one of them. It was the last thing Jenna said to Callie, and it hits differently now that she knows the facts. Jenna had been ashamed that the Caputos claimed Callie, that it looked like she was more theirs than Jenna's.

"Does Lorraine know? About you and Luke? About . . . me?"

"Ah. She knows. In her way. I don't think any of them ever really tell her a goddamned thing. But she's not stupid."

"Why didn't you tell me?"

Jenna looks around the room for a minute, long enough that Callie thinks she might not answer her. “I didn’t want to tell you at first, because it was painful. And then when you got older, I didn’t want to tell you, because I knew you’d choose them. Stable jobs, pillars of the community. I mean, look at you. Chief of fucking Police. I guess you chose them anyway.”

“And . . . Baby Doe. There was a test done, Mom, and they found out that . . .”

“Luke’s too. With Annabelle.”

“You knew that too?”

Jenna clears her throat, looks up into the corner of the room for a moment. “He used to come pick me up, when my mom first got sick and my dad was driving her to treatments and I was alone a lot. Those were his cop days. He’d put on the siren in his patrol car, say stupid shit through the PA system to make me laugh.” Jenna shakes her head, lets out a sigh. “I was young. I thought, hey, this guy is giving me attention, I thought it would give me something to write songs about. How stupid is that? But that’s what you’re taught, when you’re that age, especially back then. The thing you write about is love, a guy. And none of that had happened to me yet.”

It breaks Callie’s heart. Because it was so true. Somewhere along the line that was what girls learned. Experience meant men. They had the keys to the rest of your life.

“When did you know about Annabelle?”

“That she was pregnant? I heard Miss Hamilton, the history teacher, talking to the guidance counselor. I was there, waiting around in the hall outside the office, I was in trouble for cutting class. Anyway, she was saying something like, maybe she had it all wrong, but that she wondered . . .”

So Hamilton had her suspicions. No wonder she didn’t want to mention it to Callie when she visited her that day at the school. Not when she knew how the story turned out. Hamilton was trying to protect Annabelle after the fact, because she failed her when it counted.

“What did the guidance counselor say?”

“That unless they had proof, or Annabelle told them something, there was nothing they could do. Not like they could take her to the doctor or make her lift up one of those big sweatshirts she had started wearing."

"But how did you know she had been with Luke?"

"He told me about it. He and I met first. He picked me up that same afternoon. He was always doing that, playing one girl off another. I was fifteen, the first time."

She winces. Fifteen years old. Callie, in all the ways she was strict with herself, had never so much kissed a boy then.

"Jesus, Mom. But then why . . . if you knew about Annabelle, did you get back together with him?"

"Get back with him," Jenna says, her mouth puckered like she's bitten into something sour.

A chill works its way up Callie's spine. She's keenly aware of the quietness around them, no sound but the occasional crackle of the logs in the fireplace. "Mom?"

"Like I said. Never a good thing when anyone in that family says they want to talk." Jenna tries to manage a smile that reminds her of the way Annabelle tried to make the mood light in her living room. "But. I thought, I don't know. That I would be good at it. Being a mother. I thought it might make me become good enough. We know how that worked out."

"You went through a lot. It must have been really, really hard."

Jenna shrugs, uncomfortable. "That's life, right?" Jenna reaches out and traces the air just over Callie's stitches. "What happened here?"

"Damien happened." She isn't sure she can get into it now, the whole thing. The water. How close it had come. "He's been arrested. Confessed to the murder of Sabrina Riley."

Jenna nods. "I figured it was one of them."

"And Annabelle Riley has been arrested in connection with the Baby Doe case. It's causing something of a sensation online."

"They found Annabelle Riley? What was she doing? Circus performer? No, she was so smart. Professor? Astronaut?"

"She's a mother. Married. Runs the PTA, volunteers. It's part of the reason the media is so into her case. It makes for good headlines. Perfect Mom Hiding Ugly Secret. All that bullshit."

Jenna presses her lips together. "So she's normal. Well. That's good too. Good for her."

"A grand jury decided she's going to be charged with murder. She's out on bail but they've set a trial date for a few months from now."

Jenna's lip quivers. "Damn it," she says, and wipes her eyes. "We were all just kids. And those boys had all this protection. They were untouchable. I tried to tell Frank at the station, about Luke. The morning I went down there after I found the baby. I told him the truth. And he made it seem like I could get in trouble. He said it would be easy enough to tell everyone I was the suspect. That the baby had been mine. It sounds ridiculous now. But how was I supposed to know?"

"I'm so sorry, Mom."

"It's not like now. Now there's Twitter and YouTube and blogs and TikTok and all these ways you can tell the world that something happened to you, that someone is bad. Me? I was just a girl in a police station in the woods. Who cared what I knew? Who cared what happened to me?"

Callie has been so caught in the cesspools of the internet, reading all of the comments about Annabelle, that she forgot that it could be used this way too. A form of power, a megaphone. "No one could blame you."

"She has kids? Annabelle does?"

"A daughter and two sons. Teenagers."

"And he's out there with his business planting trees and growing his little pet pot plants in a greenhouse for kicks. Fuck that." Jenna sits up, squares her shoulders, and Callie sees something new in her, something she hadn't been able to see all this time. Her mother as a survivor. Callie doesn't want to tell her the next detail: that she talked to a friend of hers the day before, a public defender she knew from up north. In New Jersey there's no longer a statute of limitations on sexual assault, but that law wasn't put into effect until 1996. Cases five years or less before 1996 might still result in criminal charges, but it's hard to get a conviction without DNA evidence. Annabelle could go to jail for murder. Luke might walk free.

They're quiet again for a while. Jenna is the one who breaks the silence. "I know I messed up. I know I did a lot wrong, Calliope. I wasn't a good mother to you. And that I have to face that. It's been a big part of my stuff at AA. But you don't just come from me, or them; you come from this too. Okay? You come from people who didn't like one way of living and were brave enough to start over somewhere else. You come from people who can make up their own minds. That's why I named you Hauser. But I should have told you all that."

"I'm sorry too. I really, really am."

Jenna rubs her eyes, takes Callie in her arms. Callie can't remember being held this way since she was a young child bawling over a skinned knee.

"Well, look at this sobfest we have on our hands. We're a mess, huh?"

Callie laughs between her tears. "I don't know. I'd say we're doing all right."

Callie stays the night in the cabin, each of them in one of the narrow bunks under the sloped ceiling. Jenna points out the beam where her great-grandfather carved his initials as a boy, shows Callie a guitar in the corner that belonged to Jenna's mother. The hot plate where she's been cooking all of her meals. There's so much more work ahead, but for now they rest. In the morning Jenna makes them breakfast and afterward she plays the guitar, her voice bursting through the quiet, clear and radiant as a new day.

Callie takes the path back to her car while Jenna stays behind at the cabin, asking for one more day before she goes back to the real world. She promises she'll call Steve, that she'll start going to meetings again.

Callie calls her friend, Chelsea, the public defender, when she gets back home. She asks about how Jenna's allegations might stand up in court if they can get criminal charges pressed against Luke on an old rape case.

Chelsea doesn't mince words. "Fifty-fifty. She's got a spotty record. That missed court date on the DUI won't look good, no matter the circumstances. They'll try to discredit her, an addict, DUIs, mental health issues, so much time has passed, it was consensual, all that. It depends on the jury. She'll need luck, too."

"What about Annabelle?" Callie asks. "What happens in these kinds of cases?"

Chelsea exhales. "That is a tougher call. America doesn't hate anyone as much as they hate a bad mom."

"What can I do to bolster the case against Luke Caputo? To make sure he ends up behind bars?"

"She says there are more girls, right? Find them. If they'll talk, the case grows. There's momentum. It's not one woman or two standing in front of the firing squad. It's easy to discount one woman, say she was asking for it, wanted attention, that her memory is unreliable after all this time, all that shit they always pull. Numbers. Numbers will be the key."

There's Sabrina, who has been silenced. Annabelle, who is being called a murderer. And there's Jenna.

Think, Callie. *Think think think.*

The bonfire party. The friends in the woods. *She's in a lot of trouble. He hates when I get high.*

Layla.

She calls Collins, asks him for a favor. All the guys have been so solicitous to her after they heard about what happened out at the sinkhole, visiting her, dropping off trays of food their mothers or girlfriends have made. She asks him to get Layla's address. He texts it to her a moment later and she puts it into her GPS.

The girl might not trust her. And Callie's not a cop anymore. Just a woman dropping by unannounced asking her to expose the most intimate parts of her story. Layla might still be in Luke's thrall, smitten and dazzled and made to feel like she's a part of something bigger than herself, than her own life. But, she knows she hit a nerve with her the last time she saw her, that underneath her bravado is a girl who wants to be understood, wants to be free of the drugs and the men who use her, wants to find her way back to herself again. Callie will do her best to tell her about the case she wants to help build. Because Layla is the strong one, not him. Because they need her. Because she's got the power to help make things right.

BLAIR

For two weeks she sits in front of a blank piece of paper at the library. Her first attempt, when she can put a pen to the page without her hands shaking, is a little more than a desperate howl. *Please don't take her. We need her. I need her. Please please please.* She has a flashback to her first week of preschool, clinging to her mother's waist, convinced that if she let go, if her mother retreated through the door papered over with cutouts of orange-and-red leaves, she would not see Iris ever again, that she would be left in a world that felt like her classroom, unfamiliar and sterile, without her mother's presence to help her make sense of it. The world drained of color and meaning, a blur of faces but none of them the one she wanted.

She feels that way, still.

At the trial Blair does not speak about the stones in the woods or the duffel bag in the corner of the closet. She does not mention the way she dug up the box and the evidence she destroyed in the cover of night.

Instead, she talks about her mother's volunteer work. About the apple slices drizzled with honey she came home to after school. About the meals they made for the senior citizens in the public housing complex two towns over. About the sense of safety she has always felt in her mother's presence, the bright sweaters her mother wore so Blair could pick her out easily on the soccer field, so that she could always know she was there. Her mother, a flare shot up through the dark.

The paper rattles in her hands as she finishes. The judge thanks her, but she hardly hears him. Blair's eyes are on Iris. Her mother has aged, over the months of the trial preparation, and over these past few weeks, and from the distance of the witness stand to the defendant's chair, Blair can see what she'll look like as an old woman. The purple-hued bags under her eyes. Her cheekbones hard, startling out from her face, her skin splotched and creased.

Her statement might be in vain. The lawyers debated about letting her speak. The prosecution used Iris's leadership in the Westchester community, her devotion to her children, as proof of all she denied Baby Doe. They even dug up her high school report cards, a testament to her essential sense of responsibility, her conscientiousness. So, what she did all those years ago could only have been done in cold blood. With an utter disregard for life. A paradox unlike any Blair has heard before: that her mother's goodness, her abilities in school, are an argument that she is evil, that she acted with intent. Meaning, murder, first degree.

As she walks back to her seat Blair feels the gaze of someone in the back of the room. A woman with her gray hair long and loose about her shoulders. For a second she thinks it is a trick of the light, her mind scattered and her eyes seeing what's not there. Her mother's worn face transposed onto another woman's body. But she stares and it doesn't resolve into meaning. This woman with her mother's mouth and eyes. She sees Blair looking back and there is something in her expression, intimate—an apology. They watch one another for what feels like a minute, but in reality is only a few seconds, before the woman rises, turns her back, and slips through the doors at the back of the court room. Blair knows that she will never see her again, and while she'll never be able to know for sure, she thinks she's just looked into the eyes of her grandmother. Which is what she wanted when she spit into the tube. Family. Connections restored. A story that wasn't broken into fragments, but part of a whole she could understand.

This is what adulthood means, she has come to realize. Understanding that there are stories that are easy, moments strung together like beads on a necklace, fixed in place according to a certain design, and truth; those same beads rattling around in a box, shifting into unresolvable arrangements. Spit in a tube and discover the story of who you are. Write a college admissions essay with a beginning, middle, and an end. Tell a room full of strangers what it was like to be someone's daughter. Convince a grand jury that because a girl earned straight A's she must have harbored an intent to kill. We form stories about everything. But how rarely we ever know the truth, even about our own lives.

CALLIE

Collins: You hear? Fauver died of an OD. Found him three days later.

Callie: More ghost story shit.

Collins: Won't miss that sorry bastard. House stuffed with goodies, cell phone full of texts to his cronies.

Callie: . . . ?

Collins: Active investigation, not at liberty to give details to civilians.

Callie: You suck.

Collins: Charming as ever, Hauser. But let's just say I think we got our dealer. Thought you'd wanna know.

She feels an instant sense of relief. No one will miss Fauver, and as far as she knows, he was the only one who could connect the other drugs to Jane in any meaningful way. Him and Damien, who, so far, has kept his mouth shut. She'll tell Jane, next time she goes to stay with her and Opal at their apartment on Long Beach Island. Jane still does physical therapy once a week, her leg still drags a little, always will. But she can keep up with Opal, who she walks to preschool every morning. Sometimes Adrian visits alongside Callie and teaches Opal the names of the kinds of seaweed that wash in on the tide.

You should keep him, Jane says, as they sip takeout coffees and watch from down the beach.

Callie hasn't told her that they talk about it. A small ceremony by the river. Barbeque and homemade cake. Soon, though, she'll confess. Once the haunted look dims a little from Jane's face.

Lorraine comes over on Sundays. Callie hasn't seen her, tries not to cross her path. Jane says she does it for Opal, that Lorraine still shows up with her trays full of lasagna and ziti and tiramisu and keeps herself busy cleaning and cooking and rarely meets Jane's eye. Callie wonders if she still wears the charm bracelet. Or if she feels lighter without it.

Annabelle gets off on first-degree charges but is sentenced to involuntary manslaughter. Callie visits her in prison, where she'll serve one year and do another two years' probation. The first time she saw her Annabelle had a black eye. The other inmates dispatching their own haphazard ideas of justice, when they discovered what she was in for. Those other women who had to leave their babies outside the barbed wire–ringed walls.

She was quiet and shrunk into herself, but before she left she told Callie that she wanted Jenna's address, so she might send her a letter.

"Do you think she would mind that? I want to apologize. I want to say I'm sorry about what happened to her. And that I'm sorry I didn't listen. Maybe everything would have been different if I did."

Callie tells her about Jenna's new job, her sobriety, that she's even recorded a few songs and put them up online. Sorrow-soaked songs tinged with just enough hope to sound just right in her pretty voice, roughened with time and life.

Della's daughter, Wren, writes a story about Luke, and the rest of the Caputo men, that is published in the *New York Times* under a headline: *The Devil in the Pines*. It describes the way Luke preyed on young women, the way Annabelle was punished. There's a picture of

Luke that runs below the headline, and another of Jenna standing in front of her house, her hands on her hips. She dispatches Callie to buy extra copies at the deli, tapes her own photo to her fridge. When Callie brings Adrian over to meet her it's the first thing she shows them, followed by her four-month sober chip.

Callie had asked Della again what she knew the day she put the Post-it with Sabrina Riley's name on it on the bathroom mirror.

"I didn't *know* anything, other than something bad had happened to those girls. I had no idea Annabelle . . . no idea what would happen to her, of course."

Della, it turns out, was the one who sent the file on the Baby Doe case up to Healy's team, hoping they might take it upon themselves to find out where the Riley girls had gone. She hadn't wanted to do it while Frank was still chief. She knew there was something off about the way the case was handled, but it was a hard time for her family. She had just found out she was pregnant again, and her husband had been laid off. They needed her job, she couldn't rock the boat. But she admitted to talking to her girls about the case a little. About the itch it left behind. And in the end Callie is grateful for Wren, for the publicity she's stirred up. There's a huge movement online of people who are rallying behind Annabelle, a fervor to see Luke punished. Callie declined to be interviewed by Wren but she was relieved to find out that the DA was working on charging him. That the tides were finally turning against him.

Callie braces herself to find Annabelle with more injuries the next time she visits, but she appeared unscathed. She had started working in the prison kitchen. Through a letter she wrote and circulated through her husband, she had quadrupled the prison library's stock of paperback books via donations from their town.

"What's with you and libraries?" Callie asks, aiming for lightness, though of course everything turned so quickly after their first meeting among the knitters.

Annabelle offers her a thin smile but soon the look on her face turns thoughtful. "I thought for so long I was trying to be good, to atone, but it's different. Maybe there's a part of me that's doing that. But I think what I want most is to feel like I belong somewhere. It feels . . . dangerous, not to belong. You know people are helping Ben with the kids? Driving them to sports practices and school? There's a few former friends who cross the street when they see Ben, but mostly people are trying to be kind. Maybe that's what I was doing all this time. Creating spaces where I belonged, where I would never feel like I wouldn't have help."

Callie recognizes the impulse. After all, that was part of becoming a cop. A uniform that meant she was claimed, sanctioned, by the rest of the group. Even Damien acted the way he did because he was trying to belong. In a moment of desperation, Annabelle had no one to keep her from the worst, most base, version of herself. No one to claim her as theirs. The girl whom so many people failed or harmed in order for her to do what she did. And the same with Jenna. Her mother's treatment, her father tending to her day and night, and then working double shifts to pay off the medical bills. It left Jenna on her own without anyone to keep her safe. Left her to fend for herself against Luke, the Caputos. A battle she was always going to lose.

"What will you do now?" Annabelle asks her.

"I have absolutely no idea," Callie says, the admission making her edgy. She's been in touch with Chelsea about the Luke Caputo case. Luke had been arrested the week before. She thinks of what Jenna said to her that day in the cabin. Callie has, for so long, defined herself against the messiness and pain of her upbringing. Her legacy was darker than even she could have guessed. But Jenna had also given her the gift of a lineage. Of people who were willing to start over, their own way. And that's what she'll do, too. Over and over until she gets it right.

ANNABELLE

For a long time you thought that the truth coming out would be the hardest part. You thought it would hurt to be called a monster. For the world to know how you had failed the baby. Your baby.

But what you could not have known until after the news trucks left your street, after your husband came to you in tears at the edge of the bed, after your daughter returned from school quiet, ashamed, after the trial and the sentencing, was that when the fear was gone, there was only grief left.

Grief that bent you in half on the thin mattress of your prison cell cot. Grief that made your stomach empty itself. Grief that you gagged on when there was nothing left for your body to rid itself of. You had kept it at the edge of your mind for so long that you did not understand how total it was. How the fear of being revealed was only the smallest part of it. A single raindrop in a storm.

As a part of your probation you speak to a counselor every week. Her name is Laura, and she is your age, with bright blond hair and a beaded glasses chain that she runs between her fingers when she's listening.

"I don't have the words," you told Laura, after spending the first four sessions staring out the window. "I've never been good at it. Telling the truth about how I feel. I never had to. Sabrina always knew. And that was enough. One person, who understood me perfectly."

Laura had smiled at you, and you detected real, true kindness in it. "Well, now. That's where we start."

* * *

They found Sabrina's body in the water. Divers brought her up from a grave of wreckage. You had never learned to swim as girls. Later, you took lessons after you married Ben, in the brisk chlorinated rectangle of the local YMCA, while Blair was in preschool on the other side of the building. You learned to float and to kick and get from one end of the pool to another with a decent freestyle. You learned that you liked the backstroke best. You had the opportunity to learn that about yourself, and even that felt like a kind of betrayal at the time, even more so now that you know what happened to her in the end.

Callie had watched as the divers went down, and down again, and down another time, until they could bring Sabrina up from the depths, release her from a tangle of machinery. You were glad there had been someone there to bear witness. Someone to watch over Sabrina, so she would not be alone.

She told you about the case against Luke Caputo, about the other girls and women who had come forward. Nine of them in all.

It was strange, after all these years, learning the Coyote's name. Son of the former police chief, sure, but in the end, with a name, he was just another man. You saw it before that, in the photos Blair had developed. He was younger than you are now. And you could finally see something small about him. An ugly need, a weakness, that warped him and diminished him.

You had been the strong one. You know that now. You and Sabrina both.

Callie had been pregnant—early enough that there was just a slight swell under her shirt, easy enough to miss if you didn't catch the way she would let her hand rest on her belly for a moment, protecting it. Just married, in law school. Would finish that year, take the Bar. She had apologized to you for how things had gone, and you hadn't known how to say it. That the truth coming out had been the beginning of something.

Your life. Your two lives. Stitched together at that ugly seam, at last.

* * *

You stare out the passenger seat window as Ben drives, the smell of cedar and pitch pine seeping into the car. Feel the shadows of the trees fall over you as you drive deeper into the woods.

The house is yours now, no one else to claim it. Ben has asked what you want to do with it. Raze it to the ground, restore it to its former splendor. Neither feels honest. In the fall, you will sell the house but keep the land abutting it. The woods, the factory ruins. The places you and Sabrina used to hide.

The trail behind the house is overgrown, but your feet lead you. Ben and Blair and the boys follow—Blair home from college for the week on spring break, your sons with their newly broad shoulders and deep baritone voices of men. Margot is with you too, bearing a bouquet of pale pink roses shrouded in cellophane that crackles in the silence.

The rubble of the factory looks so much smaller than it had been in your mind. It was bigger, you want to tell them. Towering. But that must not be true. It must have been this small all that time.

How impossible, to tell the story of how it had been to anyone else, who wasn't there at your side. Still, you have been trying. Your promise to all of them. As much truth, the best you can.

There's the clearing just behind it. Callie did it, Ben tells you. Made sure the weeds were pulled, any debris removed before you came.

Two headstones stand side by side.

Margot unwraps the roses.

Your fingers meet Margot's as you take two of the flowers from her, and with the easy intimacy of that touch you think of something she told you when the rest of the world was calling you a monster. Margot—someone who had more right to hate you than anyone else—wrapped her hands firm around yours.

There is nothing that happens to a child that a mother does not feel. Even when the thing that happens to them is you.

Margot told you something else, too, something that helped her after the stillbirth. She said that scientists had found that a child's cells remain in the mother's body, even after a miscarriage, even decades after pregnancy, after the mother dies. The cells rove around the first few years after pregnancy. Sometimes they collect in places that need healing. Repairing tissues, fixing wounds.

But, you read later, sometimes, the cells find darker places to collect. If the mother has a tumor, the fetal cells can encourage the cancer to fester. A case-by-case scenario, whether these cells rush in to heal or destroy. Both of you marking another, shaping another, at one another's mercy, for all time.

You put the first rose on Sabrina's plot. Can't help but think of the bones below your feet, the same length and shape as the ones under your skin. The scar on your arm prickles as the breeze shifts between the trees.

You turn to the second grave. When they asked what name to carve into the stone it came to you in an instant, unlocked from the black box of your mind. As if it had always been there, waiting to be known.

Heather.

Like the Pine Barrens heather your own mother revered. Rare in so many other places but thick and dense in the understory in these woods.

Resilient in the acidic, inhospitable soil, with yellow flowers that burst forth in the spring. You—I—kneel in front of the stones, bury the amber bead I've held onto for so long in the earth between them.

ACKNOWLEDGMENTS

Thank you to Sarah Bedingfield, who encouraged me to write this book when it was just a wisp of an idea. I am so lucky to have such a dedicated, fearless, and whip-smart agent in my corner. Thanks to Rebecca Rodd at Levine Greenberg Rostan, who provided an early read and crucial feedback and helped keep everything on track with grace and aplomb while we navigated two maternity leaves.

Thank you to my editor, Ryan Doherty, who both trusted me and challenged me at every step of the editorial process. We took this book on quite the ride but your patience, wisdom, and encouragement made it a pleasure.

Thank you to Faith Tomlin for your astute edits and your enthusiasm for *Heather* and the women who populate the world of this book.

Jennifer Jackson went above and beyond and read this novel in so many forms and offered essential feedback. I'm so lucky to have had another brilliant reader on my team.

Thanks, too, to the rest of the team at Celadon for embracing *Heather* and bringing it into the world with such attention and care.

Thank you to Kristina Moore at UTA, for having a nearly supernatural ability to see to the heart of a book and imagine a life for it beyond the page and to Orly Greenberg for joining the team this time around and gamely jumping in with both feet.

Susan Scarf Merrell provided a crucial, confidence-giving early read of this book and offered support and advice through the long process of writing and publishing a second novel. Susie, your generosity and grace continue to astound me.

Thank you to my friends, especially Sheena Cook, Daisy Florin, Melanie Pierce, Stephanie Wrobel, Caitlin Waher, and the mighty women, writers, and mothers that make up the Creative Coven for the dinners, happy hours, Zoom chats, and check-in texts and calls that make this writing life so much richer and more fun.

Thank you to the day care teachers who have so lovingly watched over my children these past two years, giving me essential time to write: Meghean, Maya, Barb, Lakshmi, Abby, Luisa, Miranda, Renee, Caitlin, Lalitha, Jazmin, Vidya, Marguerite, Justin, Gabe, and Claire.

I wouldn't be able to do this work without the support of my family, especially my mom, to whom this book is dedicated; my sisters, Lauren and Meghan; and my brothers-in-law, Sean and Jon. I may write dark books but my life is filled with so much light and humor thanks to all of you.

Thank you to my in-laws, especially Karen Lucian and Carol Piraino—the best West Coast publicity team I could hope for.

Thank you to my children. I am proud and delighted to be your mother. You have made my life richer in so many ways. Raising you is humbling, hilarious, and more joyful than I ever could have imagined.

Thank you to Spencer, who has weathered so many highs and lows at my side with patience and love. Our life together continues to get bigger and messier and you are the steadiest presence through it all.

Finally, a tremendous thank-you to my readers. The gift of your attention and time is what allows me to do this work and I am so grateful to every one of you.

ABOUT THE AUTHOR

Caitlin Mullen is the author of *Please See Us*, which won the Edgar Award for Best First Novel and was named a *New York Times* Best Crime Novel in 2020. She lives in New Jersey with her husband and children.

Founded in 2017, Celadon Books, a division of Macmillan Publishers, publishes a highly curated list of twenty to twenty-five new titles a year. The list of both fiction and nonfiction is eclectic and focuses on publishing commercial and literary books and discovering and nurturing talent.